BLACK FLAGGED
VEKTOR

a novel by

Steven Konkoly

Book Four in the Black Flagged Series

First edition

Dedication

For my father, Thomas Konkoly (1943-2013)

Acknowledgments

To my wife, for reading through Vektor twice. She's become my primary sounding board for nearly every step in the process. The kitchen has become our boardroom.

To the beta reader crew. Trent, Nancy, Joe S, Jon, and Bruce. Special thanks to Nancy and Jon for providing an exhaustive list of edits.

To the multinational production crew, starting with editor extraordinaire, Felicia A. Sullivan (Maryland). No deadlines on this one…sort of. Jeroen ten Berge (New Zealand) for another stand-out cover. Stef (UK) for keeping my blood pressure in the green by taking care of the formatting. I used to set aside several days to do this, and still didn't come close to getting it right. Finally, Pauline (Canada) for another solid proofing job. As a writer, I couldn't ask for a better team. Thank you.

About the author

Steven Konkoly graduated from the United States Naval Academy and served for eight years in various roles within the Navy and Marine Corps. He currently lives with his family on the coast of southern Maine.

He published his first novel, *The Jakarta Pandemic*, in 2010, followed by three novels in the *Black Flagged* series: *Black Flagged* (2011), *Black Flagged Redux* (2012) and *Black Flagged Apex* (2012). *Black Flagged Vektor* is his fifth novel. Steve is currently working on *The Perseid Collapse*, a sequel to *The Jakarta Pandemic*, to be released later this year.

Please visit Steven's blog for updates and information regarding all of his works: www.stevenkonkoly.com

About Black Flagged Apex

Black Flagged *Vektor* is the fourth book in what I call the "core" Black Flagged series. I had originally intended to squeeze *Vektor* into *Apex*, but was stopped by good friend and writer, Joseph Souza. He kindly informed me that 1.) The book would run another 200 pages and already contained enough sub-plots to keep the most avid Clancy reader occupied 2.) The idea deserved its own, fully developed story line. After finishing *Vektor*, I'm glad he stopped me. There is no way I could have closed the loop on this aspect of the *Black Flagged* world without cheating readers. *Black Flagged Vektor* takes place a few weeks after the events of *Black Flagged Apex*.

Like the rest of the *Black Flagged* series, keep in mind that the scenes occur in chronological order and are labeled in local time. Here is a list of the time zone differences between the locations featured in the *Black Flagged Apex* and the U.S. East Coast: Argentina +2 hours, Kazakhstan +10 hours, Moscow +9 hours, Germany +6 hours, Novosibirsk +11 hours, Sweden +6 hours, Ukraine +7 hours.

Character List

In alphabetical order

Dmitry Ardankin – Director of Operations, Directorate S, Foreign Intelligence Service (SVR)

Arkady Baranov – Director, Center of Special Operations (CSN), Federation Security Service (FSB)

Sevastyan Bazin "Seva" - BF Russian Group Demolitions/Assault

Audra Bauer –Deputy Director, National Clandestine Service, CIA

Viktor Belyakov – Russian bioweapons scientist, Vektor

Karl Berg – Assistant Deputy Director, National Clandestine Service, CIA

General Robert Copely – Director, CIA

Vadim Dragunov – Zaslon operative, Directorate S, Foreign Intelligence Service (SVR)

Richard Farrington "Yuri" – Black Flag, Russian Group Leader

Alexander Filatov "Sasha" – Black Flag Russian Group Assault

Erin Foley – CIA agent assigned to Black Flag Russian Group, aka Katie Reynolds

Luc Fortier "Luke" – Black Flag Electronic Warfare Team, Europe

Lieutenant General Frank Gordon – Commander Joint Special Operations Command

Maxim Greshnev – Chief Counterterrorism Director for the Federation Security Service (FSB)

Jared Hoffman "Gosha" – Black Flag Russian Group Sniper

Konrad Hubner – Black Flag, European Group

Darryl Jackson – Brown River Security Corporation executive

Alexei Kaparov – Deputy Director, Bioweapons/Chemical Threat Assessment Division Federal Security Service (FSB)

Major General Bob Kearney – Defense Intelligence Agency Director

Reinhard Klinkman – Black Flag European Group

Dima Maksimov – Solntsevskaya Bratva, *Pakhan* (Leader)

Thomas Manning – Director, National Clandestine Service, CIA

Nikolai Mazurov – Deep cover Black Flag operative, Moscow

Mikhail Nesterov "Misha" – Black Flag Russian Group Tech/Assault

Mihail Osin – Spetsnaz operative, Directorate S, Foreign Intelligence Service (SVR)

Lucya Pavrikova – Technician, Center for Special Operations (CSN), Federation Security Service (FSB)

Matvey Penkin – Solntsevskaya Bratva, *Avtorityet* (Brigadier)*Daniel Petrovich* – Black Flag operative, retired

Jessica Petrovich – Black Flag, retired

Yuri Prerovsky – Federation Agent, Federal Security Services (FSB)

Stefan Pushnoy – Director, Russian Foreign Intelligence Service (SVR)

James Quinn – National Security Advisor

Jacob Remy – White House Chief of Staff

Anatoly Reznikov – Former scientist at Vektor

Brigadier General Terrence Sanderson - Black Flag Leader

Grigory Usenko "Grisha" – Black Flag Russian Group Assault

Feliks Yeshevsky – Field Agent, Foreign Intelligence Service (SVR)

Valery Zuyev "Viktor" – Solntsevskaya Bratva, *Boyevik* (Warrior)

PART ONE

BLACK VEIL

Chapter 1

Karl Berg walked briskly down a wide, raked gravel path bordered by weathered cedar planks. The main walkway cut directly through a rough landscape of knee-high grasses and lichen-encrusted granite chunks. Several smaller paths branched off into the thick pine trees that surrounded the clearing. He easily found path number five, which was marked by a solid-looking post displaying the number. He stopped for a moment and took in his surroundings, shaking his head slowly. If the American public ever discovered that their taxes funded places like this, the CIA would have hell to pay. Even he had a hard time coming to terms with it.

For such a small "guest" population, the Mountain Glen facility cost U.S. taxpayers an unimaginable sum of money. The compound had been designed as the final "deal" for enemy foreign nationals willing to provide information critical to U.S. national security. Enemies too dangerous for release were offered a lifetime "retirement" in exchange for their knowledge, which would be vetted and confirmed. Prior to permanent acceptance at Mountain Glen, the director of the CIA carefully reviewed each case. If the information turned out to be bogus or failed to live up to advertised expectations, the "guest" would be evicted.

1

The process involved a significant element of trust, but few prospective guests turned their back on the deal after spending a few days at Mountain Glen with its fresh air, mountain views, babbling brooks, gourmet food, and first-class accommodations. Most of them had already tasted the alternative while in regular custody. Only the most stubborn or distrustful chose to spend the rest of their lives trapped in a dank, poorly lit prison cell, pissing and shitting into a rusty coffee can that was emptied once a day.

He turned down the path and let the pristine air fill his lungs. Cold pine air. Quite a difference from the crowded confines of the Beltway. He couldn't imagine anyone turning down the offer to stay here.

The temperature dropped a few degrees as he passed through the green curtain of pines. He could see a small post-and-beam structure with two dormers and a green metal roof situated in a tight clearing fifty meters ahead. He searched the trees while he walked, trying to spot one of the cameras or sensors. He felt exposed walking to Reznikov's villa alone.

Berg approached the front door cautiously, scanning the windows for signs of life within the house. Security had assured him that Reznikov was awake. Breakfast had been delivered thirty minutes ago. He thought about that. They delivered breakfast at Mountain Glen. Reznikov certainly didn't deserve a place like this, but what other options did they have? The door opened before he could knock.

"Come in, my friend. Breakfast is waiting," said an invigorated looking Anatoly Reznikov.

"I already ate," Berg said, stepping across the threshold, fully expecting to defend himself from a hand-to-hand attack.

"Nonsense. Please, this is my treat. Welcome to my mountain *dacha*."

"It's not yours yet. We're still a long way from securing your stay, which is why I'm here," Berg said.

He followed Reznikov through a short hallway to a square, Shaker-style kitchen table. Through the windows beyond the table, they had a view of the pine wall at the edge of the backyard. A snow-covered mountain peak rose above the pines, but the view wasn't what caught Berg's attention. What did was a one-third empty bottle of Grey Goose vodka, which sat on the kitchen counter next to a small shot glass.

"Looks like you've made a remarkable recovery," Berg said.

"It must be the mountain air, and a little gift from the staff. Join me in a toast."

"A little early, don't you think?" Berg replied.

"Never too early to celebrate. Plus, it's almost noon—"

"It's 10:30," interrupted Berg.

"And I need to warm up for our chat. You won't be disappointed," Reznikov said.

While Reznikov pulled another shot glass out of a cabinet, Berg placed his leather satchel on the pine floor and sat down at the kitchen table. He surveyed the feast prepared by the lodge's kitchen staff. He hoped they were just rolling out the red carpet to loosen Reznikov's lips. Fresh fruit, orange juice, lobster Benedict, smoked salmon and toasted bagels with cream cheese.

"Please help yourself. They just showed up with all of this. Can you believe it? Only in America. I should have come to your country earlier. Maybe I wouldn't have turned out so bad," he said. He poured two full shots of vodka and set one of the glasses in front of Berg, then took a seat across the table.

"A toast. To taking down VEKTOR Labs."

Berg hesitantly raised his glass. He eyed Reznikov warily as the Russian downed his glass of clear liquid. Berg followed suit, grimacing at the sharp burn. A few seconds later, he felt a little less worn out from the previous day's travels.

"Where did you stash your beautiful assistant? I had hoped she would be part of the package. I didn't notice any women here."

"I'm sure they keep a few blow-up dolls on hand for the guests," Berg said, placing the shot glass down on the table.

Reznikov's jovial smile flattened. "Such hostility. Not exactly the kind of environment that makes me want to share the intimate details of my former employer."

The Russian reached behind him to retrieve the vodka bottle from the countertop.

"Perhaps you'd rather have your head stuffed into a diarrhea-filled toilet bowl three stories below the surface of the earth?" Berg raised his hands to simulate a balanced scale. "Fresh mountain air, nice view, gourmet food, spa-like amenities," he said, raising one hand and lowering the other. "Or…daily beatings, concrete pavement sleeping arrangements, one meal a day, and toilet bowl scuba lessons. Don't fuck with me here."

"Easy, my friend. I get it," Reznikov said, pouring another shot.

He started to move the bottle over to Berg's side of the table, but Berg grabbed it from his trembling hand. On closer inspection, Reznikov didn't look as robust as he was acting. Mention of a permanent prison cell underground had quickly flushed the color from his face.

"I'm not your friend, and you'll get this bottle back after we've made considerable progress."

Berg placed the bottle on the floor and retrieved a legal pad from his satchel, along with a digital recording device.

"Don't put the bottle on the floor. Radiant heat, you know. Feels wonderful, but you almost have to wear socks," Reznikov said.

Berg removed the chilled bottle from the floor, placing it on the table, shaking his head. Radiant fucking heat? What was next? Daily massage therapy?

"So…where do you want to start?" Reznikov asked.

"From the beginning. How did you become involved with Vektor?"

"The roots of that decision reach back to my childhood. Are you in the mood for a story?"

"As long as it has something to do with Vektor," Berg said.

"It has everything to do with Vektor and how Russia's bioweapons program long ago eclipsed their nuclear weapons program," he whispered.

Three hours later, Berg emerged from the villa with a distant look on his face. He followed the gravel path through the forest to the main clearing, hardly paying any attention to his footing. The warm late afternoon sun barely registered on his face. If Reznikov had told the truth, the United States and its allies faced the greatest threat to world stability since the Cold War. A secret race to develop bioweapons of mass destruction, and the Russians had a thirty-year head start. The reckless plan that he'd suggested to Sanderson didn't feel so outlandish anymore. The bioweapons program at Vektor Labs had to be destroyed.

๑๑๑

Anatoly Reznikov peered through the shades of his front window at the vanishing shape of Karl Berg, the enigmatic CIA agent that had miraculously rescued him from a quick death at the hands of his former masters. The past week had been confusing, hazy, and punctuated by severe fluctuations in his mental state. He'd spent most of the time feeling utterly helpless, certain that he would be brutally interrogated and discarded. His pessimistic side had taken full control of his emotions, which didn't surprise him. He'd tried to drink himself to death in Stockholm, and failing that had put a gun to his head to finish the job. And that had just been the beginning of a two-day roller coaster ride through Hell, marked by repeated cardiac arrests, torture and beatings while strapped helplessly to a bed.

Only a sheer miracle could explain his sudden moment of clarity on the jet ride back to the United States. It had probably just been a natural fluke. A random release of chemicals, possibly dopamine, to relax his anxiety long enough for him to wrestle control of his mind. Maybe the sight and smell of Karl Berg sipping scotch had triggered it. It didn't matter. Within the short span of time it took for Karl Berg to walk down the business jet's aisle, he had formulated a plan that was guaranteed to set him free.

Earning a transfer to this facility was just the first step in a plan so perfect that he considered the possibility that it had been his fate all along to fall into Berg's lap. Now that his mind had cleared enough to see the bigger picture, he couldn't think of a better scenario. He'd been despondent about Al Qaeda's betrayal and his subsequent failure to recover more of the virus canisters, but this new turn of events would take his original scheme to the next level. He just needed to place a single phone call to activate part two of his plan.

He hadn't lied to Berg. On the contrary, he had told the agent everything, except the part about how he had successfully stolen samples of every weaponized virus and bacteria created at Vektor. He hadn't been dismissed from Vektor for attempting to steal viral encephalitis samples. By that point, he had already stolen samples of everything he had seen in the bioweapons division. He had been fired for trying to access a section of the laboratory off limits to everyone except for three scientists. Rumors started circulating that the small group had created something nobody had seen before. He took the bait and attempted to sneak into the lab.

At that point, security features at Vektor relied more on humans than technology, and large sums of money helped him circumvent most of the security surrounding the isolated laboratory cell. Or so he had thought. Seconds from crossing the point of no return, he was warned off by the only security guard not infiltrated by FSB agents. Without stepping foot in the off-limits section, they couldn't shoot him on the spot like they had planned. Instead, FSB agents backed off and allowed him to continue to work at the lab, under close supervision.

A week later, he received an offer to lead a lab group at their sister institute in Kazakhstan. He knew it was a setup, and the rest was history. He'd barely escaped with his life and bioweapons samples worth millions of dollars. Fate had given him one more chance and he didn't intend to waste it. One call to some very nefarious "friends," and he could take leave of this place, free to sell his weapons to the highest bidder.

And the icing on the cake? Berg's people would target Vektor's bioweapons division and key personnel. He'd finally avenge his parents' murder at the hands of Russian security forces. Revenge was sweet, especially when it required no effort on his part.

Chapter 2

Mihail Osin stared at the glowing windows of 14 Värtavägen and considered his options. Interior lights had greeted them upon their silent arrival at the edge of the property's thick evergreen screen, but he hadn't detected any movement inside the one-story house. Still, he couldn't ignore the possibility that someone had remained in the house. Even snagging one of the safe house's "keepers" could put them back on the path to finding Reznikov. Unfortunately, his own experience with the use of foreign safe houses didn't leave him optimistic. Reznikov's abduction had occurred over two weeks ago, which was an eternity to keep a high-value target in such an exposed, but well-concealed location.

The CIA had made a wise choice with this house. The neighborhood was surprisingly rustic and eerily quiet for a suburb less than fifteen kilometers from the center of Stockholm. Close enough to the city for quick access, yet isolated enough to ensure natural privacy. Judging by the amount of time it took the Russian Foreign Intelligence Service to uncover the location, the CIA had gone to great lengths to bury this place in the open. Hidden in plain sight.

His team of four operatives had been deposited on the street behind the safe house a few minutes before dusk, their van joining a rented Volvo sedan parked at a church less than two minutes away. The two-man team in the Volvo had conducted the initial reconnaissance of the neighborhood, quickly determining that street parking was either prohibited or discouraged in the residential areas of Viggbyholm. They hadn't seen a single car parked on any of the nearby streets. Parking one of their vans on the street for any length of time or lingering nearby would invite disaster. Sitting in a church parking lot after dark probably wasn't the best idea either, but it was the only non-residential parking zone with quick access to the safe house.

Mihail shifted his knees and removed a hand-sized black electronic device from the open nylon backpack next to him. The device had two stubby antennas and a muted orange LCD screen. He examined the screen, which cast a barely detectable glow on his face. The multi-channel, wireless radio frequency (RF) detector showed a few faint wireless signals in the 2400-2480 MHz range, which was typical for commercial home wireless routers. He was more interested in anything using the 800-1000 MHz frequency range, specifically the sub-ranges most commonly used by wireless motion sensors. Anything lower than 800 MHz would similarly pique his attention.

The RF detector had passively collected data since their arrival twenty minutes earlier, twice detecting a short frequency burst at 910 MHz, which was one of the most common frequencies associated with the local GSM-900 cellular network. The short transmissions resembled what he'd expect to see when a cell phone registers to a local cell tower. At this point, he felt satisfied that neither the yard nor the house was protected by motion detectors. He stood up and signaled for the team to move forward, placing the detector in the pack before slipping it over his shoulders. He disengaged the safety on his PP2000 submachine gun and stepped into the backyard.

Three of the four Spetsnaz operatives converged on the back door from different points in the yard, while the fourth slid along the right side of the house, looking for the power line connection. Mihail listened intently near one of the illuminated windows, but heard nothing beyond the distant hum of a car motor. He decided that they would try to pick the lock and deadbolt, instead of forcing the door open. He desperately wanted to avoid making noise in this neighborhood. If the house was unoccupied, he wanted time to inspect it for anything useful. While one of his operatives worked the locks with a small tool kit, he listened underneath a different window. The house was still. By the time he returned less than one minute later, the two locks had been opened.

He lowered his PN21K night vision monocular into place over his right eye and spoke softly into the microphone attached to his headgear. Two seconds later, the house went dark. On cue with the sudden darkness, the lead member of his team shouldered the door with enough force to dislodge any chain lock barring their entrance. The door opened unhindered, and his team slipped inside. Mihail followed the second man through the door, scanning the darkness with his goggles. Once the two doorways leading out of the kitchen had been secured, he whispered orders for the team to go silent and listen. Roughly two minutes later, he raised his night vision goggles and ordered the fourth operative to return electrical power to the house.

When the lights reenergized, they could plainly see what the rough green images cast by their night vision had indicated. The house had been cleared of everything, "sanitized" all the way down to the toilet paper rolls. He recalled the fourth member of his team to the house, and they spent the next five minutes checking closets, opening drawers and prying at wallpaper in a futile attempt to find anything. Each operative returned to the kitchen cradling his submachine gun and quickly shaking his head. Nothing. He opened his backpack and scanned the radio frequency detector. He found a strong reading at 1621 MHz, which had started a few minutes ago. This was an L-band frequency used for satellite communications. Someone knew they were here, and would very likely receive a video feed of their foray through the house.

He signaled for the team to evacuate the structure and contacted the van once they were outside. On their way to the front of the house, he ordered the power to be permanently cut. Once the power line had been cut, he checked the RF detector again and saw that the device hidden in the house continued to transmit, indicating an independent power source. He thought he had committed an error restoring power while they were inside, but it wouldn't have mattered. His big mistake tonight had been assuming that they might find anything useful in the CIA safe house. Now the CIA knew for certain that they hadn't lost interest in Anatoly Reznikov.

As they waited for the van in the shadows, Mihail pulled out his encrypted cell phone and placed a call to SVR headquarters. It was time to exercise the least desirable option on the table. As he had anticipated, their night had just begun.

Chapter 3

Karl Berg reviewed the last few slides from the PowerPoint presentation he would present to Thomas Manning. He had been awake much of the night putting together the first draft of his urgent appeal for the CIA to take action against Vektor Laboratory's bioweapons department. With Reznikov's inside information, they could send General Sanderson's Russian Group to destroy the facility and eliminate key personnel involved in the program. Reznikov felt confident that a small, properly equipped, elite force could successfully execute the mission, given the right tactical intelligence, which he could provide.

Audra Bauer had joined him for part of the morning, helping him to modify most of the slides he had hastily cobbled together. She had already spoken at length with Manning about the threat posed by Vektor Labs. Israeli intelligence assets had repeatedly warned them about the Iranians' continued efforts to secure research positions within Vektor, despite Israel's best efforts to dissuade Iranian scientists from studying abroad. Iranian scientists died from sudden natural causes at a startlingly higher rate than their counterparts in other nations. A scientific career in the fields of biology, chemistry, or physics currently ranked as one of the most hazardous occupations in Iran.

The Israelis expressed little doubt that the Iranians intended to steal bioweapons samples from the lab or collaborate with Russian scientists associated with the program. Recent grumblings from Wiljam Minkowitz, their Mossad liaison, left Manning and Bauer with the distinct impression that Israel was no longer satisfied with the CIA's backseat approach to curbing Iran's unquenchable thirst for weapons of mass destruction. Manning had already dodged three meeting requests from the Mossad liaison since the president had appeared on national television to explain the domestic terrorist attack on the nation's water supply. They all knew what Minkowitz would say: *It's time for the U.S. to step up to the plate and take care of the problem.*

Berg's job today wouldn't be to convince Manning of the necessity of targeting Vektor. Manning was already primed to take their efforts to the next level. Berg's presentation was designed to convince Manning that they could win the director's approval, which would ultimately impact their chances of winning over the president. Without the president's approval, Berg would have to make some difficult choices. Drop the topic entirely, or take the operation "off the books."

He didn't think an unsanctioned black op would be feasible in this situation. Novosibirsk was the third largest city in Russia, nearly two hundred miles beyond the Kazakhstan border. Getting Sanderson's team to the target wasn't the problem. Evading the massive military and police response from the Novosibirsk Oblast would be impossible without significant, targeted intervention.

The feasibility of this operation depended upon White House support, which shouldn't be entirely difficult to win given the fact that a weaponized virus from Vektor Labs had nearly decapitated the U.S. government.

Berg's STE (Secure Terminal Equipment) desk set rang, indicating a call from the operations watch center. He picked up the handset, which triggered the automatic negotiation of cryptographic protocols within the removable Fortezza Crypto Card inserted into his phone. Unique identifiers built into the card's cryptographic processor verified that Karl Berg was on one end of the call and that the operations watch center was on the other. STE technology represented a major improvement over the STU-III system, where the cryptographic processor was built into the phone and provided no unique identification procedures. With the STE system, Karl Berg could insert his card into any STE phone and conduct a secure, encrypted conversation.

"Karl Berg," he answered.

"Good afternoon, Mr. Berg. I have a Flash Alert data package designated for your eyes only. How do you want me to proceed?"

"You can send it through my secure feed. I don't have time to review the package in the ops center," Berg said.

Berg knew where the package had originated, but he was dying to see the contents.

"Understood. You now have access to the package."

"Thank you," Berg said.

He navigated to the CIA operations intranet gateway and entered a long string of passwords that enabled access to his secure feed. He quickly found the data package in question. A separate screen opened, showing eight data sets, all of which contained a hyperlink. He opened the one showing the longest period of time, which ended three minutes ago in Sweden. "19:17.24GMT/13:17.24EST-19:23.53GMT/13:23.53EST."

The hyperlink activated a data recording captured by one of the motion-activated, night vision-capable cameras hidden in the Viggbyholm safe house's fire detectors. Located on the ceiling of each room, the cameras provided a searchable three-hundred-and-sixty-degree view within each space. The recording showed a three-man team enter the kitchen from the door leading into the backyard and proceed to wait for two minutes. Each operative wore the latest generation Russian night vision monocles and carried the same type of submachine guns used by the Zaslon Spetsnaz team in Stockholm. Definitely not your garden-variety operatives. He guessed they were some variation of SVR Spetsnaz.

After two minutes, the house lights came on, momentarily blinding the camera as the smart-sensor switched camera lens inputs. A fourth operative entered through the back door, and they proceeded to search the house. Berg toggled through the other hyperlinks, which showed the team conducting a quick, yet thorough investigation. He returned to the first link, which was still running, and almost missed the most important part of the data feed. The lead operative removed a small electronic device from his backpack and immediately ordered the team's evacuation. Less than fifteen seconds later, the scene went dark, replaced by the green image of an empty kitchen. The team leader knew that their raid hadn't gone unnoticed.

Berg sat back in his chair and considered the situation. He hadn't expected the Russians to forget about Reznikov. Given what the crazed scientist had told him over vodka shots and gourmet food, he was surprised that they hadn't heard more from the Russians by now. Of course, Moscow was still buried under the staggering fallout left by Reznikov's manmade disaster in Monchegorsk, compounded by Reznikov's link to the terrorist plot in the United States. The Russians didn't have a basis to object on any level. Everything led back to a program that supposedly didn't exist.

As predicted, the Russians would dig around quietly for Reznikov. But how long would their efforts remain below the surface? The Spetsnaz team in the video didn't look like they would have passed up the opportunity to take down anyone found in the house. The big question was where would they go next? If Berg were pulling the strings, he'd start with the Stockholm embassy.

Three members of the CIA station knew critical details about Petrovich's operation. One of them was temporarily assigned to his staff while she awaited her next assignment, which took her out of play. This left the Stockholm embassy's CIA station chief and her assistant station chief. The Russians wouldn't dare touch the station chief, but if pressed, they might make a move on the station's second-in-charge. This was the only move that made sense.

Given the sensitivity of Reznikov's circumstances, it would be reasonable for the Russians to assume that the details of the operation had been restricted to the most senior CIA officer at the station. In this case, neither the station chief nor her assistant knew the identity of the target, but this wasn't something he could pass on to the Russians to dissuade them from taking regrettable action. All he could do was warn Emily Bradshaw that the Russians were actively prowling the streets of Stockholm. He opened a different internet directory and located the station chief's after hours contact information.

Chapter 4

Thomas Manning cracked his knuckles and nodded at Berg, shifting his attention to Audra Bauer. Karl Berg put the projector in standby mode and exhaled, waiting for Manning to start.

"I can sell this to the director. Do we have a confirmed link to the Iranians, beyond what the Israelis have hinted?" Manning asked.

"Reznikov didn't specifically mention any Iranians in the facility. He just said that he'd been approached on the outside by what he assumed were Iranian intelligence agents," Berg said.

"For all we know, those could have been Mossad agents testing the waters at Vektor. This wouldn't be the first time we've mistaken Mossad operatives for Middle East terrorists," Manning countered.

"It's always a possibility. I could run this by our liaison and see what our Israeli friends might be willing to confirm."

"If we're willing to share the information provided by Reznikov with the Israelis, I'm sure Mr. Minkowitz would be amenable to steering us in the right direction," Bauer said.

"The director will never approve that," Manning interjected. "Reznikov's information stays with us for now. We'll need to come up with a different angle to garner Israeli support."

"If we can convince them that we plan to take action against Vektor, they'll pass information," Berg said.

"Let's take this up the chain of command without trying to involve the Israelis. If the plan gets kicked back, we'll take steps to solidify the Iranian connection," Manning said.

Berg's phone buzzed, breaking his concentration. He'd set the phone to silent for this meeting, with the exception of high-priority calls from the operations center.

"Late for dinner?" Manning said.

"My apologies. It's the operations center. This might have something to do with Stockholm," he said, and Manning nodded for him to take the call.

"Karl Berg," he answered.

"Mr. Berg, I have a priority, encrypted call from Stockholm. Source station confirms Emily Bradshaw originated the call."

"Stand by. I'll call you right back from an encrypted terminal," Berg said. "Call from the Stockholm station chief," he said to Manning and Bauer.

"Shit," Bauer mumbled.

He pulled his crypto card from his front pocket and inserted it into a slot on the front of the STE desk set next to Manning. After entering his PIN into the set, he dialed the operations center and the call was connected.

"Is Ian in a secure location?" Berg asked.

"We have a situation," Bradshaw responded.

"How bad?"

"I tried to contact Ian via cell phone and landline immediately after your call, but he didn't answer. I tried a few more times before heading out to his flat myself," Bradshaw said.

"You went out there alone?" he said.

"What choice did I have? Send the police to investigate a CIA officer's residence? Wake up one my officers and burn another CIA employee?" she said and paused. "I found his apartment door damaged and half of the apartment in disarray. He put up quite a struggle," she said flatly.

"Jesus. I'm sorry, Emily. I called you as soon as they hit the safe house."

"I know. They either had a second team on Ian, or they drove straight to his flat from the safe house. I was at his place within the hour. I should have gone straight over."

"Based on what I saw in the digital feed from the safe house, your presence might have complicated matters even further," Berg said.

He looked up at Manning and Bauer and shook his head.

"Is there anything we can do?" Bradshaw said.

"No. We can't afford to let this spiral out of control, and I can't imagine any scenario leading to Ian's recovery. You'll have to treat Ian's disappearance like any other embassy employ—"

"I understand what's required," she interrupted.

Berg paused before speaking again. "I'm really sorry, Emily. This is a shitty situation made worse by the politics."

"How bad will it be for him?" she asked.

"What do you mean?" Berg said.

"You know exactly what I mean," she hissed.

"The worst," he said.

"I need to recall all of my people to the embassy. Frankly, I don't trust your assessment that the rest of us are off limits. Let's hope nobody else has disappeared." She hung up.

Berg removed his crypto card and looked up at Bauer and Manning, who appeared speechless.

"Not good. Ian Reese disappeared. Bradshaw found signs of forcible entry and a struggle at his apartment. We can assume that the Russians will strip the information out of him in a short period of time," Berg said.

"Beyond Erin Foley's involvement as a surveillance asset during the raid, he really doesn't know anything," Manning said.

"Yes and no. In terms of raw data, both the station chief and Reese were kept in the dark. The only damning thing they could confirm is the timeline for the raid. He knew that our team arrived in Stockholm the day before and that the team didn't learn the address until the next morning. They'll connect the dots pretty quickly."

He had never divulged any information regarding Kaparov, nor would he ever betray that trust in any way. If Manning or Bauer knew Kaparov's position, they would immediately try to leverage the Russian for information regarding Vektor. As director of the Bioweapons/Chemical Threat Assessment Division, Kaparov should have detailed information regarding the operations and physical security of Russia's premier virology and biotechnology research center.

Vektor, or the Vektor Institute, served as Russia's equivalent to the U.S.'s Centers for Disease Control and Prevention and the U.S. Army's Chemical Biological Defense Command. In fact, the World Health Organization recognized the Vektor Institute as one of the world's premier virology research centers. Vektor and the CDC were the only WHO-authorized repositories of the smallpox virus, which indicated the significant level of trust and prestige bestowed on the institute.

Like the CDC, other infectious diseases would be kept at Vektor for "research" purposes, representing a possible biological threat to Russia that would fall under Kaparov's sphere of concern. When and if the time was right, he would ask his friend for help, but until then, Berg had no intention of exposing this secret.

"Obviously, I'll let you decide how to handle your source. Let me know if a warning isn't enough," Manning said.

"Extraction?" Berg said, clearly surprised by Manning's suggestion.

"I'd support something like that in this case. Your source has more than paid his or her dues. Keep it in mind. Give me until tomorrow to redline your presentation and get it back to you with more detailed thoughts. Until then, you have some preliminary notes to work from. I'll schedule a meeting with Director Copley for the late afternoon."

"Sounds like a plan. We'll be on standby," Bauer said.

"Thomas?" Berg said, stopping the National Security Branch director in his tracks at the door. "I think we might want to consider bringing Emily Bradshaw back to the States. The Russians aren't likely to be satisfied with Ian's level of information."

"There's absolutely no way they would abduct a station chief," Manning said.

"I sense the rules changing. I'd strongly consider it," Berg said.

Manning stared at him for a few seconds and opened the secure conference room door, disappearing from sight. Bauer gathered her materials and packed her briefcase.

"I'll talk to you later. Sounds like you have a call to make and some slides to fix."

"Not fix, modify. None of them were broken," he said, closing his laptop.

"That's because I helped you with them. I'll be by tomorrow morning to fix the rest of them," she said, walking toward the door.

"Your office or mine?"

"Mine, of course. Your office is still a pit. As deputy director, I get to have someone unload all of my boxes," Bauer said.

"Sifting through the boxes is half the fun," Berg said.

"Then I suggest you schedule some time to have fun. Catch you tomorrow," she said and vanished.

"Yep," he said to no one.

Berg glanced at his watch. It would be nearly midnight in Moscow. He'd call Kaparov later tonight and hopefully catch him at the office. This would make it impossible for the CIA or NSA to use their magic and find him. If they could somehow triangulate Kaparov's cell phone, nobody would be surprised to learn that his office was at Lubyanka Square. He seriously doubted that his own agency would attempt such a backhanded trick, but he'd take the steps to minimize the risk on Kaparov's end. It was the least he could do for an old enemy turned wary friend.

Chapter 5

Berg sat at a modest kitchen table in his townhouse and dialed the latest number provided by his friend in Moscow. He'd purchased several new prepaid Tracfones recently and activated them using dummy email accounts through an untraceable laptop at Wi-Fi hotspots located across the D.C. area. Prior to entering Kaparov's cell number, he had dialed the CIA's phone redirect service, which would send Berg's call through a random, unencrypted phone number, usually a business, within the same Moscow call area. Caller ID on Kaparov's phone would show a local call, instead of a Virginia area code that would immediately raise eyebrows.

"This must be important. It's past your bedtime," said a thickly accented, Russian voice.

"It's important," Berg said.

"Call me back in five minutes. I need to throw on a coat and head out for a smoke," he said.

"I thought you smoked in your office?" Berg said.

"I'm trying to reform my ways."

Berg counted the seconds, considering the possible direction of their conversation. He needed to speak with Kaparov about two issues, but had to be careful with how he proceeded. He needed to warn Kaparov about the CIA officer's abduction, but he also needed to prep Kaparov for the possibility that the U.S. government might strike a blow against Vektor. They'd likely need Kaparov's assistance to pull off a fully successful mission. Unfortunately, the significance of the CIA officer's abduction wouldn't be lost on Kaparov, and Berg ran the risk of permanently losing him. He wouldn't be shocked if Kaparov tossed his cellphone into the nearest sewer opening and never talked to him again. He'd have to tread lightly. A few minutes later, he tried the number again, hoping Kaparov hadn't disposed of the phone.

"Deputy Director, how can I be of assistance?"

"I try to play that down around here, comrade."

"The infamous Karl Berg claims to be modest? This is disappointing," Kaparov said.

"I try not to attract too much attention in my twilight years. It's bad for the career," Berg said.

"Apparently not so bad. Every time I read the cables, you are once again promoted. After last week's events, I expect you to be running the show over there," Kaparov said.

Berg could hear traffic and distant voices in the background. Possibly a light breeze blowing across Kaparov's cell phone.

"I had little to do with this one. Our domestic security forces took the lead. Plus, I'm starting to get the feeling that this promotion is more about keeping an eye on me and less about my wildly lucky hunches."

"Instinct, my friend. There's no such thing as a hunch in this business, which leads me to a rather delicate matter. My instinct tells me that you haven't been completely forthcoming about Stockholm's grand prize," Kaparov said.

"And I thought I could still slip one by you after all of these years."

"You couldn't do it back in the day. What made you think anything had changed?" Kaparov said, followed by roaring laughter.

Since Kaparov had brought up Reznikov, Berg felt comfortable moving forward with news about Vektor first, followed by the warning about the abduction.

"Funny you should mention this prize. We need to discuss an ongoing problem in your neck of the woods. Something that shouldn't exist."

"Confirmed by our mutual friend?"

"Confirmed with details. I'm going to need some help with this one," Berg said.

"We'll see. Timeline?"

"Nobody seems keen about waiting for the next incident."

"Be careful with your guest. He's a slippery one. Our Arab friends weren't the only parties interested in his services."

"He's in a safe place," Berg said.

"I hope so."

"Now it's my turn to warn you about something," Berg said.

"Should I start running for the nearest Metro station?"

"Not yet, but you'll definitely need to raise your guard. Someone in Stockholm disappeared last night. He didn't have any detailed information about the surprise party, but he does know that most of the guests received last-minute invitations."

"I see," Kaparov said, pausing for several moments.

"Are we still friends?" Berg said.

"For now. I'll need to see what comes of this before I make any promises about the future."

"I understand. The vacation offer still stands, if the climate changes too drastically."

"You'd like that, wouldn't you?" Kaparov said.

"From a practical standpoint, I prefer that you stay in Moscow," he said, and they both started laughing.

"If you had said anything else, I would have hung up on your dishonest ass. We need to figure out a better way to keep in touch. Throwing cell phones into the Moscow River can be expensive, especially on my salary."

"I can't believe you would pollute the river like that. I thought they were cleaning up the Moscow," Berg said.

"Throwing phones into the river is the new national pastime. Putin has resurrected the paranoia in our DNA. Even the kids throw their phones in, and they don't even know why they're doing it."

"As long as it keeps *you* out of the Moscow River, I approve."

"Nobody is going to throw me in this river. No calls in my office or my home. If what you say is true, neither location will be safe. This time of the year, I like to walk every evening from six-thirty to seven, right after dinner. I stop off to buy vodka and cigarettes. It's my usual routine. This would be the best time to call."

"I can give you a Moscow number that will redirect your calls. Just in case."

"Sounds good. Call me in a few days, and I'll take that number. Until then, be careful with your new friend and stay out of trouble."

"That goes double for you, comrade," Berg said and hung up the phone.

He stared at the clock on the microwave and shook his head, taking in what Kaparov had said about Reznikov. His hint that the scientist had attracted attention beyond Al Qaeda disturbed Berg to the core. Given Reznikov's outlaw status in Russia and Europe, he would have been forced to rely on Russian organized crime contacts for false paperwork or "off the books" travel. The Russian mafiya would have undoubtedly surmised his potential. The market for bioweapons among desperate rogue states represented an untapped economic resource for organized crime networks. The thought sent a chill through his body. He'd incorporate this revelation into the presentation, in the hopes that it would emphasize the importance of putting Vektor out of business.

Few would ever truly realize how important it had been to take Reznikov out of circulation. If the raid on Vektor succeeded, he would permanently "retire" the scientist. Reznikov wouldn't be the first "retiree" to take a walk in the forest and never return. The term "retirement" had more than one meaning at the Mountain Glen facility.

Chapter 6

9:24 AM
Federal Security Service (FSB) Headquarters
Lubyanka Square, Moscow

Alexei Kaparov extinguished his cigarette and lit another one immediately, inhaling deeply. He turned toward the Internal Affairs investigators and released the noxious smoke in their direction. The younger agent grimaced, while his seasoned partner stared through the haze unimpressed. At least they had the respect to send an old-timer to question him.

"Smoking has been prohibited in this building for two years," the younger agent said.

"My habit was grandfathered," Kaparov said.

"By who?"

"By someone old enough to be your grandfather. Are we done here? I've told you everything I know about Monchegorsk, which is nothing. I know this is hard for your superiors to understand given my position as director of this division," Kaparov said, placing the cigarette in his overfilled ashtray.

"What bearing would that have on Monchegorsk?" the older agent said.

"Back to square one, eh? How many interrogations have we been through, and we can't seem to get past this," Kaparov said.

Kaparov shook his head. He really didn't need this shit, but it was necessary in the long run. He'd continued to seek information about Monchegorsk long after everyone else had stopped asking questions. He didn't see any other option. He had a reputation for tenacity and defiance, which had obligated him to pursue his initial line of questioning about the possible use of bioweapons in Monchegorsk for a reasonable period of time.

Before the government's ironfisted clampdown on information pertaining to the "situation" in the Kola Peninsula, his office had received more than enough warning signs to warrant further investigation of a possible "biological incident." The video smuggled out of Monchegorsk and released worldwide by Reuters cast serious doubt on the government's assertion that employees of Norval Nickel had formed an armed insurgency. If he'd suddenly dropped his inquiry, he would have drawn even more attention to himself.

"Interviews," the younger agent corrected him.

"That's right. Interrogations were banned along with the cigarettes. Comrades, I have work to do, so if you don't have any new questions, I don't have time to give you the same answers to the old ones," he said and started typing on his keyboard.

The older agent forced a smile, which Kaparov returned before turning back to the computer monitor, pretending to open emails. At least they weren't asking questions about Stockholm. He could play this little bullshit cat-and-mouse game for the rest of his career if it suited them. He wondered how many times they would be required to return before someone interceded on his behalf.

"Thank you for your time, Alexei," the gray-haired investigator said, sharing a glance that acknowledged the futility of this game.

"My pleasure, Boris," he said.

Less than a minute later, his deputy walked in, closing the door behind him. Yuri Prerovsky crossed his arms and stared at Kaparov.

"Yes?" Kaparov said.

"What did they want?"

"The same thing they wanted three days ago. The same thing they talk to you about. Monchegorsk. It's the same conversation every time. Why do you keep asking questions about Monchegorsk? I don't ask questions anymore. Why did you keep asking questions after the government explained what happened? Because I'm not a fucking idiot. What does that mean? It means you're all fucking idiots for thinking the government explanation has satisfied the population. And round and round we go."

"Nothing more, huh?" Prerovsky said.

"No. Nothing more. We've discussed this."

Kaparov was starting to get annoyed by everyone at this point. He'd shared his strategy with the nervous youngster, assuring him that as long as his "friend" in operations covered her tracks, they could not be linked to Stockholm. He'd draw a little heat with the Monchegorsk questions, which would divert any other attention away from them. Why would a veteran of the KGB era keep bringing up Monchegorsk and Reznikov if he had anything to do with Reznikov's abduction? That's the question he wanted internal affairs to ask themselves.

"I know. It just makes me nervous," Prerovsky said.

"Internal affairs should make you nervous. They make me nervous…"

His statement was interrupted by the phone on his desk. He held up a finger and answered the call.

"Director Kaparov."

He listened as Prerovsky glanced around at the piles of folders stacked haphazardly throughout the office.

"I'll be right up, sir," he said and replaced the receiver.

"That was Greshnev. He wants me upstairs immediately," Kaparov said.

An audience with the Counterterrorism Director was something he typically avoided at all costs, but in this case, he relished the opportunity. His obstinate refusal to play along with Internal Affairs' nonsensical semantics game had finally earned him the chance to put this nonsense to rest. He could simply throw his hands up and ask what his boss wanted from him.

"Did he say what he wanted?" Prerovsky said.

"Of course not. I guarantee you that Boris flipped open his cell phone once they were out of our section and reported that the interview went nowhere as usual. Maybe five interviews is the magic number for a crusty dog like myself."

Kaparov reached into the ashtray on his desk and smothered the cigarette he had lit to annoy the younger Internal Affairs agent.

"Do you want me to wait here?" Prerovsky said.

"Don't you have a fucking job to do?"

"Keeping you out of trouble is a full-time job," he said and stood up to get the door for Kaparov.

Kaparov retrieved his suit jacket from a tree stand next to the door and squeezed the ill-fitting brown jacket over his saggy frame. He pulled down on the lapels out of habit, which did little to flatten the wrinkles.

"I think it's time for a new suit," his deputy said.

"Maybe it's time for a new deputy director," Kaparov said, raising an eyebrow.

"If you're not back within the hour, I'll start looking for my new deputy," Prerovsky said, dusting off the shoulders of Kaparov's jacket.

"If succeeding me gives you hope, who am I to crush the dream?"

"You can't blame a young man for dreaming. See you in few minutes. Greshnev isn't one for many words," Prerovsky said.

Kaparov walked through the cluster of cubicles and workstations that defined his turf on the third floor. Few of his analysts looked up from their work to greet him, which was to be expected. His true mood, or whatever he chose to display, was rarely established before lunch, and nobody wanted to push their luck, especially after a visit from Internal Affairs. This suited him fine. He wasn't in the mood for small talk on most days, and today was no exception. Despite this preference, he'd have to put on a smile and do some public relations work, regardless of the meeting's outcome.

In a few seconds, word would spread like wildfire that he was meeting with Greshnev, fueling rumors limited only by their wildest imagination. Within two minutes, half of them will be despondent, convinced that the entire section would be dismissed, their careers forever tainted by Kaparov's stubbornness. The other half would start to prepare their transfer requests, certain that Greshnev would appoint a ruthlessly cruel director to replace Kaparov and reform the section. He'd spend half of the remaining day smiling and assuring them that everything was fine. The smiling was the worst part. Kaparov hated smiling.

He proceeded past the boundary of his section and turned onto a central thoroughfare leading to the staircase. A few minutes later, he was standing in front of Greshnev's secretary like a schoolboy waiting to see the principal for a spanking. She barely acknowledged his presence, and he silently refused to take one of the wooden chairs against the wall.

Inga Soyev, as her desk placard indicated, had apparently been a fixture in this building before Kaparov started his career with the KGB in 1973. With silver hair and graying skin, she looked old enough to have served as a secretary under Stalin's regime. Despite her years, she looked sturdy. When she stood up to open the door to announce Kaparov to Greshnev, she showed no signs of advanced age so common among senior Muscovites. Wearing a pressed knee-length gray skirt and starched white blouse, she moved steadily and surely, with perfect posture. Kaparov suddenly felt self-conscious about his shabby appearance and unhealthy aura.

"The director will see you now," she stated without smiling.

"Thank you," Kaparov said, moving past her scornful gaze as quickly as possible without breaking into a run.

The door closed behind him.

"Alexei. Have a seat, please," Greshnev said, indicating the cushioned, straight-back chair in front of his desk.

"Thank you, sir."

He wondered if he would have the opportunity to say more than "thank you" to Greshnev. Actually, if that was all he was required to say, the meeting would be a success.

"I just spoke with Internal Affairs," Greshnev began.

"So did I. Less than five minutes ago, coincidentally," Kaparov replied.

Greshnev showed the faintest hint of a smile, which faded as quickly as it arrived. "Monchegorsk is a closed issue."

"I couldn't agree more. I haven't asked any questions or made any suggestions in nearly two weeks."

"Let's keep it that way. This comes from above. Far above me," Greshnev added.

"I never look any higher than your office, comrade. If it comes from you, that's all I need to hear," Kaparov said.

"All right then. Do you need anything from me?"

Here was the moment of truth. He didn't want to piss off Greshnev, but it was necessary to keep him off the suspects list, should the missing CIA officer from Stockholm end up in a dank, SVR-sponsored torture chamber.

"How should I proceed with Anatoly Reznikov? I forwarded my assessment of the information captured in Dagestan, but never heard back. If he's working with Chechen separatists, this could represent a major bioweapons threat to the Russian Federation."

"I have it on good authority that Reznikov is no longer a threat. SVR wouldn't release any details, which leads me to believe that he met an untimely death."

"The only thing untimely is that it didn't happen years ago. I'll close Reznikov's file," Kaparov said.

"Good work making that connection. Russia is much safer because of your diligence in that matter," Greshnev said, standing up. He held out his hand, signifying the end of the meeting.

"Thank you, sir. That's all I've ever persevered to do on behalf of our government."

Chapter 7

Mihail Osin walked toward the door at the back of the dimly lit room. He stopped and glanced over his shoulder at the sagging, bloodied CIA officer zip-tied by his hands and feet to a high-backed wooden chair in the center of the room before continuing to the door. He heard the door's external deadbolts slide, followed by a sudden bright light. Mihail stepped into the well-lit hallway and shut the door behind him, shaking his head at Stepka, one of the operatives assigned to his team. Stepka uttered an expletive and relocked the deadbolts. None of them wanted to spend any more time in this building.

Acquired over a decade ago by a shell company associated with the Russian Foreign Intelligence Service, the warehouse served as a Directorate "S" way station for northern European operations, and provided the perfect location for a discreet interrogation. Located on Oxelösund's working waterfront, the warehouse was one of few serviceable buildings left on the sparse north dock. Most of Oxelösund's ironworks exports passed through structures on the more accessible and modernized southern dock, leaving the north dock largely ignored.

Warehouse 42 was maintained in decent enough shape to keep Swedish public safety authorities from demanding a detailed inspection of the grounds, but not well enough to attract the attention of local criminals. Most of the money allocated to the warehouse by Directorate S went into an internal expansion of the "corporate offices." The internal structure consisted of several soundproofed interrogation rooms, stocked with every tool or device needed to extract information from its unfortunate guests. Mercifully, Warehouse 42 represented the last stop for most guests. The unluckiest among them were transferred by boat to a coastal site near St. Petersburg, where they could be sent anywhere within Russia for a more thorough interrogation.

Additional rooms beyond the interrogation cells served as temporary lodging for transiting teams of "illegals" or Spetsnaz; complete with showers, locally sourced clothing and a stocked kitchen.

The last room, known as the "bath house," served the most nefarious purpose, and few within Directorate S knew what was kept inside. Once a guest expired in Warehouse 42, they were taken to the "bath house," where the team that "sponsored" the guest would dispose of the body. One look inside the room would test the personal resolve of the hardest operative.

Unlike the rest of the "office suite," the interior walls of the "bath house" were lined with floor to ceiling cinderblock, matching the ugly gray concrete floor. An industrial-grade stainless-steel ventilation hood reached down from the center of the tall ceiling. A 55-gallon stainless-steel barrel mounted to a wheeled frame sat next to a Teflon-coated 20-gallon rectangular bin along the wall opposite the door. A small sewer drain sat in the furthest corner of the room, flanked by a water spigot on one side and a neatly coiled, wall-mounted garden hose on the other. A sturdy plastic shelving unit next to the door held several one-gallon jugs of hydrofluoric acid. Larger, five-gallon, military-style plastic jugs labeled "sodium hydroxide," lye, were stacked side by side on the lowest shelf next to three neatly arranged propane tanks.

The most gruesome spectacle was the "work bench," a thick, wooden four-foot-by-three-foot tabletop set upon solid, stubby square legs. The table was pushed up against the wall next to the plastic shelving unit. A blue industrial pegboard covered the wall above the table, suspending two small chainsaws and an electric skill saw.

The process for disposing of Warehouse 42's guests was relatively simple. The bodies were cut into smaller pieces and placed in the stainless-steel drum, which was wheeled into the center of the room under the ventilation hood. The drum was filled with enough sodium hydroxide and water to cover the body parts, and a sizable propane burner was placed under the drum. The burner slowly brought the drum's contents to a boil, accelerating the alkaline hydrolysis process and completely dissolving the body within seven to eight hours.

The resulting alkaline soup was poured down the drain in the corner and washed down with the hose. Hydrofluoric acid was used in the Teflon-coated bin to dissolve metal remnants like knee pins or any stubborn bone material that failed to completely dissolve in the heated lye. The guest's clothing and shoes were often burned in a metal barrel outside of the warehouse or taken along by the "sponsors" to be deposited in a city dumpster.

Upon completion of the process, nothing remained of the guest in question. Sixty-seven guests had disappeared at Warehouse 42 during its twelve-year operational period, designating the cement-lined room in Oxelösund, Sweden, as the most active "bath house" operated on foreign soil by Directorate S. Within Russia, several notorious "bath houses" far exceeded Warehouse 42's productivity level, forming the backbone of an expansive network of clandestine torture chambers commissioned after the dissolution of the KGB in 1991. Nearly all of the KGB's secret locations had been exposed when the organization was split into the Foreign Intelligence Service (SVR) and the Federal Security Service (FSB). The SVR's Directorate S, which operated under considerably less oversight than any of the other branches, took the lead in reestablishing the KGB's legendary interrogation apparatus.

Mihail turned left and walked down the concrete hallway, past a door leading to another windowless interrogation room. He leaned against the cold wall and dialed his control station on a small, encrypted satellite phone kept in his coat pocket. After negotiating a few layers of SVR security, he was connected with Dmitry Ardankin, Director of Operations for Directorate S. Ardankin's voice sounded like a whisper.

"What do we know?"

"The CIA station at the embassy provided ground surveillance for the operation. Several officers were staged throughout the city to put eyes on the target when the location was passed."

"When did they put these officers in the field?"

"The night before the raid. The station chief turned over control of the agents to NCS operations. The assault team arrived separately, but he doesn't think the assault team was CIA."

"What does that mean?" Ardankin asked.

"He maintains that the station didn't know anything about the target or the team. CIA headquarters was in direct communication with the agents on the street, effectively compartmentalizing the operation. At this point, I don't think he's hiding anything from us. We've worked on him all night."

"Did he shed any light on the mission source?"

"Karl Berg was the only end user identified."

"Yes. That would make sense. What about the missing female CIA officer? Erin Foley?"

"According to Reese, Foley never returned to the embassy. She must have been situated the closest to Reznikov's apartment in Södermalm."

"And the CIA station chief?" Ardankin demanded.

"Reese was sitting with the station chief at the embassy, waiting for word. They received a call from headquarters around 7:30 AM, notifying them that the operation had succeeded."

"Did he take the call?"

"No. It was the station chief."

"Did he know the location of the safe house?"

"No. He was not aware of any secure facilities within Sweden. Should we prepare for a return trip to Stockholm? It sounds like we should have grabbed the station chief," Mihail said.

"We don't grab station chiefs, or any CIA employees, for that matter. This was a one-time exception. We'll have to approach this from a different angle," Ardankin said.

"What should we do with Mr. Reese?"

"Pack him up for shipment. There's no sense in wasting the resource. What's done is done. It's not every day we grab a station officer. I'll pass the pickup information shortly. Once the pickup is complete, head to Munich and stand by for further orders. We may have located one of the shooters in Stockholm."

"Understood," Mihail said, and the connection ended

He looked down the hallway toward Stepka and saw that the operative had been joined by the rest of the team.

"We prep him for transport," Mihail said.

"That's a first," one of the operatives remarked.

"Beats the alternative. I hate that fucking room," Stepka replied.

"The situation is unique. Events like this cause ripples that tend to come back as tidal waves," Mihail said.

"As long as I don't have to pour him down a drain, I don't care what they do with him," Stepka added.

Mihail regarded his comment with feigned disinterest. The young operative had no idea what this meant. Grabbing an "illegal" off the street was one thing, nabbing a station officer was another. There would be repercussions.

Chapter 8

12:50 PM
Foreign Intelligence Service (SVR) Headquarters
Yasanevo Suburb, Moscow, Russian Federation

Dmitry Ardankin stood up from the small desk in his private communications room and took a few steps to the sealed door leading out of the chamber. He paused for a moment before sitting back down in front of the secure telephone set. He had another call to make that would require the use of this space. The closet-sized room was located at the front of his office, taking up most of the right corner. Resembling a walk-in closet, the standalone chamber had been designed to thwart any possible efforts to electronically eavesdrop on his conversations from the outside, despite the elaborate amount of effort put into the building itself. Laser detection and jamming technology had been mounted to every building in the SVR campus in order to augment the countermeasures integrated directly into the buildings.

The exterior windows had been designed to passively defeat attempts to use laser technology. Each window held two panes of glass separated by a spacer frame. The area between the frames was filled with a gas mixture denser than air, effectively damping sound waves travelling from one pane to the next. An integrated sound generator was applied directly to the outer pane, creating thermal noise over a wide frequency range, which superimposed vibrations equivalent to a forty-decibel level of sound. This created the unusual humming effect heard throughout the campus. Unless Ardankin yelled during a conversation at his desk, a laser-based listening device targeting his office window would register white noise. Finally, a coating on the outer pane prevented the laser from reaching the inner pane, where the glass vibrated with his voice. All of this, and they had still insisted on a soundproof room within a soundproof building.

He rarely used the chamber, but this morning's call from Mihail Osin had been different. The room also provided him an extra layer of security against internal eavesdropping, which was highly unlikely. Still, the ongoing operation in Sweden required the strictest compartmentalization. Beyond Osin's team, only the director of the Foreign Intelligence Service knew about the kidnapping. Unfortunately, the risky gamble didn't shed much light on the situation, beyond confirming that either the SVR or FSB had been compromised. The only other way to explain the security breach involved a more frightening possibility.

The Americans may have developed a new generation of surveillance technology without their knowledge. He hoped it wasn't the latter. His people could uncover a leak, but a significant shift in electronic espionage technology represented a devastating challenge to Russian's intelligence community. He didn't look forward to the next call. The director would report these findings directly to Putin, and nobody could predict how he would react.

Dmitry Ardankin suddenly didn't relish the privilege of sharing Russia's darkest secrets anymore. Putin had an ironfisted reputation for keeping these secrets from ever reaching daylight, regardless of rank or position. Putin and his cronies continued to take a bizarre and unhealthy interest in Reznikov. Unhealthy for anyone but Putin. Ardankin decided he would watch his back on this one. He hadn't made it this far to be poured down a drain on the outskirts of Moscow.

Chapter 9

Maxim Greshnev continued to examine a recent report on Monchegorsk when the door opened. He heard Inga go through her solemn routine of making anyone who stood outside of his door feel uncomfortable.

"The director will see you now," she said.

He looked up when the door closed and frowned, motioning for Arkady Baranov to take a seat. He waited until the Center of Special Operations (CSN) director was seated before placing the report on his desk. He regarded Baranov for a moment, knowing that his usual gruff scare tactics would have little effect on the man. Baranov still looked like an active Spetsnaz operative, athletic and grizzled, his muscular frame evident under his navy blue suit. The only telltale sign that Baranov had reached his fifties was graying hair, which he kept in a smart buzz cut. He'd known Baranov for nearly twenty years, having helped the ambitious Spetsnaz colonel transition from the KGB to the Federal Security Service.

Colonel Baranov's distinguished career started in Afghanistan as a young "Alpha Group" lieutenant. He led a squad of KGB Spetsnaz during *Operation Storm-333*, an ambitious raid launched against Afghan President Hafizullah Amin, at Tajbeg Palace in 1979. The operation killed the anti-Soviet leader, along with his entire two-hundred-guard contingent, successfully opening the door for the Soviet occupation of Afghanistan. Baranov successfully negotiated a transfer to the newly formed "Vympel Group" in 1981 and returned to Afghanistan, where he led sabotage groups against the Mujahideen until the bitter end of the Soviet occupation in 1989.

After Afghanistan, the newly minted full colonel took command of the Vympel Group, which was gutted and tossed around from agency to agency upon the collapse of the Soviet Union two years later. Colonel Baranov's group eventually landed in the hands of the Interior Ministry (MVD), with only sixty of its original three hundred operatives. In 1993, Maxim Greshnev plucked Baranov out of the MVD on his meteoric rise up the FSB hierarchy ladder, placing him as the assistant deputy director of Greshnev's newly formed Center of Special Operations. By 1995, Baranov had consolidated control of CSN, showing little motivation or ambition to rise any further, which suited Greshnev fine. He had little doubt that Baranov could easily outmaneuver him on the way to the top. Fortunately for him, Baranov was Spetsnaz to the core and couldn't step away from the action to be bothered with politics.

"We have a problem," Greshnev grumbled.

Baranov cocked his head slightly and waited for Greshnev to continue.

"I just got off the phone with the director of the Foreign Intelligence Service, and he's not happy—"

"He's never happy," Baranov interrupted, drawing a critical stare from Greshnev.

"Apparently, they have confirmed that Reznikov's address in Stockholm was leaked to the CIA."

Baranov shook his head. "Let me guess. They think it came from my division."

"This was the first joint operation with SVR in years, and it ended in disaster. It's only natural for them to react this way."

"Joint operation? We had a grand total of four people in the Ops Room for that fiasco. Myself, two others that I trust explicitly, and one of the senior techs," Baranov said.

"Then our investigation shouldn't take too long," Greshnev said.

"That won't satisfy our friends in the SVR," Baranov said.

"No. It probably won't. We can expect them to start surveillance on your entire department," Greshnev said.

"Maybe we should put Directorate S under surveillance. How many fucking people did they have involved in the operation?"

"Given the unit involved, not as many as you might think. Ardankin won't ignore the possibility that the leak came from his side, and neither will his boss," Greshnev said.

"It's the Security Service's job to investigate issues like this," Baranov said.

"Not when Zaslon is involved. I can't hand this over to the Counterintelligence Service and let them swarm CSN. I'll handpick a team from Internal Affairs' (IA) special investigative unit. We'll keep this low profile for now, and I'll actively liaison with Ardankin's SVR goons. Give them what they want, and get them out of our business," Greshnev said.

"I'll tolerate surveillance by our SVR comrades, but that's all. If they make a move against any of my people, they'll have a war on their hands...and I'm good at fighting wars," Baranov said.

"I know you are, and so do they. I'll make sure they understand the ground rules. Do you have any ideas beyond the four agents present in the Operations Room during the raid?" Greshnev asked.

"Our weakest link is technology. In the old days, we had telephones and status boards marked by grease pencil. Throw in a few TVs hooked to video players. Now we have twenty widescreen monitors, hundreds of computers, videoconferencing equipment, visual data boards...all controlled by a network of servers and optics cables that I couldn't dream of comprehending. The whole setup requires an army of technicians, many of whom I've never personally met. The whole fucking place is a liability, which is why I kept the number of people involved in that operation to an absolute minimum. Those fucking idiots at SVR could have updated me over the phone, instead of insisting on a live joint feed. All we needed to know is whether the mission succeeded or failed...and even that didn't really matter. Unless Reznikov steps foot on Russian soil, we're on the sideline."

"The joint involvement was my idea," Greshnev said.

Baranov cracked a smile before responding. "I know."

"You haven't changed since I met you. Always a ball breaker," Greshnev said.

"That's my job these days."

Greshnev smiled in return. "That's why I keep you around. Promoting you out here would catapult this place into chaos. We'll investigate the techs associated with the Operations Room in this building, leaving your headquarters out of it, for now. Internal Affairs has a group that specializes in technology investigation. I have to bring the heat down on everyone that was in the Operations Room at the time."

"Including me?"

"Especially you. I can't afford to have you sneak up and kill one of their surveillance agents. The sooner I convince them that you're clean, the better."

"Am I that transparent in my old age?" Baranov said.

"Quite the opposite. I have no fucking idea what you are thinking these days. Make sure none of your operatives kill any of their new shadows. All right?"

"Understood," Baranov said, standing up to take his leave. "This Reznikov business…there's more to this than meets the eye."

Greshnev stared at him blankly. He agreed with Baranov's assessment, but would never acknowledge the fact in front of him, or anyone, for that matter. Pure instinct told him to steer clear of pursuing the matter. Even though he truly possessed no information suggesting that Reznikov was anything more than a rogue scientist offering the prospect of bioweapons to terrorists, he sensed there was more to this story. Way more.

His Directorate had chased down men like Reznikov before, but the effort and resources spent on finding Reznikov had been disproportionately higher than any of those previous efforts, and this calculation didn't account for the diplomatic risks inherent to operating larger than usual teams on foreign soil.

Sending a regional military Spetznaz platoon into Kazakhstan turned into a disaster of epic proportions, somehow explained away as a training exercise gone seriously awry. Fortunately for the Center of Special Operations, someone at the highest levels didn't think their Alpha Group team in Novosibirsk would be large enough to deal with the five Americans snooping around the former site of Reznikov's suspected laboratory. Apparently, an entire platoon hadn't been enough.

The most damning evidence came from the operation in Stockholm. Neither of them could fathom the circumstances leading to the loss of ten Zaslon Spetznaz operatives. Frankly, he had been shocked to learn that the SVR had assembled so many Zaslon operatives in one place. They had never been informed of the actual number, but he had little trouble putting the pieces together based on Swedish news reports and crime scene information leaked by their sources in the Swedish National Bureau of Investigation and Stockholm County Police Department. The importance of this mission to Putin must have been unprecedented. He could think of no other reason why Dmitry Ardankin would have authorized such a large-scale Zaslon operation.

Zaslon operatives typically worked alone under deep cover, conducting sensitive missions abroad related to "state security." This euphemism covered a wide spectrum of nefarious activities, from kidnapping to assassination. Most of their operations were carried out against Russian citizens who had betrayed Russia in one way or another. Of course, this was all purely rumor. Government officials had never acknowledged the existence of the Zaslon program, which was why the Stockholm mess underscored the importance of Reznikov. The Americans had wanted the scientist just as badly, which added another layer of intrigue to the entire fiasco. He didn't believe that Reznikov had been terminated, regardless of what he'd been directly told by Dmitry Ardankin. This business wasn't finished.

"It's a done deal. Reznikov is dead, and this isn't our business anymore," Greshnev said.

"I can live with that," he said, reaching for the door handle. He turned around again. "If the leak turns out to be one of mine. I'll take care of it personally."

"I would expect nothing less from the legendary Arkady Baranov."

When the door closed, Greshnev stood up and stared out of the window at Lubyanka Square. He could never understand why foreign tourists went out of their way to see the square, which had to be the most uninteresting piece of real estate in all of Moscow. Paved over years ago, and barely resembling anything more than a glorified parking lot, visitors were treated to a shitty patch of grass and flowers surrounded by traffic. He supposed they could visit the Solovetsky Stone in the equally uninspiring park next to the square. The stone was placed there as part of the Gulag memorial, adding to the collective misery of Lubyanka Square, which housed its own share of tragedy.

He watched a gaggle of Westerners mill across the concrete expanse, staring up at the iconic building, which represented past horrors of the Soviet regime. Unknown to most, the repressive terror hadn't truly ended. The government had simply relocated that apparatus to a less public location, south of the city. He really shouldn't cast stones at the Foreign Intelligence Service. His own service had its share of problems, and as a chief director for the Terrorism and Political Extremism Control

Directorate, he often dipped his hands into affairs that had more to do with politics than protecting the Russian Federation.

Even worse, he was often told to stay out of business that clearly fell under his purview, like Monchegorsk. He didn't want to think about that city. If digging around the Reznikov story carried health risks, asking questions about Monchegorsk was like swimming through radioactive sludge. Prior to Kaparov bringing certain reports to his attention about a month ago, his office hadn't paid much attention to the Kola Peninsula. Its geographic isolation on the Barents Sea and shared border with Finland had kept the peninsula quiet. Upon forwarding a report suggesting the possible use of bioweapons against Monchegorsk, the entire peninsula was shut down.

A day later, he learned from one of Putin's key Federation Council lackeys that the entire city had revolted against Moscow in a labor-related dispute. Of course, the military would handle the operation to regain control of the city. Little else was said, and nothing else needed to be said. The story was so preposterous that Greshnev immediately decided he would never mention it again. Kaparov's stubborn insistence on pressing the issue had unnerved him to the point of needing anti-anxiety medication. At least Kaparov had the sense not to bring up Reznikov and Monchegorsk in the same breath. The old-timer might be thick-headed, but he hadn't lost his ability to read between the lines. He needed more agents like Kaparov and Baranov. Effective, reliable and trustworthy.

He sat back down in his thick black leather executive chair and took a deep breath. He had to initiate the investigation into Baranov's people immediately. Fortunately, the investigation would be confined to this building. The leak could only have come from the Operations Room on the third floor, which served as a temporary location to monitor the joint operation in Stockholm. The Center of Special Operations headquarters was located outside of the Moscow ring in Balashikha, and encompassed a vast complex with training facilities for FSB Spetsnaz. Keeping the investigation out of CSN headquarters would be one of his priorities. He reached for the phone and steeled himself for a series of painful conversations.

Chapter 10

2:45 PM
Leopold Strasse
Munich, Germany

Konrad Hubner sipped the remains of his lukewarm cappuccino and glanced around at the lively tables in Café Centrum's outdoor terrace. This was one of his favorite cafés, mainly for the local female scenery, which proliferated as summer approached. Not that the café ever suffered from a lack of pleasant background. He loved May in Bavaria. The weather was mild and constantly improving, dragging Bavarians outside in droves to the biergartens, cafés and parks.

Located west of the English Garden on the southern border of the Schwabing district, the café on Leopold Strasse took in a constant flow of university students and wealthy patrons who could afford to live in the upscale neighborhood. As he set down his cup on the table, a mixed group of well-dressed students carrying book bags walked onto the patio from Leopold Strasse, searching for an empty table. He didn't want to make them wait any longer than necessary and had no intention of pulling the creepy move of inviting them to sit at his table. He picked up his cup and saucer, nodding to a tall, male student, who led the group to the table, thanking him as they passed. He walked inside and settled the bill directly before walking onto Leopold Strasse and turning south.

He wasn't sure what he'd do with the rest of the day. A few analytical projects awaited completion, but none of them involved pressing deadlines. His client base consisted of a few handpicked, undemanding European Union financial houses that passed on collaborative, long-term economic forecasting projects. He had attended Munich Business School in 2001 at the suggestion of General Sanderson, who had assured him that their unit would recommence operations by the time he had finished. The degree would open doors in Europe and serve to enhance his cover, allowing him to take on professional work and justify his far-from-modest lifestyle.

Hubner strolled along the wide, tree-lined sidewalk, scanning his surroundings. Despite the appearance of a relaxed lifestyle in Munich, he remained ever vigilant for threats. Turning onto Georgen Strasse, headed for his apartment two buildings away, his eyes were drawn to the red umbrellas of a comfortable biergarten nestled away behind the trees near the street corner. The gated patio served light food and excellent beer in generous one-liter, frosted glass mugs. He felt the pull of a crisp Augustiner Edelstoff and started to angle toward the gate. A sharp pain in his left thigh snapped him out of his reverie.

He turned his head left and noticed a student continuing up the street toward Leopold Strasse. The man's face was hidden, but the backpack, dark corduroy pants and untucked shirttails gave him the distinct impression that he was a student. White headphone wires trailed down his neck, appearing from the bottom of his bushy, brown hair. The pain in his thigh had disappeared by the time he reached down to caress and examine the spot. He didn't see a rip in his dark blue, designer jeans, and started to wonder if he had experienced a cramp or some kind of transient nerve impingement. The kid turned right and crossed Georgen Strasse, headed south on Leopold Strasse, toward the university. He disappeared behind a thick stand of trees next to the tall apartment building on the corner. Hubner shrugged and continued on his walk, distracted from his thoughts of cold beer.

He made it halfway to his apartment building before the first wave of sluggishness struck, signaling that he was in serious trouble. He felt like he was pushing his legs and arms through a viscous pool of petroleum. He started to turn his head to stare back at the corner of the Leopold Strasse, in what he knew was a futile attempt to spot the cleverly disguised fucker that injected him with some kind of toxin.

There wasn't much he could do at this point. He would either be dead or incapacitated within a short period of time, and death might be his better option. Defying his body's newly defined gravitational attraction to the earth's core, he struggled to reach his jacket's inside pocket, straining as his vision started to narrow. He found the phone just as his body toppled to the stonework walkway, trapping his arm under his torso. There was no way he could pull his phone out at this point. He could barely move his fingers.

The last thing he registered as his vision closed was the sound of footsteps approaching.

❧

Vadim Dragunov continued walking along Leopold Strasse, slowing his pace. He glanced behind him, just in case something had gone awry, leaving Hubner capable of pursuit. He saw nothing. He turned to face south on Leopold, catching sight of the Siegestor, or Victory Gate, a few hundred meters down the wide boulevard. The three-arched structure, similar in style to the Arc de Triomphe in Paris and Arch of Constantine in Rome, was crowned with a statue of Bavaria riding a lion-quadriga. Dragunov appreciated the simple, yet masculine architecture of the one-hundred-and-fifty-year-old landmark looming ahead. The Siegestor was dwarfed in size and significance compared to the Brandenburg gate. Berlin reminded him of Moscow, where each successive ruler felt compelled to make a bigger mark on the architectural landscape.

He heard a motor vehicle slow on the street next to him, which drew his attention away from the gate. The SVR team's silver minivan pulled into the bicycle lane several feet in front of him and stopped. The right sliding door opened, and he casually walked into the van, glancing around one last time for the police before closing the door. Blocking a bicycle lane in Munich, even for a few seconds, could attract more attention from the police than running a red light. These fucking Germans were obsessed with their bicycles, and it was a matter of pride to get from one place to another without using a car. In Moscow, only the poorest migrant workers rode bicycles, and even that was a rarity.

"Are you trying to get us arrested?" he asked in Russian. "You have to pay close attention to the roads here. There's a parking strip, clearly marked by a solid white line. You can pull over and park on the other side of the line, as long as you don't block the bike path."

The driver protested as he drove the van forward, continuing down the bike path. "How the hell was I supposed to know it was a bike path?"

The van crossed over a small lip in the road as he merged back into traffic.

"By observing the damn curb," Dragunov said.

"I barely felt that," the driver continued.

Dragunov shook his head and stared at the lead agent, who he only knew as Mihail.

"Take it easy, Stepka. This man's observations will keep us out of trouble," the leader said.

Dragunov leaned his head over the headrest, glancing into the third row. Konrad Hubner lay crumpled on the seat cushion next to a detached-looking agent. He hoped this team wasn't filled with sociopaths. They were all sociopaths on some level, but so far this crew's attitude hadn't impressed him. Maybe he was misjudging them, since he had become more accustomed to working alone. He would have preferred to keep walking down Leopold Strasse, but his order had been crystal clear. He would lead Hubner's interrogation.

The German businessman had been photographed in Stockholm, driving the van involved in the Zaslon massacre. SVR got lucky with a traffic camera, which took a clear picture of the driver and front passenger. Konrad Hubner had been the driver, and a Serbian war criminal named Marko Resja had been his passenger. None of it made sense, which was why headquarters wanted Dragunov personally involved in the interrogation. Not only was he a Zaslon operative, but he was considered to be one of the organization's top interrogators, specializing in long, drawn-out torture. Everybody confessed to Dragunov, eventually.

"No problems on the street?" Dragunov asked.

"Everything was perfectly timed. Nobody on the street saw us load him into the van," Mihail said.

"Good. The next step is to get us to a secure location east of the city. If your driver can follow simple directions, I can have us there in less than an hour. Another hour beyond that will put us at the Czech border."

The driver didn't take the bait and allowed his team leader to respond, which was the proper response under these circumstances.

"He's extremely capable, as long as we don't run into anymore bike paths," Mihail said, trying to alleviate the tension.

"I never saw a bike path before coming to Germany," Dragunov admitted. "Who the fuck has time to ride a bike?"

Chapter 11

Vadim Dragunov squeezed out of the two-story barn and took in a deep breath, savoring the rich mixture of forest scents. The sharp fragrance of the occasional spruce or fir tree faintly stabbed through the overwhelming smell of new foliage from the ever-present towering beech trees beyond the clearing. The fresh smell of spring competed with the musty aroma of moist, decaying leaves from last fall's seasonal shedding. He missed spending time in the countryside. He glanced toward the dirt path leading from the forest into the tight clearing and nodded at an SVR agent leaning against a thick tree alongside the road.

Movement inside the barn drew his attention, and he turned to see two agents carrying a bloodied body into the light cast through the half-opened barn door. He pushed the heavy, reinforced steel door along its well-lubricated track, giving the team a larger opening. Dragunov stood aside and paid his respects as the men struggled with the corpse. Whoever this man had been, he was by far the most skilled and resilient operative Dragunov had come across in a long time. A worthy adversary on every level.

They had arrived at the safe house during the early evening hours and wasted no time commencing Konrad Hubner's interrogation. The interrogation had yielded scant details. Hubner had expertly twisted and

46

turned them in multiple false directions throughout the night, wasting precious time and exhausting them as the dawn approached. Just when they thought they had achieved a breakthrough, they found themselves thirty minutes into another dead end, with Hubner smirking. Even without lips, which agent Osin had removed at an early point in the night, the man still managed to smirk.

Around nine in the morning, they took a short break to eat some breakfast and formulate a new game plan. Unendurable pain and agony would continue to be the centerpiece of their strategy. There was only so much a human could withstand, and they still had some evil-looking tools in the kit they had unearthed from the barn, along with a vial of acid. They had re-entered the barn, expecting a long morning, but Hubner had other plans. Without warning, he managed to impale his neck on Osin's knife, severing the carotid artery. In less than a minute, he bled out onto the concrete floor of the small cinderblock room, taking the rest of his knowledge down the metal drain under his chair.

The two agents carrying Hubner's body had been given specific instructions regarding the preferred disposal method for this site. The stand-alone barn structure did not contain a proper "bath house," so bodies had to be buried at least two hundred meters into the forest, in a westerly direction. A poorly maintained, lightly used trail had been discovered several hundred meters to the southeast, tracking north, so they avoided any unnatural activity east of the site.

The property itself enjoyed a high degree of privacy, buried deep within the national preserve. Only accessible by foot, they had parked their new van in a cleverly constructed hide site a few hundred meters south of the clearing, slugging their way along a relatively unfriendly, twisting path until they reached the barn. Motion detectors hidden along the barn's roofline had confirmed the location's privacy, recording mainly twilight activity commonly associated with deer. This was Dragunov's second visit to Site 93, and Mihail Osin's team's first. He'd uploaded coordinates to an encrypted GPS device to locate both the vehicle hide-site and the barn. Site 93 hadn't seen much activity since the end of the Cold War, which was why Dragunov had chosen it. He liked isolation for jobs like these.

Mihail Osin trailed the body by several feet and stopped in the doorway. Dragunov glanced in his direction, expecting the agent to make an unnecessary excuse for Hubner's early demise. A few moments passed, but the agent remained quiet. He was impressed with Osin. Directorate S Spetsnaz were an impressive group, but this agent was different. He carried himself extremely well, exuded an unspoken leadership influence on his team, and had natural interrogation skills...aside from the rookie mistake that prematurely killed Hubner. He might recommend Osin for consideration within the Zaslon ranks.

"What happened to Hubner is extremely rare. I've seen suspects attempt to choke themselves on their own restraints or try to enrage their interrogators to the point of murder. I've never seen or heard of one cutting their throat like that. Lesson learned. No need to include this in the report. The suspect expired on his own...which is true," Dragunov said.

"That was a first for me. Fuck. This guy was something different altogether," Osin said, stepping into the rays of light peeking through the eastern tree line.

"Very different. At least we got a few new names out of him. Headquarters should be very interested in this Sanderson guy. We also confirmed that they were given Reznikov's address at the last second."

"Either the FSB has a mole, or we do. That alone made this trip well worth the effort."

"He was holding out on us about Marko Resja. Something was off. I could smell it," Osin said.

Dragunov considered his comment for a few moments, staring off into the forest. He agreed with Osin's assessment about Hubner's partner in Stockholm. Whoever they had captured on camera in the passenger seat was a mystery that Hubner didn't care to expose.

"He wasn't familiar with the name, which leads me to believe Marko Resja might have been an alias he'd never heard of. I'm starting to wonder if the entire team in Stockholm had been assembled from multiple sources. It doesn't matter at this point. We pass the information on to Directorate S, and let them sort it out," Dragunov said.

"I'm getting a bad feeling about this one. This isn't a typical setup for the Americans. This is something very different," Osin said.

"We don't even know if the Americans are behind this. That's the real problem here. The U.S. embassy was involved, but even those details are sketchy. Hubner never confirmed that the address was passed by the CIA station chief," Dragunov said.

"I led the assistant station chief's interrogation. He confirmed that this was a CIA operation. They were never given the address. That came directly from another source," Osin said.

"That's what the station chief told him?" Dragunov said.

Osin nodded. "Correct."

"The link to the Americans keeps thinning," Dragunov said, shaking his head. "The station chief could have been working for anyone. Reznikov represents an unchecked financial opportunity for some extremely dangerous, well-funded groups. If this was a mercenary crew working for one of these groups, Russia could end up in the deepest shit pile imaginable. Our job is to shed some light on who was behind the abduction. At this point, I hope to hell it was the Americans, but I'm no longer optimistic."

Both of them turned their heads toward the sound of crackling underbrush and swearing at the edge of the clearing. The burial team had begun their long trek through the forest.

Chapter 12

The president sat back with a bleak face. He glanced at his National Security Advisor and raised both eyebrows, but Karl Berg could tell that James Quinn didn't plan to make the first comment on their proposal. Jacob Remy, the president's chief of staff looked eager to take the first shot in what Berg expected to be a concentrated salvo of opposition against the plan. The president didn't wait.

"I don't like the timing. The nation still hasn't recovered from True America's attack. Public outcry about our apparent lack of infrastructure security has kicked up a storm of Congressional inquiries, none of which appears coordinated...yet. Congressmen and senators are tripping over each other to satisfy their constituents, threatening to open fact-finding investigations into every organization with an acronym. When they get their collective act together and start cooperating, the 9/11 Commission Report will look like a one page intel summary. The Department of Justice has fielded over twenty-two thousand Freedom of Information Act requests over the past two weeks alone. Last year they processed sixty-one thousand in total. It's going to be a long year for all of us, gentlemen, especially the CIA. I have it on good authority that the Senate Select Committee on Intelligence plans to dig deep. I don't think we can afford to have the operation you've suggested on the books."

The CIA director nodded and tapped his pencil on the table. "I've been assured that this operation can be accomplished off the books," he said. "The facility can be destroyed and the principals neutralized by a small team. No agency assets will be used. The facility appears to be a soft target."

"How can you be sure it's a 'soft target'?" Jacob Remy asked, mimicking quotation marks with both hands to emphasize "soft target." "A secret Russian bioweapons facility? I think you're underestimating the security involved. We can't afford an international incident. Not now."

Karl Berg couldn't resist interrupting the conversation. Selling them on the mechanics of a plan that hadn't been developed was pointless if they didn't agree that the facility represented a clear and present danger to the United States. He wasn't sure they had reached this consensus yet.

"Mr. President, may I?"

Jacob Remy looked annoyed by the interruption.

"Please," the president assented.

"During the Cold War, Vektor Labs was part of the Biopreparat system, a vast network of secret laboratories, each focused on a different pathogenic weapon. Vektor produced smallpox. Biopreparat dissolved with the collapse of the Soviet Union, and most of the facilities were abandoned. Vektor survived and became the State Research Center of Virology and Biotechnology, hosting international scientists and serving as Russia's equivalent to our CDC. The elite army regiment that guarded the facility during the Cold War no longer exists. Our information suggests that security is provided by a small contract force consisting of Russian ex-special forces and—"

"That doesn't sound like a soft target," Remy interrupted.

"It's soft for the group we'll use. Beyond contract security, response to a facility breach would be reactive in nature. A regional Spetsnaz group is tasked to provide a rapid response team in case of emergency, but it won't arrive in time to make a difference. They're hiding an illegal bioweapons lab in plain sight. It's a soft target because they're trying to draw attention away from the facility. The team can destroy the lab. I have no doubt about that. The real question is do we believe that this facility needs to be destroyed? Based on what I've seen in the past month, I firmly believe that this facility spells trouble. Weaponized encephalitis is just one of many WMDs in the works at Vektor. The Russians are developing offensive weapons, and as we can clearly see by their cover-up of Monchegorsk, they're taking extreme measures to keep this a secret. I say we bury their secret before even scarier groups get their hands on their work."

"Do you have evidence to suggest other groups are actively pursuing that angle?" the president asked, turning to the National Security Advisor.

"The Iranians have been aggressively pursuing multiple WMD routes."

"I'm not asking about the perpetual quest by Islamic fundamentalists for weapons of mass destruction. I need a specific, actionable reason to authorize an attack on this facility. If you told me Iranian agents were headed there in two hours to take possession of biological weapons, I'd vaporize the site. I don't disagree that this is a nasty place that would be better off as a smoldering ruin, but I need to put an end to our little low-intensity conflict with the Russians before it spirals out of control. I understand we've lost a CIA officer in Stockholm? What happens to our people when Vektor labs is attacked?"

Thomas Manning stepped in to answer the president's question. "Mr. President, I don't believe Mr. Reese's disappearance is a retribution-style action. Too much time has elapsed since Stockholm. They're still trying to piece together what happened to the Russian scientist that could blow the lid off their secret. The Russians can't afford to draw any attention to this. They're still sitting on a powder keg up in the Kola Peninsula. Our analysts believe that they won't respond to a surgical strike limited to the bioweapons facility. This may even give the Russians a way out of the mess they've created in the Kola Peninsula. We could even congratulate certain counterparts in their Foreign Intelligence Service on a job well done."

"A job well done?" Remy asked.

"They uncovered and destroyed a rogue bioweapons program responsible for creating the weapon used in Monchegorsk to turn the population homicidal. They had no choice but to suppress the population using military force. At the same time, Putin can publicly express his outrage against the development of biological weapons and announce that Russia will host a summit to develop plans to prevent this kind of a tragedy in the future. Something like that," Manning said.

"Or he'll do nothing and simply stare at me with emotionless eyes the next time we meet," the president said.

"Either way, Mr. President, the United States and the world will be a safer place. Frankly, this mission is worth the risks involved, even if it gets messy afterward. What if we fail to stop the next attack against the U.S.?"

"That's why we hire the best and brightest to work for our intelligence agencies. To stop these attacks."

"It won't always be enough," Berg said, creating an awkward pause in the conference.

"Mr. President, I stand by my team's assessment. The value of taking this fight to Vektor Labs far outweighs the risks, which can be mitigated the sooner we act," Director Copley said.

The president rubbed his face and stared at Karl Berg for a few seconds. The answer had been evident on the president's face as soon as he lowered his hands, but something caused him some hesitation. Berg wondered how much the president had been told about the missions and decisions leading to the discovery of True America's plot. Did he know that Berg had initiated a series of questionable covert activities that put the FBI in a position to stop the insane vision of domestic terrorists? Was he trying to gauge whether his words would have any impact on Berg's course of action?

"Director Copley," the president began, "the nation owes this team a debt of gratitude that can never be fully explained, or adequately paid, but I won't authorize this raid without credible evidence of a more immediate threat. I'd like to approach this from a different angle, using diplomacy instead of mercenaries. If that fails, I will reconsider taking direct action. Until then, all planning activities related to a raid on Vektor Labs must cease."

Berg had expected the president to reject their plan, but he hadn't expected the overt slapdown that came with his less than subtle use of the word *mercenaries*. He felt his blood begin to rise, and had to use every ounce of restraint he possessed not to respond. These "mercenaries" had saved countless lives and prevented the United States from spiraling into utter chaos. They had sacrificed without hesitation, against near suicidal odds. General Sanderson may be a devious son of a bitch on many levels, but his loyalty and commitment to the United States remained untarnished, which was more than Berg could say for the men sitting across from him.

"I understand, Mr. President. We'll monitor the situation at Vektor closely. If a threat emerges, we'll be in a position to offer a solution," Director Copley said.

The president stood up from the small conference table, along with Jacob Remy, signifying the end of their meeting. Berg stood respectfully and kept silent. A secret service agent escorted them past the security station inside the West Wing lobby, where Director Copley separated from Manning and Berg. He had arranged a few additional meetings to coincide with his trip to Capitol Hill, most likely to spare himself the discomfort of riding back to McLean with the two of them. This suited Berg fine, since he had no intention of dropping the issue of Vektor labs. The director didn't reinforce the president's decree while they weaved their way through the hectic hallways of the West Wing. They engaged in small talk about the White House and some of the historically significant pieces located throughout the living museum. Maybe that was Director Copley's intention. Manning waited until they were safely behind the thick bullet-resistant glass and armored chassis of an agency Suburban before speaking.

"That didn't turn out like I expected," Manning said.

"Yes, it did," Berg said, staring out of the window at the White House.

"Maybe you're right. The president left us some wiggle room, and Copley conveniently disappeared. I want you to contact Minkowitz and see what the Israelis can offer about the Iranians."

"We'll need more than that. The Israelis whispering sweet nothings about Iranian WMD projects won't sway the president or his National Security Council. I'll take another trip to Vermont. Reznikov isn't the type to give us everything up front. He never mentioned Iranians at the facility. Maybe he can verify one of these sweet nothings."

"If you can make that kind of connection, I'll take this right back to Copley."

"And if Copley can't convince the president?" Berg asked.

"We need the president's support to get Sanderson's people out of there. With the president on board, I can put together a package that will give them a fighting chance to reach the Kazakhstan border. Two hundred plus miles is a long journey without help."

"Sanderson's people will take the mission…regardless," Berg said.

"That's his choice. Our job is to identify the threats and match them up with the appropriate solution," Manning said.

Berg sighed. "We owe Sanderson more than that."

"I agree," Manning said, "which is why we need to find a way to gain the president's approval."

"And if that fails?"

"We go with Plan B."

"I wasn't aware of a Plan B," Berg replied.

"Plan B is whatever we can cobble together using your vast network of friends and favors."

"Let's hope it doesn't come down to Plan B. The past month has exhausted my supply of favors."

Chapter 13

Karl Berg carried two double espressos to a table in the back corner of the café and gently placed the saucers on the table in front of Wiljam Minkowitz. The serious-looking Mossad liaison regarded the small porcelain cup for a moment and stared up at him with a neutral expression until he sat down. The table was isolated enough from the other seating choices to allow a private conversation. Less than twenty minutes from closing, only one other table was occupied. As Berg had observed previously, the window table at this location was always the last to clear before the baristas locked the door. Aside from a few to-go orders, they would have few interruptions.

"Thank you for making a trip out into the suburbs at short notice," Berg said.

Minkowitz responded in a New England accent that sounded as natural as Berg's. "My pleasure. Receiving an invitation to coffee by a rising star piqued my curiosity," he said, radiating a false smile.

"Still," Berg said, "considering the fact that Thomas Manning has been avoiding you, I appreciate this."

"I know exactly why Thomas is dodging me…and so do you. That's why I'm here," Minkowitz said, relaxing with a sip of espresso.

"We need help with something related to your Persian friends."

The Israeli lifted his right eyebrow and pushed his wire-rim glasses back with his index finger. "We're doing all we can in that arena…by ourselves, I might add."

"We'd like to make a contribution to that cause. How familiar are you with Vektor Labs?"

"How serious are you about making a contribution?" Minkowitz asked.

"Deadly serious. I'd like to put Building Six out of business…permanently," Berg said.

"So what's stopping you? I'm still afraid to drink your tap water."

"Vektor doesn't fit the criteria of a clear and present danger to the United States," Berg said.

"I don't understand your politicians. They declare war on threats that don't exist, against enemies that they can control…but they don't have the stomach to take action against the threats right in front of their faces."

"That's where I come in," Berg said.

"And how exactly can I help?"

"If I can definitively link the Iranians to Vektor, the president will green light my operation. We're talking about more than a simple strike against Building Six. I want to permanently shut down the program."

"And any Iranian connection?" Minkowitz asked.

"Yes. If there are Iranians involved, they will cease to be a threat to Israel and the United States. This happens even if a strike against Vektor is prohibited. I promise you that much."

Wiljam Minkowitz finished his espresso and studied Berg. He started nodding slowly, then a genuine smile formed on his thin lips. He extended his hand. "We have a deal. I will provide you with two dossiers. One for a scientist, and one for the Iranian intelligence agent assigned to watch over him. We can't confirm exactly what the scientist is doing inside the lab, but I can assure you he's not studying chicken pox vaccines."

"I might have a source that can help fill in those gaps," Berg said.

"I hear that source came at considerable price," Minkowitz said.

"And we just received another bill."

"The Russians continue to play a dangerous game with our enemies. The Cold War never really ended for them. They just outsourced it. The end of the Cold War was a false notion the politicians managed to sell wholesale," Minkowitz said.

"Most people believe it."

"They chose to look the other way. Most people don't want to see the threats that pose them the most danger. I'll deliver the electronic dossiers tomorrow morning."

They both stood up, and the Israeli leaned over the table to Berg.

"A word of advice? Don't hold onto Reznikov for very long. Vermont isn't as remote as your agency likes to think."

He patted Berg on the shoulder and walked out of the café, leaving the CIA officer speechless. The quicker they destroyed Vektor Labs, the sooner he could permanently close the entire loop. Killing Reznikov was the only way he would be able to sleep soundly again.

Chapter 14

Daniel Petrovich took a long swig of beer from an amber bottle and leaned his head back into the white Adirondack chair. He kept the bottle in a loose grip on the wide chair arm and stared out at the calm ocean. Despite the slowly healing bullet wound to his left shoulder, the past few weeks had been the most relaxing time he had spent with Jessica since they abruptly departed Maine two years earlier. His vacation was interrupted every other day by physical therapy visits and a weekly trip to a Charleston orthopedic center to make sure his shoulder was healing correctly. At least he could wade out into the pleasantly warm waters of the Atlantic.

His peripheral vision caught some movement on the wide porch of the thatched cottage next door. He turned his head and watched a solitary figure walk down the steps leading from the deck to the beach. He had wondered how long they would wait. The man reached the bottom of the stairs and turned right, heading south along the beach. He wore a dark blue polo shirt tucked into khaki pants and a white golfing hat. Even from a distance of thirty yards, the outfit looked brand new. Daniel drained the rest of his beer and set the bottle down onto the faded decking next to his chair. He eased the hand back toward a blue soft-cooler housing several more beers and removed a SIG Sauer P250 from one of the outer pouches, placing the pistol on the chair along his right leg.

Chambered in 9mm, the ambidextrous P250 represented the latest in modular pistol technology, allowing the owner to change the pistol from subcompact to full size to suit different situational needs. The P250 eliminated the need to buy two or three different pistols, or compromise on one. By purchasing different-sized polymer grips and slide assemblies, the user could quickly switch between pistol categories. The pistol resting in the crease of Daniel's olive green cargo shorts had been configured for concealed, subcompact use.

Daniel watched the figure move purposefully toward the stairs leading up to his beach rental, not bothering to feign any interest in the tidal boundary that attracted even the most seasoned tourists. Two weeks. That's all his past would allow. He considered opening another beer, but the man had already reached the stairs and started climbing. Unbelievable. He gripped the pistol and extended it along his right leg, pointing the barrel at the top of the stairs. The gradual rise of the weathered stairway over the rocky seawall eventually brought his uninvited guest's head into view. A few more steps and the head would be exposed to the pistol's barrel. When he recognized the face, he was glad Jessica had decided to go shopping in Savannah for a few hours. He lifted the pistol and rested it on the chair's armrest.

"You could have called," Petrovich said.

"Sanderson said neither of you were taking calls," Karl Berg said, arriving on the deck.

"You missed Jessica. She left for town about ten minutes ago," Petrovich said.

"Twelve to be precise."

"This ought to be good if you didn't want her around. Beer?" Petrovich said, reaching into the cooler.

"Why not. May I?" Berg said, motioning to the chair next to Petrovich.

"Suit yourself," Petrovich said.

He handed a bottle to Berg and took another out for himself.

"How's your shoulder?" Berg said.

"Not bad enough to keep me from drinking beer on the beach," Daniel said, transferring the bottle to his immobilized left hand.

He held the bottle tight, experiencing a sharp pain up and down his arm when he used his good hand to twist the cap free.

"Here's to a polite rejection of whatever you have in mind. You were smart to wait for Jess to leave," Daniel said.

Berg laughed and reached over to meet Daniel's bottle.

"More of a coincidence than anything. How is she doing?" Berg said.

"Better," he said. "Oddly enough, the work we did a few weeks ago had a therapeutic effect on her."

"I'm glad to hear that. She deserves a fair shot at putting as much of this behind her as possible," Berg said.

"I hope the irony of that statement, compounded by your sitting here, isn't lost on you," Petrovich said.

"I'm not here to ask either of you back into the game. I need your consulting services for less than twenty-four hours. A short trip to Vermont for a reunion of sorts," Berg said.

"I'm pretty sure all of the ski resorts are closed at this point."

"This trip won't require a doctor's note. Sanderson agrees that your presence will make a big difference..."

"The last time I came out of retirement for Sanderson, we ended up on the run in South America."

"And that series of events put you in a position to stop one of the worst terrorist attacks in history," Berg finished.

"And nearly killed Jessica," Petrovich said.

Berg took an extra-long swig of beer, which signified that Daniel had struck a nerve with the comment about Jessica. He knew that Berg served as her training mentor at the CIA, eventually recommending her for assignment to the Special Activities Division (SAD). Berg would have been in a position to monitor her progress against a carefully constructed psychological profile. Letting her board an airplane for Paris had been a tragic miscalculation. Traces of Jessica still existed when he found her in Belgrade, but most of them were buried deep inside the hard, superficial shell known as Zorana Zekulic. The young college student he had fallen deeply in love with several years earlier had gone into hibernation. Saving Jessica became his primary mission in Serbia, and in rescuing her, he ensured his own survival. Berg's show of concern for her came fifteen years too late.

"Yeah. She's spent most of her life one degree of separation away from something horrible," Berg said.

Petrovich didn't respond, letting the silence settle between them. Berg finished his beer before speaking.

"Anatoly Reznikov is cooperating with us to provide detailed information about Vektor Labs. I'm putting together an operation to destroy the bioweapons program at the facility, which will be led by your protégé, Richard Farrington. Sanderson would like you to represent Farrington at my next meeting with Reznikov. I'll give you everything we have on Vektor so far, so you can put yourself in Farrington's shoes and fill in the blanks. I'm also hoping that your presence has a unique psychological impact. I don't want him holding anything back."

"Surely he's been exposed to nastier company than me by now," Petrovich said.

"Not exactly."

"Why do I get the distinct feeling I'm not going to like what I'm about to hear?"

"Given his deteriorated physical and mental condition, I couldn't risk putting him in the hell hole he truly deserves to—"

"He deserves to be dead," Petrovich stated.

"He's been inside the bioweapons facility at Vektor, which makes him temporarily invaluable. I'll take him for a long walk after we destroy Vektor."

Petrovich turned his head slightly to look at Berg. The CIA officer stared out at the water, focused, but clearly troubled by something. Possibly disturbed by a fleeting image of what he'd just suggested. He had little doubt that Berg would tie up that loose end when the time was appropriate. He'd come to respect Jessica's former mentor as a man of action and decisiveness. He just didn't care to be sitting next to one of the agency instruments responsible for luring her away from him. Sadly for both of them, the promise of a prestigious and exotic career had been too much for her to resist…and he really couldn't blame her. College had been the only bright spot in an ugly, depressing life as the only child of physically and mentally abusive parents. Out of one frying pan, right into another.

"I'll make the trip. When is your next meeting with Reznikov?"

"Tomorrow morning. I have a charter plane waiting in Savannah. You can read over the files en route. I've booked hotel rooms in Burlington for tonight. It takes about two hours to get out to the site, so we need to start early. I can answer any questions on the way," Berg said.

"I don't suppose you can just give me the directions and I'll meet you there?"

Berg laughed and shook his head. "The CIA has secrets, and then they have secrets. This facility doesn't exist."

"I've been to a few places like that in my career," Petrovich said.

"I guarantee you've never been to a place like this," Berg said, standing up and facing him.

"Now you have me curious. Jessica never spends more than an hour or two in town. I'll be ready to leave when she returns. Should I walk next door?"

"Just step outside and wave. I'll pick you up," Berg said.

"Say hi to my guardian angel," Petrovich said.

Berg stared at his broadening smile.

"She's not the only one with a pair of binoculars and a healthy dose of paranoia. You shortened her hair and colored it black, but I recognized her immediately by the way she carries herself. Stockholm. Did I miss the fine print in my rental contract, or are these houses owned by the CIA?"

"Everything is owned by the CIA," Berg said, turning toward the staircase.

"Certainly feels that way sometimes," Petrovich grumbled.

"Where is she headed after her vacation?"

"To Argentina…then Russia. She's part of the operation," Berg answered.

"She'll certainly fit in," Petrovich said.

"That's what I thought. See you in an hour or so."

He watched Karl Berg amble down the stairs and onto the beach. The CIA officer immediately turned left and proceeded directly to the house next door, not even momentarily stopping to let a warm breeze pass over his face. He disappeared into the cottage, leaving Petrovich to wonder if Berg ever took a break from this work. He'd clearly purchased his tragic golf outfit at one of the airport tourist traps, which led him to believe that Berg was a stranger to leisure activity. The next twenty-four hours promised to be miserably interesting, not to mention the brief, tumultuous outburst he could expect from Jessica.

Chapter 15

Daniel Petrovich fidgeted in the front passenger seat of Karl Berg's BMW 3 Series sedan and stared past the windshield at the sea of pine trees enveloping the road. He'd stayed up past midnight examining the Vektor files provided by Berg, continuing to arrive at the same conclusion. The U.S. would be better off bombing the site from a standoff distance. He knew this wasn't an option, but Farrington's team faced a serious challenge after destroying Vektor, traversing over 150 miles of unfamiliar territory with most of the Novosibirsk Oblast's military hot on their trail. He didn't see an easy way to handle the team's withdrawal, unless the CIA could convince the president to invade Russian airspace and pick them up deep within Russian territory. Berg's less-than-optimistic response to this suggestion indicated that the president was barely on board with the plan as it stood. He'd discuss this in detail with Sanderson after meeting with Reznikov. Farrington's team would need a highly creative escape and evasion plan to get out of Russia alive.

The car slowed, and Berg scrutinized a handheld GPS unit, alternating his gaze between the GPS and the road ahead. He placed the small gadget in the center console and stared into the rearview mirror. Daniel watched him out of the corner of his left eye, curious about their next move. They had spent nearly two hours travelling northeast out of Burlington, trading one scenic, two-lane road for another, gradually downgrading the road quality as they delved deep into heavily forested territory. Now they were about to turn onto an unmarked road in Berg's pristine silver BMW. Interesting.

Apparently satisfied that nobody was in sight behind them, Berg glanced at the road ahead for a few seconds before turning onto a tightly packed dirt road barely wide enough to accommodate their vehicle. They passed two unmistakably visible signs marking the road as private, each immediately followed by a generous turnaround point burrowed into the forest. Berg had placed a call with his smartphone roughly an hour out of Burlington, as the last vestiges of civilization streamed past their car. He wondered if the entrance to this road had been camouflaged prior to that phone call.

Their car continued down the dark, claustrophobic forest growth until the silver glint of a vehicle caught his eye. He instinctively placed a hand on Berg's right arm, reaching for the passenger door handle with his other hand.

"No worries. This is our ride to the compound," Berg said, navigating his car into a tree-covered clearing.

The clearing held a single Yukon SUV, with tinted rear compartment windows. The tinting didn't allow any light to penetrate the back seats, giving Petrovich an uneasy feeling. He could see two men in the front seats. Berg parked the BMW next to the SUV, and they took a few minutes to organize the material that Petrovich had continued to study in an attempt to avoid conversation with Berg.

"Shall we?" Berg said, opening his car door.

The two men in the SUV joined them in front of Berg's BMW, exchanging a few words. Berg seemed to know the procedure, handing his keys, phone and GPS unit over to one of the men, who pulled a chip out of the GPS unit and placed it in his front coat pocket. The other items were stuffed in a small black bag, which was placed on the hood of the SUV.

Petrovich studied each man, quickly concluding that they were paramilitary. They moved with a purpose, studying Berg and Petrovich in the careful, detached trademark manner of an ex-special forces operator. Each carried a concealed pistol on their right belt line, tucked just behind the hip and loosely covered by their waist-level windbreakers. By the way their clothing fit, he could tell they were in optimal shape. The only variable Daniel couldn't determine was their experience level, and in his line of work, this was often the most important variable. He wondered if they were running through the same mental drill, sizing him up and calculating their odds of surviving an encounter.

Daniel's mind constantly assessed these odds, regardless of the environment. He never stopped identifying potential threats around him. Escape routes appeared to him automatically, and possible courses of action were analyzed like a computer. Even life's simplest tasks were processed this way. This mindset had been drilled into him by Sanderson's training program and honed to perfection as an operative in Serbia, where his daily survival often depended on the speed and efficacy of basic decision-making. Experience sharpened this skill to a razor. Without this experience, you were just another fitness buff with weapons and martial arts training. He couldn't tell if the men in front of him had spent most of their professional careers at Planet Fitness or in Afghanistan. They looked authentic, but looks could be deceiving.

Both men brushed past them and started to search the car. He figured they were looking for any additional GPS units or cell phones that could be used to determine their final destination. Satisfied that the car was clean, the two men returned and asked them to step inside the vehicle.

Daniel opened the door and saw that the window was opaque. A black panel ran from the ceiling to floor and separated the rear compartment from the front seats, completely blocking their view of the front compartment windows. He leaned his head in and confirmed that the rest of the windows were opaque, forming a visionless box to keep the final destination a secret. Karl Berg opened the door on the other side and stepped up on the running board, preparing to enter the SUV.

"Fuck this. I'm not riding in a coffin," Daniel said.

"It's non-negotiable, Daniel. If the director came out to visit, he'd be required to follow the same procedure," Berg said.

"Somehow I really doubt that," he said, considering his options.

"It is what it is. You either take it or leave it," Berg said, nestling himself into the far seat.

Daniel looked past the opaque window and caught a glimpse of one of their escorts. He stood with his arms folded at the front of the SUV, staring at Daniel impassively.

"They won't get in until both of the back doors are closed and locked. They'll stand around all day," Berg said.

Daniel hopped into his seat and shut the door, which automatically activated the interior lights. Before either of the front compartment doors opened, he heard his door lock. He shared a look with Berg.

"This facility is our securest for three reasons. Isolation, secrecy and physical security. The detachment assigned to Mountain Glen takes each aspect very seriously. Follow directions, and don't fuck around up there," Berg said.

The vehicle jolted forward, pushing Daniel into his seat.

"What makes you think I won't take this seriously?" Petrovich said, securing his seatbelt.

"I have it on good authority."

Sixty-four minutes later, the SUV stopped for several seconds and continued. *Perimeter fence*, Daniel thought. A few minutes after that, the vehicle turned and suddenly halted. The engine stopped running, and the door unlocked.

"We may proceed," Berg said.

"So much for two hours," Petrovich said.

"Sanderson told me to shave an hour off the advertised time."

"Uhhh…I think we stopped in the wrong place," he called out, opening the door and stepping down onto the packed gravel. He walked briskly past their escorts, who no longer appeared interested in them. "This looks more like a mountain retreat than a maximum security prison for the worst dregs of society."

"It gets a little complicated when you rank this high on our list of enemies," Berg said, catching up with him.

Petrovich surveyed the grounds. They had parked in front of a two-story colonial-style home that bristled with antennas and featured a satellite communications dome at the apex of the roof. The house stood in the center of a round clearing the size of three football fields. A natural stream ran through the northern edge of the clearing, visible among the jagged rocks along the water's edge. A massive post-and-beam lodge dominated the western edge of the clearing, complete with a wide covered porch and Adirondack deck chairs.

Fifty meters to the left of the lodge sat a white, one-story building that looked more utilitarian than luxurious. The squat structure featured two garage bay doors and a crushed gravel driveway leading toward the dirt road they had arrived on. He saw several ATV-sized trails leading in multiple directions from the center of the clearing, but no motorized equipment beyond the SUV that had transported them to the compound.

He raised his view above the tree line to admire the rocky face of a mountain several miles away. Faint traces of snow could still be seen in some of the sheltered crags. Anatoly Reznikov had been delivered to paradise for causing the death of thousands in Russia and selling his designer virus to Al Qaeda. Unbelievable.

Daniel's gaze returned to the house just as the front door opened. Berg filled him in as they walked over to meet the camp commandant, or whoever had decided to greet them.

"The house ahead is the security station. It's home to roughly a dozen security specialists, all former special operations personnel. It houses the state-of-the-art equipment used to keep track of the compound's 'guests.' Every aspect of the guests' lives is monitored and analyzed, from heartbeats to toilet flushes. Dozens of active and passive measures are taken to ensure each guest's compliance with the rules.

"The guests stay in residences situated beyond the thick tree line that surrounds the clearing. Each residence is bugged and monitored by several cameras mounted in nearby trees. Motion detectors track movement inside and outside of each structure, guiding the sophisticated array of night vision and thermal imaging equipped cameras assigned to each guest. Patterns are recorded, analyzed and anticipated. Anything out of the ordinary is immediately investigated by a mobile security team. Normally, you'd see a few ATVs around here. They must be busy."

"What the fuck is that place? A goddamn resort lodge?" Petrovich asked, pointing at the post-and-beam structure.

"The lodge holds the facility's gourmet kitchen, common dining area, recreation room, indoor pool and exercise facilities…trust me, I think it's a fucking crock of shit, but the promise of a life here has motivated some of our most hardened enemies to cooperate. The small white building houses the compound's backup generator, water distribution system and main electricity breaker. The garages hold ATVs for patrolling the grounds, plowing snow and transporting guests."

"I lost three good men capturing that motherfucker, and now he's eating crème brule after dinner?"

"And after lunch if so desired," Berg said.

"I'm not finding any of this to be amusing. You have to be kidding me?" Daniel said, stopping Berg before their welcoming committee arrived. "He gets to live out the rest of his life here? Seriously?"

"That's the general concept, but in the case of Anatoly Reznikov, I might throw him an early retirement party. Those lives weren't wasted."

Berg cast him a deadly serious look that Petrovich recognized immediately. For the moment, he was satisfied that Reznikov wouldn't get to live out his golden years snacking on fresh cheese and drinking Green Mountain coffee. He risked one more glance at the lodge's porch and saw someone take a seat in one of the Adirondack chairs with a cup and saucer.

"They can roam the place freely?"

The man joining them from the house answered his question. "Guests are allowed free run of the compound, as long as they don't bother another guest or interfere with the staff. Or try to escape. Violations result in a remotely activated lockdown. Gary Sheffield," he said, shaking hands with Petrovich first.

"Daniel Petrovich," he responded, stuck in Sheffield's iron grip.

Unlike his Members Only jacket adorned security staff, Sheffield looked like he had embraced the Vermont mountain life. The bottoms of his worn quilted flannel shirt flapped in the breeze, lapping gently against his reinforced khaki pants. A pair of rugged dark brown hiking boots stood firmly planted in the ground in front of them. His face betrayed a four to five day growth of graying hair, which had the potential to sprout into a proper beard if left unchecked, but like Petrovich, the man couldn't completely abandon the ritual of shaving. Give Sheffield another year or two out here, and he'd look like Grizzly Adams. He wondered how a CIA officer pulled duty out here…if the guy was even CIA.

"Welcome back, Karl. Looks like Mr. Reznikov is keeping you busy," Sheffield said.

"It's a refreshing break from the pollution."

"I didn't think D.C. was that bad," Sheffield remarked.

"I wasn't talking about the air," Berg replied.

"Neither was I," Sheffield said, smirking, and the two men shook hands.

"Gary and I served together in Eastern Europe back in the day," Berg said to Daniel. "He headed up one of our most successful Special Operations groups behind the Iron Curtain. How he ended up with a cushy assignment like this is unfathomable."

"Beyond the cameras and motion detectors, what keeps the prisoners from walking to the nearest town?" Petrovich asked.

Sheffield put a hand on his hip and pointed at the forest with the other, sweeping his hand in a grand gesture at the tree line. "The final immediate security precaution consists of a reinforced, twelve-foot-tall razor-wire fence that encircles the entire compound. The fence is located three hundred meters beyond the edge of the clearing, and the entire fence line is monitored by cameras and motion detectors. If one of the compound's guests or an outside party decided to scale the fence, security personnel could deliver a substantial electrical charge to that specific section of fence. Beyond the fence, the last deterrent to an escape is isolation. Anyone finding themselves on the other side of that fence would face a fifty-mile trek through unforgiving wilderness to reach the first signs of civilization."

"Has anyone tried to go over the fence?" Daniel said.

"Fuck no. The average guest puts on thirty to forty pounds within the first three months here…and most of them arrive already showing the signs of an excessive lifestyle. The gourmet food serves a purpose. Most of them would have a heart attack getting to the fence. Speaking of heart conditions, Mr. Reznikov's health is improving."

"That's a shame," Berg said.

"Good food. Fresh air. Works wonders. I'll notify him that you've arrived. Should I announce Mr. Petrovich?"

"No. I'd like to surprise him. Maybe set his health back a few notches. The two of them have met before," Berg said.

"Very well. I'll send his usual breakfast over. Can I get the two of you anything?"

"Lobster Benedict with homefries?"

"How do you like the egg yolks?" Sheffield asked.

"Wow, I was just kidding," Petrovich said. "Cooked through."

"Karl?"

"I'll have the same, but runny."

"Give it about thirty minutes. Here's the code to cut the audio feeds. Input at the door touch pad," Sheffield said, removing a notecard from his trouser pocket.

"Thanks, Gary. See you on the way out," Berg said.

Sheffield nodded at his security officers, who followed him into the security station as Berg and Petrovich walked down the raked gravel path toward Reznikov's residence. They arrived at the cozy Cape Cod-style cottage a few minutes later after a short walk through the forest. Without stopping to examine any of the trees, Daniel failed to detect any of the surveillance equipment installed to keep Reznikov from wandering off the reservation. Either the gear had been expertly hidden or the whole system was a carefully crafted lie to keep the inmates guessing. Either method could be equally effective. He maneuvered himself behind Berg as they approached the cottage.

Petrovich saw one of the curtains flutter as they walked onto the small covered porch. Less than a second later, the door flashed open, and Reznikov bellowed in a deep Russian voice, welcoming Karl Berg. When Daniel stepped onto the porch, clearing Berg's shadow, the pallid Russian's face lost any last vestiges of color. He imagined that Sheffield and his crew were getting their monthly dose of entertainment watching Reznikov's vital signs spike.

"Good morning, Dr. Reznikov," Petrovich said in his cheeriest voice.

"What is *he* doing here?" Reznikov asked, looking betrayed.

"Emotional support…and to reinforce the fact that you are not out of the woods by a long shot. Stand back from the door," Berg ordered.

Reznikov retreated into the house, and Petrovich followed him, glancing around at the modestly appointed residence. Comfortable, inexpensive furniture adorned the family room to the right, reminding him of the mountain cottage he had rented for a week with Jessica in New Hampshire. He heard Berg type his code into the keypad on the porch, which piqued Reznikov's interest.

"What are you doing?"

"He's cutting the surveillance feeds so I can beat you senseless without interruption from the warden," Petrovich said.

"Director," Reznikov countered.

"Warden. You're an inmate. This is a prison…albeit a nice one."

"I like to think of it as my well-earned retirement."

Berg slammed the door shut and walked past Petrovich, causing Reznikov to retreat into the kitchen area ahead of him.

"Well, I have bad news about your retirement plan. Have a seat," Berg said.

Reznikov swiped a half-finished bottle of Ketel One vodka from the kitchen counter and started to dig through one of his cabinets for shot glasses. He set the glasses and the bottle on the kitchen table and took a seat. Karl Berg sat across from him, but Petrovich opted to stand with his back against the kitchen island countertop with his arms crossed. He stared at Reznikov, watching the Russian's trembling hand reach out with the bottle. He heard the mouth of the bottle chatter against the first glass and wondered if Reznikov might collapse from the strain of seeing him again.

"I wouldn't waste any more of that until you hear what I have to say. This isn't going to be a celebratory moment for you or me. The president doesn't feel that Vektor Labs is a clear and present danger to the United States, and will not authorize action against the facility or its personnel. I hope you've been practicing the art of holding your breath. I hear the toilet bowls are deep where you'll likely end up," Berg said.

"Wait a minute. Wait. He just dismissed the bioweapons program with the wave of a hand? After his country was attacked? It's only a matter of time before another scientist makes a deal. Trust me, there are many interested parties," Reznikov said, finally steadying his hand enough to pour three shots of vodka.

"A toast..."

"At eight in the morning?" Petrovich said.

"I'm still on Moscow time, which means I can drink whenever I want," Reznikov replied, reaching for one of the glasses.

Berg preemptively stopped him by covering the three glasses with the palm of his hand and sliding them to his side of the oak table. This quick denial caused the Russian to rise out of his seat momentarily. Petrovich's glare put him back in the chair without protest.

"I'd like to hear about some of those interested parties, especially any that might be intimately involved with the program. A little birdie told me that Vektor Labs hosts a whole array of foreign scientists, some of whom with questionable motives."

"Well played, my friend," Reznikov said.

"I'm not your friend," Berg countered.

"Just an expression. You give, I give. That's the way this works, no?"

"Time to open up door number three, or I'm going to bury you alive in the deepest, darkest prison I can find."

Petrovich admired the way Berg controlled the situation. From Berg's appearance and general demeanor, he'd expected the CIA officer to behave more like a reserved college professor. Instead, he was witnessing an interrogation disguised as bargaining.

"What is door number three?" the Russian asked.

"Just an expression. Time to show me all of your cards."

The Russian shook his head.

"Lay it on the table."

Reznikov looked around, confused. Apparently these phrases didn't translate well into Russian. Berg looked over to Petrovich and forced a smile, returning his gaze to Reznikov to hiss the next statement.

"Time to tell us every fucking thing you know, or you're gonna spend the rest of your short, miserable life in a hellhole."

Reznikov recoiled at the sudden change in Berg's persona, glancing around nervously. "Iranians," he blurted.

"What about the Iranians?" Berg prodded.

"I was approached by Iranian intelligence agents while employed at Vektor, but at that point I hadn't fully come to terms with my own plans to steal virus samples. They scared the hell out of me. Showing up in the least expected places at the oddest times. Hints were dropped about potential financial arrangements. After a while, they left me alone. I heard they were scrambling to find me when I left Vektor. Of course, that stopped once they finally got someone inside the facility. Is this what you might find behind door number three?"

"You're getting closer. What do you mean by inside? Inside the P4 containment building? Inside the bioweapons program? What are we talking about here?"

Petrovich thought Berg sounded overeager, sensing a shift in the bargaining power.

"I'm told they have a scientist assigned to the infectious disease fellowship program. He's been seen offsite with a likely Iranian intelligence agent. Not too many Persians in Novosibirsk. Not many outsiders at all. Now it's time for a toast."

Petrovich leaned in to take one of the shots off the table, wondering what Jessica would think of him drinking vodka at nine in the morning. He wasn't driving, though, so what did it matter? After spending hours in Berg's company, he could use a drink.

"To keeping your head out of a dirty toilet," Petrovich said.

Reznikov didn't look amused by his impromptu salutation. Neither did Berg. He shrugged his shoulders and drained the vodka down his throat, slamming the glass back down on the table like a fraternity pledge.

"Rude and uncivilized. Here's to a long retirement in the mountains and a successful mission against Vektor," Reznikov said.

Petrovich waited for both of them to finish their shots before interjecting. "I liked my toast better."

Reznikov grabbed the bottle and poured another shot for himself, placing the bottle near Berg's glass. The CIA officer declined.

"Maybe later. I need to make a phone call. If my boss isn't willing to walk this back up the chain of command, this might be your last drink," Berg said.

"Don't tell him that," Petrovich said. "He'll end up just like we found him in Stockholm."

Petrovich's statement caused Reznikov to tense for a moment before he took another shot of vodka. He placed the glass on the table, and his grimace melted into a smile. He refilled Daniel's glass.

"My friend, you need to lighten up a little. What happened to your arm?" he asked, waving the bottle at his shoulder.

"Dislocated my shoulder beating another prisoner to death," Petrovich said.

"Come on. This is going to work out for everybody. Door number three I give to you!"

"We'll see," Petrovich said, taking him up on the offer of another shot. "Here's to the miracle of automated defibrillators. Without them, our friend would be dead."

"I don't have to take this abuse," Reznikov said.

"Take it easy on him, Daniel. We have a long day ahead of us," Berg said, walking toward the front door to make his call in private.

"To your health," Petrovich said, raising his glass to meet Reznikov's.

"That's better."

The vodka burned slightly less going down the second time, leaving him with a warm buzz. Reznikov immediately poured another shot for each of them.

"I think that's enough," Petrovich said.

"Fine. Two for me, then."

Petrovich walked over to the kitchen and waited for Berg to finish the phone call. He heard the bottle clink against glass again, which worried him. If Reznikov passed out from drinking, he had no intention of sticking around the compound to continue their conversation when he woke up. By the time Berg returned, he'd heard at least two more shots poured. He intercepted him in the hallway leading to the kitchen.

"I think our friend will be hallucinating within the hour if he keeps drinking like this."

"The last time I visited him, he put away a bottle and a half in three hours. It kept him talking."

"It's your call. What did the home office say?"

"They're walking it up to the director this morning. We might have an answer before we leave. My goal now is to get enough information to adequately plan the attack, regardless of the ultimate decision."

Petrovich shook his head and grinned. Berg truly impressed him. Time to have some fun. When the two of them turned the corner, Reznikov screwed the cap on the bottle of vodka, which stood on the table half-empty. The serious look on his face betrayed a slight change in his attitude. Daniel guessed they were in for a request. The frightened scientist had found confidence in the clear liquid sitting at the bottom of his stomach. Not the kind of liquid courage found at a late-night karaoke bar, but something different. Berg sensed it too as they entered the kitchen nook.

"This ought to be good," Berg mumbled.

"Gentlemen, before we proceed, I need assurances," Reznikov said.

Berg sat at the table and sighed. "This isn't a negotiation. We've been through this already. When and if your information is confirmed, you'll be offered permanent residence at this wonderful facility. Signed and sealed by the director of the CIA. If your information is deemed deceitful or purposely jeopardizes the safety of my people, the deal is off."

"That's what I'm worried about…"

"What? The possibility that the mission will succeed and I'll still throw you in a hole?" Berg said.

"I'd be worried about that," Petrovich added.

"We both know I don't have any control over your personal integrity, but I can drastically improve your team's chance of success with a single phone call. I think we both can agree that it's in my best interest for the team to succeed."

"I'm listening," Berg said.

"You're going to need connections on the inside…"

"Not inside Vektor. It's far too risky. Try again," Berg said.

"I'm not talking about Vektor. I'm talking about inside Russia," Reznikov said.

"Our team is perfectly capable of handling that aspect of the mission," Petrovich said.

"Really? How much time have they spent in Russia, particularly Novosibirsk?"

They kept silent until Reznikov continued.

"Novosibirsk is a provincial Siberian city, with few foreigners…"

"The team is trained for that," Berg said.

"Trained? You'll only get one shot at this, Mr. Berg. Novosibirsk is still a Soviet city in many respects, unlike Moscow or Saint Petersburg. Less cosmopolitan, more bureaucracy. In order to pull this off, you're going to need specialized equipment, weapons, explosives and hard-to-acquire transportation. You're going to need a way to grease palms without raising eyebrows. If you don't believe what I'm saying, get in touch with your analysts. I'm sure they'll confirm what I've told you."

"What are you suggesting?"

"I have contacts in the *bratva* that can pave the way for your team. Take care of the logistical details and conduct preliminary surveillance," Reznikov said, unscrewing the bottle.

"The Russian mafiya? You have to be kidding me. Why would the brotherhood help us…or help you?"

"Money, of course, and a favor I did for one of the Solntsevskaya brigadiers a few years ago. I provided a small amount of natural neurotoxin that targets the body's respiratory muscles. Something I smuggled out of Vektor on their behalf. They had no idea what I was really working on back then. Anyway, he used it to quietly kill several rival mafiya 'boyeviks' over the course of a six-month period, while the Solntsevskaya gang solidified control of organized crime activity in the Novosibirsk Oblast. That favor will get me an audience. A large sum of money will get you the support you need to take down Vektor."

"The Solntsevkaya Bratva is a nasty group that I'm not keen to trust. I think I'll pass on your offer," Berg said.

"It's non-negotiable. They're your only hope of pulling this off and getting your people out alive. One hundred and fifty miles is a long trip. A very unpredictable trip without local support. I can't afford to take the chance. Either you put me in touch with my *bratva* contact, or I'm not saying another word. And you still need my help. I haven't told you half of what you'll need to know about Vektor."

"How much money do you think it will take?" Berg said.

"Several million U.S. dollars. Maybe more," Reznikov said.

Petrovich whistled. He couldn't wait to hear Berg's response to this. Maybe Reznikov was smarter than he acted. He certainly hadn't expected this wrinkle in their plan, but oddly enough, it made sense. Trust would be a major issue, but enough money could always solidify temporary loyalty in organizations like these. He'd seen more than his share of deals sealed over large payoffs that trumped long-standing personal disagreements. The Serbians under Milosevic had perfected the concept of purchasing loyalty. The trick to buying loyalty always remained the same. Make your first offer higher than expected, and be prepared to pay out more at the last minute. Never start out with a lowball offer, or you're likely find yourself standing at the end of a steel barrel...sold out to a competitor willing to pay more. He'd make sure to speak with Sanderson at length about the payment amount, reinforcing its importance to the mission. Sanderson might have to shell out some of his own cash to keep the team out of trouble.

"That sounds like a lot of money. I'm not sure how I'm going to come up with several million dollars for an operation that never happened," Berg said.

"Oh, give me a break. One of your new Tomahawk missiles would cost you close to one million dollars, and I think you'd need to use three or four to make absolutely certain that the building was obliterated. Even then, you'd never know. The beauty here is that the Russians will probably blame the Israelis, especially if you take out the Iranians. Several million dollars is a bargain! I can get this started immediately. All I need is access to a cell phone."

"That's not going to happen. No outside contact is allowed," Berg said.

"I'm not asking to keep the phone here. I just need periodic access, to make sure the relationship is going smoothly. No cell phone, no deal. Good luck trying to destroy a P4 containment building with Semtex. I hope you can rent a dump truck in Novosibirsk, because that's how much explosives you'll need…unless I get what I want."

"I'll give you limited, strictly monitored satellite phone access. Five calls. One to establish contact. One to negotiate the deal. Three to confirm whatever it is that you feel the need to confirm. I will personally oversee the calls, along with several translators. If anything is screwy, I'll bury you myself. No questions asked. Does this sound fair to you?"

Petrovich was glad to hear that Berg wouldn't agree to the use of a cell phone. He figured they had some kind of scrambling device or way to reroute calls from the compound, but computer hackers could work miracles these days, as he had witnessed firsthand a few weeks ago. There was no reason to assume that Russian hackers couldn't do the same thing. Satellite communication was the safest method available. The radio waves couldn't be intercepted without sophisticated land or space-based SIGINT (Signals Intelligence) technology, which, in the case of Reznikov's limited use, would be like finding a needle in a haystack without looking.

"Yes. Five calls will be sufficient. The final call will be made right before I give you the most important piece of information, so don't think of playing any games," Reznikov said.

"How important?" Berg said.

"They won't need it until right before the attack on the facility. I will tell you how to destroy the bioweapons laboratory without using explosives. Very easy. Very complete."

Berg stared at him for a few seconds before standing up. Reznikov offered his hand, which Berg regarded icily.

"Only children require a handshake to seal a bargain. You'll get your phone calls. I'd like you to make the first one this morning."

Reznikov retracted his hand with a scowl and poured three shots of vodka.

"A toast to the destruction of Vektor," he said.

Petrovich picked up the shot glass, still slightly woozy from the first two drinks. A few seconds later, his throat ached as he slammed the shot glass down. No more shots for him. One more and he'd nap through the rest of the interrogation. He heard Berg ask the security station for a satellite phone to be delivered with breakfast. Berg took a seat at the table and watched Reznikov take another shot.

"Good news. Breakfast is on the way, along with a satellite phone. I hope your friends in Novosibirsk don't hang up. You get five calls."

Petrovich walked toward the kitchen, looking for the bathroom. He spied several more bottles of vodka tucked away under a row of kitchen cabinets, which prompted him to open the refrigerator. Nothing. A few seconds later, he heard the buzz of an ATV approaching. Special fucking delivery. He really hoped Berg didn't intend to honor any deal to let Reznikov stay here. The thought of that psychopath enjoying personally delivered gourmet food for the rest of his life didn't sit well with him.

Chapter 16

Sergei Dubinin parked his AvtoVAZ sedan and surveyed the sidewalks in front of the bank for any obvious signs of trouble. He had been abruptly interrupted from drinks at his new favorite lounge atop the Swiss Hotel Krasnye Holmy and ordered to run a quick errand nearby. Such requests were not unusual from his boss, but they usually came late at night, when he was busy working the streets. He wasn't pleased to be yanked away from the company of his newly acquired admirers at the chic and ridiculously expensive rooftop hotel bar.

He'd been recently promoted from *Shestyorka* (associate) to *Vor* (thief) within the Solntsevskaya Bratva, which was the equivalent to becoming a "made" man within Sicilian mafia organizations. Accepting the *Vor* code meant greater responsibility, increased respect and more money.

He reported to a *Boyevik* (warrior) who led the business extortion efforts for their *Brigadier*, who in turn reported directly to Mr. Dima Maksimov, the organization's *Pakhan* (boss). It was a long list of intermediaries, with numerous cut outs designed to prevent direct links back to the higher-ranking members. Security up the chain-of-command even featured "ghosts," who watched over everybody and served as an informal version of mafiya internal affairs.

He'd thought his errand boy days were over, but it had only intensified with his new position. He no longer stood lookout outside of the stores or apartment buildings. Now he went inside and made the collections while someone else looked tough on the steps. The only benefit so far had been money to fuel his hunger for the finer things in life. His new errands almost always involved large quantities of cash, either payoffs from local businesses or debt collection.

He learned early in his career never to skim off the top, but instead to insist on an additional collection consisting of petty cash. A small tribute to keep him in a good mood and ensure that his next visit would be just as peaceful. He didn't push the amounts, purposely setting his sights low to avoid attracting attention. He made several dozen collections a week, so the money added up quickly. No reason to shake down the wealthier "clients" for larger sums that might result in a phone call to his boss. Any money made at any level was subject to a "tax" up the chain of command. Eventually, his *Boyevik* would tactfully bring up the subject of his extra collections, and he would have to cough up money on a monthly basis. This was a natural part of the process and understood by everyone within the ranks.

He hoped this inevitable taxation didn't impact his newly found place among society's elite. There was an incredible amount of money to be made from these people, and he planned to tap into it. The combination of wealth and naivety sang to him as they regaled him with stories about yachts and third homes in the Swiss Alps. He felt like a shark in a fish tank as he laughed along with them, flashing the latest luxury watches and buying overpriced drinks with reckless abandon.

But first, another fucking errand…and this time to a bank. His unit didn't do business with the banks. That was handled by a high-level *Boyevik* that specialized in bribes and government affairs. Maybe this was a good thing for him. A sign that they might be considering him for a special track within the *bratva*.

He opened the car door and stepped into the street, careful to examine the door mirror before making the near suicidal leap of faith into traffic. At six in the evening, Leninsky Avenue was packed with edgy drivers trying to race home. Fortunately, the bank was located on the eastern side of the ten-lane boulevard that carried traffic toward Moscow, and was slightly less packed than the other side. After quickly navigating to the sidewalk, he approached the bank, mindful of the time. The bank closed at six, and his boss would have a fit if he screwed this up. As a new member of the *bratva*, his actions were more closely scrutinized than ever before. Everything was a test of loyalty and commitment. He wondered if the downward pressure ever stopped.

He found the bank door unlocked, which was a relief. He had three minutes to spare until closing, which in Russia didn't guarantee anything. He'd protested the time constraint, having received the phone call less than twenty minutes ago. If the bank manager wanted to go home at 5:30, the bank closed early. The last thing he wanted to do was visit the bank manager at home. Things were certain to get ugly if that happened, but orders were orders, and he was expected to return with the contents of the safety deposit box.

Sergei pulled on the heavy reinforced steel door and entered the bank, drawing a few stares from the staff. He saw one of them grimace, apparently unsatisfied that the bank might not close on time tonight. A guard armed with a shortened military carbine eyed him from the front corner of the lobby as he approached the more attractive of the two blond tellers. Bank robberies were relatively common in Moscow, though they were rare along this stretch of Leninsky Avenue. His *bratva* didn't look kindly upon this kind of activity here, and transgressors were punished severely and publicly. Only the most desperate criminal upstarts dared to try and pull off a robbery in this district of Moscow.

The teller avoided eye contact with him, likely hoping that he'd turn to the other teller and let her continue to close out her station. No such luck, though he wouldn't keep her for long, unless she wanted to join him for a drink later. Always a possibility. Handsomely dressed in a ridiculously expensive suit, tailored to his fit ex-military frame, he looked sharp and could easily pass for one of the hundred thousand millionaires living in Moscow. When the blue-eyed blonde finally looked up at him, a look of relief flashed, which quickly transformed into a flirtatious smile. The evening just got more interesting.

"Can I be of assistance to you?" she said.

Maybe later, he thought. Out loud, he said, "I need to access one of your digital safety deposit boxes. The circumstances are unique, and I believe arrangements have been made for me."

She seemed confused for a moment, asking him to hold on while she contacted the bank manager. A few seconds later, the manager emerged from one of the glass-encased offices on the far right side of the bank.

"Good evening. My name is Yakov Krutin. I received a call about twenty minutes ago with one of two remote access codes to a safety deposit box. Do you have the second code?"

"Yes. A twenty-four digit code," he said, reaching into his pocket for his cell phone.

The number had been sent to him via text by his immediate boss. The order to retrieve the box's contents had been sent straight to him a few minutes ago by their *Brigadier*, Matvey Penkin, which made this a priority task.

"Please follow me," the manager said and started walking toward a hallway leading deeper into the bank.

They pushed through a set of rich wooden doors into a harsh fluorescent environment that stood in stark contrast to the welcome, subtle lighting of the lobby. A second guard stood up from a chair at a small computer station and picked up an assault rifle similar to the one held by the guard in the lobby. Sergei guessed it was an AKS-74U, a short barreled, folding stock version of the Russian service rifle he'd carried as a conscript. The guard cradled it in a non-threatening manner and nodded as they passed through another set of doors into the safety deposit area.

The room extended at least twenty feet into the building, measuring at least fifteen feet wide. Boxes of varying size lined the walls, flush with each other. The larger boxes were located at the bottom, extending upward to several rows of standard sized boxes. The boxes on the flanking walls contained the same dual key mechanism typically used by banks to open safety deposit boxes. Once the key holder's identity was confirmed as the owner of the box, the bank manager and key holder would simultaneously insert their keys, opening the drawer. Another metal container typically sat inside the drawer, providing immediate privacy from the bank staff. The contents of the box were examined by the key holder in a nearby, private room.

In this case, the door to this private area stood in the center of the room's far wall. The rest of the wall contained digital safety deposit boxes, one of which contained the items he had been sent to retrieve. He had never heard of a digital safety deposit box until tonight. A curious development in the world of banking, they offered more flexibility in terms of content retrieval, since a digital code replaced the need to present a physical key. The box's owner could still request the additional security layer of identity confirmation, but this had become less common and didn't serve the most common purpose of these boxes. Money drops.

The proliferation of digital boxes across Europe, and particularly Moscow, served organized crime well, allowing them to not only hide money effectively, but to disburse it anonymously to anyone given the second code. Born in Russia, the idea was quickly spreading west, creating serious difficulty for federal law enforcement agencies investigating the major drug cartels and organized crime gangs. The days of staking out the big money drops were evaporating, as money changed hands behind vault doors, free from the prying eyes and ears of the police.

The bank manager approached a row of boxes at chest height to the right of the door and slid open a small keypad on the front of the box.

"I'll enter the first code, and then you'll have three tries to enter your code. The box will automatically lock after a third unsuccessful attempt, so please take you time. There is no rush. Make sure to press enter after all of the digits appear. If you don't mind," he said, waiting patiently for Sergei to face a different direction.

He heard the man pushing the buttons on the keypad and wondered what would happen if the first code was entered incorrectly. A few moments later, the manager asked him to enter the code. He removed his cell phone and approached the box, glancing over his shoulder at the manager, who had started to pace toward the center of the room with his hands behind his back. He eyed the phone's screen and carefully entered the code, confirming that the red numbers on the small, thin digital screen matched the numbers on his cell phone. He pressed enter, and a green light blinked, followed by several beeps and the hushed rumbling of mechanisms in the wall. The bank official appeared out of nowhere next to him.

"Most excellent. You may open the drawer and retrieve the contents. The room through this door will assure you complete privacy. When you are finished, there is a telephone mounted on the wall. Simply pick up the phone and let whomever answers know that you are done. I will arrive shortly after that to escort you to the lobby. Do you anticipate needing a bag to carry the contents?"

"Yes."

"You will find a low cabinet on the far side of this room filled with a variety of sturdy bags. Take whichever best suits your needs. If you have any questions after I leave, you can reach me on the phone," he said and nodded, stepping back.

"Thank you," Sergei said.

When the outer doors to the room clicked shut, Sergei opened the one-foot-by-one-foot drawer and reached inside, removing a metal case. He glanced at the door again, wondering what the low-wage security guard thought of the wealth concentrated in this room. The thought made him uneasy. The money and secrets stashed in this room remained frustratingly out of the guard's grasp most of the day, until someone like Sergei arrived. It had to drive the guard insane with curiosity. Was Sergei here to collect ten million rubles or some old rich geezer's last will and testament? Diamonds? Gold? He could never work a job like this. Every person that walked through those doors represented a life-changing gamble.

He entered the private room, which contained a simple metal table surrounded by four equally utilitarian metal chairs. The cabinet sat against the far wall as promised, just a few feet from the table, and a single black phone hung on the wall to the left of the door. Out of habit, he scanned the room for cameras or any other surveillance devices and found none. Time to verify the contents and get the fuck out of here. He was expected to meet his boss at an apartment complex in the Tverskoy District by six-thirty, which would take a near superhuman effort at this time of the day.

The metal slid open to reveal three individually secured stacks of one hundred dollar bills, a worn three-by-five inch notebook, and a small thumb drive. Exactly what he had been told to expect. He picked up one of the stacks, which measured roughly three inches thick, and thumbed through one of the corners slowly. As far as he could tell, the entire stack contained crisp one hundred dollar bills. He repeated the process for the two remaining stacks. Two hundred thousand U.S. dollars was one of the largest amounts he had been tasked to handle, and he had no intention of fucking this up. Anything could go wrong with a drop like this, robbery being the least of his problems.

If one of the stacks had been padded with one dollar bills, and he didn't document the fact immediately upon discovery, he'd likely end up in the Moscow river with his throat slashed, or even worse, dissolved alive in some warehouse on the outskirts of the city. Satisfied that all of the bills were hundreds, he selected a small faux leather tote bag from the cabinet and placed the contents of the box inside. A quick call to Mr. Krutin put him back into his car on Leninsky Avenue without incident. The time on his watch read six-twelve. No way in hell he would make it to Tverskoy during rush hour.

༒

Matvey Penkin thumbed through the journal sitting at a sleek metal-framed glass table in his penthouse suite overlooking Tverskaya Street. He'd read the first several pages with rapt attention. What Anatoly Reznikov had proposed could make the Solntsevskaya Bratva a veritable fortune on several fronts, opening the doors to a new stratosphere of power and respect on the international scene. The contents of this box represented one of the largest business opportunities in decades, and his greatest chance to secure his place as Dima Maksimov's right-hand man in the organization.

Of course, seizing an opportunity like this carried serious risks and required careful maneuvering. Penkin had to decide whether to seek his Pakhan's blessing for the operation or simply deliver the goods. Conspiring with an American mercenary group to destroy a sensitive government facility was unheard of, but so was the payoff. Exclusive access to bioweapons production capabilities, which Reznikov insisted he could deliver.

With Vektor Labs destroyed, they would have no competition in the bioweapons market and could demand exorbitant prices from countries like Iran, North Korea or China for the production and delivery of the weapons. Once word hit the back channels that these nations possessed bioweapons, other nations would be willing to acquire the same capabilities to participate in a secret bioweapons *détente*. The entire scheme seemed farfetched, but with minimal effort, they could actively explore the option. He decided to move forward without alerting anyone else in the leadership structure. The fewer that knew about this, the better.

If the operation failed or backfired on him, Maksimov and the rest would be insulated from the damage. If it succeeded, he alone would be in a position to present the grand prize to his Pakhan.

"How long did your man have this package in his possession?" he asked the stocky, brown-haired man seated next to him at the table.

"Thirty minutes or so. He was adamant that he didn't waste any time getting here. Traffic and all," said Valery Zuyev, Sergei's boss.

"Who else knows about the pickup?"

"Nobody. I sent the closest guy. Sergei's new, but he's shown initiative and an enterprising spirit."

"Unfortunately, I would have been happier if you had told me the opposite. The last-minute nature of the pickup and the contents would attract anyone's attention, especially someone with, as you say, an enterprising spirit. I trust you implicitly, Valery, but this guy?" Matvey Penkin shook his head slowly.

"I understand," Valery said.

"Good. I'll need you here tomorrow at four in the afternoon. You and I are about to embark on a journey that will require most of your attention, I'm afraid."

"I like the sound of this. Is there anything I can do to prepare before we meet tomorrow?" Valery asked.

"Yes. I need you to think hard about whom you can trust in Novosibirsk. We're going to need a small core group to take care of some very secretive logistics."

"We have good people out there. I'll come up with a list," he said.

"Tomorrow, then," Penkin said, politely dismissing Valery.

When his Boyevik left the room, escorted by two of Penkin's omnipresent bodyguards, he opened the notebook again. The thumb drive found in the safety deposit box held a software program that would decode random words from future conversations with Reznikov. The scientist had instructed them to record each call and transcribe it exactly into the program.

Reznikov would call them tomorrow at 5 o'clock p.m. According to the journal, a particular word would be used to indicate the use of a satellite phone. Additional words would narrow the location down as far as possible, providing geographic features, temperature, sunrise/sunset, moon phase, and weather. He hoped Reznikov would be given access to a cell phone. This would provide the easiest method of determining the location. Penkin had access to some of the most sophisticated hackers in the world and could very likely pinpoint the location within two phone calls.

A satellite phone presented a few unique challenges that weren't insurmountable, but would likely eat up most of the money recovered from the safety deposit box. The worst-case scenario involved bringing another Brigadier onboard with the scheme. He loathed the idea of sharing this with another high-ranking member of the *bratva*, but unfortunately, his business dealings didn't bring him into contact with anyone within the GRU's Sixth Directorate, responsible for Signals Intelligence intercept.

He regarded the thumb drive and placed it on the table. Fate had paid him a curious visit today, promising one of two extremes. There was no middle ground once he committed to this opportunity. He would either die a horrible death or be responsible for ushering in a new era of prosperity for the Solntsevskaya Bratva.

⁂

Sergei Dubinin stepped out of his car in the parking garage of the Swiss Hotel Krasnye Holmy. The last-minute errand had only kept him away from his swank audience for about an hour. The trip back to the hotel had been mercifully quicker than the interminable drive through the heart of Moscow to deliver the package. All the better, actually. His lady friends would be two or three drinks closer to getting fucked in one of the bathrooms, like usual, and if he played his cards right, he might even bang the fashion model that had recently started showing up regularly. All before his night really started. He'd join another colleague to make the rounds through restaurants and clubs, collecting money on the spot. They found the establishment owners much more willing to pay extra in order to avoid a scene.

He shut the car door and walked toward the parking garage elevator bank, pressing the only button available between the two shiny metal doors. A few minutes later, the right door opened and he stepped inside, shifting left to press the button for the top floor of the hotel. Movement outside of the elevator caught his eye, causing him to pause before pressing the button. No more movement. The doors started to close, and he walked to the center of the car, confident that he would be the only passenger. When the doors stopped halfway and started to reopen, he snapped open the knife that had already found its way into his right hand from his belt.

His serrated folding knife proved to be no match against the sawed-off, double barrel shotgun that poked between the doors and unceremoniously discharged at head level. When the elevator door opened on the thirty-fourth floor of the hotel, happy-hour patrons crowded around the entrance to City Space had a hard time processing the expansive, stark red pattern on the back wall of the elevator, until their eyes followed the stain to the body slumped on the floor and the screaming began.

Chapter 17

Karl Berg alternated staring between the road and Daniel Petrovich, trying desperately to read his face. Petrovich played with the radio controls, settling in on a faint signal from Burlington playing Tom Petty. He'd done the same thing driving out, preferring to listen to static instead of country music or, worse yet, Berg's voice. He almost looked disaffected, like a sociopath, but Berg knew better. Petrovich's gears were spinning at full speed trying to process the information gathered from Reznikov's interrogation. Sanderson would want a full assessment, and he wasn't the type to take this lightly. Lives would be at stake during the operation, the lives of people he had worked with and trained.

"What do you think?" Berg asked.

Petrovich surprised him by answering immediately. "I think you have a problem."

"How so?"

"There's something wrong with Reznikov," Petrovich said.

"That's obvious."

"And you trust his information?"

"Trust but verify. He has the most to lose from a failed operation. Is this what's bothering you?" Berg asked.

90

"No. The mission looks straightforward enough going in. Getting out is going to take a miracle, unless the agency has an ace up its sleeve. The Russian mafiya support will dissolve as soon as the alarm is raised at various 41st Army barracks around Novosibirsk."

"We're working on that," Berg said.

"There's no way the president will authorize a stealth incursion with the entire Siberian Military District mobilized," Petrovich said.

"Our analysts don't think the Russians will want to publicize the event. Response will be limited to Special Forces, light motorized units and possibly fighter aircraft. The nearest sizable helicopter brigade is too far away to make a difference," Berg said.

"I seem to recall the rather sudden arrival of three Russian helicopters in Kazakhstan, not far from the proposed crossing point. One of them was a Havoc," Petrovich replied.

"True, but we believe that the helicopters were part of a special task force stationed in Novosibirsk from another district. One of the hull numbers matched a unit that had been recently pulled from Georgia and was normally stationed outside of Moscow. I'm not discounting the possibility of helicopters responding to the attack, but it won't be the type of coordinated effort that I'd consider a showstopper," Berg said.

"What *would* you consider to be a showstopper?" Petrovich said, glaring at him.

Berg suppressed a grin. Petrovich was extremely perceptive and had probably long ago answered that question for himself. He'd just been waiting for the right time to ask it. Berg had sent his team on one suicide mission after another across Europe and Russia in pursuit of Anatoly Reznikov, but the threat unleashed by Reznikov still lingered at Vektor Labs. The show must go on.

"That's why the good general insisted that I bring you along. To provide an unbiased assessment of the situation," Berg said.

"And to keep you from bullshitting him," Petrovich said.

"Same thing, pretty much. So really, what do you think?"

"I think you better start talking to your Department of Defense buddies. Without some kind of helicopter or drone support near the Kazakh border, the team will never make it across. I'm not sure how you pulled off your drone miracle before, but that's the kind of magic this team will need to get out of Russia. Aside from that? I can't see any reason to sideline this op, assuming that Sanderson doesn't mind relying on the Russian mafiya."

"Once I set the terms of cooperation—"

"The price of cooperation," Petrovich corrected.

"Correct. The price. Once this is agreed upon, I'm going to step away and let Sanderson handle all levels of coordination with the Russians."

"Smart move. How much is the CIA willing to pony up for this operation?"

"Let me worry about that."

Berg observed Petrovich raise his eyebrows and go back to fumbling with the radio. The conversation was almost over, leaving a long, two-hour drive ahead of them.

"Anything else you can think of?" Berg prodded, hoping to keep him talking.

"Yes. You need satellite radio. This is borderline torture," he said, turning the radio off.

Chapter 18

Alexei Kaparov walked directly to his favorite shelf at the back of the liquor store, where they sold the absurdly inexpensive brands of vodka at prices decreed by the Federal Service for Alcohol Market Regulation. The minimum price of vodka sold in Moscow was seventy-five rubles, less than three dollars, and the further you drove out of Moscow, the less expensive it became. It was not uncommon for the less affluent Muscovites to take public transportation outside of the city to take advantage of the pricing, and any family trips to other regions always ended with a trip to one of the state-sponsored liquor stores where a half-liter bottle could be acquired for thirty-five rubles, nearly half of the Moscow price. Kaparov didn't get out of the city much these days, so he gladly paid a little more for the iconic beverage that he drank straight from a shot glass.

The rear aisle filled the entire back wall of the store, and at nearly ten o'clock at night, he was the store's only customer, so he thought. The sudden appearance of his assistant, Yuri Prerovsky, caused his breath to stop. The young agent stepped out from behind one of the display stands near the end cap of a long row of red wines. Whatever Prerovsky wanted, it wouldn't be good. Kaparov knew for a fact that the agent lived on the other side of the city, east of Moscow. He glanced back down the aisle he had just walked, half-expecting to see several additional agents headed in his direction. The paranoid look on Prerovsky's face eased his fear that the young agent had betrayed him. He continued to the back wall, pretending to examine the different bottles while talking.

"Are you trying to give me a fucking heart attack? There are easier ways to take my job. Just ask. You can have it," he said.

Prerovsky mimicked his actions, standing close enough for conversation.

"Sorry about this, but we have a problem that can no longer be discussed or even hinted about at headquarters. I remember you mentioning your nighttime trips to pick up vodka at this place. You should avoid this wall. Spend another thirty rubles for some decent vodka. This stuff will kill you," Prerovsky said.

"I could never tell the difference between vodkas. As long as it keeps me warm on cold nights and numb on warm nights, I'm satisfied. What kind of a problem are we facing?"

"Lucya. They have her under twenty-four-hour surveillance. She detected them on the way home from headquarters yesterday and is pretty sure they are watching her apartment. She's been part of the routine investigation by internal affairs, but she thinks this is different. She's panicky," Prerovsky said.

"She detected them so easily?"

"It didn't sound like they were trying to conceal their activity," Prerovsky said.

"Fuck. I was wondering how long we had until the Foreign Intelligence Service stepped up their investigation. I received a warning that our friends in the SVR have been busy in Sweden. They must have uncovered something."

"Damn it, why didn't you tell me this? My ass is on the line here," Prerovsky whispered forcefully.

"And have you acting suspiciously, glancing over your shoulder and running off to warn Lucya? I need you to continue acting as natural as possible, and ten o'clock trips across the city is far from normal, Yuri. How is Lucya holding up?"

"Not good. That's the real problem. She'll crumble under any pressure, and…I don't know," he said, hesitating.

"What is it?" Kaparov demanded.

"She suggested that we turn you in and say that you forced us to conspire in this," he whispered.

"Fuck me. A few days of surveillance, and she's ready to roll over. Damn it," he hissed.

He picked out two bottles of vodka, not even bothering to read the green label. Based on the information just shared with him, he might finish an entire bottle tonight, contemplating his fate. He should have known better than to think that Directorate S would let this one slide. Ultimately, the Federal Security Service leadership wouldn't stand in the way of the Foreign Intelligence Service witch-hunt, which would gain momentum as the initial round of pushback expired.

Something had gone severely wrong in Stockholm, resulting in the unprecedented, simultaneous loss of several "illegal" Spetsnaz operatives. Once the investigation picked up speed and the remaining roadblocks were removed, surveillance would turn into arrests. Everyone involved with the Lubyanka building's Center of Special Operations (CSN) group would be detained and interrogated. Lucya wouldn't last five minutes in custody. She'd probably spill their names in the windowless van that snatched her off the street.

Prerovsky remained silent while he thought about their options. A few seconds later, Kaparov had made a decision. It might be a long shot, but the Americans, specifically Karl Berg, owed him a favor. A big favor. He'd call Berg on the walk home, if he wasn't already being followed by SVR agents.

"All right. I have an idea," Kaparov said.

"Please tell me that this doesn't involve getting rid of Lucya. I don't think I could do that," Prerovsky said.

Kaparov regarded him for a moment, surprised by his suggestion that they might have to kill her. The thought had crossed Kaparov's mind, and it still lingered.

"Unfortunately, Lucya has to go…but not to the bottom of the Moscow. She knew the risks involved here. We all did. I need to make a phone call."

"Where will she go?" Prerovsky said.

"Anywhere but here. Her life as a Russian citizen is done. She either accepts that, or…let's just hope she accepts her new reality. Don't say a word to her about anything. If she comes to you again, explain to her that turning us in will not save her life. You need to buy me some time to put my plan into motion."

"I can do that. Keep me posted. I don't like being kept in the dark, Alexei," Prerovsky said.

"That's the first time you've ever called me Alexei," Kaparov said.

"Deputy Director didn't sound like an appropriate title for a conversation between two traitors," Prerovsky said.

"Get that out of your head immediately. The real traitors tried to snuff out Reznikov in Stockholm, and they're still hard at work trying to conceal the fact that Mother Russia is still producing bioweapons. Their handiwork killed thousands of Russian's up north. I don't feel a twinge of guilt about what we accomplished," Kaparov said.

"Neither do I, but I'd rather not spend the rest of my life in prison," Prerovsky said.

"Don't worry. If they catch us, we'll never see the inside of a prison. Hurry up and grab a bottle of your fancy wine. We should leave separately," Kaparov said.

Prerovsky shook his head and departed, grabbing the nearest bottle of wine on the way down the aisle. After Kaparov heard the familiar jingle of the bells mounted to the door to alert the cashier, he took his two bottles to the register and paid a mere one hundred and fifty rubles for a complete liter of forty-proof alcohol. Not a bad deal. He shook a dented cigarette out of a crumpled pack fished from his jacket and deftly maneuvered the brown bag to light the cigarette with his silver butane lighter. After inhaling deeply, he turned north and walked along the wide, tree-lined sidewalk.

Pedestrian traffic was light at that time of the night. That part of Brateyevo mostly held large apartment buildings built during the Soviet era. Beyond a few grocery stores and liquor shops, the district remained devoid of commercial business, which Kaparov preferred. The wide streets and open spaces were difficult to find this close to Moscow, even if the district didn't cater to the wealthy.

Brateyevo had remained a middle class to lower middle class enclave close to the heart of Moscow, though more and more younger affluent Russian couples had started to migrate into the community, driving up the apartment prices for new contracts. Most of the districts denizens took advantage of rent control provisions, which hadn't been eliminated like in other districts. One of these days, the government would level this place to make room for mansions and expensive condominium complexes. The face of corruption in Moscow was often disguised as "progress," according to city politicians. Until then, Kaparov would continue to enjoy peaceful nighttime walks along the district's well-lit streets.

Halfway down Alma-Atinskaya Boulevard, mostly convinced that he was not being followed, he turned onto an unfamiliar walkway and pulled out one of his prepaid cell phones. Another two thousand rubles to be thrown in the Moscow River. In this case, the phone call would be worth far more than the price he had paid for the phone. He checked his watch and calculated the time difference. Karl Berg should be finished with lunch, or whatever he did with his noon hour. He heard that many of the CIA employees exercised or took yoga classes instead of eating lunch. Right inside the facility. He couldn't imagine the day that they installed a full gym at Lubyanka Square, or had people standing on their heads contemplating their inner self in the same rooms that still echoed with the screams of the purged.

It took longer than usual for Berg to answer, which made Kaparov nervous. He kept walking toward the towering apartment building ahead of him, occasionally checking to see if anyone else had followed. He wasn't surprised to see the walkway clear. Lucya was the only link to his deception, and she was still in the surveillance phase. Once they decided to pick her up, it was over for him.

Damn it, where are you, Karl!

"What in hell is holding this up?" he said, unaware that the line had been answered.

"And good afternoon to you, comrade. Everything all right over there?" the voice asked in Russian.

"Far from it. No names. We have a big problem here," Kaparov said, stopping near a tree.

"I was about to call you with some interesting news about our mutual friend. It seems that your people have been playing with the Iranians and—"

"I don't give a fuck who is playing with who right now. Forget all of that and listen closely. Whatever recently happened in Scandinavia has caused a reaction here in Moscow. A bad reaction. The source responsible for saving America's ass is under surveillance. Overt surveillance, and they're not from my organization. Do you understand what this means?"

The line remained silent for a few seconds longer than Kaparov expected, leaving him with the distinct impression that it might go silent forever, leaving him to fend for himself.

"This source is the nexus. Correct?"

"Correct," Kaparov said.

"Electronically, everyone is clear. Correct?" Berg said.

"So I am told."

"Then there is only one solution," Berg said.

"I was afraid you might say that," Kaparov said.

"You didn't need me for that, comrade. I assume you have another reason for calling? My offer of a cushy retirement still stands."

"I'd like to avoid that if possible, which is why I need your help. I'd like to remove the source in question. Permanent relocation," Kaparov said.

"I assume that's not a euphemism for termination," Berg said.

"Correct. She'd be a valuable source for your organization. One way or the other, she can't stay. I'm asking for this as your return favor."

"It's an awfully big favor," Berg said.

"Ha! Always the negotiator. I sense that you still want something from me. Take care of our problem, and I'll be able to better concentrate on what you have to say," Kaparov said, throwing his cigarette to the ground in a flurry of sparking ashes.

"Let me make a quick call. I might be able to do this without using in-house assets. What is our timeline?" Berg said.

"Forty-eight hours maximum. More like twenty-four. Once they consistently notice that the subject is visibly shaken, they'll move in for the grab. This one isn't faring well, so I predict it will happen sooner than later. How close are these assets?"

"Close. I'll contact you at the next phone number as soon as I know anything," Berg said.

"This is getting expensive for me," Kaparov said.

"I can have someone drop off some phones for you," Berg said.

"You'd like that, wouldn't you?"

"It's the closest I could ever come to recruiting you."

Kaparov roared with laughter at the comment, knowing exactly where Berg was coming from. The two of them had traded jabs for three years in Moscow, each subtly suggesting the same thing on numerous occasions. They had an odd relationship as adversaries. They probably trusted each other's motives better than their own masters' chameleon-like agendas.

"Well, if this plan of yours doesn't work, you might ultimately win our decades-old showdown," Kaparov said.

"As much as I'd like that, I don't think we could afford your vodka habit."

"Probably not," Kaparov said.

"Stay safe. You know how to reach me if things take a turn for the worse. I'll be in touch," Berg said.

Kaparov started walking back toward the street with the intention of turning left and continuing past his featureless apartment building. He'd take a quick stroll down the tree-lined boulevard, crossing into the park that adjoined the Moscow River, where he'd sink the financial equivalent of thirty vodka bottles to its muddy bottom. There, he would remind himself how easily his own body could be tossed into the murky depths if he wasn't careful.

Chapter 19

General Sanderson picked one of the closest human silhouettes and swiftly raised the MK12 rifle, finding the target's head through the EOTech holographic sight. He placed two quick holes in the paper less than an inch apart and shifted his aim to a target two hundred yards downrange, simultaneously flipping a Switch-To-Side 3X magnifier in place and taking a second to line up his shot. He fired two rounds at the distant target, using the magnifier.

"Two hits. Center mass. Three MOA, possibly less," stated Jared Hoffman, his observer.

Hoffman was the Russian Group's dedicated marksman, and in the absence of Daniel Petrovich had taken over as one of their primary weapons evaluators. Richard Farrington put their weapons to the test in a more practical environment, taking them off the static ranges and trying to destroy them on the live fire maneuver ranges. "Combat Town" was his favorite, where he would instruct teams to throw all of their weapons from the top floor onto the hard-packed ground. The teams would follow, rappelling from the windows to retrieve the weapons, which would be immediately used to engage pop-up targets down the street. A wide variety of optics and rifles failed this test, honing their selection of weapons and optics platforms. So far, the EOTech sights passed with flying colors. The flip-up magnifier didn't hold as much promise.

"I don't know. A six-inch spread at two hundred yards under stable conditions…"

"Six inches is being generous. Your last batch was more like four MOA. I can't get it any better without cheating," Hoffman said.

General Sanderson grunted. "Three to four MOA on an eighteen-inch barrel isn't good enough to justify this flip-up contraption. I can't imagine it would survive Richard's field assessment. Let me see the other configuration again."

Sanderson removed the magazine and ejected the chambered round, letting it tumble into the dirt. He leaned the cleared rifle against the firing range stand as Hoffman handed him another MK12, this one configured with a Trijicon 4X ACOG and an offset red dot sight. After inserting the magazine in the new rifle, he engaged the targets in reverse order. He quickly lined up two shots at a new distant target using the scope before twisting the rifle forty-five degrees to use the red dot sight. A rapid double tap punctured the twenty-five yard target, keeping the tight pattern formed by previous firing. He lowered the rifle and raised it again, repeating the drill starting with the twenty-five yard target.

"Two MOA at 200 yards. All four rounds pretty tight. Results at twenty-five yards are the same," Hoffman said.

"Well, it was a nice concept. We just haven't been able to replicate the accuracy of a dedicated battle scope. Canting the rifle to use the red dot doesn't impede progress. I think this combination is the winner for our mid-range rifles. Start equipping different platforms with these optics. Farrington has done everything but take a blowtorch to the ACOG. See if he has any real heartache with the offset red dot sight."

"Easy enough, General. I wish we could take the MK12s out on a real op. Fucking amazing weapon," Hoffman said.

"That's the irony of our situation. Aside from local work on behalf of Galenden, none of our weapons ever leave the compound, and in most situations, we have to use locally sourced equipment," Sanderson said.

"It's a shame," Hoffman said, taking the rifle back from Sanderson and clearing it.

"I'm pretty sure you're stuck with the trusty AK family of rifles. They've served us well up to this point. Ask Farrington," the general said.

What he didn't add to his statement was the fact that Farrington was the only member of the first Russian team alive, besides Petrovich, who was more of a last-minute addition to the group. The first team fielded by Sanderson's new program had suffered heavy casualties. Two killed and one severely wounded. Of the five men sent to Kazakhstan, only Farrington and Petrovich had survived intact. Setting these grim statistics aside, the team had achieved the impossible, which always came with a high price tag. The program had been designed to produce teams that would deliver results against overwhelming odds, and it had repeatedly proven to be successful.

"Speak of the devil," Hoffman said, nodding toward the tree line behind them.

Richard Farrington approached them dressed like a Russian street thug. Tight black jeans and a gray turtleneck sweater under a worn leather bomber jacket with thick lapels complemented the look, which he never abandoned in the compound. He required the same of every member under his charge in the Russian Group.

"General, we have a special request from the CIA. You left your phone back in the lodge," he said, tossing the satellite phone to Sanderson.

"Sanderson," he said into the phone's receiver.

"General, Karl Berg here. I have a situation in Moscow that may be directly related to the disappearance of your operative in Munich. My contact has reported an unexpected increase in SVR activity. The source of the Stockholm leak is under aggressive surveillance, and my guy doesn't think she has more than twenty-four hours before they pick her up. He's fairly certain she won't last five minutes under interrogation. She's already suggested preemptively turning my contact over to SVR in exchange for a deal."

"They won't make a deal with her. They'll just torture the information out of her and discard her corpse in a dumpster," Sanderson said.

"If she's lucky. I think she's watched one too many Western television shows. She's responsible for the death of at least eight of their best, so I have a feeling she won't get off that easy. I need your help pulling her out of Moscow. If she disappears, the whole problem goes away."

"When you say *gone*, what exactly do you mean?" Sanderson said.

"Safe from Russian hands. By my count, you have at least one operative left in the nearby area of operations."

"He's likely compromised," Sanderson replied.

"All the more reason to give him one more mission and get him the hell out of Europe. This is important, Terrence. My source is aware of our intentions to strike Vektor. He's an old-school Cold War type who would rather die than tell them anything, but we can't take the risk," Berg said.

"I get the sense that you have a personal stake in this," Sanderson said.

"The United States owes him everything. I can't leave him hanging like this," Berg said.

"Tell me why the CIA can't yank her off the streets?"

"Tensions are high right now. The Russians grabbed a high-level CIA officer from our embassy in Stockholm. We can't afford an escalation, and the director will not authorize the use of Special Activities Division assets on Russian soil," Berg said.

"Have you asked the director?"

"I don't need to ask him. They will not authorize the kidnapping of a Russian citizen."

"What about the other option?"

Karl Berg's silence answered the question.

"The CIA would be willing to kill her to protect this secret?" Sanderson said.

"I can't really speak for what the CIA might do. I only learned about this problem a few minutes ago. I do know that a street killing would be a hell of a lot simpler than kidnapping someone under active surveillance. I called you first because your operatives have proven to be extremely effective with this type of operation…and because I'm fairly confident that the CIA will scrap the raid on Vektor if I present these new facts. We can't let that happen. The Iranians have infiltrated the program, and it's only a matter of time before something worse than the Zulu virus finds its way into their hands."

"My operatives will not assassinate a noncombatant. If she can't be taken alive, I suggest you start working on your travel plans to Moscow. What kind of surveillance are we talking about?" Sanderson asked.

"Most likely on the lower end of the spectrum. They've made themselves fairly obvious, which doesn't require a great deal of skill. Plus, they're probably doing the same thing to at least a dozen other suspects."

"I'm going to burn two operatives with this," Sanderson said.

"I've faced the same decision point before, so I know it sucks. All the time and investment wasted on something seemingly insignificant. I'm intimately familiar with the feeling," Berg said.

"I trust your assessment of the situation. If anything, you've demonstrated an uncanny talent for predicting the future. I'll make the arrangements. Barring unforeseen circumstances, I can have two operatives in place by noon tomorrow. I'll need specific information about the target and limited logistical support from your agency. Be prepared for a handoff. Snatching her off the street is my problem. Getting her out of Russia is yours."

"Perfect. I'll start working on my end immediately. My contact will be able to provide most of the information you'll need to locate and identify the target. I'll pass this on immediately. Have you heard from Petrovich yet? We had an interesting meeting with Dr. Evil."

"He's scheduled for a videoconference tomorrow morning. I'll have the entire team assembled, to include the young woman from Langley. I plan to recruit her, by the way. I'm not sure where you find these femme fatales, but I'd like a tour of the factory. With a little additional training, she could give Jessica Petrovich a run for her money. She's already broken one nose. The second batch of 'Russians' is a little rowdier than the first. It was well deserved," Sanderson said.

"Sounds like they would fit in perfectly on the Moscow subway," Berg said, obviously ducking the rest of Sanderson's comments.

Sanderson had lost both of the program's women during the domestic operation to stop True America, and saw little chance that either would ever return. Dhiya Castillo survived her gunshot wounds, but permanently lost the full use of her primary shooting hand. Beyond that, the full impact of her injuries couldn't be determined without extensive physical therapy. For all practical purposes, she was done with the program. This left Jessica, who may or may not continue to serve the program in a limited capacity. He suspected that Daniel and Jessica wouldn't be able to stay away from the action for long, but he wasn't about to push them for an answer. He was satisfied just knowing that they hadn't officially told him to "fuck off." Yet.

"Let's hope they don't have to ride the subway to escape. I assume these mafiya contacts will be able to provide something more substantial than Metro tickets?"

"Petrovich already shared that gem?" Berg asked.

"He felt we would need to have an in-depth discussion about this prior to his teleconference. I'm not sure how I feel about it," Sanderson said.

"Neither am I, frankly," Berg said. "Daniel's biggest concern was the exfil. Your boy isn't that talkative, but we came to the same conclusion during the drive back to Burlington. The safest way to the Kazakh border will likely involve the use of a boat and several pre-staged vehicles. Reznikov also made a good point about Novosibirsk. We're dealing with a unique part of the country. Novosibirsk is the third largest city in Russia, but it doesn't resemble Moscow or any of the western cities. The language, customs...everything is a little different. The less contact your crew has with local vendors the better. Putin's reforms may be mostly lip service, but my Russian area analysts say that the areas beyond Moscow's grasp don't even bother to read his lips. We can't afford to attract the wrong kind of attention. Nobody questions the mafiya, inside or outside of the major cities. I've received approval from my director to offer up to ten million dollars in exchange for their cooperation and support."

"That's a hefty price tag. I assume you'll start negotiations lower?"

"Of course," Berg said. "I fully expect to be blackmailed at the last moment."

"What if they insist on ten?" Sanderson asked, now knowing exactly why Berg had broached the topic of money.

"Well," Berg admitted, "I was hoping that you might be willing to cover any expenses exceeding my budget."

Sanderson shook his head and laughed. "Let me get this straight. Not only am I providing you with the car for your road trip, but now I'm expected to pitch in for gas money?"

"What can I say? There's only so much money in the covert foreign invasion budget."

"And it's only May." Sanderson sighed.

"Maybe we'll get lucky, and they only ask for five million."

"Don't count on it. Make sure to pass me any bank routing information they provide. I can cover the shortfall."

"One of these days, you and I will sit down and share that drink. I owe you more than one at this point," Berg said.

"I suspect you'll owe me the entire distillery before this is over, Karl. Call me when an agreement is reached with the Russians. We'll start the planning phase tomorrow based on Daniel's input."

"Sounds good. Reznikov will place a call to his *bratva* contact tomorrow. I will monitor this call and take over if they are interested. At that point,

Reznikov's involvement will be limited to two additional calls to verify that we're cooperating with the mafiya."

"That's an odd arrangement. How are you routing the call?"

"Satellite. I had the same thought at first, but Reznikov didn't balk at the use of satcom for the check-ins. He's worried that I'll revoke his deal if the team doesn't make it back in one piece. He claims to be withholding a piece of mission-critical information that won't be revealed until his last call is completed," Berg said.

"Has it crossed his mind that you'll just blow his brains out regardless of what happens?"

Berg hesitated with his answer, which confirmed his other suspicion. "He's trying to exert some control over the end result. Ease of mind, I guess."

"Nothing wrong with a little hope," Sanderson said.

Sanderson disconnected the call and turned to Hoffman.

"This is going to be the stuff of legends, Jared. A once-in-a-lifetime mission."

"That seems to be par for the course around here," Hoffman said.

"That's what happens when you're the final option."

Chapter 20

Nikolai Mazurov edged around the corner of the building and spotted the black sedan. He kept his body hidden, only allowing a small fraction of his head to break the plane of the building. Having just scurried along the western side of the apartment building, scraping through the tight walkway that connected the rear alley with Raskovoy Boulevard, he didn't detect any traffic coming from either direction on the road. The empty street matched his own intelligence assessment of this distant northwest suburb of Moscow. Mostly consisting of Soviet Bloc apartment buildings, it catered to lower middle class families or recent college graduates, most of whom could not afford the luxury of an automobile. He'd have to be infinitely more cautious of pedestrians, though it really wouldn't matter one way or the other who saw them on the street. His time as a deep-cover operative in Russia ended tonight.

He had been assured by General Sanderson that Lucya Pavrikova's abduction would become the Russian Foreign Intelligence Service's number one priority in the upcoming days, leaving no stones unturned in Moscow or the surrounding areas. He would depart Europe with Reinhard Klinkman and eventually find his way to Sanderson's new Argentinian hideaway.

The thought of warmer weather suited Nikolai fine. He had grown accustomed to his life in Moscow, but yearned for more. He was in his mid-thirties, having spent nearly all of his service time in Moscow, simply waiting in the shadows. He attended Moscow University, earning a teaching degree with a concentration in foreign language. Not surprisingly, he took to English like a native speaker and was able to secure a position in a suburban Moscow secondary school, teaching English to middle graders. Attending college and teaching English to fourteen-year-olds wasn't exactly what he had in mind after spending nearly four years training in Sanderson's hellish program. On the flip side, he was one of the few surviving graduates of the original Black Flag program. The survival rate had been abysmally low according to Sanderson, and most that survived had endured hell on earth to return. Because of this, he really couldn't complain about walking away from his life in Moscow. It had never really been his from the beginning.

He raised a suppressed OTs-14 assault rifle to the chipped concrete edge of the building and tucked the "bullpup" configured weapon tightly into his shoulder. The OTs-14 "Groza" was used exclusively by Russian Spetsnaz or Interior Ministry units, chambered to fire 9X39mm subsonic ammunition. Fitted with a suppressor, the subsonic rounds made the "Groza" one of the quietest Russian assault weapons on the market.

Nikolai peered through the 3X scope attached to the rifle's carrying handle and sighted in on one of two heads visible through the sedan's rear window. Unlike the car parked in the alley, he could not approach the sedan on Raskovoy Boulevard unseen. The four-lane road was well lit by Russian standards, and curb space on both sides of the street was mostly empty. The black sedan was one of few cars parked in front of Pavrikova's apartment building.

He'd been able to shoot the two agents in the back alley at point-blank range, from the driver's side window. He wouldn't have that kind of luxury with these two, and he needed to hit both of them in rapid succession. He chose the head on the left, since it was already partially obscured by the sedan's frame. Take the hardest shot first. He braced the suppressor against the building and steadied the green-illuminated crosshairs. Nikolai applied pressure to the trigger as he had been taught many years ago, continuing to focus on the target in the crosshairs. The scope's point-of-aim and point-of-impact would be the same at this range. Under fifty meters, the subsonic ammo kept a flat trajectory.

The Groza cracked, biting into the concrete as the first projectile raced toward its target. The rear window turned white, obscuring his view of the second target, as the round's impact with the safety glass caused the entire rear window to shatter in place. He had anticipated this problem. The scope's field of view allowed him to see most of the second man's head as he took the first shot, giving him a frame of reference for the blind shooting about to take place. He shifted the scope's crosshairs from the small hole in the opaque window to the previous location of the second head. He used the crosshair's mil-dots to measure the shift and pulled the trigger twice. The rest of the window collapsed from the impact of the two rifle rounds. Through the scope, he could see that a third shot would not be necessary. Two large red stains covered the spider-cracked front windshield a few feet apart.

Nikolai glanced around the city street and listened for a few seconds. The rifle's suppressor had distorted the sound of small arms fire to a low-grade firecracker, which still had the potential to attract significant attention. Nothing. He stared up at the various windows visible from his position. Curtains remained in place and unlit windows stayed dark. Even if anyone had decided to take a look, they would think twice about calling the police. A street shooting usually meant one thing: Russian mafiya. Contacting the police only served one purpose—to identify yourself as a possible witness, and witnesses to mafiya crimes in Russia had a very short life span. For the average citizen, it was better to let the police stumble upon the crime scene.

Satisfied that the shooting had escaped overt attention, he jogged up to the car to confirm his handiwork. A quick look inside verified that his shooting had been accurate. Both bodies were slumped against each other, tangled over the car's center console. Dark fluid poured out of the gaping holes that once resembled human faces. He started jogging to the side street corner used by the third SVR surveillance vehicle.

"Surveillance team two neutralized," he whispered.

His throat microphone translated the vibrations from his vocal cords into sound, which was passed on to Klinkman and the driver of his own support vehicle.

"Copy. Team two neutralized. I have the door unlocked. Standing by," Klinkman replied.

"Breach and remove target. I'm moving to cover the third surveillance team," Nikolai said.

"Better move fast. I'm going in."

࿇

Lucya Pavrikova poured a glass of white wine from an inexpensive bottle she had picked up on her transit home that evening. She'd left at six-thirty, later than most, hoping to get a reprieve from her new shadows. No fewer than two agents followed her wherever she'd go, regardless of the time. At this point, she was afraid to leave her apartment outside of the busy hours in the morning or evening, when the rest of her building's inhabitants travelled back and forth to work, hopefully deterring a street-side abduction. She knew this was mostly wishful thinking. If the SVR wanted her in custody, they wouldn't hesitate to take her in the middle of Red Square on May Day. The only place they would avoid for now was the FSB building at Lubyanka Square. She knew they were fishing for leads, overtly sweating everyone possibly connected to the Center for Special Operations at Lubyanka. They hadn't moved on anyone yet, but the death of several SVR agents guaranteed that the rulebook would be suspended until they discovered the leak. It was only a matter of time before they started rounding them up, and once they disappeared, she didn't feel hopeful that they'd ever see the light of day again.

She took a long sip of the harsh chardonnay and refilled the glass, deciding to check on her shadows. She walked past the television, briefly blocking her roommate's view of some mindless reality show based on the lives of several Russian millionaires' wives. *Dacha Princesses* or something equally inane. Her roommate spent most of the evening brainlessly pining away for the life represented on the show, which aired every weeknight. With over one hundred thousand millionaires in Moscow alone, Katya had yet to score her knight in shining Mercedes. Katya's concerns paled in comparison to Lucya's own at the moment, and she prayed that her roommate didn't feel like small talk tonight. If she was lucky, the television station would rerun last night's episode immediately following this one, and Katya would be locked into another hour of brain drain. By then, Lucya would be passed out in their shared bedroom.

Lucya pulled back the flimsy curtain covering their living room window and peered five stories down at the crowded street. Through the dark windshield of the familiar black sedan parked below, she caught the faint orange glow of a cigarette, which burned brightly for a second. The car was parked several vehicles away from the nearest streetlamp, swallowed by the darkness which had only minutes ago consumed the city. A faint bluish-red light on the horizon could still be seen between the twisted maze of apartment buildings visible from her window. She hated the night now. Only two days of this shit, and she was afraid to go to sleep. She'd have to drink herself into a semi-stupor to get any sleep at all. She knew there was nothing she could do to stop the agents if they decided to take her, but the thought of them kicking her door in during the middle of the night terrified her.

The reality of her situation still hadn't fully registered, and she hadn't really come up with any kind of game plan. Her time at work was too hectic to stop and focus on the situation. CSN had several ongoing operations that required her undivided attention, and her commute was mostly spent looking over her shoulder at the thugs assigned to follow her. Time spent in the apartment had been clouded by a perpetual blood alcohol content that probably disqualified her from microwaving her own dinner. If their tactic was to scare the shit out of her, she had to give them credit.

Her only consolation was that they were also doing this to everyone else in her office. Most of her colleagues didn't openly discuss it, but a few had opened up to her, figuring that the leak had come from the SVR. This seemed to be the prevailing theory among the agents in her office, but she still sensed the barely palpable tension associated with doubt, which fueled alienation. This was the worst part for her. Aside from a few close friends in her division, everyone at headquarters now avoided her. She was tainted until they figured this out.

She glanced at the sedan one more time, wondering what they would do if she walked down the stairs and offered up Kaparov. Would they be lenient? Her boyfriend didn't think so. He had cornered her in the stairwell after she cleared security in the morning and started her journey to the fourth floor. Their rendezvous lasted less than a minute, but he had made it clear that selling out Kaparov wouldn't ease her burden. She'd be tortured mercilessly until they had everything, then she'd be dissolved alive in a tub of acid. She'd suffer immeasurably, and no trace of her body would ever be found. Prerovsky had just as much at stake, so she wasn't sure if his words were meant to put her situation in perspective or threaten her. Based on his sudden appearance and tone, she tended to believe it was the latter. So much for their relationship.

She decided on another refill, smiling at her roommate, who looked up from the television and almost asked her what was bothering her. She could read it on her face, but something had mercifully dragged her back into the drama unfolding on the screen. Outside of *Dacha Princess* hour, Katya was a compassionate friend and good roommate. Lucya had purposely timed her return to the kitchen to avoid commercials. Her friend would have asked her what was wrong, and she was in no emotional shape to refuse a sympathetic shoulder. She preferred to pass out and wake up to a new day. A day that didn't include black sedans and serious-looking men following her onto the Metro.

She gripped the wine bottle and prepared to drain its contents into her glass, when the door to her apartment suddenly opened to reveal a dark-haired man wearing black pants and a gray windbreaker.

ॐॐ

Reinhard Klinkman felt the locking mechanism's tumbler move and tested the doorknob, which turned freely. Easy enough. He removed a pistol-sized compressed air gun from his backpack and thumbed the safety switch. The gun was loaded with six self-actuating darts. Upon contact, each dart would discharge enough neurotoxin to instantly disable a three-hundred-pound human being, primarily targeting the skeletal muscle system. The toxin affected its target immediately, preventing fine motor skill almost instantly, graduating to full paralysis seconds later.

In this case, he didn't want to hit the wrong target. Intelligence indicated that Lucya had a roommate who looked remarkably similar. Both had long blond hair, blue eyes and similar builds. The picture provided by their contact wouldn't help in this situation. He'd have to take his time with this one. He couldn't afford to carry Lucya down five flights of stairs given their tight timeline. Then again, if Lucya didn't immediately come to terms with the situation he presented, he'd have to refamiliarize himself with the fireman's carry. He really hoped she would be reasonable. He tightened the backpack straps and took a deep breath before opening the door.

The scene registered before he physically responded. The woman on the couch glanced in his direction with her mouth open, but made no immediate attempt to get up. The other one reacted without hesitation. She knocked a bottle of wine out of the way to reach for the small knife rack

112

next to the sink. He raised the pistol and fired a single dart at the woman on the couch, freezing the dumb look on her face. By the time he aimed at Lucya, the agent had retrieved a thick handled, five-inch blade from the rack, holding it in front of her in a desperate attempt to establish dominance. He hoped his Russian didn't leave anything lost in translation.

"Lucya, the darts in this gun work instantly. You wouldn't get past the kitchen counter. I need to get you out of here right now, so please drop the knife and follow me. My instructions are simple. One way or the other, you leave with me."

"I won't tell you anything," Lucya said, threatening him with the knife.

"I'm not asking any questions. You're in grave danger, and I have been sent to bring you to a safe place."

"Who sent you?" she demanded.

"I can't disclose that. Someone may be listening. I need you to trust me, Lucya. You played and you lost. Your life here is over if you want to stay alive. There's no other way. If you don't walk out with me in the next three seconds, we do this the hard way," Klinkman said.

"Is she all right?" Lucya said, looking at her roommate.

"She's fine. She'll wake up within the hour with a nasty headache. Time to go."

Lucya placed the knife back on the rack and walked forward. "Do I need my purse?"

"No. Lucya Pavrikova no longer exists," Klinkman said, pulling her through the doorway.

෴

Agent Boris Shelepin focused the high-magnification scope and stared through the low-intensity light optics into their target apartment. The Pavrikova woman had just stared down at the surveillance car located on the main street across from her apartment building's entrance. The sight of the omnipresent car had triggered a long sip from the glass of white wine she had been pouring most of the evening. He wished they had been given a proper surveillance post in one of the surrounding apartments. Pavrikova's roommate was equally as easy on his eyes, and he wouldn't have minded getting a better view into their apartment. From the street, their view was limited. They'd parked the van as far down the side street as possible to increase the depth of their view, but he still couldn't see past the front door, which was located halfway across the cramped common area that served as their kitchen and family room.

He didn't bother to ask his SVR section head for permission to "requisition" one of the apartments facing Pavrikova's. His boss had made it clear that his surveillance detail's purpose was intimidation. They were to maintain an obvious presence in Lucya Pavrikova's life outside of the FSB's Lubyanka headquarters. *Physical surveillance* had been the term used by his superiors. Foreign Intelligence Service assets had the rest of Pavrikova covered from an electronic standpoint. Apartment phone. Cell phone. Email. Eavesdropping devices. Remote cameras. All of this would be monitored from a distance. His team would do the grunt work, which suited him fine. He just wished he could get a better view of Pavrikova's ass, or her roommate's. Either one would work for him.

He could see the top of her blond ponytail in front of the refrigerator, which meant she would reappear at the window with a refilled wine glass in a minute or two. He lowered the scope and turned to his comrade, who had nodded off in the driver's seat. He nudged the agent.

"Hang in there a little longer. She's going to drink herself to sleep at this rate," Shelepin said.

"We're headed back when the apartment goes dark?" the driver asked.

"Yeah. We'll leave the two cars to keep an eye on the exits," Shelepin said.

In addition to the car parked on the street in front of the apartment, they had another jammed into the tight service alley behind the building. The alley led to a rear service entrance that allowed easy access to the large trash collection bins located in the dingy area off the main stairwell. The doors had been padlocked from the inside since they started Pavrikova's surveillance, which was standard procedure in many of the apartment buildings. The landlord or building owner would meet the trash removal crew in person and unlock the door, at the same time passing a weekly payment to the crew…most of which would eventually find its way into the hands of the local mafiya. Still, local fire ordinances required two working ground-floor exits, so several of the occupants would have the key to the padlock. They couldn't risk Lucya being one of them.

He stretched his arms in his seat, twisting his body to look into the pitch-black recesses of the van. The shadowy figure sitting directly behind the driver cracked his knuckles.

"You're going to give yourself arthritis doing that," Shelepin said.

"That's an old wives' tale," the agent said.

A cell phone lit up the inside of the drink holder on the van's center console tray, bathing all of them in a soft blue light and exposing the agent in the van's second row of seats, who squinted. Shelepin grabbed the phone and answered.

"Agent Shelepin."

"Why the fuck aren't you answering your radio? The apartment was just breached! Nobody is answering the radios!"

Shelepin didn't bother to raise the surveillance scope to view the apartment. Training and instinct took over, telling him not to waste the time. He hissed at the driver and grabbed his handheld radio.

"Let's go. Front door," he said before speaking into the handheld. "Surveillance units report. This is Shelepin! Report your status now!"

The van lurched forward, racing toward the main street. He received no reply from either unit. Seconds from turning the corner, he put the cell phone back to his ear.

"What happened in the apartment?"

"One man kicked the door in and shot the roommate. Your target left willingly. What is the status of the other agents?"

"I don't know," Shelepin replied just before the van turned sharply right onto Raskovoy Boulevard, pinning him against the passenger door.

∫∼∫

Nikolai Mazurov reached the corner in time to hear the van's tires screech, validating one of their most critical assumptions about the SVR operation. Their electronics tech had studied the neighborhood's electronic signature for hours and had found several suspicious bandwidths that could signify the presence of listening devices or wireless camera feeds. He couldn't be sure, since every household in this lower income neighborhood utilized some form of pirated electronics. Because these devices were mostly illegal on the international market, the manufacturers weren't concerned with conforming their products to recognized international bandwidth spectrums. Bandwidth ranges varied wildly with these unregulated devices, creating an electronic signature that looked like a "fucking mosaic," according to their tech. Even this mosaic had a pattern that could be interpreted given enough time, but time wasn't one of the luxuries on their menu today. They had arrived shortly before six o'clock, several minutes before their target exited the nearest Metro station. They simply assumed that the apartment had been rigged with video feeds, which meant their countdown started when Klinkman kicked down Pavrikova's door.

Nikolai risked a quick peek and saw the silver van barreling toward the intersection. He wouldn't have time for any well-aimed semi-automatic shots. He thumbed the fire rate selector switch to automatic and raised the rifle, jamming the suppressor against the building's corner and tilting the weapon forty-five degrees to use a small custom red dot sight affixed to the side.

"Engaging hostile van. Request pickup on Raskovoy in front of target building."

Not waiting for a response, Nikolai fired a sustained but controlled burst of fire at the front windshield, peppering the glass directly in front of the driver with several rounds. His next burst collapsed a large section of windshield on the passenger side. The van lurched to the left and accelerated through the intersection, barely missing the corner that concealed him. The unguided vehicle raced past him and slammed into a streetlight on the opposite side of Raskovoy Boulevard, casting a dark shadow over the area.

Nikolai quickly shifted to the protected side of the building's corner and fired the rifle's remaining rounds into the back of the van. While swiftly changing rifle magazines, he noticed several lights appear in the windows above. Their timeline had just been hyper-accelerated. Without hesitation, he leveled the Groza and systematically punctured the van's rear compartment with the thirty rounds supplied by the fresh magazine. He reloaded the rifle, keeping it leveled toward the van, and used his peripheral vision to navigate the street. Any movement within the wrecked vehicle would conjure another maelstrom of steel from Nikolai's weapon. His earphone crackled.

"Coming out of the apartment with our package."

He detected movement to his left and quickly glanced over his shoulder to confirm that Klinkman and Pavrikova had walked through the front door.

"The street is clear. Where the fuck is the van?" Nikolai said.

"Turning onto Raskovoy," his earpiece responded.

A pair of headlights appeared on Raskovoy, moving rapidly toward them. Nikolai tensed, and Klinkman eased back into the building's alcove. The lights flashed twice, allaying their concern and drawing them back into the open.

"Let's go," he said, still focused on the last remaining immediate threat.

He started walking backward along the sidewalk, while Klinkman and Lucya jogged toward the speeding van. By the time Nikolai climbed inside the van a few seconds later, Klinkman had replaced the electronics tech as their driver. The van sped down Raskovoy and turned onto a side street. If their plan was still intact, Klinkman would find the next major road heading north.

He extended his hand to Lucya Pavrikova. "It's a pleasure to meet you, Lucya."

The tears streaming down her face were illuminated by the soft green glow of a small laptop computer mounted to a table behind the second row of seats. She shook his hand tentatively, but said nothing.

"How are we looking?" he said to the technician kneeling in front of the computer.

The technician typed for a few seconds before looking up.

"SVR units were pulled from the nearest surveillance job to respond. They're fifteen minutes out. Police units have been dispatched. They should arrive within five minutes. It'll take them time to sort out the mess. We'll be in a different vehicle by the time they issue an alert," Luke Fortier replied.

"Keep a close eye on that. If we need to change vehicles sooner, we'll improvise," Nikolai said.

He turned back to Pavrikova, who stared out of her window. "Did my associate fully explain your situation?" he asked.

She nodded.

"Do you have any questions?"

"What happens to my family?"

"They'll be questioned. Watched for a while, but nothing beyond that. This isn't your father's Soviet Union."

"Will I see them again?"

"That's not up to me. You'll have to work that out with your new friends," he said.

"And who exactly are my new friends?"

"I'm not authorized to share that information. We're just the delivery team. I will caution you to accept their proposal," Nikolai said.

"What if I don't accept?"

"Then your broken body will turn up somewhere outside of Moscow a few days from now," Nikolai said.

"I should have known better than to trust Yuri. He's so far up that Cold War dinosaur's ass, he probably never stopped to consider the possibility that Kaparov was working for the CIA. Saving Mother Russia, my ass. Kaparov is a CIA mole," she spat at him.

"If I were you, I wouldn't repeat that again. Ever," he said and placed the business end of the OTs-14's suppressor against her forehead. "Unless your specific intent is to nullify any arrangements that have been made on your behalf. And for the record, Yuri Prerovsky and his Cold War dinosaur boss saved your ass from a miserable death. They insisted that you be given a second chance."

"How generous of them. I disappear and nothing changes for them," she uttered, sniffling and wiping her face.

"Exposing Kaparov would have put you in the hands of some very pissed off Directorate S operatives. Did you think they would grant you some kind of immunity deal?" he asked, staring into her face.

She averted her eyes, which told him everything he needed to know. He was surprised that she could have been so naïve, even for a technical agent.

"You did. Well, you're the luckiest woman in Moscow right now. Up until five minutes ago, you were on course to be brutally tortured and gang raped to death in some undisclosed, dank warehouse. I'd say your options have significantly improved thanks to your friends."

She started sobbing uncontrollably, which suited Nikolai fine. She needed to get as much of this emotional outburst out of the way before they handed her off to the CIA. She'd need to be as levelheaded as possible during the transfer. The full bottle of wine she had consumed over the past hour compounded this problem. He'd make sure they understood this, though he hoped she might sober up slightly by the time they made the delivery. She had a chance to come out of this unscathed, and he was happy to steer her away from her certain fate at the hands of the Foreign Intelligence Service.

Even more so, he was pleased to learn that his ten-year undercover stint hadn't been compromised for a trivial reason. Sanderson didn't know which FSB agents would benefit from Lucya's abduction, but Nikolai had always made it a priority to learn the names and ranks of the senior agents at the Federation Security Service. The mere mention of Kaparov and his direct subordinate tied the entire scenario together for him. If the FSB's deputy director of the Bioweapons/Chemical Threat Assessment Division was assisting the CIA, the removal of Lucya Pavrikova had everything to do with enabling a future operation to deal with the bioweapons mess that had been unleashed on the world.

His only regret was that he would not be able to directly participate in the operation. He had been officially recalled from Russian soil, to return to Argentina. Since Luke couldn't determine with one hundred percent certainty that no external cameras had been used by the SVR near Pavrikova's apartment building, they had to assume that both he and Klinkman would eventually be identified. Sanderson strongly suspected that images taken by street security cameras in Stockholm had led to the recent disappearance of one of their operatives. Until their identities could be significantly changed, they would be confined to the Americas.

Chapter 21

Upon entering the secure conference room, Dmitry Ardankin stood at attention in front of the Foreign Intelligence Service Director and waited for permission to take a seat. As deputy director of Directorate S, Ardankin made the trip to the director's office on a daily basis, and not always under welcome terms. His directorate had experienced its share of failures, mishaps and defections during his tenure, but it had also pulled off some of the most notoriously successful foreign operations in the Directorate's recent history. Not to mention the weekly, if not daily "tasks" performed by his Zaslon operatives on behalf of the Federation's more connected government officials.

He wasn't sure what had angered Pushnoy more, losing Reznikov or losing eight of Putin's errand boys. Probably the latter. The Zaslon group had devolved into Putin's "business compliance" enforcers over the past several years, spending most of their time pressuring or assassinating Russian citizens abroad. Most of their targets were business types or entrepreneurs that had fallen out of favor with one of Putin's key government or industry allies.

Zaslon was a throwback to the sleeper-cell program initiated during the Cold War and grossly overestimated by the Americans, often romanticized in Western espionage novels. The program had existed, but on a much smaller scale and mostly in Europe. Kremlin leadership had long ago determined that the decisive battle would be fought and won on European soil, so GRU and KGB programs focused on disrupting strategic and tactical NATO targets in western Europe by inserting Spetsnaz teams prior to the anticipated start of hostilities. Sleeper cells comprised a tiny portion of the Cold War plan, just as Zaslon operatives barely factored in the Foreign Intelligence Service's global espionage network.

Still, they were extremely valuable, nearly irreplaceable assets, and the loss of a single member was treated as a disaster. The loss of eight Zaslon operatives at one time was an unmitigated catastrophe, and this didn't even begin to address the implications associated with Reznikov's disappearance. Unfortunately, their mess had fallen in his lap, and he'd managed to make matters worse, through no fault of his own. He'd sent eight of his best operatives, double what had been suggested by the director himself, and it hadn't been enough. The best they could figure at this point was that the Americans had a similar "illegals" program, and that their operatives were possibly better trained. Of course, all of this would have been a moot point if the FSB hadn't been compromised. Pavrikova's deception had put the two teams on a fatal collision course, in which the better team had clearly prevailed.

At least all of the attention wouldn't be focused solely on his Directorate. He'd take his lumps, but Federation Security Service leadership would take the brunt of the blame for this debacle. Pavrikova couldn't have been more perfectly placed within the Center for Special Operations to spy on high-level joint operations.

He took his eyes off the wall behind Stephan Pushnoy for a brief moment to see if the director had finished scrutinizing the files he had forwarded an hour earlier. If Pushnoy was staring at him, then the meeting wouldn't go well. The director's cold blue eyes didn't meet his glance. He was still absorbing the details of last night's abduction.

"Dmitry, please take a seat," he said, without looking up.

Ardankin started to feel better about the meeting. Pushnoy never invited one of his deputies to sit during an ass-chewing. He would have preferred that the director looked up at him, but this was better than the interminable silence that inevitably preceded the director's wrath. He got halfway into the seat next to Pushnoy before the first question erupted.

"Reinhard Klinkman. What do we know about him?"

"Not very much. German citizen. Lives in Hamburg—"

Pushnoy looked up at him, which stopped him from continuing. He knew the look. The director was interested in simple, conclusive statements.

"Nothing in his publicly available record raised any red flags. There is no record of him entering or exiting Russia," Ardankin said.

"I assume you found nothing unusual surrounding Nikolai Mazurov?"

"Aside from his involvement in the kidnapping of a Russian national and the murder of seven SVR agents? No."

Pushnoy looked up at him again, and he could see the start of a sinister grin. He had to admit, the director looked intimidating. He had thick, dark brown hair, which contrasted starkly with his light blue eyes and pale skin. The imbalance made it nearly impossible to determine his age. Only the thick crow's feet around the outside of his eyes and the deep wrinkles on his forehead suggested the kind of advanced age one could assume by his position as the senior ranking member of the Foreign Intelligence Service. He met the director's gaze and held it, knowing from experience that the former KGB officer expected his subordinates to look him in the eye while speaking. He interpreted an aversion to eye contact as weakness or deception. Ardankin had no intention of falling under either label.

"I don't expect they'll turn up in Russia or Europe. The remote operations team reports that none of the surveillance teams responded to their radio calls. What is your theory about that?" Pushnoy asked.

"Klinkman and Mazurov had technical support. All P25 encryption systems are vulnerable to detection and jamming. Signal interception and hijacking is also possible, but requires an extremely sophisticated electronics presence. The camera feeds remained functional, so I suspect they targeted the radio network. Smart. If they had played around with any of the remote video feeds, our technicians in the Operations Center might have detected the intrusion."

"Tech savvy and lethal. A dangerous and admirable combination," Pushnoy said.

"Our agents have the same capabilities," Ardankin reminded him.

"Then why are we losing so many agents?"

"This group operates in a radically different—"

"You mean they win!"

"I'm not making excuses," Ardankin began. "What I mean is that—"

"I know what you are trying to say. Even the Americans' Special Activities Division adheres to basic rules of engagement. This group appears to have no rules or boundaries. We've been spoiled for a long time, Dmitry, taking advantage of the West's misguided sense of morality and ethics. I fear those days have passed. Hubner said he was sent to Stockholm by Sanderson. Brigadier General Terrence Sanderson, United States Army, retired. His name didn't come up in any of our classified files. How did this man escape our attention for all of these years? Klinkman, Hubner and Mazurov were deep-cover operatives."

"Here's what we have so far," Ardankin said. "The three you just mentioned are mystery men. We found established public records in Germany and the Russian Federation reaching back to the mid to late nineties. University records to start, followed by the usual markings of a citizen from that point forward. Utility bills, car registrations, city permits…everything you would expect. Hubner's name came up in connection with several black market weapons dealers in Eastern Europe. He started small and worked his way onto the international scene, but promptly vanished in 2001, apparently deciding to pursue an advanced business degree in Munich. This sudden change of heart coincided with General Sanderson's fall from grace back in the United States." Ardankin paused to allow Pushnoy ask questions.

"You suspect a connection?"

"Absolutely. General Sanderson appeared briefly in 2001 to testify before the American Congress. Specifically, the Senate Select Committee on Intelligence. He retired from the army shortly thereafter. We know that Sanderson spent over a decade attached to the 1st Special Forces Operational Detachment-Delta, commanding the unit for nearly two years before taking a relatively obscure position at the Pentagon in 1991. He spent the next ten years in that position, which is extremely unusual. Our analysts found no mention of Sanderson during that ten-year period. He basically disappeared with a paycheck."

"Unusual indeed. The CIA had nothing on him?"

"Nothing, which is why his program never drew our attention," Ardankin said.

"Assuming he created a program," Pushnoy added.

"Of course, but here's where it gets interesting. Cameras in Stockholm captured images of Hubner and another operative involved with Reznikov's abduction," Ardankin said.

"Petrovich."

Ardankin nodded as Pushnoy shuffled the papers in front of him, removing two full-page photographs and setting them side by side.

"Daniel Petrovich. Now this is a complicated individual. His public record is sketchy at best. Graduated from Northwestern University in 1991. Commissioned in the United States Navy immediately upon graduation. Hometown news releases indicate that he was trained in Newport, Rhode Island as a surface warfare officer and—"

"Precisely what is a surface warfare officer?" Pushnoy interrupted.

"Shipboard naval officer. He was assigned to a frigate based out of Japan after completing about nine months of training at the surface warfare school in Newport. Nothing unusual about this training or his follow-on assignments. However, our analysts found nothing on Daniel Petrovich in the public domain after he reported to Japan—"

"Do you suspect he never reported?"

"We're pretty sure he reported to Japan. Analysts found press releases filed by the ship's public affairs officer and subsequently carried by his hometown newspaper. The latest date for one of these releases is November of 1993. At some point during this tour, he vanished. Daniel Petrovich didn't reemerge until the fall of 2000. He attended business school at Boston University, followed by a corporate job in Portland, Maine, at a technology company. We found a Massachusetts marriage license dated in 2001. He got married during business school to Jessica Petrovich—"

"What was her maiden name?" Pushnoy asked.

"None listed."

"Odd," Pushnoy said.

"Very odd, but minor in the grand scheme of things," Ardankin said.

Pushnoy raised a single eyebrow and stared at him.

"In the course of trying to identify Petrovich from the images taken in Stockholm, we discovered an amazing coincidence through Interpol. Daniel Petrovich bears a 93% resemblance to Marko Resja, a Serbian paramilitary sniper wanted by the International Criminal Tribunal for the former Yugoslavia. The charges leveled against him are highly specific, which is unusual for this tribunal. Torture and murder, to include a beheading. According to the documents, he fled Serbia in 1999, never to be seen again."

"When did he first appear in Serbia?"

"The exact timeline is unknown. Tribunal documents state that he operated with the Panthers from early 1998, until he disappeared in the late spring of 1999."

"Four years," Pushnoy muttered.

"Four years?"

"His training lasted nearly four years. 1994 to 1998. That's unheard of, even for CIA deep-cover agents."

"We found two more possible members of this group. Richard Farrington and Jeffrey Munoz appeared on FBI wanted lists at the same time as Sanderson and the Petroviches."

"Petroviches?"

"Daniel and Jessica Petrovich were placed on FBI wanted lists right around the time of the high-profile assassination spree in the United States," Ardankin clarified. "Several Muslim businessmen were killed in one evening."

"I remember that. This is nearly unbelievable. What about Farrington and Munoz?"

"Both of them were regular military. Lieutenant Colonel Farrington started his career in 1987 as an infantry officer and remained on active duty until he appeared on the FBI watch list in 2005. The details of his arrest warrant are sealed. Munoz's profile resembles Petrovich's. Entered active duty as a Marine artillery officer in 1992 and melted away, reemerging in early 2002 as a civilian. He was wanted in connection with the murder of one of the eight Muslim businessmen."

"Was?" Pushnoy remarked, looking up from the files.

"That's the most interesting aspect of this entire case. They all disappeared from the FBI wanted lists in late April of this year. A little more than three weeks ago," Ardankin said.

"All of them?" Pushnoy said.

"All of them," he replied blankly.

"This is all highly irregular. Were they taken off the FBI lists before or after Stockholm?"

"Archived snapshot data indicates that they were removed from the lists the day after the ambush in Stockholm."

"You would think that if Sanderson's group had been turned into a legitimate extension of the United States government, they would have been removed from the lists prior to the CIA-sanctioned attack on our agents," Pushnoy said.

"The CIA has been known to utilize questionable assets. Maybe Sanderson's group conducted the attack in exchange for some kind of immunity."

"I'm not so sure. This group is homegrown. Not the kind of degenerate outside scum we use for missions requiring no links. The operative captured in Munich could have shed more light on this mystery."

Ardankin noted the subtle implication that his agents had mishandled the opportunity. Unfortunately, this wasn't far from the truth, though in all fairness, the Directorate "S" agents assigned to the abduction couldn't have predicted their captive's steely resilience and unnatural commitment to this newly discovered program.

"He killed himself on an agent's knife. Careless, yet completely unexpected," Ardankin said.

"It seems that General Terrence Sanderson has created a new breed of American operatives. We can expect nothing but the unexpected from this point forward."

"Perhaps all was not lost with Pavrikova. Her kidnapping—"

"Defection. Though I'm surprised they didn't just kill her. It would have been a lot simpler," Pushnoy interjected.

"The Americans have always been soft when it comes to their contacts," Ardankin said.

"Indeed. Have you notified FSB Special Operations?"

"Not yet."

"I'm surprised they haven't contacted you. Miss Pavrikova's absence must have been duly noted this morning."

"Arkady Baranov will tiptoe around this—" Ardankin started.

"Baranov? Tiptoeing? Hardly. If anyone is worried right now, it's his boss, Greshnev. He'll be concerned about my reaction, but infinitely more troubled about Baranov's," Pushnoy said. "Baranov is hardcore, old-school Spetsnaz. If he suspects that we made a direct move against one of his people, he might retaliate. Pavrikova was part of the Center for Special Operations."

"She was a technician. Hardly the same as an agent," Ardankin said.

"Baranov is a warrior. He doesn't need much of a reason to pick a fight. Especially with us. Make sure you contact him immediately to explain the situation. And put an immediate end to any continuing surveillance of his personnel," Pushnoy said.

"What if he doesn't believe me?"

"You need to *make* him believe you. We can't afford to have him as an enemy. Sooner or later, it will cost us more than just a few operatives."

"I'll take care of this immediately. How much information should I share regarding Sanderson's program?"

"Nothing about Sanderson. You can give him the names of the men involved in the abduction and their biographical information, but nothing connecting them to Stockholm. Let him draw his own conclusions, while we formulate a strategy to deal with this new threat," Pushnoy said.

"Understood. Shall I consider Pavrikova a dead end at this point?"

"I think so. We'll issue a capture-kill bulletin abroad, but I'd be surprised if we ever saw her again."

"What a fucking mess this has been. The Americans crossed the line on this one," Ardankin said.

"Everyone went over the line on this one," Pushnoy corrected. "At least something good came of it. We've uncovered a potent threat to Russian Federation security."

"Potent indeed," Ardankin said, waiting for Pushnoy to dismiss him.

The director cast his eyes down, examining the file for a few seconds before closing it. "I'll prepare a briefing for the Prime Minister. Make sure you call Baranov immediately. Don't bullshit with him. The sooner he's off your case, the better."

"Of course, sir," Ardankin said.

"Don't wander too far today. I may need you to fill in some of the details for my briefing. Putin will not be pleased with this update. That will be all."

Ardankin simply nodded, keeping his thoughts, or any visual betrayal of these sentiments, to himself. Pushnoy opened his laptop, which meant the meeting was officially finished. At this point, Ardankin ceased to exist. He turned unceremoniously and approached the conference room door, thinking dangerous thoughts about why Putin wanted Reznikov erased so badly.

Chapter 22

Richard Farrington leaned over the rustic lacquered conference table and examined the map, tracing the routes leading south out of Novosibirsk. He was still unsettled by the clear lack of options for their escape and evasion plan. As always, Petrovich's assessment had been a "no holds barred," concise summary of their situation. The first words out of his mouth had been, *"I'm glad I won't be in attendance."* What followed summed up Farrington's first impression of the job. *"Looks like a straightforward deal going in…getting out promises to be a motherfucker. Good luck."* Not exactly the words Sanderson wanted broadcast to the team during the videoconference, but at least his sentiments cleared the air. The group selected for this mission didn't balk at his pessimism. If anything, they embraced the challenge, which resulted in a robust, yet deeply flawed escape plan.

Heading north through Novosibirsk was quickly eliminated due to the location of a sizable military garrison northeast of the city. The possibility of going north was considered solely on the merits that it would be the least expected route. Vektor Labs was located south of the city in a small urban settlement called Koltsovo, which had easy access to the M52 Highway. The highway led south to several smaller roads that reached the Kazakhstan border and provided the quickest path out of Russia. They had little doubt

128

that the Russians would focus their search efforts south along these routes, leaving the northern roads relatively unguarded. The trick to heading north would be Novosibirsk.

Situated twenty-five kilometers north of Koltsovo, road options were limited and would no doubt be heavily patrolled once the alarm was raised. The key highway northwest of the city was only accessible by crossing the Ob River at one of two bridges located well within Novosibirsk city limits. They could imagine few scenarios in which those crossings would be left unguarded once they completed their handiwork at Vektor. The critical question for the northern attempt centered on whether they could travel roughly twenty-five kilometers before the police and military response became organized enough to establish roadblocks. Nobody felt optimistic about their chances to break through Novosibirsk.

With a northern escape off the table, all of their efforts became focused on a southern escape and evasion plan. Farrington liked what his team had devised, but they would be forced to rely on some sketchy variables to reach the border area. Getting across the border was another story. One that would likely require a small, U.S. military sponsored miracle…or a series of them. He'd leave that part of the equation to General Sanderson, who had an uncanny ability to produce miracles on a near biblical level.

"My biggest concern is trusting our escape to the *bratva*. One lapse, whether intentional or unintentional, will put us out of business," Farrington said, glancing up at Sanderson.

"We either trust that money buys their loyalty, or we try to figure out a way to do this without them," Sanderson said.

"Reznikov's holding back key information. I don't see us having a choice."

"There's always a choice. This is your team, so it's your call. My gut tells me the Russian brotherhood will honor their end of the deal, though I have no doubt they will hit us up for more money right at the end. Mafiya is mafiya," Sanderson said.

"And we'll cover that?"

"We'll have to. I'll send the CIA a bill later."

"Good luck collecting," Farrington said.

The general exposed a thin smile.

"Equipment won't be an issue?" Farrington said.

"Not at these prices. I've been assured top-of-the-line gear. Latest generation Russian military hardware and high-quality commercial-grade electronics. All included. Berg has given them a basic list of items based on our earliest assessment, so they can start to source the equipment. You can fine-tune that list with your *bratva* contact before the team departs."

"Sounds good," Farrington said. "What about border crossing?"

"I'm working on that with Berg and my DoD friends."

"You still have friends at the Pentagon?" Farrington asked, raising an eyebrow.

"Christ. Are you taking over Petrovich's role as camp comedian too?"

"His personality rubs off on you after a while."

"Wonderful. As long as some of his skill rubbed off at the same time, I can deal with it. Anyway...I can't guarantee what we'll muster from Uncle Sam, but we'll get you something decisive," Sanderson said.

"Worst-case scenario, we split up and go to ground. Wait for opportunities to cross, or double back into Russia and blend into the population," Farrington said.

"Besides Novosibirsk, you're not looking at any major population areas," Sanderson said. "Options will be very limited with the Russian government on your heels. I'll get you out of there. I have Parker working with Admiral DeSantos in D.C. to push the case, along with Berg and a few other allies. I'm sure Berg has a few surprises left in him."

"He's been pretty resourceful in the past."

"I wouldn't want to get on his bad side," Sanderson said.

Farrington heard a knock at the lodge door and turned in time to see the screen door swing inward. One of the Russian Group operatives poked his head inside and spoke to someone standing on the porch.

"They're inside. Good luck," he said and disappeared.

Erin Foley stepped inside the post-and-beam structure, surveying her surroundings. "It's a little more rustic than I expected, but I like what you've done with the place," she said, not waiting to be invited to the table.

She shook hands with Sanderson first, then Farrington. Her grip was strong and cold, which didn't match what his visual senses had predicted. He had been too preoccupied in Stockholm to take in many of the salient details. He remembered her wearing gray, carrying a red purse and sporting blond hair. The woman standing in front of him looked drastically different. A jet-black, shoulder-length bob had replaced the golden locks sported in

Scandinavia. She wore stylish, functional clothing, a mix of J Crew and Patagonia that had probably been purchased in a boutique mall somewhere in Buenos Aires.

She looked more like a highly primped adventure traveler than a hardened espionage operative, but looks could be deceiving. Berg had assured them that she was the real deal. Another Jessica Petrovich in the making. He highly doubted that, but Daniel had vouched for her lethality based on what he had witnessed in Stockholm, and that was good enough to earn her a place on the team. Her skills and attractiveness would play a critical role in the early phase of their plan.

"It appears that I'm a little overdressed for the camp," she said.

"Welcome to the team, Ms. Foley," Sanderson said. "I trust your trip went smoothly, but most importantly, unnoticed?"

"My journey west from Buenos Aires was unremarkable, beyond the antics of Rico Suave and Julio Iglesias," she said.

"Munoz and Melendez escorted her from the airport and kept an eye out for unwanted attention," Farrington explained.

"You were in capable hands," Sanderson assured her, "despite the comedy routine, which seems to be the only bad habit I can't eliminate here."

"Oh, they weren't cracking jokes. The two of them bickered like a married couple throughout the entire ride. I think they need to get out more often," she said.

Sanderson broke out laughing, catching Farrington off guard.

"They get out plenty. Mostly together, which is the real problem. They've been joined at the hip for over a month now," he said, pausing to glance at Farrington.

"So, Ms. Foley," Farrington said, "are you ready to take your field craft to the next level? Your role in this operation will be unlike anything you've experienced. You'll work hand in hand with the Russian mafiya to execute your objectives."

"I won't be working with the rest of the team?"

"Once you leave this compound, you may not see any of the team again…unless I can persuade you to permanently join our modest operation," Sanderson said.

"I don't know. I'm not big into nature," she said, glancing around the lodge.

"Very well. Would you like to go over the basic concept of your role in the operation, or do you need to freshen up after the trip?" Sanderson asked.

"You're kidding, right?" She brushed past Farrington to examine the map, staring at it for several seconds before looking up.

"It's a little over four days on the train from Vladivostok. Don't you think it might be easier to fly me into Kiev? I could drive or take a shorter train to Novosibirsk."

"We thought about that," Sanderson said, "but Karl Berg thinks that a western entry would be too risky at this point. Several recent developments lead him to believe that the chance of you being intercepted is too high. I'm not sure if you're aware of this, but the deputy station chief in Stockholm disappeared. The Russians are getting desperate, and you're no doubt on their short list of people they would like to interview. The CIA is putting together cover paperwork that will pass scrutiny in Vladivostok. The details haven't crystalized, but you'll likely pose as an Australian travel blogger taking the Trans-Siberian Railway. You'll find plenty of tourists onboard the train, along with little scrutiny. The rail system still operates in a relatively archaic mode. There's very little technology involved. If all goes according to plan, you'll be on a flight back to the States before the fireworks start."

"Like Stockholm? That was supposed to be a simple surveillance job, but I did the math and decided to stick around. I was apparently the only operative who could count," she said.

"Actually, Ms. Foley," Farrington said, "Stockholm went precisely as planned."

Foley regarded him for a moment. "You purposely drove your vehicle into a Spetsnaz crossfire?"

"Yes. Everybody on that team knew exactly what was at stake, and nobody hesitated. That's how it works here. While your role in this mission isn't a cakewalk, your situation is vastly different than the rest of the team's. When you're finished with your part, you'll board the next available flight out of Russia, presumably flying first class. Nobody on my team will have that luxury. Once we hit Vektor Labs, it'll take a miracle to get us safely to the Kazakhstan border. I tell you this to provide some perspective. The men you'll get to know over the next day or two are a fairly optimistic and highly capable group, but they harbor no delusions about their chances of escape. Be careful what you say around them. They know you're holding the golden ticket out of there."

Erin Foley maintained her unreadable facade, but he could see a fire ignite beyond her eyes. He was glad to see this. She was angry that she wouldn't share the same risks as the rest of the team and was hungry to prove something.

"I get it. I didn't mean any disrespect. How much time do we have before I leave for Vladivostok?"

"We're still waiting for Berg and his masters to convince the White House. They're bringing new information to the president tomorrow," Sanderson said. "We expect a green light shortly after that. Full mission briefing and talk-through at 1700 hours. Expect a long night. You can eat with the team at the Russia House. No more pickled herring, fancy baked goods and good coffee for you."

"No more smorgasbord." She sighed.

"Watery cabbage, potato-based soups, unseasoned boiled meats, salted fish, porridge...it grows on you," Farrington said.

"What about *blini* or *pirozhki?*"

"We haven't hired a pastry chef, yet," Farrington grumbled.

"Might be a future condition of my employment," Foley said to Sanderson.

"You pull this off for us, and I'll send our cook to a few fine Russian cuisine classes," Sanderson replied.

"Deal."

Foley nodded and turned for the door, hesitating before facing them again. "What if I don't want to take a flight out of Novosibirsk?"

Foley was starting to grow on him. She had a slightly irreverent sense of humor and cold affect, but he sensed that she would never back down from a fight. Her decision to stay on Bondegaten Street after fulfilling her assigned role in Reznikov's takedown wasn't a fluke. He could see it in her eyes. He now wondered if he'd gone too far with his dressing down and implication that she had the easy job. This clearly didn't sit well with Foley. He'd have to keep a close eye on her and make sure she didn't try to expand her role. He had no doubt that she was a capable, intelligent operative, but her skill set would require an extensive retrofit to match the team selected to breach Vektor Labs. Her job would be just as critical to their success, but he needed to keep her at a distance.

"Ms. Foley, you have a long, arduous path ahead of you. Your role is critical to the operation," Farrington told her. "You'll gain a much better appreciation for your importance to the mission tonight. Trust me. And for the record…everybody here knows what you did for us in Stockholm. You've already earned their respect…and mine."

"All right," she said, faltering to say anything beyond that.

"Grisha will show you to your accommodations," Sanderson said.

On cue, the same operative that had shown her inside minutes earlier materialized in the doorway. Grisha, aka Grigory Usenko, stood an in inch short of six feet, built on a sinewy, muscular frame. His drab, loose-fitting clothing gave the impression that he was simply thin, which in terms of body mass and height to weight ratio would be an accurate surface observation. Under the surface, Grisha was pound for pound one of the strongest and quickest human beings Farrington had ever met. The first generation Belarusian looked indistinguishable from the average East European male, with short, faded brown hair and blue eyes. He nodded with a disaffected look plastered to his thin, angular face.

While Farrington commanded the overall team, Grisha was the de facto assault element lead. His lightning reflexes and unmatched quick decision-making capacity made him a natural choice for this role. With Grisha on point, Farrington could concentrate on the bigger tactical picture, satisfied that all immediate threats would be assessed and dispatched flawlessly. Grisha had trained exclusively with three other operatives for the past two years, forming a tightly knit team that operated on a near subconscious level.

Watching them conduct drills reminded him of the team assembled to check out the abandoned laboratory in Kazakhstan. Andrei, Sergei and Leo had been his first team, and like Grisha's crew, he had trained alongside them for nearly two years before they were sent out with Petrovich to unravel the madness created by Vektor Lab's star scientist, Anatoly Reznikov. Andrei and Sergei had been killed during their mad trek across Russia and Europe. Leo had been severely wounded in Stockholm, losing the full use of his right shoulder. He was unlikely to be reintegrated into the program at this point.

Farrington would like to return as many of Grisha's comrades as possible from this operation, but he wasn't overly optimistic. At this point, without U.S. military assistance, taking down Vektor was tantamount to a suicide mission. Nobody on the Russian team had said a word about the final stage of the evasion and extract plan. Sanderson had created a pervasive and unequivocal cult of loyalty and service among his operatives.

Like Farrington, everyone knew that he would work tirelessly behind the scenes to get them what they needed for every aspect of their assigned missions. It was also implicitly understood that their personal safety was secondary to mission accomplishment, and nobody questioned or balked at this key premise of their existence as Black Flag operatives. Lives would never be cast away on worthless causes. If Sanderson's operatives were put into action, their mission objectives represented the solution to an essential national security problem that required the use of untraceable, "off the books" assets.

The Vektor Labs raid fit all of the above criteria, but took the concept a step further. Sanderson had made it clear to Farrington that there would be no middle ground for operatives sent against Vektor, meaning that capture by Russian Federation forces was not an option under any circumstances. He hadn't decided when to broach this non-negotiable term with the team. Ultimately it would be his responsibility to ensure compliance with this directive, which meant that it was unlikely that he could allow the team to split up and try to make their own way across the border if Sanderson failed to arrange an extraction. As if reading his mind, Sanderson addressed him as soon as the steps faded from the porch.

"Have you decided when to tell them?" Sanderson said.

"Not tonight. I think this will be part of the final brief. I don't need this clouding their thoughts. They'll be pumped full of adrenaline at that point. Less chance to register and cause them to hesitate or falter."

"I'd recommend telling Grisha and letting him make the final decision. He knows that crew like the back of his hand. I'm willing to bet that he won't want to tell them at all."

Farrington knew what that meant. Bringing two of them in on the secret ensured that the final directive could be carried out if one of them was taken down. He didn't want to spend any more mental energy on the worst-case scenario, but he agreed with Sanderson.

"I'll talk to Grisha tonight. Let him weigh in on the decision."

"We'll get you the support. Berg has something up his sleeve, I can tell by his tone. He won't let me in on it, but if I know Berg, this promises to be a good one," Sanderson said.

"Sounds like a plan. See you at 1700."

Farrington didn't push the issue. He knew better than anyone that Sanderson would sell his soul to the devil to get the support they needed. His only concern was that Sanderson didn't have any of his soul left to leverage. To have brought the Black Flag program this far, through two iterations, he'd likely signed it over several times. Farrington had been working with Sanderson ever since the two of them reconnected outside of a Senate hearing on April 12, 2000, when Sanderson's original program came under fire from the Senate Select Committee on Intelligence.

With a disgruntled former Black Flag operative's help, one of Sanderson's career enemies, Brigadier General William Tierney, started to stir up trouble from his comfortable, dead-end perch in the army's Plans and Resources Division. Farrington never learned why Tierney hated Sanderson, but something had clearly gone awry between the two of them and had festered for years. With Tierney raising difficult questions, Pentagon supporters of Sanderson's classified program started to shy away, taking their budget with them. Derren McKie had turned on the Black Flag program, following a precipitous fall from grace for his role in attempting to arrange and ultimately conceal a sizable arms shipment destined for elements of the Irish Republican Army.

McKie had committed two cardinal sins. First, he had violated one of Sanderson's non-negotiable rules of engagement for Black Flag operatives: *No direct action will be taken against U.S. or allied military, law enforcement or civilian entities, nor shall indirect courses of action be set in motion that would do the same.* McKie's illicit weapons shipment would most certainly be used to fuel Provisional Irish Republican Army attacks against British interests, which violated Sanderson's directive. The general set down very few rules for his operatives, but the few he established were considered sacrosanct.

Most of the operatives had been sent to their assignments to infiltrate and provide intelligence for the Department of Defense. If their roles allowed them to participate in direct or indirect action against the regimes and criminal groups they had infiltrated, such action was encouraged as long as it did not jeopardize their undercover status. Similarly, any action taken within the regime against other criminals or regime members was fair game. Theft was encouraged, if the payoff was big enough.

Petrovich's plan to abscond with nearly one hundred and thirty million dollars had been deemed significant enough to warrant an early end to his undercover operation. Money had continuously flowed in large quantities from Sanderson's Central American operatives, but nothing on the scale of what Petrovich proposed. Sanderson hadn't balked at Petrovich's proposed finder's fee of thirty million. The remaining one hundred million dollars could permanently bankroll the Black Flag program if invested properly.

This was where McKie made his second mistake. Knowing that Sanderson would never approve of the shipment and not wanting to lose out on a one-point-three million dollar payoff, he proceeded anyway, trying to keep the entire transaction under the radar. Fortunately for Sanderson, McKie's acquisition efforts were far from subtle. The operative's "legend" as an arms dealer put him in a position to seize the stockpile through a series of high-profile assassinations and double-crosses that attracted the attention of U.S. Embassy officials in Nuoachott, Mauritania. It didn't take long for word to filter through the appropriate Department of Defense contacts, landing on Sanderson's desk. He immediately recalled McKie and purged him from the program, making the mistake of assuming McKie would go quietly into the night.

Instead, he went noisily into General Tierney's arms and blew the whistle on the Black Flag program. Within six months, Sanderson was tap dancing in front of Congress, and the Black Flag program was running on fumes. Petrovich's windfall hit right about the time Sanderson decided to withdraw most of his operatives. The bulk of Petrovich's money was disseminated into accounts that would be accessed when Sanderson was ready to start the second program.

Major Richard Farrington's chance meeting with General Terrence Sanderson set in motion a series of events leading to the killing of Black Flag's Judas, Derren McKie, in a baptism by fire that christened their new group, raising Black Flag from the ashes.

Chapter 23

Karl Berg shuffled a few manila file holders into his worn leather messenger bag and surveyed the top of his desk for anything he had forgotten. Satisfied that he was ready, the veteran CIA officer closed the bag's cover flap and latched the brass buckle to secure the contents. He didn't need the physical files, since the entire presentation had been forwarded to the White House late last night, but he felt secure knowing that the contents of the briefing could be handed directly to the president, via Director Copley, if interest in the PowerPoint slides started to wane. Berg would scrutinize the president and his tightly knit cabal closely for signs of wear, producing the documents at the necessary moment to resuscitate the briefing and achieve his true purpose for hand-carrying them into the White House.

Nothing demanded the respect and attention of politicians more than files stamped with red block letters spelling "TOP SECRET." In Berg's experience, once he started distributing classified memoranda, he could pretty much say whatever he pleased with little interruption. In corporate America, MBAs were taught never to distribute handouts during their PowerPoint presentations. Attendees might start reading the material and stop giving their undivided attention to your boardroom soliloquy. Berg preferred to divide his audience's attention from the start, especially for his more controversial pitches. The last thing he truly wanted during a briefing like this was a bureaucrat's full attention. He found it more useful to keep their concentration slightly scattered, so he had room to maneuver the facts and fictions ever so gently to achieve the desired result. And if one thing could be said about his upcoming audience with the president, he'd be blending fiction with fact.

He stared at the brown leather bag standing upright on his desk and took a deep breath. He'd stretched the truth before…stretched it pretty far in some cases. He'd just never pulled off a stunt of this magnitude in front of the president and his own chain of command. A key element to the briefing had been essentially fabricated from scratch, with the hope of sealing the president's support for the mission. He already had the CIA director's support for covert action against Vektor, so he didn't feel that he was deceiving his own organization in any way. Audra Bauer might raise an eyebrow, but she'd probably know better than to say anything in front of Manning or the director. She might not say anything at all, writing it off as one of Berg's harmless little subversions. He remained fairly certain that she would never fit the pieces together to determine the ultimate reason for his subterfuge. Lives depended on the perfect choreography of his latest masterpiece, and he had every intention of playing Carnegie Hall this morning.

His cell phone chirped from his suit coat. He reached inside his jacket and checked the caller ID. *Speak of the devil.*

"I am just about to perjure myself in front of the president on your behalf. This isn't a good time. I'm on my way out the door," Berg answered.

"It's the perfect time. We conducted our final mission talk-through last night and we're still coming up short in a few areas," Sanderson countered. "First and foremost, exfiltration remains an issue. Do I need to elaborate?"

"Negative. I have that covered," Berg said.

"Does that mean solved?"

"No. But I have something cooked up that should seal the deal when push comes to shove. Have you worked this from your end? My little concerto only works if the assets are in place," Berg said.

"I've received assurances that the assets will be in place if the president approves the overall mission, regardless of whether he agrees with our concept of final extraction," Sanderson replied.

"Then I suggest you let me concentrate on this meeting. Is there anything else?"

"Two things, both related. Details regarding the installation are sketchy at best and—"

"I've sent you everything we have on Vektor. Satellite photos, Reznikov's assessment, and intelligence data. I don't have anything else to give you. Your people are good at improvising. This mission should suit them well," Berg said.

"Not funny. I suggest you dig deeper. Reznikov hasn't been employed by Vektor for a number of years, and I'm seeing several new structures at the facility. The satellite shots alone show considerable change over the past five years. This doesn't concern you?"

"A separate intelligence asset has verified that the P4 building remains the same and has not been expanded. I'm not a tactical expert, but the building is located in an isolated section of the compound, easily accessible from surrounding ground cover. This is as good as it gets," Berg said.

"Construction. Upgrades. Who knows what else has changed since Reznikov's days? His assessment of the local security response seems sketchy on top of that."

"Why are you throwing this at me right now?" Berg asked.

"Because my operatives need every advantage possible to survive this operation," Sanderson shot back. "I have no doubt whatsoever that my team can infiltrate the site and destroy the facility, even without Reznikov's supposedly critical final piece of information. The trick is getting out. Even with the most perfect extraction plan that you and I can envision, they're going to face some long odds. The fewer bumps along the road the better, starting with the raid itself."

"I really have to go, Terrence. I can't conjure up information I don't possess, and I'm not holding anything back."

"Maybe you just haven't considered all of your sources."

Berg remained silent, trying to process the general's statement. The man didn't waste words, which led him to the worst possible assumption. Sanderson had resources and friends hidden in high places, but not high enough to uncover Kaparov's identity. Maybe he was just overanalyzing the comment. He doubted it.

"I'm fairly confident that the drawers have been emptied," Berg finally replied.

"I think one of the drawers hasn't been opened. In fact, I'm pretty sure you have your foot up against it to keep it closed. To be honest, I didn't put it together until recently. I always assumed your source was Spetsnaz, which goes to show how dangerous an assumption can be. Ms. Pavrikova was a little intoxicated when we grabbed her. She let her anger spill out, along with a few name—"

"You can never repeat any of the names," Berg cut in.

"That goes without saying, and I understand why you're protecting him. You're not the only Cold War relic with old enemies for friends," Sanderson said, pausing for a moment. "Time to ask your friend for another favor. With the heat off his back, he should be able to give us an update of the facility. He should have the appropriate clearances for that, given his position."

"I get it," Berg said. "I'll give him a call. He's not going to be happy."

"Who's happy these days? Good luck in your meeting," Sanderson said, disconnecting the call.

"Fuck you too, General," Berg muttered to the dead line.

He replaced the phone and grabbed the messenger bag, rushing out of his office to meet with Audra Bauer.

Chapter 24

The president leaned over to accept a thin manila folder that the CIA officer had produced from his satchel and handed to the director. Several folders had been prepared for the meeting's participants, and within a few seconds, everyone seated around the mahogany table was thumbing through documents, including himself.

"Is this all summarized in the presentation?" he asked.

"Mr. President, the top secret memos in the file expand on the presentation and hold key insights regarding the various sources used to derive the information. Of particular interest is the background on the Israelis. Diplomatic tensions between the two nations have been strained for years, compounded by the discovery of Russian made Kornet-E and Metis-M systems in Hizbullah's possession within southern Lebanon two years ago. Mossad has been watching the Vektor situation with great interest and has provided us with actionable intelligence regarding two confirmed Iranian intelligence operatives assigned to Vektor," Karl Berg said.

The president glanced at James Quinn, his National Security Advisor, who was still sifting through the documents to find the one Berg had referenced. Quinn sensed his stare and looked down the table at the president, nodding.

"This is a significant development, Mr. President, especially in light of the recent attack on the U.S. by domestic terrorists. Mossad confirms that one of the operatives is working inside of Vektor?" Quinn asked.

"That's correct. Like our own CDC, Vektor hosts international scientists. They just don't have the same selection standards," Berg explained.

"Wouldn't it be easier to get rid of the Iranians?" the president suggested. "Cut off the nexus between Iran and Vektor?"

The CIA director stepped into the conversation, which relieved the president. He was starting to get the impression that this previously unknown CIA officer was running the show at Langley.

"Mr. President, neutralizing the two Iranian operatives would be a temporary fix. Iran would send more scientists, and we'd be back to square one. On top of that, the Israelis would be blamed for the killings, which would further strain Russian-Israeli relations. Mossad appears extremely hesitant to conduct operations on Russian soil," Copley said.

"So they get us to do their dirty work," the president said.

"They've done the lion's share of the dirty work for as long as I can remember. With all due respect, Mr. President, it's our turn to take up this fight."

"I agree, Director Copley," the president said, "I just wish our turn didn't involve blowing up Russia's equivalent to the CDC."

"The raid will be confined to the bioweapons facility. Unlike the CDC's P4 containment labs, which are buried within a massive multi-story building situated in an urban center, Vektor Labs remains isolated, and its different research labs are well separated. The P4 containment facility housing the bioweapons program is at the far end of the virology campus. The raid itself will be surgical, with highly specific objectives. Non-lethal methods will be employed if practical. We anticipate minimal local casualties at the site. Best of all, we get our hands dirty from a distance. Sanderson's crew is untraceable."

"They also have a habit of churning up a high body count," Jacob Remy said. "This is a high-stakes game we're playing here."

"They understand the stakes better than the rest of us," Berg said.

"Good," the president said, "because I won't allow U.S. military assets to violate Russian sovereignty. I've spoken with General Frank Gordon, and SOCOM will provide helicopter support for the extraction, but only in Kazakhstan. Sanderson's people are on their own until they cross the Kazakhstan border."

"Can they count on drone support?" the CIA director asked.

"Not over Russian airspace. If General Gordon needs drones for surveillance, he can have them, but the same rules of engagement apply to unmanned vehicles," the president said.

"They shouldn't experience any problems getting to the border," Berg said, hoping to steer the conversation away from drones. "Sanderson's crew will be guided by local sympathizers during their exfiltration."

The president looked up from one of the documents in time to see Director Copley flash Berg a faintly quizzical look. Thomas Manning, the CIA's National Security Branch director remained stoic, almost too stoic compared to the normal array of facial expressions he had previously displayed throughout the briefing. This should be interesting. He decided to take whatever bait Berg was offering.

"Sympathizers?" Remy asked. "Do we have a massive sleeper cell network in the Novosibirsk region?"

"That would be nice, wouldn't it? We're looking at something homegrown. Since the dawn of time, a nation state's internal enemies served as its external enemies' best friends. These are turbulent and corrupt times for Russia, and they have no shortage of internal enemies. One in particular will be extremely valuable. If you'll turn to the memo with the subject line 'Kola Activist Group,' you'll see that our intelligence analysts have linked two very recent car bombings and three murders to a Russian-based eco-terrorist group.

"Historically, this group has been active in the northern regions around Monchegorsk and Norilsk, where widespread ecosystem poisoning by industrial pollutants has been a contentious, often violent issue for decades. In response to the Russian Federation's brutal crackdown on Monchegorsk, the eco-terrorist group has renewed attacks and promised continued reprisals against the government until the truth surrounding Monchegorsk is revealed. Monchegorsk has brought them back to life. Initial contact with their leadership indicates a willingness to provide internal logistical support for the team, especially during the exfiltration phase," Berg said.

"The Russians aren't going to believe that this eco-terrorist group destroyed Vektor Labs," Remy cautioned.

"It doesn't matter. Even if they don't help at all, this group's implied involvement could complicate matters exponentially for the Russians, putting Monchegorsk back in the spotlight. This will help with any political fallout from the mission. The Russians will look for any excuse to sweep this whole thing under the rug as quickly as possible, knowing that we have a connection to this group…and not wanting to reignite Monchegorsk."

The president looked to his National Security Advisor for any final thoughts. "James. Anything to add? Can you see any reason why we shouldn't proceed?"

"No, Mr. President. With the Iranians involved at Vektor, we can assume it's only a matter of time before they get their hands on something similar to the Zulu virus or develop the expertise to start their own program. The use of Sanderson's team keeps official U.S. assets off Russian Federation soil, maintaining the requisite amount of plausible deniability and distance required on the diplomatic front. I don't see any impediments. The State Department will have to prepare a special song and dance for this one, but I don't foresee any unmanageable fallout. The Russians got caught with their hands in the cookie jar with this one."

"Jacob?" the president asked.

"They're going to know we did this. I'm worried about an escalation. The Russians have already taken the unprecedented step of abducting a high-ranking CIA officer. Can we keep this from escalating?" Remy said.

"We've had a development in the overall situation related to Stockholm," Director Copley said. "Their trail just went cold."

The president didn't like Copley's choice of words. Dead bodies "went cold." Berg suddenly looked uncomfortable for the first time since walking through the door.

"Is this something we need to be worried about?" the president said.

"Negative. It's a complicated maneuver, but it should stop the SVR investigation in its tracks," Berg said.

"The last time their investigation stalled, they kick-started it by kidnapping a CIA officer," Remy said.

"There's no chance of the Russians repeating that," Berg said.

"And how, exactly, can you be so sure?" Remy said.

The president knew the answer to his chief of staff's question, calculating that Berg had floated the statement in an attempt to goad his often-overzealous chief into stepping on another landmine.

"Because Ian Reese isn't tied to a chair in a dark basement, praying for some kind of negotiation that will secure his release. He's dead, and his body will never be recovered. Ian Reese was off limits, and the Russians knew it from the start. He was dead as soon as they kicked in his apartment door. Since he was marked for death, the Russians had no reason to hold back on his interrogation. I guarantee he told them everything the station knew about the operation, which wasn't much. They likely confirmed the timing of our leaked information, which helped focus their internal investigation...but we just yanked the rug out from under that."

"Is it your assessment that the Vektor raid will be interpreted as a standalone event?" the president asked.

"Like Mr. Remy stated, the Russians will connect it to the overall situation, Mr. President, but it won't escalate the SVR's blood vendetta. This will fall squarely in the Federal Security Service's lap...and of course Putin's, who is unlikely to overreact," the director said.

"Director Copley, you are authorized to proceed with this operation. What are we looking at in terms of timeline?"

"The first elements will depart tonight. We could have this wrapped up within a week. Two weeks at the most."

The president regarded the three CIA officers seated in front of him: Director Copley, Thomas Manning and their new agent provocateur, Karl Berg. Until their first meeting a few days back, Berg's name had never materialized in the White House. He couldn't figure out what he didn't like about the man, but something set off his internal alarm. Nothing substantial, just a gut feeling. James Quinn had never heard of him either, which surprised the president. Quinn knew everybody with political capital inside the Beltway...and outside. It was almost like they had dragged this guy out of the basement for the first time. Whoever he might be, the president could assume one thing—the man was deeply connected to the operation, which meant he was linked to Sanderson. Maybe that was his hesitation with Berg. How did a CIA deputy director get embroiled with someone like Sanderson? The answer to that question would likely explain why a small voice inside his head kept whispering that he'd just made a mistake.

"Very well. I want daily updates while the team is moving into place, graduating to more frequent communication as we approach the raid. I'll monitor the final raid from the Situation Room. This will be a very limited audience. Similar to Stockholm."

"Understood, Mr. President," Director Copley said.

The president stood, signaling an end to the meeting. He walked around the table and shook hands, careful not to betray his distrust of Berg. When he reached Copley, he held the grip a few seconds longer than the rest.

"Robert, keep a close eye on this one," he said, looking back at Manning and Berg. "You have good people working behind the scenes, but I need your personal supervision to ensure this goes by the book."

"Of course, Mr. President. Though I don't think we have a book that covers this kind of operation. We're writing it as we go," Copley said.

"Make sure it goes by my book."

Copley nodded, and the president released his hand. Once the CIA entourage had departed the president's study, James Quinn, Jacob Remy and the president reconvened at the table.

"So, what do you really think?" the president asked, interlocking his fingers and placing them on the bare table.

"I think we need to make sure that General Gordon and anyone else with tactical authority over the extraction force understands that U.S. forces are not to cross the Kazakhstan-Russian border under any circumstances. Our CIA friends didn't put up any resistance when you reiterated this position, which gives me an uneasy feeling. Sanderson still has connections high up in the Department of Defense. That much is clear. We might need some kind of additional failsafe to keep our forces out of Russia."

"I agree with your assessment, Jacob. I trust Copley will follow my rules. Manning will follow suit. I don't know what to think about Karl Berg. Until recently, his name has never surfaced, which leads me to believe that he has been intimately involved in the planning of this mission—"

"Which means he knows the players all too well," Remy said.

"Exactly," the president agreed. "If he's been working with Sanderson since Stockholm, we have to assume their history goes back even further."

"How far?" Remy said.

"That's the question. How far is Berg willing to go for Sanderson and his people?" the president asked.

Chapter 25

Karl Berg hunched over his desk and stared at the mess of notes chronicling his efforts to keep "Operation Black Fist" on track. He'd just brokered one of Reznikov's calls to his *bratva* contact in Moscow, who had assured the scientist that a sizable sum of money had been transferred to seal the deal between the Solntsevskaya Bratva and foreign mercenary operatives assigned to carry out the raid against Vektor Laboratories. Sizable was an understatement. Berg had just wired the largest sum he'd ever handled to a Panamanian bank account, which would no doubt bounce around between several discreet international accounts before finally landing in a Russian bank account.

If the *bratva* contact brokering this deal wasn't already one of the 150,000 or so millionaires living in Moscow, he could now add that distinction to his title. A grand total of five-point-two million dollars secured a personal assurance of cooperation from a mystery voice at the other end of a completely untraceable phone number. Audra Bauer had suggested they make their best attempt to confirm the general location of the *bratva* contact in order to provide Manning and the director with some kind of reasonable assurance that they weren't feeding five million dollars to one of Reznikov's close friends.

As expected, the NSA's best efforts to trace the call resulted in a scattershot of locations that changed several times every second as the data signal was redirected through dozens of networks internationally. The

NSA's best guess based on the signal's travel patterns indicated continental Europe, which was good enough for Berg to pass on his own assurances through Bauer.

Berg didn't suspect this was a money scam on Reznikov's part. He'd made it perfectly clear to the scientist that he would die swiftly if his *bratva* contacts betrayed them in any way. Reznikov remained adamant that they would uphold their end of the bargain if the CIA met their price. He'd negotiated them down from their initial request for six million dollars, which he knew was more than they expected to receive up front. He played the game, working them down to the exorbitant price of five-point-two million dollars. A king's ransom under normal circumstances, but less than he anticipated paying in the end. He fully expected a last-minute "glitch" requiring another eight hundred thousand dollars. He was prepared to spread around some of Sanderson's money when that phone call came.

Involving the Russian mob had been a necessary compromise that had been vetted on several levels. The CIA's own analysts had assured Berg that the Solntsevskaya Bratva had a notorious reputation for honoring contracts, or more specifically, punishing those that didn't honor their commitments. Recent historical cases indicated that this informal code worked both ways and that the Solntsevskaya Bratva enforced breeches of agreement made by their own members. Reputation was everything to them, and this included business dealings outside of their inner circle. Still, analysts warned him that high-level *bratva* members displayed opportunistic tendencies when confronted with large sums of money.

He couldn't give the analysts any specific details of the operation, but their final warning fueled Berg's sole fear regarding the mafiya. He could envision an enterprising *bratva* soldier selling them out to the Russian government in exchange for more money and other lucrative favors. Sanderson's team would remain on high alert throughout every stage of the operation, searching for signs of betrayal. Farrington had been ordered to abandon the mission at the first sign of trouble related to their mafiya contacts. They simply couldn't take any chances once they were on Russian soil. Getting out of Novosibirsk would be difficult enough under the best of circumstances.

He shuffled one of the papers to the top of the mess on his desk. Sanderson's request for detailed information regarding Vektor Labs. Onsite security protocols. Recent facility upgrades. Military response procedures.

Anything and everything that Alexei Kaparov, director of the Bioweapons/Chemical Threat Assessment Division, should know about Russia's premiere virology and biotechnology research center and former Biopreparat site. He couldn't blame Sanderson for demanding more information, especially regarding the P4 containment building and any security response protocols. CIA intelligence confirmed a reduced security posture in terms of onsite personnel with the addition of automated cameras and an additional perimeter fence, but this just meant that the real threats could be better concealed. For all they knew, the number of security personnel remained the same, but the number of visible patrols had decreased due to expanded visual coverage provided by the cameras.

Kaparov should be able to shed some final light on the security arrangements. He hated to put this kind of pressure on him, but "Operation Black Fist" was gaining critical momentum and he couldn't afford to lose Sanderson's enthusiasm. Farrington's crew was less than twenty-four hours from crossing the line of departure. He picked up the phone and called a redirect number designated to ring the most recent cell phone number provided by Kaparov. He just hoped that his friend hadn't decided to throw all of his remaining cell phones in the Moscow River. There was no way he could risk calling Kaparov's desk. Pavrikova's kidnapping wouldn't fade from FSB or SVR attention for quite some time, and he couldn't assume that her sudden departure would be interpreted to mean that she was the sole leak at Lubyanka Square.

He let the phone ring nearly a dozen times before hanging up. This wasn't a good sign. In the past, Kaparov's cell phones always went to voice mail in half that time. He tried the number one more time, achieving the same dismal result. His next call went to Sanderson, who picked up immediately.

"How are we looking?" Sanderson said.

"Everything is on track. The *bratva* deal has been sealed. Five-point-two million dollars. Just for the record, nobody is happy about that number on my end."

"Of course not. The concept of 'you get what you pay for' is anathema to bureaucrats. Frankly, I'm surprised you got off that easy," Sanderson said.

"Oh, I fully expect to be shaken down for more as we get closer to the objective. You'll have to cough up the rest. Given the look on Manning's face when I gave him the figure, I can't imagine wrangling another dollar out of them…let alone a million," Berg said.

"I'll cover the rest. If my guess is right, they won't call you directly. They'll shake the team down at the worst possible moment. I've prepared Farrington for this possibility."

"Good. Farrington will contact 'Viktor' directly from this point forward."

"Viktor. Vektor. That's the best he could do?"

"Viktor doesn't sound like much of a conversationalist. He's been my direct contact from the start, but he isn't the brigadier that Reznikov originally contacted. He's probably someone highly trusted within this brigadier's own personal network. One of his most loyal *boyeviks*," Berg said. "Viktor will personally oversee *bratva* operations in Novosibirsk, so Farrington can expect to meet him face to face. He expects to hear from you once the team is assembled in Russia."

"That works fine. Any progress with your friend in Moscow?"

Berg winced at the mere suggestion of Kaparov's existence. He knew that his own line was secure and that Sanderson's satellite phone couldn't be intercepted by anyone outside of the NSA, but it still made him nervous. It was bad enough that Sanderson was leveraging his knowledge of Kaparov. He didn't need anyone within his own organization leaning on him in the future. His agency had a bad habit of applying too much pressure to valuable sources. They squeezed and squeezed until the source popped, which was an easy thing to do sitting behind a desk, where no real dangers existed.

"He's not answering his phone at the moment. Give him some time. I know he'll come through. He knows the stakes," he answered.

"All too well perhaps," Sanderson said. "My people took one hell of a risk in Moscow on his behalf."

"On my behalf. He's invaluable to us. I'll bring him around, even if I have to fly to Moscow myself to convince him."

"Cold War old-timers' reunion?" Sanderson asked.

"I'll make sure you get an invitation."

Berg's desk phone rang. The digital readout screen of the STE (Secure Terminal Equipment) phone unit indicated that the call was encrypted. Further examination of the data presented confirmed that the call had been rerouted through the CIA's call redirection center.

"Terrence, let me call you back. I have an important call from Moscow," Berg said.

"My team needs that information before leaving Argentina," Sanderson stated.

"I understand. You sound like a fucking broken record sometimes."

He quickly transferred calls.

"You're still at work?" he said as a greeting. "I thought you might have been on the Metro."

"Of course I'm still at work. I don't work lazy capitalist hours. What is it you have there? Working nine to five? Ridiculous," Kaparov said.

"I think that was a movie starring Dolly Parton," Berg said.

"Country music combined with massive tits. Now there is something America can be proud of," Kaparov said.

"Sounds like you're in a good mood. Out for a walk?" Berg asked, noting the sound of car horns and buzzing motors in the background.

"I'm just enjoying a peaceful cigarette amidst the carbon monoxide cloud of Moscow's interminable rush-hour traffic."

"Very poetic," Berg said.

"Literature was never one of my strong suits in school. Why do I get the feeling that my time out of the frying pan was short lived?"

"Am I that transparent?" Berg asked. "I might be calling to wish you well."

"I'm doing wonderful," Kaparov replied. "Shall I hang up now?"

"I'd appreciate if you didn't. We're very close to crossing the point of no return with the operation we discussed, but there are still quite a few unknowns."

"Even with our mutual friend's information?"

"He provided enough details to get the operation approved, but he hasn't set foot on the grounds in over three years," Berg said.

"Damn it! Do you understand the level of scrutiny surrounding that program? Especially now?"

"I can imagine," Berg said.

"No! You cannot! I have already been personally warned by my director not to pry into a certain northern city. Accessing information regarding the facility in question would certainly raise alarms."

"And exactly how are you supposed to do your job as director of the Bioweapons/Chemical Threat Assessment Division?"

"Very fucking carefully, that's how. For now, I'd prefer to avoid initiating any inquiries having the faintest connection to our mutual friend," Kaparov said.

"Do you have any personal knowledge that could shed some light on security protocols or response procedures?"

"Sure. I spend all of my time analyzing and assessing the vulnerabilities of locations that pose no threat to Russia. Maybe you've forgotten, but the facility in question isn't exactly advertised for its true purpose."

"But it's one of two legitimate repositories for something that concerns your division," Berg said.

"If I suddenly show an interest in the facility, it will raise eyebrows. If the facility in question is breached soon after, I'll face a firing squad...if I'm lucky."

"We can always get you out," Berg stated.

"Two in one month? Do you get a prize if you reach a certain number?"

"You know I wouldn't ask if it wasn't important. Is there any way to do this without attracting attention?"

"I might have some paper files with the information you seek. I'll have to do the digging myself. We conducted a routine security assessment of the facility sixteen months ago, about five months after they upgraded to a more automated security posture. Contract security force, cameras, motion detectors. Nothing too exotic."

"Why didn't you tell me this from the beginning? This is exactly what I'm looking for."

"Because I wanted you to sweat a little. See how long it would take you to try and leverage the favor your friends did on my behalf," Kaparov said.

"I wouldn't have leveraged that."

"I didn't sweat you long enough," Kaparov replied.

"True. How long will it take you to retrieve the files?"

"I should be able to pass along the information sometime tomorrow. If you can wait that long."

"We can wait. I'll put my people in Moscow on notice. Your choice of drop method?"

"One time dead drop. I'll call you with the location. Expect a digital format."

"Digital. Not microfiche? I'm impressed," Berg said.

"You'd have to dig the reader out of your museum, and I don't want to delay the process. My cigarette is finished. Back to work."

"You really should give up smoking. Takes years off your life," Berg said.

"So does talking to you, but I still return your calls. I'll be in touch."

Berg replaced the receiver and smiled. This was good news. All of the pieces were falling into place. Within the next twenty-four to forty-eight hours, the operation would be on autopilot until exfiltration. Unfortunately, the final pieces of the "exfil" puzzle couldn't be snapped into place until the very last moment. All he could do right now was move the pieces closer together. Even then, there was no guarantee that they wouldn't be left without the last piece.

Chapter 26

Matvey Penkin turned in his black leather office chair and faced Valery, who was seated at a sleek metal conference desk toward the back of Penkin's inner sanctum. Deep, rust-colored rays of light from the day's fading sun streamed through the partially canted vertical blinds that covered the penthouse's bullet-resistant windows, slicing across the rear wall to dissect his young associate.

"It's done. We've found Reznikov," he said.

"Unbelievable," Valery said, looking up from his own laptop.

"Money and leverage works miracles," Penkin said.

He'd spent more than a decade carefully collecting intelligence regarding the other brigadiers under his boss, filing the knowledge and evidence away for future use. The brigadier responsible for maintaining the *bratva's* network of military contacts made a habit of underreporting the value of the military hardware that passed through his hands. He'd served their boss well, turning out an endless supply of hard-to-acquire weapons from unscrupulous and previously underpaid non-commissioned and commissioned army officers, but by Penkin's estimation, he didn't kick back nearly enough to Maksimov. Based on his own personal experience with their boss, there was simply no way the math worked out in his colleague's favor. The only explanation was a clever system of underreporting.

This blackmail alone would have been enough to force his cooperation, but strong-arm tactics like that yielded short-term gains and longtime enemies. Penkin didn't want to start a war, especially around such a controversial operation. He offered the brigadier a quarter of a million dollars, along with a gentle reminder that his cooperation was not optional. He got the message and took the money without asking a single question. Within several hours, he was back, requesting an additional fifty thousand dollars. Redirecting a Sixth Directorate GRU satellite apparently commanded a hefty price. The additional money was well worth the payoff.

Not only did the Sixth Directorate contact intercept the conversation, but more importantly, they were able to pinpoint the location of Reznikov's satellite phone. Positioning the Russian SIGINT satellite among the geostationary government communications satellites dedicated to handling traffic out of Vermont and most of upper New England, proprietary software stolen from the Americans and installed aboard the satellite enabled a technological miracle that defied conventional navigation logic.

The software ordered the satellite to intermittently slow itself below geostationary orbital speed, while frequently altering course during the satellite call. Hundreds of minute adjustments were made throughout the duration of the satellite call, allowing the software to combine several navigational techniques in reverse to locate the L-Band satellite signal. By the end of the thirteen-minute call, they had narrowed his location down to a ten-kilometer by ten-kilometer area in northeastern Vermont.

The GRU contact even provided them with several high-resolution, multi-angle imagery overlays of the area. It took Penkin less than two minutes to identify the compound, which had been cleverly disguised to attract little attention from the sky. Unfortunately for Reznikov's hosts, the compound turned out to be the only sizable cluster of buildings inside the search area. In fact, the CIA had done such a good job of isolating the compound from the outside world the nearest small cluster of houses sat more than twenty kilometers away on the outskirts of a tiny village called Lowell. Luck had smiled on them today. Then again, three hundred thousand dollars had a way of forcing anyone to smile.

"Take a look at this," he said, beckoning Valery to join him.

Valery dragged one of the thick metal chairs from the table and placed it next to him. Penkin manipulated the computer mouse to display one of the satellite images on the center screen of his triple, thirty-inch flat-screen array. Sitting less than three feet away, the satellite image took up most of his field of vision, floating crisply in front of him. He magnified the image and quickly navigated to the compound located within the outlined search area. Even without Reznikov's proposed partnership, knowledge of this location could turn a tidy profit on his investment. He could likely blackmail the CIA for a one-time payment far exceeding his three hundred thousand dollar stake. Of course, the CIA would raze the site and relocate the prisoners to an equally isolated and hidden compound. No. He had bigger plans for the information. More profitable, long-term plans.

"It looks like a mountain retreat. Very clever of them. Who else do you suppose they are hiding there?" he asked.

"Ha! My thoughts exactly," Penkin hissed before continuing. "But we'll have to stay focused on the grand prize. Washed-up dictators, terrorists or genocidal war criminals don't hold a candle to our scientist. We may have to fly some specialized talent into America for this one. Our brothers in America are hardcore on the streets, but this is more of a military-style operation. Deep penetration, coordinated timing, multiple skill sets."

"I know a group suitable for the job," Valery said. "Semion recently recruited a team of former GRU Spetznaz. All six men served together for a number of years until their unit was subordinated to one of the military districts. Their battalion was slashed by military reforms. One of Semion's associates put him in touch with the group's leader. They've been working miracles for Semion."

Penkin gave this some thought. He'd heard of this group. He encouraged his subordinates to actively pursue the recruitment of GRU Spetznaz. Their unique military-style training better suited the organization's needs than the elite federal units. KGB and Interior Ministry Spetznaz displaced after the failed coup attempt against Mikhail Gorbachev routinely gave them more hassle than they were worth. Most of the KGB agents worth their salt had found employment in the newly formed Federal Security Service or the Federation Government. The rest plagued the streets already owned and run by the *bratva*.

The Russian military intelligence service (GRU) had become a fertile recruiting ground for the Solntsevskaya Bratva over the past decade. Trained for infiltration, sabotage and assassination, GRU Spetznaz brought an entirely new skillset to their group, expanding their range of criminal activity. Simple break-ins and extortion were augmented by sophisticated heists and coordinated attacks in remote locations. The presence of former GRU Spetznaz in the *bratva* had been good for business. Their "business targets" no longer felt completely safe at their secure dachas outside of Moscow or their heavily guarded mansions within the city. Valery's suggestion would be their best shot at retrieving Reznikov.

"I'll call Semion immediately. As for you," he said, raising an eyebrow, "it is time for you to travel east."

Valery nodded once and met his steely gaze. "We need to ensure that the American team destroys this bioweapons laboratory...without leaving any traces of our involvement."

"Provide anything they request, as long as it is untraceable. Money is not an issue, but take care not to attract undue attention. Under no circumstances are any of your men to participate in the actual attack on Vektor. The Americans must do the dirty work. If the government suspects our involvement, all hell will break loose. I will trust your judgment on how to proceed. You are my most trusted associate, Valery. The potential reward for our success is immeasurable. I don't have to remind you about the consequences for our failure. We sink or swim together on this one, my friend," Penkin said.

"I won't fail you, brother," Valery assured him. "The crew in Novosibirsk is rock solid."

Penkin stood up from his chair, prompting Yuri to do the same out of respect. He placed a hand on Yuri's left shoulder and pulled him in for a hug, whispering into his ear.

"Keep a close eye on everyone involved during the operation. Trust nobody. Word of this must not filter back to our Pakhan. Not yet. Make sure to take a few highly trusted soldiers with you, but keep them out of sight," Penkin said.

Valery cocked his head in a quizzical manner.

"I may require a more permanent solution to keep the Novosibirsk crew silent," Penkin said.

He could tell that Valery was uncomfortable with the suggestion, and rightly so. Killing their own people to keep this secret left broader implications. Once it started, where did it stop? He was no doubt wondering about his own longevity, which could only be expected.

"We will strive to avoid this, but the secret must be contained for our plan to work. And this is *our* plan now," he said, hoping that this provided a modicum of reassurance.

He had no intention of eliminating Valery, unless his most trusted *boyevik* decided to take advantage of the situation. Needless to say, he'd keep a close eye on the young man. Matvey Penkin had risen to the rank of brigadier in the Solntsevskaya Bratva by taking risks and following one simple mantra: Trust nobody.

PART TWO

BET IT ALL ON BLACK

Chapter 27

Darryl Jackson stared at his BlackBerry screen for several moments, listening to the artificial sound of crickets chirping. He seriously debated whether to take the call. Reluctantly, he pressed the green receive button.

"No," he said into the phone.

"Is that any way to treat a good friend?" the familiar voice asked.

"The answer to whatever you are about to ask is no. Actually, it's more like hell no," Jackson said.

"What makes you think this isn't a social call? I'm not allowed to call a longtime friend anymore?"

"Karl, including today, I can count the number of times you've called my office at eight in the morning on my middle finger, which is currently extended facing north toward your office. You can redirect one of your surveillance satellites to confirm this, unless you need my help with that too," Jackson said.

"I've called you at the office before," Berg said.

"That's right. I remember a late afternoon just a few years ago when you called asking for a favor. That didn't work out very well for me. Then it happened again a few months ago. Same result. Less than a month ago, another call comes through and suddenly I'm sitting on an airplane headed to bum fuck Pennsylvania with a cache of illegal weapons, which was returned to me dirty," he whispered. "So the answer is fuck no, to whatever you are asking."

162

"I need help with something overseas. I wouldn't ask if it wasn't important," Berg said.

"Does your agency have *any* organic assets at its disposal? Why the fuck am I still paying taxes to the government?"

"Here's the situation," Berg started.

"I didn't say I wanted to hear about it," Jackson cut in.

"Of course you do. I'm running a critical national security operation out of Kazakhst—"

"Sorry. Can't help you. I'm not exactly on good terms with our office in Astana after the unfortunate loss of several assault rifles. That was your fault by the way. Just wanted to remind you in case your memory doesn't extend more than two months into the past. Look. I'm due in a meeting here shortly and—"

"I need six men at the minimum. They can split four hundred thousand dollars. I just need them to babysit some important equipment in southeastern Kazakhstan. This is a middle-of-fucking-nowhere camping trip," Berg said.

"Six contractors won't be easy to swing," Jackson said, suddenly interested in the proposal. "The office isn't that big."

"Four hundred and fifty thousand. All you have to do is find six guys willing to give up a week of vacation to sit in the middle of nowhere and make half of their annual salary. Tax-free. I know these guys pull this kind of shit all the time. Seventy-five grand for sitting on their asses, cradling AK-74s. I'd be willing to bet that the entire office would close down for thirty thousand apiece."

Jackson sighed. "No funny bullshit on this one?"

"Not for them. They'll keep an eye on some refueling gear and about 2000 gallons of aviation fuel. No smoking."

"What the hell have you gotten yourself into this time?"

"We're closing the loop on this whole Zulu virus thing," Berg said.

"I thought you took care of that in Kazakhstan."

"We did, but it wasn't the original source of the virus," Berg said.

"Shit," Jackson muttered.

"Shit might be an understatement when this is finished. I'll pass you the coordinates when available. I expect them soon. We'll do our best to make the site accessible by vehicle. No promises."

"Timeline?" Jackson asked.

"Your people on site within forty-eight hours. We have a limited window for the use of some very specialized helicopters, which is why your people might have to spend some time out in the desert. I have to put this gear out there before that window closes. I don't have a solid execution time for the rest of my operation, but I'm told no more than five to seven days from now. Combat controllers will relieve your men roughly twenty-four hours prior to the raid."

"I thought you were close to retirement age, Karl."

"Oh, I'll probably be forced into retirement after this one," Berg said.

"Or into hiding."

"The thought has crossed my mind. Now that your kids are out of the house, how do you feel about house guests?"

"Let me run that by Cheryl." Jackson chuckled. "I'll get back to you next year."

"I'm still waiting for that dinner invitation," Berg said.

"Yeah, well, I'm still trying to explain why Cheryl could hear a jet taking off in the background of one of my phone calls...when I was supposed to be watching over my daughter in Princeton. There's no fucking airport in Princeton, Karl."

"You called her from the airport in Pennsylvania?"

"Unlike you, I can't disappear for days on end without answering questions," Jackson said.

"That whole diversion took less than eight hours."

"What can I say? I'm on a tight leash."

"That's not a bad thing. I'll be in touch shortly. Thank you again, my friend. You always come through for me. I owe you big time," Berg said.

"No worries. Friends help out friends, even if they are a pain in the ass. I'll get the ball rolling in Kazakhstan. I have to get going here," Jackson said.

"I'll get you the coordinates. Talk to you soon."

Darryl Jackson placed his phone on the desk and drummed his fingers. On a micro scale, he owned Berg's ass for all of these risky favors, but Darryl was never one to forget the bigger picture. Without Berg's intervention years ago, he would have died a miserable death at the hands of the Taliban outside of Kabul. Karl Berg had stepped in and done the right thing on his behalf, before they were friends. He'd never forget that, which is why he'd always help out, even if it meant trouble for him at home or with Brown River. Berg would do the same for him if the tables were turned.

He picked up his phone and scrolled through his contacts list, quickly finding the number he needed. His relationship with the detachment chief in Astana was a little strained after Berg's crew ditched several government-registered and easily traceable AK-74s, but nothing came of the screwup.

Fortunately for Brown River Security's Kazakhstan detachment, the site was strewn with nearly three dozen additional AK-74s belonging to the Russian Spetznaz platoon that mysteriously ended up massacred on Kazakh soil. Apparently, the presence of a few extra weapons never climbed high enough on the government's list of "shit that doesn't make sense here" to warrant further investigation. They had bigger questions to contend with, and most of these questions were directed at the Russian government. Specifically, they focused on uncovering a reasonable explanation why a small Kazakh village located over 400 miles from the Russian border had been subjected to a small-scale invasion, which included 30mm cannon fire from a Russian attack helicopter.

With the heat off Brown River, Darryl funded new weapons, in addition to some expensive gear previously denied to the detachment. This cleared the air enough that he felt comfortable asking for the chief's help with this. With $450,000 to spread around, he felt certain that the chief would have no trouble mustering volunteers, most likely to include himself. Berg had tossed around a half-million dollars like pocket change. With money like that flying around, Jackson shuddered to think about the implications. Something big was going down.

Chapter 28

7:45 PM
Vokzal-Gravny Railway Station
Novosibirsk, Russian Federation

"Katie Reynolds", aka Erin Foley, felt the train slow to a crawl, eventually jolting to a stop several minutes later at her destination. She glanced at her watch, impressed that the train had arrived only five minutes late after a four-day journey across Siberia. Despite historical grumblings about Soviet inefficiencies, she got the distinct feeling during her trip that the Trans-Siberian Railway had always run on time. She looked around at her first-class compartment, making sure that she didn't leave anything behind. Novosibirsk was one of the biggest stops "1 Rossiya" would make on its westbound journey to Moscow, so she would have plenty of time to debark, but a few close calls at smaller stations along the way had made her paranoid.

The train had almost left without her in Birobidzhan, where a supposed ten-minute stop turned into a three-minute pause at the platform. This had been her first attempt to buy food from a local vendor outside of the railway platform. Dashing out to buy food and snacks was a common activity for passengers on the train, especially foreigners who hadn't adjusted to the limited cuisine available in the restaurant car. She'd never eaten mutton before and had no intention of trying it. Grilled ham and cheese sandwiches had started to wear thin on her by that point, and she had only been on the train for a day. She never reached the front of the line to buy anything, having to scramble back to the train with several other travelers. She had been warned by Berg to stay on the train. The next westbound train didn't run for two days.

Her next attempt brought her closer to salvation, but still left her empty handed. At the Slyudyanka station, on the shores of Lake Baikal, she ventured out to acquire the much-talked-about smoked fish. Once again, she had been assured that she could have the fish in her hands within minutes, leaving plenty of time to return. When the train whistle sounded, she was in the middle of a transaction, forcing her to throw money at the vendor and grab the tinfoil-wrapped fish. Upon returning to her compartment, she discovered that she had absconded with a chunk of meat vaguely resembling the mutton served onboard. That was her last venture off the train.

After four days of ham and cheese sandwiches, accompanied by potatoes, Erin was ready for a four-course meal at Novosibirsk's finest restaurant. Of course, her cover as a struggling Australian travel blogger didn't exactly permit such indulgences. If her hotel accommodations in Vladivostok were any indication of what she could expect in Novosibirsk, she'd have to set her sights lower.

The train car remained still long enough for her to be sure that the engineer had finished making any final adjustments at the platform. She grabbed her oversized rucksack and heaved it onto her shoulders, adjusting the straps for a snug fit. Her black nylon, theft-proof travel bag followed, slung over her right shoulder. Pickpocketing and petty theft didn't top the list of tourist concerns in Novosibirsk, but she wasn't taking any chances. Her Australian passport and Russian tourist visa were irreplaceable at this point, providing her the only legitimate way to depart Russian soil. If these were stolen, she'd have to take her chances with Farrington's team or find a way to slip over the border into Kazakhstan. Either choice presented dangers.

Erin wasn't fooled by the faux optimism back at Sanderson's camp. The destruction of Vektor's bioweapons facility would be difficult enough. Successful exfiltration of the team would require a miracle. As much as she yearned to be part of the direct raid on Vektor, she wasn't suicidal. She'd gladly take a first-class seat on whatever flight would take her as far away from Novosibirsk as possible.

She opened the door and joined a few passengers in the hallway. Most of them had no plans to spend more than the train's allotted thirty-minute stop in Novosibirsk. A few of them asked her if she had already purchased nonconsecutive trip tickets, worried that she might not be able to secure tickets to continue her trip on a different train. The Trans-Siberian didn't function like many of Europe's railways, where passengers could buy passes for unlimited travel. Stops on the Trans-Siberian had to be planned in advance, or a wayward traveler could find themself stranded, unable to negotiate the bureaucracy and language barrier needed to purchase another ticket.

She tipped the first-class car attendant, who acted surprised and distraught by her departure. He had enjoyed her company over the past four days, fawning over her ability to speak flawless Russian and complimenting her "limited" knowledge of Russian history. She neglected to mention her international relations degree, with a concentration in Russo-Soviet history, from Boston University, or her follow-on graduate degree in post-Cold War Russian politics. She played the role of decently informed travel writer, listening to his history lectures while they stood in the hallway sipping tea. All part of her cover, though she wondered what he really thought about her.

Mikhail had been an attendant on the Trans-Siberian for nearly thirty-three years, many of those during the Cold War, when the railway took on a near mystical and legendary reputation for intrigue and espionage. It was inconceivable to imagine that he hadn't been embroiled in KBG schemes to observe passengers and report suspicious activity. For all she knew, he might have been a former KGB proxy-agent. Hotels, trains, stores, all were plagued with proxy-agents, who were given ranks, job security and additional privileges in return for their additional duties.

Erin shook the attendant's hand and accepted a hug, presenting him with an overly generous tip for his four days of service. Glancing quickly at the money, he nodded and gave her a knowing look, which told her everything she needed to know. Any suspicions he might harbor had been instantly erased. She smiled and turned toward the station, shielding her eyes from the glare reflected off the massive two-story window arch that formed the center of the building's facade.

The Vokzal-Gravny station loomed directly across the tracks, all of its windows showing traces of the deep orange sun low on the western horizon. The sun's deep color darkened the building's eggshell blue exterior, giving it more of a green appearance. She had been told that the station would be the most colorful building in Novosibirsk, which she could confirm by what she witnessed through her compartment window. The station stood out in a sea of drab gray buildings, featuring an incredibly incongruous blue paint job and white trim, which conjured a Scandinavian impression. Erin took in the view for a moment before turning toward the elevated walkway that would take her over a few tracks and deposit her in the building. As she cleared the train's diesel engine, the sun struck her face, warming her slightly.

The temperature had been predicted to be in the low sixties throughout the week, leaving her grateful that the operation's timing coincided with early summer. She couldn't imagine a deep winter operation on the outskirts of Siberia. Sweden had been cold enough for her, but nothing compared to the average temperatures experienced here. The high temperatures in Novosibirsk for January peaked in the low single digits. Combined with the constant winds blowing in from either the Kazakhstan steppes to the west, or the Western Siberian Plain to the east, the wind chill factor rarely rose above negative ten degrees Fahrenheit during winter months.

Several minutes later, Erin found herself standing in the shadow of the building, waiting for a taxi to take her to her hotel. She'd clean up and seek massive quantities of decently prepared food, careful not to draw undue attention. She had to remember that she was an underpaid travel writer on a modest stipend to cover the Trans-Siberian Railway for an upstart travel blog. She even had business cards that linked to a real website, where several of Katie Reynolds' previous articles were prominently featured, along with other writers, whom she suspected were real. Her picture appeared on the website, with a gracious biography chronicling her travels and accolades. Overall, the CIA had done a decent job with a fairly simple cover. The only real weakness to the cover was her spotty Australian accent, which Berg had assured her would not be an issue in Novosibirsk. Tourists were still a rarity in the city, and as long as she steered clear of the obvious "expat" haunts, her accent wouldn't become an issue.

She reached the front of the queue and opened the door to the next taxi, placing her hiking backpack next to her in the back seat.

"Tsentralnaya Hotel, please," she requested in passable Russian.

The driver nodded and drove her less than a kilometer to the hotel. She could have walked, but hadn't felt like navigating the streets with the backpack. As the taxi approached the featureless gray building, she started to question her cover as a struggling writer who specialized in travelling on a budget. The hotel didn't look promising. She should have vetoed the budget travel aspect of her cover and booked herself at one of several chain hotels in the city. It was too late to make the change at this point. Her tourist visa was connected to an "invitation" issued by the Tsentralnaya Hotel, which was a requirement to travel in the Russian Federation.

She paid the driver and hauled her backpack onto the curb. Nobody rushed out of the hotel entrance to help her with her bags. All she required was a clean room, bug-free bed and her own bathroom. That had been non-negotiable, regardless of her supposed "budget-minded nature." As long as she didn't have to share a bathroom, she'd be fine. She picked up her backpack and travel bag and proceeded to check into her base of operations for the next few days. She'd notify Farrington that she had arrived, and wait for him to arrange her first meeting with the Solntsevskaya Bratva. Until then, she'd do a little sightseeing and a lot of eating. She had four days' worth of cheese sandwiches and vodka to clean out of her system.

Chapter 29

Mike McFarland scanned the southern horizon with a powerful night vision spotting scope, fighting against the stiff wind blowing in from west. The sky was clear, providing his scope with ample ambient starlight to illuminate the horizon, which yielded nothing but a bright green image of the Kazakhstan steppes. He had his doubts about the helicopters arriving tonight. Heavy gusts accompanied the warmer European air, playing havoc with their encampment. He couldn't imagine how the wind would affect the aircraft. The landscape was flat, which was ideal for a makeshift helicopter landing zone, but the proposed refueling site was exposed to the elements on all four sides. The pilots could expect no mercy on their approach.

Despite the open terrain immediately surrounding the landing zone, the team could expect full privacy during their babysitting gig. The twisted, rugged drive to the site from Highway A345 had tested the limits of their 70 Series Land Cruisers, flattening two tires and most certainly damaging the alignment of both vehicles. Mission planners for the operation had done their research. Not only would the drive from the highway disable most vehicles, the landing zone sat in the middle of a small raised plateau, forcing the team to hide their vehicles and hike three miles to arrive at the given GPS coordinates.

The hike had been expected based on his terrain assessment, along with the flat tires. They had brought six full-size spare tires, since he had no intention of losing one of his trucks out here. They were a long way from Astana, and the only help they could count on was a salvage contract, which would require him to pay nearly seventy percent of the vehicle's value to have it towed to the nearest repair garage. Of course, repairs would eat up the remaining value of the vehicle, so in many cases, you were better off leaving the vehicle where it died. Abandoning one of the trucks wasn't an option on this mission. He'd greased enough palms to keep this little side venture off the books, but the unwritten rules were clear. If he lost company gear, it came out of his own pocket, which meant he'd have to take some unsavory side jobs to compensate for the lost income.

McFarland checked his watch again. 0132. The birds were late. He lowered the scope and peered through the impenetrable darkness at the rest of his team scattered around the LZ. He could barely distinguish their darkened forms against the unlit background, spread in an oval along the periphery of the proposed site. They had been instructed to sweep their sectors with night vision, searching for any possible witnesses to the landing. Prior to dispersing to take position around the LZ, they had formed a line to conduct a FOD (Foreign Object Detection) walk.

Unlike the FOD walks conducted on pristine aircraft carrier decks or concrete flight lines, his men wouldn't clear rocks, chewing gum wrappers or discarded cigarette lighters from the ground. Instead, they would use heavy duty spray canisters to paint large rocks with an infrared paint visible to each helicopter's Forward Looking Infrared Pods (FLIR). Anything larger than a watermelon was marked, so the pilots could pick the best locations for the initial landing.

"Sector reports," he said, speaking into a small handheld radio clipped high on his field vest.

One by one, his team reported "all clear," confirming what his senses detected. No lights were visible from any of the surrounding villages due to the distances involved. The largest town in the area, Ayogoz, was just below the visible horizon to the northeast, once again giving McFarland the distinct impression that the mission planners involved in this operation knew what they were doing. Settlements along the highway to the west were blocked by a range of low mountains running parallel to the highway, and the local road they used to travel through the mountains showed no signs of permanent inhabitants. Even at its closest point of approach, this washed-out road never came closer than twelve miles from the plateau, and traffic between Ayagoz and the southern town had been minimal. All in all, they were nicely tucked away in the middle of nowhere.

Satisfied that they were alone for the moment, he leaned his head back and took in the vast, brilliant array of stars. McFarland had served in the army at remote outposts around the world, finding little comfort in the harsh, inhospitable locations during the day. He took his solace at night, when night vision and sophisticated listening devices provided a distinct advantage over their enemies, tipping the odds overwhelmingly in their favor. The insurgents rarely bothered them at night, which afforded him the opportunity to enjoy the tranquility and raw beauty of an unspoiled sky, something he could never enjoy living amidst pervasive fields of artificial lighting back home or at a major Forward Operating Base. His reverie was cut short by a growing gust of wind, which he had learned to predict during their twenty-two-hour stay on the exposed plateau.

He started to reach for the goggles hanging loosely around his neck, but decided to shift his AK-74 from a stowed position across his back to a ready position along his chest. The transition took less than a second, which was one half of a second longer than it took for him to figure out why he had instinctively gone into self-preservation mode. The gust of wind came from the wrong direction, preceded by a deep thumping.

"They're right on top of us. Fuck!" said one of his team members on the radio circuit.

McFarland turned his body, looking frantically in every direction as artificial gusts of wind buffeted his body, stinging his face with pebbles and dirt. He quickly brought the goggles to his face and continued his search for the helicopters. Through the dust storm, he spotted them hovering fifty feet in the air over the eastern half of the plateau. They had approached the LZ from the leeward side, which he had expected.

Helicopter pilots preferred to land and take off into the wind, though this was not a requirement, especially for skilled pilots. What he hadn't expected was a mission altitude lower than the plateau, which was why he never spotted their approach. They arrived from a downwind position, below the nearby visible horizon, masking the sounds of the rotors and blocking his line of sight.

Not bad at all, he thought as he pulled three high-intensity chem sticks from his front right cargo pocket. He cracked all three sticks at once and proceeded to wave them overhead for several moments in a specific order.

Red. Green. Blue. Once finished, he raised his night vision goggles and waited for the return signal. Three infrared lasers, one from each helicopter, reached out and intersected at his feet, confirming that his signal had been verified. If he had waved the chem lights in a different order or tried some other method of attracting their attention, the same infrared lasers would have guided hundreds of 7.62mm projectiles into his body.

Satisfied that he wouldn't be cut to pieces by the miniguns, he started to jog to their encampment, which had likely been turned upside down by the rotor wash. He didn't need to issue orders to his team. Everyone would return to the tents and let their guests run the show from this point forward. Darryl Jackson had made one aspect of this mission clear. They would have no contact with the helicopter assets upon arrival. Personnel onboard the helicopters would arrange the refueling gear within the LZ and promptly depart, leaving his team to guard the site until Combat Controllers relieved them at a still undecided point in the near future. Easy money he hoped.

Examining the helicopters through his night vision, he could tell that the operation supported by this refueling station would be anything but easy money. Two KCH-53K Dragon Cows followed a MH-53 Pave Low into position over the LZ, spreading out over the center to give plenty of distance between rotors. He'd never seen one of the Dragon Cows in person, but could easily recognize the rare refueling variant of the CH-53K by its refueling probe and extended fuselage. Instead of airlifting bladders of fuel in a sling underneath one of these behemoth helicopters, the Dragon Cows would fill empty bladders with their own internal fuel tanks. This had been another reason he had expected to easily spot the helicopters on their approach. He had anticipated that they would be forced to fly at a higher altitude due to externally slung bladders.

The Dragon Cow gave mission planners more flexibility, putting an incredible amount of mobile fuel in one place. Employing the Marine Corps' Tactical Bulk Fuel Delivery System, this helicopter variant could add an additional 2400 gallons of fuel as internal cargo to its expansive 3000 gallon built-in capacity. Two Dragon Cows could refuel twenty helicopters on the way in to their objective, with plenty left over to top them off on the way home. Whatever was in the works out here had the potential to be huge.

McFarland sat down near a small outcropping of rocks that served to shield their tents from some of the wind and observed the operation. Less than an hour later, the helicopters departed, leaving one Advanced Aviation Forward Area Refueling Station (AAFARS) behind, configured to receive four helicopters simultaneously. The station was oriented east to west, to best take advantage of the most common prevailing winds, though helicopters could approach the individual stations from the south, avoiding the fuel bladders and pumping equipment. Four bladders stood behind the main pumping equipment, significantly higher than the rest of the equipment. His best guess regarding their capacity was 500 gallons, but he wouldn't know for sure until the morning, when he could read the nomenclature stamped to the equipment.

Overall, it represented less fuel than he had estimated, given the presence of two Dragon Cows in the refuel task force. It did give him a good idea of what might be headed through the refueling station en route to some nasty business. If he had to guess, he'd say some variation of the Sikorsky H-60 frame. The army and navy versions of the venerable airframe sported a two hundred gallon fuel tank, giving them roughly a 350 mile round trip fully loaded. The smaller fuel bladders made sense when considering the smaller H-60 tanks. Average tank size for the H-53 frame measured over 1300 gallons. The refueling station in its current configuration could easily support a round trip for up to four UH-60 Blackhawks. That was his bet, but unfortunately, he would never know. His team would be long gone when the helicopter strike force came through.

Chapter 30

Katie Reynolds felt less secure the further they travelled from the center of Novosibirsk. She had no weapons and no backup, which was compounded by the fact that she had lost track of any recognizable landmarks. She knew they had started off in an easterly direction based on her knowledge of the city streets within central Novosibirsk, but as they drove deeper into the outskirts of the bleak city, she couldn't be sure they were still headed east. An overcast sky kept her from making the most basic calculations.

As city streets transformed into a rundown business-residential district, most vestiges of her personal safety net, real or perceived, slipped away. Trust was all that remained. Trust in operatives she barely knew, and reliance on mafiya thugs who would cut a businessman's throat on the off chance that the Rolex he sported was real. At least she wasn't squeezed between two *bratva* soldiers. She had her own seat, which gave her some confidence in the situation cooked up by Berg and Sanderson's crew.

She had been instructed by Farrington to meet their Solntsevskaya contact in a modest café near her hotel, where she would be given further instructions. Farrington told her that she would likely be put into action tonight. The *bratva* had identified a unique opportunity that fit the overall mission profile, but the window was transient, requiring her to meet her new friends sooner than expected.

Viktor arrived promptly at 9:30, joining her at the small table with an espresso and a grim face. Without saying a word, he downed the small cup and stood, waiting impatiently for her to finish. She took a deep swig of her strong coffee and joined him for a short walk around the block. Minutes later she sat firmly pressed into the worn leather seat of a black vintage E30 class BMW, heading east out of the city. Fifteen minutes into the drive and nobody had said a word to her. She sat silently next to a murderous-looking man, whose emotionless face displayed a crisscross of several short scars. Deep blue tattoo work crept up his neck, peeking over the collar of his black leather jacket. He took a deep drag on his cigarette, exhaling through his nose. Hard men that chain-smoked shitty cigarettes and bathed in strong cologne. She couldn't wait to get out of the car.

A few minutes later, after she had completely abandoned the idea of jumping out of the car into this completely unfamiliar and markedly rougher neighborhood, Viktor snubbed his cigarette into the car's overflowing ashtray and turned to her.

"I need you to put this over your head," he said, extending a hand between the front seats.

He gripped a thick black piece of cloth, which she assumed was some kind of hood or bag.

"I'll cover my eyes," she replied in Russian, meeting his serious glare.

The man next to her took another drag on his cigarette, not appearing to tense for action. She kept staring at him until he spoke again.

"It's a security precaution. Standard procedure. Two minutes," he said.

"I'm not putting a bag over my head," she said.

"Then we're not going any further," he said, and the vehicle pulled over to the side of the road.

The BMW nestled under a thick tree next to a tall, rusted fence. The unmarked street resembled more of an alley, bordered by persistent, untrimmed bushes and trees that scraped the right side of the car at times. Half of the asphalt had crumbled, leaving wide, washed-out portions containing potholes that required the driver to constantly maneuver the vehicle from side to side. A weathered brick building with a corrugated tin roof sat across the street from the car, separated from the road by a six-foot, gated cinderblock wall. The residence stood next to a collapsed wooden structure that had fallen victim to fire long ago.

She figured the fire had destroyed the brick building's roof, explaining the new tin roof. Measuring the cinderblock wall mentally, she calculated an easy jump and lift to get over in one swift movement. She could probably be over the wall before they could level their weapons for a shot. Glancing up and down the street, this appeared to be her only option if she was forced to fight her way out of here. What she would do once she landed on the other side was another story.

"They told me you wouldn't be a problem," Viktor said.

"And nobody said anything about putting a bag over my head."

"Would you prefer to ride in the trunk?" he countered.

She slowly shook her head, sensing a shift from the seat next to her. The man rolled down his window and tossed the cigarette. She moved her hand slowly for the door handle, just in case the situation spiraled out of control.

"Then we have a problem," he said, eyes drifting to her hand.

"Feel free to step out, Ms. Reynolds. Nobody will stop you, but I'm not kidding when I say that this car will not drive any further toward our destination unless you wear this hood…or ride in the trunk. Nobody else is in the trunk, right?" Viktor asked, addressing the driver.

They all started laughing, which caught her off guard. They had been deadly serious up until this point. The sudden shift heightened her tension.

"See? We're not so bad. We make jokes, just like the Sopranos. Right?" Viktor said.

She eased her shoulders and caught herself smiling vaguely, unsure what to make of the sudden change in behavior.

"Look, Ms. Reynolds. If you can't trust me for two minutes, we'll have to hire a prostitute like I suggested and hope for the best. I don't think Yuri will be happy with that scenario. We've come up with a solution to one of your group's hurdles. You're infinitely more qualified to pull this off than one of our drugged-up hookers. We need to get you some new clothes for the job. We have a wide selection at one of our warehouses," he said.

Now she was intrigued. Farrington, aka "Yuri," hadn't provided any of the details for tonight's mission. She didn't like the implications for her role in whatever they had planned, but she'd play by their rules for now. She couldn't possibly let them trust any aspect of the overall mission to a prostitute.

"I saw some nice clothing boutiques near the hotel. Wouldn't that be easier?"

"Don't you think shopping in clothing boutiques might attract unwanted attention?"

Viktor had a point, though she wondered how careful they had been with her pickup. Shopping for designer clothes in a Novosibirsk boutique had to rank lower on the list of suspicious actions than getting in a car with three gangsters. It all came down to a little trust. She took the black hood from Viktor and placed it over her head, waiting for someone to start choking her. Nothing happened beyond the car lurching back onto the broken street, moving toward what she envisioned to be the *bratva's* version of the Bat Cave.

Chapter 31

Foreign Intelligence Service (SVR) Headquarters
Yasanevo Suburb, Moscow, Russian Federation

Dmitry Ardankin hung up the phone and immediately dialed Director Pushnoy's direct line. The secure telephone system prompted him for a passcode, which he entered. The passcode enabled his call to bypass Pushnoy's secretary and ring directly at his desk, or whatever phone the director had designated to receive calls. Only a few of the Foreign Intelligence Service's deputy directors had been given this number, and none of them abused it. Ardankin reserved the use of Pushnoy's direct line for emergencies. He wasn't sure if this qualified as an emergency—yet, but it was without a doubt headed in that direction.

He waited tensely as the phone rang, hoping that it would go to the director's voicemail. He hated answering Pushnoy's one-word questions, often fired in rapid succession like a machine gun.

"Speak quickly, Dmitry. I'm in the middle of something," the director said as a greeting.

"One of General Sanderson's operatives walked off a flight in Kiev on Tuesday and disappeared," Ardankin said.

Several seconds passed in utter silence, which was unusual for the director. Just as Ardankin considered the possibility that their connection had been severed, Pushnoy spoke.

"Three days ago?" Pushnoy asked, his tone clearly implying that the time delay was unforgiveable.

Ardankin chose his words carefully. The Federal Customs Service had reluctantly agreed to add "sanitized" profile photos to their computerized watch list, which was directly linked to Ukrainian Customs. These requests were normally relayed by the Federation Security Service's counterintelligence branch, but Ardankin wanted to bypass the FSB in this case. He had spent the better part of an hour negotiating a truce with Arkady Baranov, director of the Center for Special Operations (CSN), which included assurances that the Foreign Intelligence Service had closed the case regarding the leak at CSN. He had been instructed not to share information regarding the discovery of a new American covert intelligence group, so it was in his best interest to contact Customs directly to add suspected members of this group to their database.

The downside to concealing the additions to the Customs database came in the form of resource priority. Since the profiles were sanitized, containing no information beyond known aliases and photographs, they would be entered as low priority in the system. The faces would not appear at Customs terminals or be shown to Customs agents at a shift briefing. Customs required information to elevate priority and allocate limited human resources. Ardankin's hands were tied, since the information would raise eyebrows and result in an immediate phone call to the Customs Service's FSB liaison, exposing his sidestep. The best they could expect was a possible match through automated facial recognition sweeps of passport and Customs checkpoint photos. Frankly, Ardankin was surprised they got a hit on one of the profiles at all.

"Bureaucracy at its worst, sir. Customs is 82% sure that Richard Farrington presented an Australian passport at Kiev Zhuliany International," Ardankin said finally.

"And he disappeared?"

"His Australian cover hasn't been used since the airport, sir."

"Disturbing," Pushnoy stated.

"How do you want me to proceed?"

"This stays internal. Activate and deploy everyone at your disposal and start working Kiev. Train stations, rental car agencies, buses…I want to know where he is headed."

"Understood. We'll start in Kiev and expand. I'll contact Customs and have them implement search protocols based on his Australian cover. I doubt he is alone. We may get lucky," Ardankin said.

"Don't count on it. I want this man in custody before he can do any damage. Contact me directly regarding your progress. I have to go."

The line went dead, leaving Ardankin with his mouth open, ready to respond. He'd call Customs anyway. It was always better to cast a wider net, especially when they had no idea what they were looking for. He'd narrow the search parameters to males between the ages of 20-50 entering Russia with an Australian passport within the past five days. The list might be extensive, but the FIS had the manpower to sort through the names looking for anomalies. They'd find something.

He checked his email for the file promised by Customs, finding that it had arrived during his terse conversation with his director. He opened the email attachment, which generated a full-screen Customs layout comparing two pictures of Richard Farrington. The leftmost photograph had been provided to Customs by Ardankin, showing Farrington in a U.S. Army uniform. He'd found this picture in one of the SVR's routine archival snapshots of Pentagon personnel. Unlike the old days, when pictures like these were taken by spies with 35mm cameras, Farrington's picture came directly from the Pentagon's database.

The rightmost picture contained the slightly altered Richard Farrington. Clearly, the Americans hadn't gone to extensive lengths to alter his appearance, which surprised him, given the fact that one of their operatives had recently disappeared in Munich. This General Sanderson, or whoever was pulling the strings, should have known that Herr Hubner would eventually break, exposing details that could compromise their program. Then again, maybe information within the group was compartmentalized. They'd never know, since Herr Hubner managed to end his interrogation early.

Ardankin sat back and stared at the two photos. There was no doubt it was the same person. His eyebrows had been artificially thickened, which was one of the easiest, but most effective ways to alter an appearance. His cheeks looked fuller, indicating the use of an oral implant. Another subtle, yet effective way to throw off facial recognition software. His natural blue eyes were hidden behind brown contact lenses. Changing eye color was a tactic used to fool humans, but had little effect on computer recognition algorithms. Farrington wasn't taking the chance that his photo might have been distributed to customs checkpoints. Finally, his hair appeared darker and longer. A modest hairpiece that didn't attract attention, but significantly differed from the close-cropped military haircut in his Pentagon photo.

Surface cosmetics. Nothing that would fool sophisticated software, but not a bad effort for an operative that didn't want to undergo minor plastic surgery…or didn't have time to. This last thought lingered, hanging over Ardankin like a death threat. He shook his head slowly, agonizing over his reaction to the thought. There was something there, but he couldn't pinpoint it. He closed his eyes for a moment and cleared his mind, breathing deeply. A momentary meditation to eliminate the clutter. Less than five seconds later his eyes flashed open.

Richard Farrington hadn't been concerned with defeating facial recognition software. He knew it would take days for the system to detect his entry, at which point he had already long abandoned the identity used to arrive in Kiev. Even after discovering his entry, it could take days or weeks to generate another lead. Best-case scenario, they'd find his next travel connection within a day or two. Add more time to prosecute leads at the end of that connection, assuming he was smart and didn't travel directly to his final destination. Unless the American made a rookie mistake, it could take them a week to finally catch up with Farrington. He had to have known this. The American's mission would take place within the next few days. Ardankin had no time to waste.

First, he'd activate all of their Ukrainian-based agents, augmenting the effort with additional agents from Poland, Belarus and Romania. If necessary, he could deploy more agents from Moscow, though he preferred to use Directorate S assets stationed in the field. The last thing he needed was an out-of-practice headquarters-based agent blowing his or her cover in Kiev and casting a light on the entire operation.

He opened one of the classified directories on his computer and searched for the number he needed, quickly finding it. Feliks Yeshevsky ran their Ukrainian operations, directing the efforts of five native Ukrainian field agents based out of Kiev. He'd proven extremely resourceful in tracking down Reznikov's Stockholm address and had never failed to produce results in the past. Still, Ardankin hesitated.

Yeshevsky had a reputation for brutality that could turn into a liability during a systematic canvassing effort. His methods were better suited for a more targeted approach to acquiring intelligence. Ardankin considered the alternatives and decided that Yeshevsky represented their best hope of quickly rediscovering Farrington's trail. He'd have to trust Yeshevsky's judgment, which was a better option than importing less capable agents into a foreign country and starting them from scratch. He dialed the Ukrainian number, apprehensive about where all of this was headed.

Chapter 32

Richard Farrington stepped off the train from Yekaterinburg and examined the station, noting the odd-colored building that dominated the skyline. He wasn't interested in the color or unique architecture of Novosibirsk's railway station. His entry into Russia had been risky, starting in Kiev, where he stepped off a connecting flight from Rome. Despite eighteen years of sovereign independence from the Russian Federation, the Ukraine maintained close ties to their former master. Too close, in Farrington's opinion, but his other entry options put him at even greater risk.

Kiev gave him easy access to dozens of trains that conducted regular runs to cities throughout western Russia and drew little scrutiny from Border Control guards. At most, the train would stop at the border for a rapid examination of visas and passports. Often, the outbound Kiev trains had a section on the train reserved for Border Control officials, who would take care of this formality while en route to the first Russian station. The high volume of rail passengers between the two countries had led to streamlined procedures that worked to his advantage.

His only real concern was the possible interconnectivity between Ukrainian customs at the Kiev airport and Russian intelligence agencies. Karl Berg had warned Sanderson that the two nations' intelligence services actively and regularly shared information. Given the low-intensity conflict smoldering over Reznikov's abduction, Berg thought it was fair to assume that the Ukrainians had been asked to carefully screen for anomalies. Farrington's cover wouldn't draw any immediate attention.

He'd flown from Buenos Aires to Sidney, Australia, where he picked up a new passport and the visas needed to complete the rest of his journey as an Australian tourist. His Russian language skills were good, but might not hold up during a customs inquiry, and there was no sense taking the risk. Sanderson's new program wasn't designed to create deep-cover "illegal" operatives. He just needed to get into Russia, where he could employ his skills to temporarily melt away into the population.

Farrington adjusted his backpack and walked through the station, constantly scanning for anyone that might have taken an unhealthy interest in his arrival. Moving through the packed station, he headed directly for the transit exit located beneath a massively wide, three-story window facing the gray city. A call placed to Viktor fifteen minutes outside of Novosibirsk had confirmed his pickup. Someone would meet him at the top of the stairs outside of the station and escort him to a waiting car. The *bratva* would take him to a secluded location, where the team would stay for the duration of the trip. Everyone agreed that moving six operatives between hotels would be cumbersome and risky if any of them attracted attention while entering Russia.

The worst-case scenario involved Russian intelligence agencies detecting an anomaly in one of their profiles that warranted further investigation. Follow-on attempts to locate his operatives would quickly dead-end at various points of entry into western Russia, leaving authorities with nothing to pursue. Each operative's trail ended at their first border entry point. Like Farrington, they immediately switched to their Russian identities for follow-on travel, strictly avoiding airports. Train or rental car transit would bring them together in Novosibirsk undetected.

Well aware that he might be on an internal Russian watch list, he took advantage of an unexpected chance to change identities in Yekaterinburg, when an apathetic ticketing agent neglected to request his identity papers. The agent asked him to spell his name, and Farrington obliged, becoming Boris Ushenko for the final leg of his journey.

The only exception to this tactic had been Erin Foley. She had arrived in Vladivostok through a series of flights originating in Australia. Since she would spend four days on a train, arriving in Novosibirsk ahead of the team, Berg didn't think it would be wise to switch her identity. Too many prying eyes on the train, which he felt was their only discreet option to smuggle her into Novosibirsk. Berg and Sanderson accepted the possibility that one of the seven operatives would be flagged entering Russia, and they couldn't take the chance that it would be Foley.

Unlike the rest of the team, Foley was far from nondescript and could be easily traced by investigative teams flashing her photograph on the streets. They had changed her appearance significantly, but they could do little to hide the fact that she was an attractive, confident woman that men and women alike tended to remember. Given the notoriety of her Stockholm debut, the last thing the Russian FIS would expect was for her to voluntarily set foot on Russian soil. Routing her through Vladivostok offered additional insurance, since prying eyes would be focused on Europe and western Russia.

Unfortunately, the rest of the team had to enter through the west. Novosibirsk stood as the commercial gateway to eastern Siberia, offering the only airport in Siberia with direct flights outside of Russia, and the Trans Siberian-Mongolian Railway was the only viable commercial rail option approaching from the east.

Crossing into Russia from Europe carried a higher risk of detection, but offered hundreds of options and put them in close proximity to Novosibirsk. Each operative arrived within a day or two of crossing the border. With the mission planned for Sunday evening, they had two full days to prepare, four days in Russia. Even if the Russians detected one of their entries, he couldn't imagine any scenario that put them in a position to stop the operation.

Farrington walked through the doors and up the stairs leading to street level, immediately spotting his contact when he reached the top. A bulky man wearing a black leather jacket held a piece of tattered cardboard with a prearranged generic Russian name scribbled in black marker. The name was meaningless, one of the safeguards agreed upon earlier, and nothing that would attract attention or prove memorable to anyone at the station. He approached the gruff driver and nodded, hoping for some kind of sign that everything was all right. The thick man raised a small handheld radio to his mouth and spoke a few words, putting it to his ear for the response. Farrington noted the deep scars on his face and a trace of tattoo reaching his lower jaw, just above his gray turtleneck sweater. He dropped the radio into his pocket immediately, folding the sign in half.

"Viktor says we need to hurry if we're going to make it to dinner on time. Let's go," he said, repeating another prearranged signal.

If the man had said anything different, Farrington would have kept walking, prepared to fight his way out of whatever situation presented itself. The fight would have very likely been short-lived, since he carried no weapons at this point, but he would have made every attempt possible to escape. He hadn't expected any trouble. Everyone on his team had arrived without incident and had been ferried off to a discreet location on the outskirts of the city. Farrington started to relax a little. As far as he could tell, the first phase of the operation had been successful. His strike team had arrived intact.

He followed the *bratva* soldier across a large cement walkway to a black BMW sedan idling between two buses in the designated station pickup zone. He could see two men in the front seat. Neither of them looked in his direction as he neared the vehicle. Scarface opened the rear passenger door and nodded for him to get in. He was met by thick, noxious cigarette smoke upon entry, sliding across the back seat to the driver's side of the car. Before Scarface could lower his hulking frame into the car, the man in the front passenger seat turned and extended his hand.

"Viktor," he said simply.

Farrington accepted the gesture and they shook hands firmly. "Yuri Rastov. Thank you for the hospitality," Farrington said.

"My pleasure, Mr. Rastov. As you are probably already aware, everybody is waiting for you at one of our secure locations."

Once Scarface closed his door, the car sped away from the curb, drifting through the tangle of taxis and vans converging on passengers from nearly a dozen different trains. As the gateway to Siberia, Novosibirsk's station was the largest and busiest rail depot east of Yekaterinburg.

"It sounds like Ms. Reynolds is prepared," Farrington said.

"She is," Viktor grumbled.

"She wasn't happy being held at the warehouse," Farrington said.

"I don't suspect anyone is watching her, but it would look rather odd if she suddenly emerged from her hotel dressed like a high-priced escort and made a beeline straight for one of the city's nightclubs. Agreed?"

Farrington nodded, his attention distracted when Scarface flipped open a silver butane lighter and lit a cigarette. He offered one to Farrington, who didn't hesitate to accept it. His first drag was rough, but he managed to keep from breaking into the telltale cough of an amateur smoker. The nicotine hit his bloodstream immediately, easing his tension. He leaned back in the seat.

"You need to trust me with these things. You all may look the part, talk like locals and smoke our cigarettes without hacking up a lung, but this is a different part of the world. A different part of Russia. Even I stick out like a fucking sore thumb around here," Viktor said and turned to face the windshield.

"I'll have a talk with everyone on the team," Farrington said.

"Especially the woman," Viktor griped. "She's been giving my men shit ever since we picked her up."

"She's hardcore. That's why we brought her along."

"She's coming close to getting her ass beaten," Viktor said, eliciting a grunt from Scarface.

"I didn't realize the *bratva* beat up women," Farrington said.

"We don't hit little old ladies, but mouthy bitches like that?" Viktor shook his head.

"If you hit her, you better hit her good," Farrington warned him.

Viktor turned in his seat with a perplexed look and shrugged his shoulders. "Why is that?"

"Because you won't get another chance. I've seen her in action, and it's not a pretty sight…for the other guy," Farrington said. "I'll talk to her."

Viktor smiled and took a long drag on his cigarette, exhaling the noxious smoke onto the dashboard. Without turning, he asked, "How do you like our cigarettes?"

"Fucking horrible," Farrington grimaced. "I thought your people controlled the distribution of Western cigarettes in Russia?"

"We do, but none of our people smoke them. They taste like candy with all of the chemicals your companies add. These are *real* cigarettes."

"Well, they taste like shit. I'm surprised anyone starts smoking here."

"We make sure they start out with your cigarettes," Viktor said, laughing.

"Sounds like you've thought of everything."

Viktor poked his own head with one of his index fingers. "We're running a sophisticated, multi-platform business organization, complete with marketing and strategic planning. You'd be surprised by the level of thought that goes into these decisions."

Farrington decided not to bite on this discussion. He had little interest in listening to this thug try to compare their criminal organization to a legitimate high-end corporation. Drugs, human trafficking, extortion, protection rackets, bribery, violence and murder topped the list of "deliverables" provided by the Solntsevskaya Bratva. Controlling stakes in legitimate products were "acquired" through business transactions heavily influenced by one of the "deliverables" mentioned above. Like every version of organized crime worldwide, the *bratva* provided *nothing* in return for everything. Their collaboration with the *bratva* was an unholy alliance sanctioned by Berg and approved by Sanderson, a one-time deal sealed by a little over five million dollars. He didn't like it on any level. He especially didn't like trusting the safety of his team to a payoff.

"Viktor?"

The Russian turned his head and regarded him without speaking.

"I need you to understand something. If you decide to sell us out or sabotage our mission, you're a dead man, along with everyone involved...all the way to Mr. Penkin," Farrington said.

Viktor's eyes opened wide for a fraction of a second before his face tightened into a practiced neutral expression. His response to hearing his boss's name had achieved the desired effect.

"We're not playing games," Farrington added.

"We didn't think you were. This mission of yours carries significant risk to us, which is why I insist that you follow our rules right up until your men hit Vektor. After that, you're completely on your own."

"That's how we normally operate. This is a one-time collaboration," Farrington said.

"Which never happened," Viktor said.

"Exactly. I get the sense that we're both on the same wavelength."

Viktor didn't respond to this statement, which was meant to soften the blow of threatening his life. He could tell that Viktor was spinning Penkin's name around in his head, trying to make sense of the implications. He imagined that Viktor would place a frantic call to Matvey Penkin as soon as he could break free from Farrington. Penkin would double up the communications security procedures surrounding any of his sensitive operations and start examining anyone close to him. He wouldn't find anything of course, but the message would be received loud and clear.

The CIA knew the names of the players and wouldn't hesitate to send another team to clean up the loose ends if the mission went sideways. All the more reason for Viktor and his crew to ensure everything went smoothly right up until the moment his men breached Vektor. It also gave Farrington some assurance that none of vehicles involved in their exfiltration plan would suffer from a suspicious engine seizure or brake malfunction. Penkin's branch of the Solntsevskaya Bratva had good reason to check and double-check every piece of equipment and vehicle presented to Farrington's team. Their own lives now depended on it.

He could sense that Viktor wanted to say something, but was hesitating. Scarface betrayed no reaction to his threat, demonstrating the considerable discipline demanded by the *bratva*. Finally, Viktor turned and spoke.

"We're good, but a word of advice. Don't mention that name again, under any circumstances. Very dangerous for everyone involved."

"I understand. What time does Ms. Reynolds head out?"

"Late. Around eleven. This is like New York City, the city that never sleeps. Yes?"

"I find that hard to believe. This looks like an old-school Soviet city," Farrington remarked.

"Well, it's not exactly Moscow, but some of the clubs stay open all night," Viktor said. "Not as expensive as Moscow either. This is a sleepy corner of Russia, slowly awakening to the realities of the Federation. There are many opportunities for us here."

"Still sleeping off the hangover of communist prosperity?"

They all laughed at his joke, including the previously unreadable Scarface.

"Very good, Yuri. You have a sense of humor after all. I was beginning to worry about you. I don't trust anyone that can't laugh. This is going to work out for both of us. Trust me on that. We'll drink to this later."

"I hope your vodka is better than these cigarettes," Farrington said, flipping his out of the window.

"Worse. Your days of Grey Goose and Ketel One are over. We drink the real stuff here."

Farrington snorted. "No wonder the average Russian life expectancy is so low."

On average, Russian males fell just short of sixty-five years, compared to seventy-five years in the United States. Life expectancy had been on the rise in Russia until the fall of communism, when the state-provided healthcare system collapsed in the turmoil immediately following the transition to a quasi-capitalist system. Russian life expectancy figures never rebounded.

"You and I have bigger impediments to our life expectancy than shitty cigarettes and vodka," Viktor said.

"Very true. How much further to the warehouse?"

"Not long. I'll need you to wear this hood when we get closer," Viktor said, raising the black nylon bag from the center console.

"I don't think that will be necessary. We're past the point of fucking each other over...I hope," Farrington said.

"But if you're captured—"

"If I'm captured, we both have bigger problems than a warehouse full of stolen goods," Farrington said.

Viktor lowered the hood and laughed with his mouth closed, expelling smoke through his nose. "Hard-fucking-core might be an understatement," he said.

They rode in silence to a red brick warehouse situated behind a concrete perimeter wall topped with concertina wire. A camera stared at them outside of the gate for a few moments before the reinforced metal gates swung inward, exposing several heavily armed, rough-looking men smoking cigarettes, low-ranking *bratva* muscle known as "Shestyorka." Young men jockeying for the coveted title of "Vor." Most of them would end up dead. Rival gang shootouts or internal cleansing would eliminate all but the most trustworthy and capable, who would be inducted into the brotherhood, leaving a void that would be immediately filled by the next petty thug on the streets. There was never a shortage of Shestyorka.

"You know, Viktor? If you want to keep your warehouses a secret, you might consider something a little more low-key than a guarded fortress smack dab in the middle of a neighborhood," Farrington suggested.

"Everybody knows about this warehouse. They look the other way because we tell them to...and pay them."

"Then the hood is just a game? I don't like games."

"Not a game. A test. Your team passed the test," Viktor said.

"I don't understand."

"If you had put that over your head without any resistance, I would have had serious reservations about your team's intentions toward my organization. All of your people resisted, which is a good sign. Welcome to Novosibirsk's worst-kept, but most secure secret."

Farrington shook his head imperceptibly. His covert world was one subtle test after another, each organization or entity probing his or her enemies and friends alike. This was the hardest part of the job, where the lethality of a mistake might not materialize until much later, at the most unexpected moment. The actual assault against Vektor Labs would be a cakewalk compared to the snake-filled, cloak-and-dagger world Karl Berg continued to manipulate. The sooner they hit Vektor, the better.

Chapter 33

11:38 PM
Novosibirsk Nightclub
Novosibirsk, Russian Federation

"Katie Reynolds" (aka Erin Foley) sat impatiently in the back seat of a Renault SUV on a lifeless side street near Diesel nightclub, counting the seconds until she could step out into the brisk, clean Siberian air. The three men accompanying her had chain-smoked furiously since they departed the warehouse compound. She had rolled her window down halfway, hoping to make a dent in the pervasive ashtray and body odor medley, but it didn't seem to help. The men made no effort to exhale their smoke in the opposite direction, despite her mild protest, and she didn't bother to address the fact that they all smelled like rotting garbage. The fall of communism apparently hadn't ushered in an era of personal hygiene.

She did her best to keep her distance from these animals at the warehouse complex, but she still caught words like "whore" and "bitch" tossed around just loud enough for her to hear. Threatening insults combined with murderous stares had left her eager to meet up with the rest of her team. Until the strike team started to trickle in, she spent most of her time wondering if this unholy alliance hadn't been a serious mistake. She still wasn't convinced it was a solid idea.

Aside from Viktor, the men she'd seen so far looked and acted like unmannered trash. A few carried themselves with dignity, possibly ex-military, but the rest resembled the kind of people you hoped to never see up close and in person under any circumstances. Degenerates and psychopaths with zero moral compasses, whose appearance at your doorstep usually heralded an era of misery, pain and death. Sitting among them made her more nauseous than the toxic cigarette exhaust that endlessly poured out of them like pollution from a factory smokestack.

She turned her head and stared at the shadowy brick wall past the crooked sidewalk. Soon, she would navigate that uneven pavement in high heels and a miniskirt, on a mission suitable for a prostitute, or so the men sitting with her in the SUV told her. Viktor clearly didn't agree, likely because he was the only *bratva* soldier that could process the full scope of their involvement.

Viktor knew that the Federation Security Services would descend upon Novosibirsk in full force after Vektor's destruction, leaving no stones unturned. A drug-addled prostitute posed a security risk to the *bratva* down the line. They would have to kill her, raising questions about her disappearance, which would inevitably lead to the Vektor scientist in question. Since all of the prostitutes in Novosibirsk were owned by the Solntsevskaya Bratva, federal authorities couldn't ignore a possible connection between the mafiya and Vektor. It didn't take a lot of intelligence or imagination to envision a hardcore crackdown, something she assumed the *bratva* leadership wished to avoid at all costs in Russia's third largest commercial center.

She heard one of their radios chirp, followed by a hushed conversation. The front passenger shifted in his seat, turning his head to address her for the first time tonight.

"It's time. You get in line and pay the fee to get in. Go to the bar on the right side of the club and look for a man wearing sunglasses, drinking a Heineken. Stand directly in front of his bar stool. He'll finish the beer and leave suddenly, giving you the seat. Your mark is seated directly to the right."

"Facing the bar?" she asked.

"What the fuck do you mean facing the bar?" the man spat.

"Is he to the right of the seat, from a frame of reference defined by facing the bar?"

"Shut the fuck up and do your job," he said, which spurred the man next to her into action.

He reached across her chest with his right hand to open the door, purposely rubbing the back of his hand against her breasts. In a blur, she jabbed a pressure point on the offending arm, just behind his elbow, disabling the arm and causing him to lurch forward in pain. She hooked her left arm around his neck pulling him back and toward her in the seat, easing a three-inch serrated blade against his neck.

"Touch me again and I'll kill you," she whispered in his ear.

The man attempted to struggle, but she kept him locked in a tight grip, pushing the knife an infinitesimal distance into his neck, bringing him closer to a carotid artery rupture that would end his miserable days. She didn't flinch when a black semi-automatic pistol appeared between the headrests, aimed at her head.

"And I'll kill you," the front passenger said.

With her free, right hand, she quickly gripped his wrist at the top of the radial bone, squeezing fiercely, while pushing his hand upward and to the left. The swift pressure-point manipulation instantly opened his hand. No amount of willpower or brute strength could overcome this painless application of ancient Chinese medicine. The pistol slid out of his hand and fell, quickly snatched out of the air by Reynolds. Before the situation could spiral out of control, she released the man next to her and stepped out of the vehicle. The front passenger, known only as Ivan, kicked open his door, jumping onto the concrete sidewalk.

Reynolds unloaded and disassembled the GSh-18 pistol in less than two seconds, tossing the four major pieces onto the sidewalk and throwing the loaded magazine as far as she could manage over a wrought-iron fence on the other side of the street.

"Tell your people to stay out of my fucking way," she said, turning toward Dusya Kovalchuk Street, leaving Ivan speechless with a strange look on his face that oddly resembled respect.

৵৹৵

Pyotr Roskov took another sip of his vodka martini and stared wistfully at the group of women gyrating on the club's main dance floor. Tightly stretched body dresses dominated the crowd, leaving little to his active imagination. He was still several drinks away from joining that throng of beauties, which he knew from experience would be too late. By that point, dozens of sharply dressed, clearly wealthy men would be in the mix, leaving him no chance of scoring anything beyond a few annoyed looks. It was the same story for him every weekend, and strangely enough, he had no intention of altering his routine.

He considered this a form of penance for having left Saint Petersburg so readily after completing his graduate studies. Saint Petersburg had been a veritable international melting pot compared to Novosibirsk. The streets were packed with foreign travelers, and the city itself attracted a worldwide residential clientele. As Russia's gateway to Europe, he found the city a marvelous break from the droll of Moscow and other stiflingly gray Russian cities. Most Russians considered Saint Petersburg to be the true heart of Russia, reminiscent of the Tsarist grandeur that defined centuries of imperial prosperity, but ultimately led to the Bolshevik Revolution, which began with the storming of the Winter Palace on the banks of the city's Neva River.

The communists couldn't dull Leningrad, despite decades of uninspired construction and political marginalization. Even the Germans couldn't destroy it with an eight hundred and seventy-two day long siege. In fact, the Germans had unknowingly saved the city from becoming the shithole Moscow had become. In 1917, the German troops invaded Estonia, threatening the city with invasion and forcing the newly empowered Soviets to transfer the capitol of Russia to Moscow. The communist riff-raff spent the next seventy-four years building one "people's" structure after another in Moscow, each one bigger and less architecturally inspired than the one before it. Saint Petersburg saw its share of this Constructivist architecture, but most of this occurred on the outskirts, expanding a sea of gray blockhouse apartment buildings around the picturesque, cosmopolitan city.

Without a doubt, he was being punished for accepting a high-paid position at Vektor Laboratories in place of less lucrative offers around Saint Petersburg. Novosibirsk was the antithesis of Saint Petersburg in nearly every way. Founded a mere quarter of a century before the Revolution, solely as a transportation hub to the eastern provinces, Novosibirsk grew up under the communists, who had no interest in the city beyond exploitation. On the banks of the Ob River, Novosibirsk was developed into a massive industrial center under Stalin's industrialization dictates, eventually claiming the title of third most populous city in Russia. Boring, ugly and culturally flat, Novosibirsk still hadn't emerged from its communist shell.

Pyotr hated it, which is why he repeatedly found himself standing in line at Diesel, waiting to pay an outrageous cover charge to drink overpriced alcohol, all while staring at women doing their best to escape Novosibirsk and hoping one of them might eventually see him as that ticket out. At least until they woke up the next morning and realized that they were not in the luxury digs of an upwardly mobile Russian businessman. It was a pathetic strategy to get laid, but it was the best he could come up with in this horrible city without paying a prostitute, and he wasn't about to travel down that path. His life here was sad enough without that.

He downed half of the martini, resolved to hop off the stool and beat his competition to the punch, but that courage retreated just as quickly, replaced with the practical realization that his efforts would only result in the loss of his seat. Instead, he turned to the bartender and ordered another martini. Before his drink arrived, he spied a woman walking in his direction. This could be trouble if she belonged to the guy seated next to him at the bar.

He stole another glance at the man, careful not to stare too long. He looked like a mafiya type. Tattoos covered his thick, muscular forearm, menacingly visible under cuffed sleeves. The fact that he hadn't taken off his sunglasses was disturbing. Maybe he was high. Maybe he was hiding a black eye. Maybe he was just a badass motherfucker that never removed his sunglasses. Pyotr couldn't think of one scenario that didn't scare him.

The man arrived soon after Pyotr had taken a seat, proceeding to smoke cigarettes and pound Heinekens at an alarming rate. The last thing he needed next to him was a drunk and disgruntled member of the Solntsevskaya gang. These scumbags did whatever they wanted to whomever they wanted with no repercussions. They were above the law and seemed to thrive on finding new ways to flaunt their untouchable status. A wrong look or accidentally bumped shoulder could land you in the hospital, or dead. As much as he didn't want to give up his seat, he'd resolved to abandon his post if this guy hit five Heinekens. Now he'd leave immediately, giving up his seat to a man who could beat him within an inch of his life in front of the police.

Without staring at the woman approaching, he started to stand, ready to pay for his drink and find another perch to observe the evening's festivities.

To his surprise, Mr. Sunglasses slapped a one-thousand ruble note on the bar and walked away from his seat, headed toward the bathroom. The woman's eyes widened at the prospect of finding a seat at the packed bar, paying no attention to the mobster as he brushed past her. Now he could check her out and celebrate his unbelievable good fortune. He could count the number of times a hot woman sat next to him anywhere in public on his thumb. Judging by what he saw before she took the seat, tonight was nothing short of a miracle.

Upon first inspection, he could tell that she was different than the rest of the women at the club. Her confidence was natural, not the practiced indifference on display in every corner of the club. Her black dress was chic and form fitting, but didn't devolve into the gratuitous body-flaunting spectacle of skintight one-piece dresses dominating the dance floor. Her soft, porcelain face was framed by shiny, jet black hair that ended at the middle of her neck. He caught the attention of her light blue eyes momentarily and offered her a weak smile, which she returned without an air of superiority. That alone set her apart from every other woman in the club, and possibly all of Novosibirsk. When she spoke to the bartender in decent, yet clearly academic Russian, he almost fell off his stool.

"I'll have whatever he's having," she said, turning to Pyotr. "That's a vodka drink, right?"

He hadn't noticed that his replacement martini had already arrived. "O-of course. Y-yes. Dry martini," he stammered.

"Perfect," she said, turning her attention to the tangle of bodies on the dance floor.

Neither of them said anything for several moments. While Pyotr struggled to come up with some kind of clever line that would ensnare the young woman who had unknowingly stumbled into his presence, her drink arrived, causing her to turn back to the bar. Still unable to decide on a clever pickup line, he stalled a little longer, resigned to the likelihood that she'd pay for her drink and scurry away from him. That was the excuse he easily conjured for delaying one of his brilliant utterances. When she reached for her purse and started to pull out a jumble of ruble notes, he decided to take unprecedented action. He offered to pay for her drink.

"No, no. Please allow me. It's the least I can do for a traveler stuck in this godforsaken city," he said, not exactly happy with his delivery.

"The city's not that bad, but I'll accept your offer. Travel funds are a bit tight for this trip," she said.

"Well, you certainly picked the wrong place to conserve rubles," he added, feeling a little more at ease with himself and the situation.

"Thank you. I had to experience the famous Russian nightlife at some point during my trip. This is the first stop that offered more than a dank pub filled with shady characters," she replied, closing her tiny purse.

"You're more than welcome…though I'm afraid this club is filled with plenty of shady characters. You're riding the Trans-Siberian?"

"I'm writing a travel story about the journey, but I'm doing it backwards. I started in Vladivostok," she said.

"Ughh. Another charming Russian city."

"The downtown area was interesting. A little gloomy overall, but it was an easy introduction to Russia. I've never travelled here before."

"Where are you from?" he asked.

"Sidney, Australia. It made sense for me to start on the eastern end of the railway," she said.

"Well, you should have skipped Novosibirsk. I've been here for two years, and I ran out of things to see and do within the first few days of arrival. My name is Pyotr, by the way."

"Katie," she said, exposing her Australian accent.

He couldn't believe his luck. A seat next to him opened up at the bar and an attractive foreigner slid right in. Australian on top of that! He wished there was some way he could ask her to continue the conversation in English without sounding creepy. He loved to listen to Australian women on the television. He decided there was no way to do this that didn't end with a drink in his face. He had to play this cool.

"What do you do here that keeps you in the city against your will?" she asked, reaching for her drink on the bar.

"I'm a scientist. More of a biologist, actually."

Her eyes lit up for a moment, which he took as a good sign. He had considered adding his title and function at Vektor, or completely lying to her about what he did in Novosibirsk. Instead, he went with the truth for once, and it seemed to pay off.

"I studied biology for a year before switching to journalism. I loved the basic biology courses, but chemistry turned out to be a problem for me. I should have seen that coming," she said.

"You probably had a much better university experience with a journalism concentration. Biology kept me locked up inside the academic buildings. Not much of a social life, I'm afraid," he said, trying not to throw back his entire martini in one gulp.

"And here you are in your favorite city?" she said, teasing him.

He was starting to feel a little connection with her. Maybe she could tell that he wasn't like the rest of the crowd packed into the club. Not many molecular biologists dancing to painfully outdated '80s music on the dance floor in front of them.

"Exactly. I suppose it's not so bad, but it's nothing like Saint Petersburg," he said.

"Do you think I should make the trip out to see it? The Trans-Siberian ends in Moscow, but it seems such a waste to miss Saint Petersburg."

"You absolutely must make the trip. This may seem forward, but I would consider joining you for the journey. I spent seven years in Saint Petersburg and could be your tour guide. It's the most fascinating of all Russian cities. You can't miss it under any circumstances."

"How can I turn down an offer like that?" she said excitedly in Australian-accented English. "Sorry. I have a tendency to switch to English when I'm drinking. This is a strong drink," she said, switching back to Russian.

"Pretty much straight vodka. A little more civilized than the traditional Russian method of drinking vodka," he said, in his best English.

"You speak English? That will make things easier. I can feel this going right to my head. I don't know how you all pound shot after shot of vodka. Cheers," she said, raising her glass.

Pyotr downed his drink and watched her do the same. He could listen to her talk all night in that accent. This had worked out perfectly so far, but he still had his work cut out for him. He had so many angles to pursue. A trip on the Trans-Siberian with her to Moscow and eventually Saint Petersburg was the grand prize, guaranteed to result in multiple sexual encounters in grand fashion. He might have to play it really cool tonight and sacrifice the more immediate opportunity in order to achieve that long-term goal. A hasty sexual encounter tonight could lead to an awkward situation, dissolving his invitation to accompany her on the train. He was getting ahead of himself and overthinking the entire situation. He had a tendency to do this, and it often resulted in disaster. He wouldn't make that mistake with this young lady. He'd go with the flow on this one. The flow of alcohol to be precise, which he would facilitate.

"Two shots of vodka. The good stuff," he said to the bartender, who barely acknowledged him.

"I don't know about shots. Straight drinks hit me hard," she said, still smiling.

"One shot to toast your arrival in Novosibirsk. It's a tradition. When you drink vodka quickly, it doesn't hit you as hard. That's how we can drink so much," he said, not sure if that made any sense.

"I suppose one shot won't kill me. This is really exciting," she said.

Four vodka shots later, they departed the club for his apartment, swaying arm in arm down the chilly street. He had decided to hedge his bet on the train trip and take what he could get up front. She'd become extremely "friendly" after the second shot, resting her hand permanently on his leg and eventually holding his hand with the other. All of this could change tomorrow, when the effects of the vodka wore off and she was faced with the choice of spending the next four or five days on a train with a virtual stranger or slipping quietly out of town to continue her journey alone. Alcohol had a wonderful way of making even the most impractical suggestions or plans sound feasible for a limited period of time.

They walked for about fifteen minutes, stopping to kiss and grope each other in the shadows at random intervals along the way. When they turned onto Planovaya Street, he could see his apartment building in the distance, situated above a pleasant bakery and café. He would bring Katie some coffee and pastries in the morning. They crossed the well-lit intersection, dodging the odd car still negotiating Novosibirsk at one-thirty in the morning.

By the time they reached the door to his apartment building, he suddenly realized that Katie was supporting much of his weight. He felt dizzy, almost like he was floating. Finding the keys to the building seemed nearly impossible, though he managed to produce them. Katie helped him open the door, and they somehow made it up the stairs to the third floor. He tried to think back and count the number of shots they drank at the nightclub, but his memory was hazy. He couldn't remember the name of the last club they left. He must have overdone it at some point, which was a real shame.

He raised his watch to his face in an exaggerated manner, straining to read the dial. Placing his wrist against his nose, he was able to make sense of the watch's hands. One-thirty? He must have gotten carried away with shots. He vaguely remembered doing vodka shots with this woman. Her name slipped away as they stumbled into his apartment. Was he even in his own apartment? He tried to focus on his surroundings, but the hazy blur worsened until it darkened completely.

❧❦

Erin Foley lowered Pyotr to the ground and closed the apartment door, ensuring that it remained unlocked. She leaned over the young scientist and shook him a few times to be sure that he was unconscious. He didn't stir. Her timing had been nearly perfect. She had ordered a final round of vodka shots after he excused himself to use the bathroom, spiking his drink with gamma-Hydroxybutyric acid (GHB). The date-rape drug typically took hold within fifteen to twenty minutes after ingestion, leaving her with time to maneuver him down the street to his apartment without raising any suspicions.

He left the club without protest, clearly energized by the prospect of what she had been advertising for the past hour. It hit him right after they turned onto his street. She noticed the glassy eyes before he started losing motor control, which gave her enough advanced warning to hasten their arrival. Ivan had made it clear that it was her job to get him into the apartment. After the stunt she pulled in the car, she didn't expect any help from the *bratva*, and lugging Pyotr up two flights of stairs after five strong drinks would have been a chore in high heels.

Before exploring any further, she removed her cell phone and placed a quick call.

"He's out," she said, receiving a gruff acknowledgement.

Erin started searching in the most obvious place, removing Pyotr's wallet and thumbing through the various compartments. Nothing. She glanced around the living room, not finding what she was looking for in the open. Further observation suggested that she should start her search in the bedroom. Pyotr's apartment was immaculate and orderly, with nothing out of place on the dining room table or kitchen counter. Even the magazines were neatly stacked on the small coffee table in front of his couch. She could envision him entering the apartment at the end of a long day at the lab, and despite his exhaustion, still straining to keep his surroundings in order.

She strode across the well-appointed room toward the doorway leading into the bedroom, flipping on the light. She found his private chambers in the same condition. Pristine and organized, bed covers pulled tight and an extra blanket folded near the foot of the bed. She took a few steps into the room and spied a long mahogany dresser with a perfectly centered black valet box sitting on top. She made her way to the dresser, reaching for the top center drawer instead of the more obvious box. Inside the drawer, she found several pairs of neatly arranged socks, separated into two sides. Casual socks on the left, formal black pairs on the right. She saw something jammed between the stacks and reached down to retrieve the grand prize. She stared at the thick plastic card for a moment, grinning.

"Roskov, Pyotr. Clearance Level 4. Vektor Laboratories," she repeated.

The white card was attached to a lanyard by a small clip that penetrated a small hole punched into the plastic at the top of the identification card. The front of the card displayed a picture of Pyotr, along with the basic information she had just uttered. The back contained the words, "THIS SIDE FOR ACCESS." The back of the card was imbedded with a biometric microchip that verified Roskov's identity and security clearance, granting him mostly unlimited access to Vektor Labs, including Farrington's target building. The security clearance system at Vektor operated on a layered principle. Since Roskov worked in Building Six, the most secure location within the Vektor Laboratories compound, his security card granted him nearly unfettered access to the entire area.

She heard the apartment door open and stepped back into the main room. Two men stood inside the apartment. Ivan and the guy she had disabled in the back seat of the car. Without moving her head, she instinctually took note of the rack of knives next to the stainless-steel sink. Logic and training told her that she was in no danger at the moment, but once Farrington's team departed the warehouse, en route to Vektor, all bets were off. If either of these men harbored a grudge, they might make a move against her at that point. She hoped to be long clear of Novosibirsk by then.

She held out Pyotr Roskov's identification card to Ivan, who calmly took it and placed it in a pocket on his black leather jacket.

"How long?" she said.

"Three to four hours. You need to stay here with Mr. Roskov. The dose we provided was a small one for someone his size. He should be dead to the world for at least ten hours, but you never know. If he wakes up and finds his security card gone before we replace it, this whole plan is fucked," Ivan said.

As much as she didn't want to sit around this apartment, she couldn't argue with Ivan's logic. In fact, she had been impressed with their plan from the beginning, even if she could barely stand to be around them. Surreptitiously acquiring a high-level security card from Vektor presented several opportunities to explore. The team's electronics tech, "Misha," working alongside the *bratva's* best credit card forgery people, would reproduce Roskov's identification card with one major modification.

The new card's biometric chip would transmit a simple Trojan horse virus deep into Vektor's automated digital security system, providing Misha with a customized "backdoor" to access the system. Most biometric chips used in point-of-access security systems utilized passive authentication protocols, where the chip is simply read by the scanning device. Most of the security focus is placed on encrypting the chip, leaving the point of interface vulnerable to active data transmission from a modified microchip.

When Roskov held his new card up to one of the secure access terminals, the microchip would actively transmit the virus during the negotiated scan of the chip's stored biometric data. Misha hoped to transmit the entire virus in one transaction, but had designed the replacement chip with the capability to stop and start, monitoring its own progress to ensure all of the data found its way into the system.

Ivan's partner placed a small duffel bag on the ground and pushed it toward her with his foot.

"Everything you need," Ivan said, nodding at the bag.

"All right," she said, making no move to retrieve the bag in front of them.

She had no reason to intentionally place herself within striking distance of either man. Ivan cracked a faint grin, which under any other circumstance could be interpreted as bizarrely creepy. He had a disturbingly calm, unaffected look plastered on his face most of the time. Smiling was not one of Ivan's practiced facial expressions, and the result was unnerving.

"When we're done here, I want to learn how you did that trick with my hand," he said.

"Takes a lot of practice," she said.

"We'll have time," he said, flattening his grin.

"In that case, it's a date."

She caught both of them looking at the bag again, which was supposed to contain a portable mask system to deliver an aerosolized anesthetic in the unlikely event that Roskov roused from his deep, artificial slumber before they arrived with the replacement card. A few hits of sevoflurane, a general anesthetic, would render him unconscious again for a short period of time. She could continue to safely deliver sevoflurane in small doses until she could leave the apartment.

"All right. I give up. What's in the bag?"

"The anesthesia and a special kit. We can't have him suspicious," Ivan said, now fully grinning.

"Kit?"

"It should be self-explanatory. We'll leave you to take care of the scene," he said, signaling for the other man to leave.

She didn't like the way this sounded. When Ivan closed the door, she threw the deadbolt and cautiously retrieved the bag, placing it on the kitchen counter. She fought away all of her irrational fears about what might be waiting for her in the bag. It made little sense for them to hurt her at this point in the operation, especially at this exact moment in Roskov's apartment. She was a phone call away from the very hasty arrival of her own teammates, who had followed her to the apartment from a distance. Grudgingly, she opened the bag and started to remove the contents.

The mask and connected aerosolizing unit was intact and ready for use. A portable battery unit had been provided to ensure continuous uninterrupted power in the unlikely event that Roskov's bed wasn't near an electrical outlet. Nothing unexpected so far. She delicately lifted a large zip-lock bag out of the duffel and examined the contents, shaking her head in disgust. Now she knew why they were smiling. Ivan and his friends had been busy in the car while she worked Roskov in the club. Unfortunately, they appeared to have enjoyed themselves more than she cared to imagine. She had to hand it to Viktor's people. They were excruciatingly thorough and took a perversely twisted pride in their work.

Chapter 34

10:45 AM
Planovaya Street
Novosibirsk, Russian Federation

Pyotr Roskov slowly tried to open one of his eyes, which stayed mostly shut in protest of the sunlight pouring into his bedroom. A pounding headache and waves of nausea rippled through him simultaneously, driving his simple desire to get out of bed. He desperately needed water and aspirin, but his body wasn't responding very well to commands. He lay there for several minutes in agony, wondering what had happened to him. He vaguely remembered meeting a woman at a nightclub. An Australian woman he seemed to recall, but details were hazy beyond that. He certainly didn't remember the trip back to his apartment.

The lack of memory disturbed him. He'd never blacked out from drinking before, despite some serious partying at university. His hangover felt different, worse than before, causing him to question the night's events. Had he been drugged? Robbed? Shit. Now it made sense. He had finally been taken for a sucker by a con artist. The thought of being duped angered him enough to turn his head and stare at his alarm clock. He was normally in the lab by now, enjoying the weekend tranquility of an abandoned facility. He wondered what they took. He let this thought linger for a few moments before sitting up suddenly and sending a shockwave through his skull.

He focused his blurry vision on the top dresser drawer, which was closed. He was well paid by Russian standards, but far from wealthy. He could think of several dozen better targets than himself in that nightclub.

Regulars that would be easy to target. Maybe the thief was after something different. He struggled out of bed, feeling a little more connected to his body. He was naked, which was unusual. He typically slept in shorts and a T-shirt. He didn't want to think of what they might have done with him while he was passed out. The pictures that might surface in an email...further blackmail opportunity.

His feet found the floor, and he walked unsteadily to the dresser. Upon hesitantly sliding the top drawer open, he stared inside for a moment, not immediately finding his Vektor security card. Aside from money and some second-rate jewelry, his security card was the only other thing worth stealing. He dug between the two rows of socks and felt the plastic card. He removed it from the drawer and examined the card, half-expecting to find a low-quality fake with a picture of Lenin. Nothing was wrong with his card.

Now he felt foolish. He was clearly not as important as he'd momentarily thought. They'd apparently just taken what little money he kept on hand, along with a few watches and an heirloom ring from his grandmother. He opened his valet box, shocked that it hadn't been emptied of these petty valuables. Now he was intrigued. Had he just drank too much, while enjoying the company of a beautiful woman? It was almost more plausible to believe that he had been the victim of a plot to steal a deadly flu strain from his laboratory.

He turned toward the bed with the full intention of going back to sleep, when he saw a littered mess on the rough hardwood floor in front of the nightstand. He walked a little closer, to allow his eyes to better focus on the incongruous untidiness. He couldn't believe his eyes. Now he really felt like an idiot. An idiot for drinking enough to stay passed out long enough for that Australian beauty to leave on her own accord after such a passionately crazy night. He wondered if she was waiting downstairs in the small café. He must have mentioned that place at some point during their sexual tryst. She had probably just gone downstairs to recharge herself for more.

What a shame he had blacked out. He counted three used condoms and their associated wrappers tossed on the floor with the casual abandon of lovers that couldn't be bothered with proper waste disposal procedures. The thought energized him enough to consider an alternative to sleeping off his hangover. He was torn between cleaning up the mess and rushing downstairs to search for this incredible woman. The mess could wait, he supposed, though he had been extremely lucky to have avoided stepping on one of the condoms in his bare feet. He'd better tidy up this mess. Used condoms would be the last thing she would want to see when they returned.

Five minutes later, bleary eyed and still a little wobbly, he sat alone in the café with a hot coffee and a tiny glass of water, waiting for an order of blini. He'd clearly taken too long to wake from his drunken stupor and she'd left. The middle-aged woman behind the counter held up under interrogation, swearing that no foreigners had been in the café this morning.

He rubbed his stubble-covered chin and contemplated the day. He'd shower off and head to Vektor. He didn't want to waste the day lamenting over his loss, eventually wandering the city like a lost puppy in search of its owner. No. He'd bury himself in work for several hours, emerging for dinner. After that, he'd count down the hours until Diesel opened and he could claim his usual perch near the dance floor. Based on the mess he had found on the bedroom floor, he felt that his chances of seeing her again were better than average.

Chapter 35

Richard Farrington joined Grisha near a bank of flat-screen computer monitors mounted to a thick wooden table nestled into the far corner of the warehouse. Three forty-watt bulbs dangled precariously from wires nailed to the ceiling's vaulted beams. The Solntsevskaya Bratva didn't have to worry about building codes or surprise inspections, so everything added to the warehouse beyond the foundational structure looked half-finished and ready to collapse at any moment.

Despite the complete lack of creature comforts, he could hardly complain. From an operational standpoint, Viktor had arranged everything they needed to this point. Detailed surveillance of Pyotr Roskov and Vektor, state-of-the-art electronics and computer gear, suitable modern weapons, and working vehicles. Everything at their immediate disposal with no questions asked. He had even provided the team with Russian internal passports, in the unlikely event that one of them was pulled over and questioned while moving around the city. The *bratva* may be a veritable rogue's gallery of despicable human beings, but they were extraordinarily thorough and discreet, something he hadn't expected from street criminals. Based on what he had seen so far, he could understand why the Solntsevskaya mafiya dominated the international organized crime scene. They were organized, disciplined and skilled, a combination he could appreciate.

"Has he swiped the card?" Farrington asked.

Grisha turned his head to reply. At first glance in the dim lighting, he didn't look very different from the men guarding the warehouse complex, giving Farrington pause. He'd made it clear to Viktor that he didn't want any of the *bratva* foot soldiers in their makeshift operations center, unless specifically requested. Grisha could pass for a Russian without a question, which made Farrington feel slightly inferior on a mission deep into enemy territory.

Farrington's straight British lineage was only slightly tempered by traceable Scandinavian roots from his mother's side of the family near western Lancashire. This combination of genes provided him with little natural Slavic camouflage beyond white skin and brown hair. He felt exposed on the streets posing as a Russian. A feeling not likely to be shared by the rest of the team, except for their sniper, Jared Hoffman, a descendant of German Jews. At least Hoffman looked European, which helped his case. Farrington basically resembled an American when he wasn't wearing his cheek implants.

"He swiped it once at the main gate, but only half of the file uploaded," Viktor grumbled.

"Everything's fine," Misha said. "The biometric scanner is faster than I expected. High end shit."

Farrington didn't like the sound of that. Information provided by Berg's contact in the FSB confirmed the addition of low-tech security solutions in 2003, when responsibility for Vektor's security was put in private hands. They had assumed that internal security upgrades would follow suit. Had they made some bad assumptions? Sensing his hesitation, Misha continued to explain.

"Mr. Roskov will pass through at least eight more security points on his way to Building Six. I can't imagine any scenario in which the remaining kilobytes of virus won't be transferred…except for one."

"What?" Grisha said, clearly taken off guard.

"If he decides to turn his car around and head back into town to find the elusive Ms. Reynolds," he said, pointing his thumb in the general direction of the cots where Erin Foley was sleeping, "we're shit out of luck."

Grisha's earpiece crackled.

"Surveillance team is returning to base. I'll notify the front gate," Grisha said, "unless you need me here."

"I'll notify the gate," Farrington said, switching to a whisper. "Let me know if anything goes wrong. I'd hate to think we grabbed the card for nothing."

"I heard that. I'll be inside their system before you walk out that door," Misha said.

"I hope so, or I'm going to stuff you in a DHL package and overnight you as a low-tech version of your Trojan horse virus," Farrington said.

"Why do I believe him?" Misha said.

"Because I think he'd actually try it as a last resort," Grisha said.

"I'll be right back," Farrington said.

"Hold on. Hold on," Misha said. "Virus uploaded. He just accessed the main entrance. Look at this. My little baby is already going to work. Three. Two. One."

The screen to the far right changed to an internal Vektor Laboratories screen.

"Administrator access to Vektor Laboratories' security system," Misha said, raising his hand above his head.

Farrington stared at the hand for a few seconds before winking at Grisha and walking away.

"You're really going to leave me hanging like that? Brutal," he said, lowering the hand.

"Excellent work, Misha. Does that make you feel more appreciated?" Farrington said, already halfway across the warehouse floor.

"As a matter of fact, it does, though I could do without the sarcasm."

"File a complaint!" Farrington called back.

"Sorry, Erin, Katie…whoever you are right now," Farrington said, catching her peeking out of her sleeping bag.

"Please tell me that I touched used condoms last night for a reason," she said.

"I really don't know how to respond to that, but if you're wondering about the security card, the virus uploaded smoothly. We're in business."

"I can't get the image of those three steaming up the car windows out of my head. I'm going to need a psych eval when this is done."

"Get in line," he said and disappeared through the door.

Fifteen minutes later, he returned with the rest of the team, locking the door behind them. Grisha had spoken one of their predetermined code words over their communications network, which called for a "private" conversation. Viktor's people had provided their handheld P25 radios, leaving them with no way to ensure that the encryption protocols hadn't been compromised. As Farrington crossed the room, passing two tables stacked with weapons and gear, he raised his thumb. On cue, "Seva," their heavy weapons assault specialist, turned on a portable boom box stereo, which emitted horrible heavy metal music from a local radio station. The entire team stood around Misha at the computer station.

"We have a problem," Grisha said.

"The basement of Building Six is protected by a fingerprint scanner. I can't bypass this security protocol. The system is self-contained and can only be accessed directly at the scanner station. Very secure," Misha said.

"Basement? Reznikov said the bioweapons lab was located on the top floor. Motherfucker. Berg's guy didn't cough up anything about this either," Farrington said.

"Berg's information is pretty detailed, but the most recent update in that file is dated October 2006. They must have moved it into the basement within the past two years," said Sasha, the youngest member of the assault team.

"Damn it. Can we change plans and just blow the building? Cause it to collapse on itself? Burn it up? I know we've been over this, but..." Farrington said.

Seva shook his head. "Reznikov was right. Based on my interpretation of the original schematics, we'd need a Timothy McVeigh-sized explosion to obliterate the building. Even then, I couldn't guarantee they would be out of business. We need to get inside the lab. The best I can do with what we have on hand is hopefully breach the door. It would get us inside."

"And alert every security guard on the property," Farrington said. "We can't fight off ex-special forces and destroy the lab at the same time."

"We can, but—" Grisha started.

"But we'd kill any hope of getting out of Vektor with a head start," Farrington cut in, "if we made it out at all. As it stands, we're not looking at a big margin of time before police units arrive. Once news of the attack hits the police and government airwaves, anyone with a badge and a car will be headed in our direction. We need to come up with a less explosive backup plan."

"Or a finger. Maybe a whole hand," Foley interjected.

Farrington turned his head to stare at her.

"What? We're planning to kill the three scientists running the program. Why not take one of their hands? Or both," she said, chewing on an energy bar.

Misha shook his head. "It's not that simple. The scanner model indicated by security schematics combines a few biometric features. First, it takes an ultrasound picture of the finger and matches it with an internal database. Then, it measures temperature—"

"We can keep the hand at body temperature somehow," Grisha interrupted.

"Right. But this system measures and averages the temperature readings taken for a specific individual since its installation. Our hand donor might have peripheral vascular disease or diabetes, causing a reduction of blood flow to the extremities, or something simple, like the flu. The system accounts for the fact that not everyone's hand is going to average out to 98.6 degrees. Ever shake hands with someone whose hands are always cold?"

"Jared's hands feel like icicles," Foley said, raising a few eyebrows and eliciting a few grins. "Add sexual harassment to my list of complaints."

"She's right. My hands have to be at least five degrees below body core temperature, and I don't have diabetes...as far as I know," said Jared Hoffman—Gosha for this mission.

"We need to do some research into hand temperatures. If you can't find a satisfactory amount of information in the next hour using the internet, I'll call Berg and put him to work on this. I'm sure the CIA has a body of information on the subject of beating biometric scanners. If any doubt remains about the viability of using a detached hand, we'll have to kidnap one of the scientists," Farrington said.

"We don't have the people for that," Grisha said.

"I know. I'll talk to Viktor about adding the service, if necessary. Anything else?" he asked, looking around at the team. When no one responded, he went on. "Very well. We still have a lot of work to do before we step off tomorrow, so don't waste any time. Check and recheck the gear. If we need to replace something, I need to hear it sooner than later. Erin, can you stick around a second?" he said, nodding at Grisha, who left with the rest of the team.

"What's up?" she asked.

"Are you sure you're all right with the mission timeline? You'll be cutting it close with your flight," Farrington said.

"I'll be fine. If I miss the flight, I know where to find a ride home," Foley said.

"Trust me. You want to be on that flight."

She regarded him for a moment, and he suspected that she might try and argue her case for staying. He didn't need her at Vektor Labs, but the team could always use another capable operative during the exfiltration. She wasn't trained for the kind of combat he anticipated, but she had proven to be a decisive asset in Stockholm. He simply couldn't discount her based on the conditions he expected during their escape. He had other reasons for ensuring her safe departure.

"You have skills our program desperately needs, and from what I understand, you're slated to spend the rest of your career behind a desk in Langley. When you get back to the States, consider taking a long vacation to Argentina," he suggested.

"What makes you think I don't want a cushy desk job in the CIA's Scandinavian section?"

"Just a hunch," he said.

"I'll make the flight."

Chapter 36

1:25 PM
Dzerzhinsky City District
Novosibirsk, Russian Federation

Farrington watched Viktor closely for a reaction to his request. The stolid Russian took a long drag on his cigarette and let the smoke pour through his nose, never changing his expression.

"You do realize it will be Sunday evening? We'll have to do this in their homes," Viktor said.

"I don't see any other way. It's a timing issue for my team. They can't be in two places at once," Farrington said.

"Bullshit," Viktor said, rising from behind his desk in a cloud of smoke. "You need me to do the dirtiest part of your job." Farrington started to protest, but Viktor continued. "I wondered when you would come crawling to me for this. Your people may be super-soldiers, but they're not cut out for street murder and dismemberment."

"I call it targeted killing of enemy personnel. Assassination. You call it street murder. I guess it depends on where you're sitting," Farrington countered.

"It's murder no matter how you look at it, and I don't get the sense that your team is up for dragging people out of their homes in front of their loved ones to kill them. Two million dollars. Final price. You take it or leave it," Viktor said.

Farrington was relieved to hear him make an offer within the range he was immediately authorized to pay. He didn't feel like wasting time debating the distinction between the Solntesvskaya's concept of murder and his own.

He agreed with the basic reality of Viktor's simplistic view that "murder is murder," but differed vastly in his interpretation and justification of killing in the course of executing his duties.

Viktor's people killed to secure the dominance of their organized crime network, employing individuals that embraced murder and violence. Farrington's people killed to safeguard lives, utilizing men and women that had to be convinced and conditioned to kill without question. He was grateful to spare his team the exposure to what would be an extremely unpleasant and morally confusing job, but he wasn't the least bit swayed by Viktor's dime-store comparison.

"There won't be any room for error on this," Farrington said.

"Lucky for you, we've been watching them closely. Do we have a deal?"

"No casualties outside of the scientists," Farrington said.

"I can't promise that, but I can assure you that it is in my best interest to limit the killing to the scientists. See, I knew this wasn't your cup of tea. If this were my operation, I would make it a point to kill everyone present to send a message. How many scientists would be eager to sign up for the same job after learning what happened?"

"I think limiting the damage to the scientists will send the right message. Shall I have the money transferred to the same bank?"

"No negotiation? I should have started at three million. We'll use a different bank this time," Viktor said.

Thirty minutes later, Farrington confirmed the transfer of two million dollars from one of Sanderson's accounts in the Cayman Islands to a bank account number traceable to Switzerland. He suspected that Viktor had made this deal without permission from his superiors. The initial payment to guarantee Solntsevskaya cooperation had been made to a bank in Moscow, where the money had presumably been transferred to one of the world's more discreet banking havens. If Viktor was siphoning money into his own account, it meant that he was violating orders by helping them kill the scientists. This eased Farrington's concerns about trigger-happy Russian mobsters. Viktor couldn't afford the extra scrutiny guaranteed to come with an execution-style family massacre linked to the evening's festivities at Vektor.

Chapter 37

Pamela Travis balanced four plates of hot food using a combination of her hands and arms. She had been working at Benny's for over a decade, never missing a Saturday morning. Saturday mornings, even in the dead of winter, kept the tables packed well past noon, which in turn put good tip money in her pocket. The summers were insane, when vacationers turned up to enjoy the Lake Memphremagog waterfront and boaters drifted down the lake a few miles from Canada to dock in Newport for the afternoon.

Arriving at any time past eight in the morning on a Saturday or Sunday morning guaranteed a minimum one-hour wait for a table. Any later than that and a party of four might be stuck outside for two hours, free to wander Main Street and window shop, but under constant threat of losing their table. Benny's waiting policy was strict. Each party received one announcement followed by a half-minute wait before they moved onto the next name on the waiting list.

Frankly, she wasn't sure why anyone would wait so long for Benny's food or put up with his wait-list shenanigans. The food was standard American breakfast fare, with little variation or panache. She made better corned beef hash at home, in half the time, and her pancakes were gourmet compared to Benny's. She supposed the long lines were more a function of the competitive market than tastiness.

They were the only game in town for breakfast, having dominated the market for as long as any of the locals could remember. Every now and then a Canadian family would stop in, and a misty-eyed mother or father would reminisce about their summer vacations as children, and how they never missed a Saturday breakfast at Benny's, no matter how long they had to wait. It made her wonder if the food up in Canada was bad.

Defying gravity and several equally important laws of physics maneuvering through the crowded diner, she arrived at a cramped table of slightly unpleasant-smelling men. Russians, by the sound of them, probably up from New York City on a fishing trip. She'd heard about large pockets of Russian immigrants living in a place called Brighton Beach, near Brooklyn. A lot of New Yorkers vacationed in the area during the summer, but they typically arrived in July or August. Families from New York or Massachusetts owned a good number of the cottages ringing the lake. Judging by the look of this group, they must be up early to take advantage of cheaper rental prices. They were pleasant enough, but certainly not part of the well-heeled New York crowd.

She had to admit, they were by far her most entertaining group this season. The spokesman for the group, a stocky, muscular gentleman with a long scar running down the right side of his jaw, asked if they served alcohol. She checked her watch and laughed. 6:52 in the morning. She wished they served booze, but Benny was too cheap to seek a liquor license. Acquiring a limited license might have made sense given the number of requests for mimosas during the summer. The New York crowd seemed to be enamored with the idea of champagne and orange juice for breakfast, even during the middle of the week. Another opportunity lost. She'd quit making suggestions long ago.

Upon her arrival, one of the men furtively concealed something under the table. She gave him a slightly disapproving look, followed by a wink. He grinned and brought the flask back to his orange juice, dumping a good portion of the contents into the half-full glass. She had seen the rest of them violate Vermont's liquor laws in a similar manner over the past thirty minutes, but said nothing. Who was she to spoil their vacation?

She offloaded their meals in less than five seconds, announcing that she'd be back with the rest of the order in a minute. The men thanked her in choppy English, nodding happily. As she turned from the table, she caught one of them swigging directly from his flask.

"Discretion, boys," she said over her shoulder, headed back to the kitchen.

Looking back at the table while loading up the rest of their plates, she could see the guy with the scar explaining what she had said to a gathering of approving faces. She couldn't imagine how difficult it would be to arrive in a strange country and try to make a new life. With that thought, she delivered the rest of their food and made sure their coffees were full until they left. She hoped they enjoyed their stay in Vermont. They really looked like a group that could use a vacation.

Chapter 38

Feliks Yeshevskey's car cleared the row of gray apartment buildings towering over Nikolajeva Street, revealing the near impossibility of the task at hand. His mood instantly changed from morose to furiously enraged, led by a string of obscenities that would have offended the Federation Navy's crustiest chief ship petty officers. Desnyans'kyi Park was packed with families enjoying the unseasonably warm Saturday afternoon. Finding their man in this vast sea of trees and picnickers was going to take the rest of the afternoon.

He briefly considered abandoning the search and waiting back at the man's apartment building, but the neighbor directly across the hallway told them that Boris Ilkin liked to take his family out to dinner on Saturdays. They would typically return before sunset, when the common areas between buildings of their apartment block filled with drunks looking for trouble. Feliks dismissed the plan. He didn't have the patience to wait another five hours. It had already taken them most of the day to track down the names and addresses of service tellers that had worked shifts at Kiev Central Station on Tuesday, when Richard Farrington landed and presumably acquired transportation to Russia.

They were dealing with too many presumptions and assumptions in this case. Farrington had entered the Ukraine posing as an Australian, proceeding to vanish into thin air. No record of him beyond customs could be found, leading Feliks to assume that he had shifted identities. Ardankin was convinced that he would try to enter Russia, which made his job slightly less complicated. Transportation to Russia was plentiful on any given day, but the options were finite.

The easiest and most expedient way to enter Russia was by train, but he could also have chosen from several regular bus routes. Worse yet, he could have rented a car from any of the hundreds of rental agency locations around Kiev. They hadn't begun to explore options beyond rail travel yet. He had limited resources and had been specifically warned not to involve Ukrainian authorities. With a handful of agents, they would concentrate on one mode of transportation at a time. His agents were spread throughout the city tracking down the few remaining ticket agents on the list.

He signaled for the driver to pull over into a residential parking space across the street. Turning in his seat, he addressed the timid-looking woman in the back seat.

"We're going to walk through the park looking for your neighbor. I better not find him before you do. Understood?"

She nodded. "Yes."

"This is a matter of state security. When you see him, I need you to be discreet. You'll stand back at a distance, and once we have him in custody, you are free to go. You wait for me to signal that it's all right for you to leave. If you leave earlier, I'll assume you are involved. Are we clear?"

"Yes."

"Very good. Let's go for a walk in the park," he said, stepping out of the vehicle.

Forty minutes into their search, Feliks had lost any remaining vestige of patience for the woman, who pinched her face together and squinted looking for their target like she needed glasses to see more than five feet in front of her. This had become intolerable, made worse by the citizens of Kiev, lounging around on scattered blankets, not making the slightest effort to get out of their way. He was about to kick a bottle of vodka out of a rather insolent-looking man's mouth, hoping to remove most of his teeth with the gesture, when the woman grabbed his shirtsleeve.

"I see him. We almost walked past. He's directly to our right, maybe thirty meters. Dark red blanket with white tassel ends. He's kicking a soccer ball with his son," she whispered.

"White collared shirt. Untucked. Brown pants?"

"Yes. That's him. Can I go now?" she pleaded.

"Not until we verify," Feliks said.

"Why would I lie to you? You know where I live," she said.

"That's right. I know exactly where you live. You wait, or we'll pay you a visit. Maybe smash your husband's skull with that bottle he lives in," Feliks said.

"Promise?"

For the first time today, Feliks allowed his face to change expression, displaying the faintest hint of a smile. He would have preferred to bring her husband, but judging by his belligerent demeanor at the door and the bottle in his hand, the man would have been more trouble than help. Besides, he was probably seeing double at this point, judging from the bright red glow plastered on his face. He had little doubt that Elena would take a beating when she returned. The kids too, probably. He'd like to escort her back and threaten the husband with a life sentence in a wheelchair, but he didn't have the time. She would have to fend for herself. He just hoped that this unusual disruption of their weekend routine didn't lead to something outside of the normal abuse that she and her children surely suffered on a daily basis.

"Wait here," he said, pressing several banknotes into her coat pocket. "Those are for the ride back."

He had given her five times the amount it would cost to take a cab back to their apartment block, hoping she would use the money to seek a little happiness with her kids during the day. He could tell by the look on her husband's face that they saw no peace at night. He signaled for the other agent to proceed, and they walked over to have what he hoped would be a friendly chat with Boris Ilkin. He didn't want to get heavy-handed in front of the Ilkin family in such a serene setting, but he was running out of time. A rogue CIA agent responsible for the recent deaths of several FIS operatives had resurfaced, raising the frightening specter of an even deadlier operation on Russian soil.

"Mr. Ilkin?"

He spoke loudly enough to be heard by the family, hoping to avoid additional unwanted attention from the civilians nearby. He harbored no illusions about appearing to be just another carefree Ukrainian out for an early June stroll. He wore a dark brown suit over a light blue shirt. The absence of a tie was the only concession he allowed in his disguise as a Ukrainian Security Service agent. Since it was Saturday, the sight of two nearby men in suits, with or without ties, broadcast one word: Police. Mr. Ilkin nodded and whispered to his son, patting him on the back. While Ilkin was distracted with his son, Feliks nodded discreetly to the woman waiting behind a tree in the distance.

"Is everything all right?" the man's wife asked.

"I'm sure it's fine, honey," he said, forcing a smile before turning to Feliks and nodding in respect.

"Officers. How can I help you?"

Feliks came closer and produced his fake credentials, holding them low in a useless gesture of discretion. Anyone watching this interaction knew exactly what was happening. Ilkin was being questioned by the police in the middle of Desnyans'kyi Park, right in front of his family. He could feel the stares and whispers. People shrinking away from them slowly. Memories died hard in these former Soviet puppet states, where police and militia were liberally used to repress the people.

"Vadim Salenko. Security Service counterterrorism division. I need your help to identify a foreign operative that may have passed through your ticket station on Thursday," he said.

"Absolutely," Ilkin said, barely glancing at his credentials, "but I don't know how much help I can be. The station serves more than 170,000 passengers every day. It gets crazy in there."

"I'll try to narrow the possibilities for you. We know that the agent initially posed as an Australian tourist and landed in Kiev. I'm fairly certain he is headed to Russia, so I suspect that he presented himself to the ticket gate with a Russian internal passport."

"Sure…" he said, hesitating.

Feliks could tell that he struck a chord. He had run the scenario through his head a thousand times before coming up with the few encounters that might "stick" with a ticket agent that processed hundreds, if not thousands of transactions per day. He was testing one of these theories now.

"I have several photographs I would like to show you."

His partner handed him the file containing several 8X10 photos of Richard Farrington. He started with the photograph taken at the customs station inside Kiev International Airport. He saw a flash of recognition on Ilkin's face.

"You remember him?" Feliks said.

"Oddly enough, I do. He…uh. Let me think for a moment…yes. He presented an international passport, and I remember telling him he could use his internal Federation passport when he reached the customs stop near the border. He apologized, saying that he'd just returned from Europe, which I thought was odd, given his destination."

"Please explain," Feliks said, exhilarated by what he had stumbled upon.

"He was headed to Yekaterinburg. I know for a fact that it's cheaper to fly into Moscow from anywhere west of here. From there you have a wide selection of flights to Yekaterinburg that probably cost less than what he paid to ride the train. I think flying to Yekaterinburg from Kiev is less expensive."

"What are you, some kind of travel agent in disguise?"

"It's part of my job in a way," Ilkin replied.

"Do you remember his name?"

"I don't think I can recall his name. I'm lucky to have remembered him at all. He doesn't look very Russian, does he?" he said, further examining the photo.

"How many trains leave for Yekaterinburg daily?" Feliks said, not in any mood to waste a second with small talk.

"None. The only way to get out there is to connect with an eastbound train out of Moscow. We have nine trains running daily out of Kiev to Moscow. Most leave in the early evening. It's an overnight trip. I don't remember which one I booked him on. There's an express train that leaves daily at 8:52 and arrives in Moscow at 6:30 in the morning. This is the earliest arrival, which would put him in a position to leave on one of the few mid-morning departures. Save him some time if he was in a hurry to get to Yekaterinburg."

"None of this is ringing a bell for you," Feliks said.

Ilkin shook his head.

"How many passengers can the express train carry?"

"Six hundred," he said.

"Trains for Moscow to Yekaterinburg?"

"Fourteen. Roughly the same passenger count."

Feliks didn't respond immediately. His mind was swimming through the options. He didn't have the time to repeat this process again at the Yaroslavlsky Station in Moscow, though he would certainly have the manpower at his disposal. Once inside Russia, the SVR could muster hundreds of agents to assist him...assuming they let him continue as lead investigator, which he doubted.

With the information provided by Ilkin, he didn't think it would be necessary to mobilize half of the headquarters building in Moscow. They didn't have a name, but they knew his final destination. With the passenger manifests for all trains leaving Kiev for Moscow last Tuesday, they could compare passenger names with all trains leaving Moscow for Yekaterinburg on Wednesday. This would significantly narrow their search. Armed with the matching names, they would have a fighting chance of finding Richard Farrington. Of course, all of this was predicated on the assumption that Farrington hadn't switched identities more than once. If he changed identities in Yekaterinburg, they would be left with nothing but the scattered memories of a dozen ticket agents. He doubted they would get this lucky again.

"Do you know the name of the supervisor on duty at the station today?"

"Sure. Mr. Gleba. Stas Gleba. He gives me weekend shifts when I ask, so we can save up for vacation."

"Let's go," he said to his partner, not the least bit interested in hearing about this man's vacation plans.

Walking briskly toward his car, Feliks stared up at the sun and allowed himself a moment to enjoy its warmth. Despite the embarrassment of having a known terrorist enter the motherland through his own backyard, he had to admit that the day had gone well. He had acquired a solid lead on Farrington sooner than expected, without having to break any bones or crack any skulls. Unfortunately, the day was still young, and he wasn't optimistic about the station supervisor. Coughing up passenger manifests for State Security was serious business, and if Mr. Gleba required a warrant or insisted on verifying his request with the State Security watch officer, he wouldn't be able to keep his promise to Ardankin. Too much was at stake to let a hyperextended finger or a broken nose stand in the way.

PART THREE

BLACK FIST

Chapter 39

Dmitry Ardankin could tell by the sheer volume of swear words uttered during the first ten seconds of his one-way conversation with Feliks Yeshevsky that the search for Richard Farrington was not making progress. Impressed with Yeshevsky's results in Kiev, he had flown the cantankerous agent, with a small entourage, to Yekaterinburg to pick up Farrington's trail once they cross-matched passengers from Kiev with the list of Russians continuing to Yekaterinburg. 5,700 passengers had been narrowed to 1,700 male Russian citizens, one of whom was Farrington. Of those 1,700, only twenty-two had purchased transfers to Yekaterinburg. Everything was shaping up nicely, until Yeshevsky started poring through the train manifests.

Fifteen of the passengers came up in the system with Yekaterinburg addresses. Yeshevsky's men, along with a dozen additional agents sent from Moscow, started knocking on doors at 2:00 in the morning. None of the fifteen turned out to be Farrington. While his men turned Yekaterinburg inside out, he painstakingly examined the passenger manifests of every train that Farrington could have taken, and matched all of the remaining passengers, except for one. Mikhail Ivanov.

Since Ivanov's passport had not been swiped by customs at an airport, they would have no convenient photograph to match against Jeffrey Mayer, the Australian tourist recently arrived from Brisbane, Australia. It didn't matter. Ivanov ceased to exist at Yekaterinburg Central Station. His name didn't appear on any of the corresponding outbound train manifests.

Yeshevsky would have to contact all of the ticketing agents and hope for a repeat of yesterday's miracle, then he'd hit the rental car agencies. For all they knew, Farrington's mission objective might be in Yekaterinburg. The Volga-Ural Military District headquarters was located outside of the city at the military base housing the 34th Motor Rifle Division. Somehow he doubted it.

"Feliks, Feliks... please take a deep breath and calm yourself. We need to come up with a new strategy," Ardankin said.

"The new strategy is me interviewing every ticket agent in the hopes that one of them has enough brain cells to understand what I'm saying. We're talking a needle in a fucking haystack here. This guy could be back in Moscow for all we know, having led us on a wild goose chase to fucking nowhere and back. Has Customs come up with any other possible operatives?"

"Nothing yet. I've expanded the data parameters, so we'll have a fresh batch of profiles to run within the hour. The director has given me the authority to increase the number of people working on this. I've called in over a hundred agents and technicians across several directorates. We'll get you something," Ardankin said.

"By the time they stumble across something useful, the Kremlin could be a smoking ruin," Yeshevsky said.

"I'm sure this isn't a plot to blow up Moscow," Ardankin said. "He may be working alone, in which case we might never discover what Farrington was doing here. He's a highly specialized operative. People like this are used for covert assassinations or kidnappings, not the destruction of national landmarks."

Like most of the FIS, Yeshevsky didn't officially know that the Zaslon branch of Directorate S existed. Yeshevsky was similarly unaware of Farrington's involvement in the Zaslon massacre, which is why he chose to downplay the American's possible reasons for being here. The connection would send Yeshevsky into overdrive and more than likely result in the beating deaths of several Russian citizens.

"Whatever he is here for, I've made it my mission to find him," Yeshevsky said.

"That's exactly why I flew you over from Kiev, instead of letting some headquarters agent run the show. If Farrington can be located, you'll be the one to find him. Start tracking down the station employees. I'll notify you if we find anything on our end."

"Understood," Yeshevsky said, followed by a barrage of obscenities directed at someone standing near him at the station.

Ardankin hung up the phone and pondered the day ahead of him. His own Directorate's technicians and analysts were in the process of readying one of the largest operations response centers for the influx of personnel. He'd need everyone under one roof to coordinate the massive data analysis, relying heavily on the other Directorate's talent. Data crunching wasn't one of his strong suits, and everybody knew it. Dmitry Ardankin was head of the "Illegal Intelligence" Directorate because he had spent most of his career overseas or in Europe, running covert operations. Unfortunately, with Farrington's trail cold, it appeared that hardcore data analysis might be their only chance to find another lead.

Chapter 40

Karl Berg sat back in his chair at one of the terminals in the CIA Operations Center and took a deep breath. His stomach had churned mercilessly for the past hour, while they confirmed that everything was in place. Confronted with nothing to do but wait, he found himself fidgeting constantly. Tapping his fingers, moving his legs, even humming old show tunes. Good lives were at stake, and they depended on a gamble he had yet to take. A secretive play he had orchestrated under everyone's noses.

"You all right, Karl?" Audra Bauer said, hovering over him.

Even Audra had no idea what was coming, which pained him. His contingency plan for extracting Sanderson's team could irreparably damage all of their careers. Berg could care less about his own recent meteoric rise through the ranks. He'd gladly trade his new office to safeguard the lives of their operatives, and he knew Audra and Manning felt the same way. He just felt guilty about making such an impactful decision without their knowledge. He might not have to put the plan into action, but he wasn't hopeful. He seriously doubted that Sanderson's crew could get across the border without a little friendly intervention, not with half of the region's military assets chasing them down.

"Yeah, I'm fine. I just hate this waiting game. Foley is a few minutes out. Her assigned time on target is 7:15 PM local time. Seven minutes."

"She'll be fine. She'll be in Mongolian airspace by the time Vektor goes up in flames," Audra said.

"I'm not worried about Foley," Berg said. "Where is Manning? He should be here by now."

"He's with the director at the White House," Bauer said.

"What? When did that change?"

"Less than an hour ago. The president wanted both of them in the Situation Room to keep him apprised."

"More like holding them hostage," Berg said.

He didn't like the sound of this. He could understand the CIA director, but keeping the National Clandestine Service director close at hand and out of the operations center indicated that the president might flip-flop on this mission. With the two highest-ranking members of the CIA in his immediate presence, there would be little room for interpretation of the president's orders. He didn't envy Manning's position in that room.

"That's what they get paid to do," Bauer reminded him, "run interference for us."

"Among other things," Berg mumbled.

"Have you contacted Reznikov?"

"Not until Foley's job is done. He won't tell me his big secret without hearing a prearranged code. We get the code from Viktor after the first phase of Black Fist is complete."

"Reznikov seems really paranoid about this," Bauer said.

"He's been eating lobster Benedict and crème brule for the past few weeks. I've made it clear what he can expect to be served at the alternative location. He has every reason to see Black Fist succeed."

"I know, but something about it doesn't sit right with me."

"Pampering a disturbed asshole like that for the rest of his life doesn't sit well with me either, but this was the easiest way to elicit the details needed for Black Fist."

He neglected to mention that he didn't intend to honor the agreement.

"Mr. Berg," the watch floor coordinator said, "Blackbird is in position. It sounds like they're kicking this off a few minutes early."

He nodded at the young woman and grabbed his headphones. Like most covert operations, they would have limited communications with the team. In this case, the communication would be filtered even further, since the team would communicate directly with General Sanderson under most circumstances. Sanderson had an open voice channel to the CIA Operations Center, which would be monitored by the watch floor supervisor, along with Bauer and himself. Sanderson would pass all relevant or requested information to him over the voice line or transmit lengthier data packets, like pictures or files, via secure internet connection.

The CIA's job was to monitor progress and coordinate assets beyond Sanderson's control. Specifically, they would interpret SIGINT information related to the Russian response to the attack, and most importantly in his view, they would direct the exfiltration package to Sanderson's team.

The White House Situation Room would receive their updates through direct communication by Berg or Bauer to Thomas Manning. Any direct requests from the White House would have to be filtered through Berg to Sanderson, which accomplished two important goals. First, it prevented the White House from attempting to hijack the mission. The last thing any of them needed was for the president to start armchair quarterbacking tactical decisions. Sanderson's team required complete on-the-ground autonomy.

Secondly, it gave the president some distance from the operation. If the mission failed spectacularly, the White House would have a disaster on their hands. Fallout from the mess would be compounded if anyone discovered that the president was calling the shots directly. He wouldn't have much plausible deniability either way, but keeping him off the line was the best damage control move the White House could manage.

He pressed the headset transmit button. "Berg on line. I copy Blackbird is at assigned target," he said, indicating that he was aware of Foley's status.

"Roger. Stand by," the digitally garbled voice announced through his headset. Several seconds later, the voice returned. "Blackjack, this is base. Commence Black Fist."

"This is Blackjack. Commencing Black Fist."

He recognized the voice of the second transmission. Richard Farrington.

Chapter 41

The president glanced at the clock on the wall in his private office, noting the time in Novosibirsk. 7:09 PM. The first phase of the operation would commence in six minutes. He had been told it would be finished quickly, but he wanted to be there to hear it for himself. He would have no dilutions of the truth today. The stakes were far too high. If everything went as planned, the secretary of state would still face an uncomfortable Monday. If the plan went sideways, they could wake up with a low-intensity war on their hands, jeopardizing their hopes of reelection in the fall.

His chief of staff had game-planned this from every angle and remained optimistic that even a total catastrophe today could be spun in their favor. Russia was ultimately responsible for the bioweapons attack a few weeks ago. A covert operation to destroy Russia's current bioweapons program could be sold to the public as a drastic but necessary course of action in light of the devastating potential of True America's attack. He preferred the first option.

His phone buzzed, indicating a call from the Situation Room watch floor. He picked up the phone and listened.

"Mr. President, I have Director Copley on the line."

"Connect us, please," he said and waited a second before continuing. "Director, this is the president."

"Sir, they started Black Fist a few minutes early. Blackbird is moving to eliminate the first targets," the CIA director said.

"We'll be right there," he said, hanging up the phone and moving toward his office door.

"They started early," he said, before Remy could ask.

Jacob Remy shot up from the couch along the far wall, swiping his insulated coffee mug from the end table.

"Nice of them to wait for us," his chief of staff said.

The president simply shook his head, signaling his agreement with Remy's comment.

"After these targets are taken out, I want a private meeting with General Gordon. I need to personally communicate the role of his units in this operation. SOCOM will play absolutely no role on Russian soil, directly or indirectly, no matter how bad it gets for Sanderson's team."

"I'll pull him aside," Remy said.

"Thank you. Shall we see what our friends are up to in Russia?"

Chapter 42

Erin Foley crouched in the dark hallway, oblivious to the smell of garbage and lingering body odor that had nearly overtaken her moments earlier in the stairwell. The apartment building showed signs of neglect and wear from the outside—five stories of chipped paint, bent gutter downspouts and rusted balcony railings—but nothing had prepared her for the stench inside. Exacerbating her already unsettled stomach, she fought the urge to vomit until she arrived at the target apartment and narrowed her focus to the door.

The door handle's locking mechanism turned out to be a basic cylinder design, which was highly vulnerable to picking. Unfortunately, the apartment had one more safeguard. A handheld metal scanner told her she would have to deal with an internal deadbolt two thirds of the way up the door. Finesse would cease to be an option once she finished with the door handle...if she ever got the damn thing open.

She had started the lock-picking process by raking the pins, hoping to catch most of them in the upper housing. No such luck. At least two of the pins dropped back into place. She manipulated one of the pins into place within a few seconds, but the last pin was proving to be a real bitch. Like everything in this building, the lock was showing signs of wear and probably gave the occupants a hassle every time they put their key in the door.

She placed her left ear close to the knob and listened, slowly easing up on the tension wrench inserted in the keyhole. With a little more wiggle room for the lock's cylinder pin, she used the pick to push the final pin into the upper housing. As she moved the pick, she heard a faint click. That was it. She kept the tension on the wrench and slowly turned the doorknob all the way to the right, simultaneously listening for any sudden movements inside the apartment.

Satisfied that her efforts hadn't been detected, she pocketed the tools and removed a small explosives package from one of her cargo pockets. Roughly the size of her thumb, the shaped Semtex charge would impart enough energy inward to pop the door's second lock without destroying the door. The "popper" charge would also temporarily stun anyone in the immediate area behind the door, giving her a slight advantage. The only downside was the noise, which was sure to draw neighbors into the hallway. She placed the charge into the door jamb at the point indicated by the metal scanner and inserted a quick delay fuse. Almost ready.

Foley glanced around to confirm that no witnesses had surreptitiously appeared in the hallway and removed a dark gray ski mask from her other cargo pocket, pulling it over her head. Next, she hastily removed her reversible tan jacket and turned it inside out, sliding it back on to reveal large yellow Cyrillic letters superimposed on the front and back of the black nylon jacket. "FSB" to anyone interested.

She removed a Russian GSH-18 semi-automatic pistol from a concealed holster near the small of her back and attached a black suppressor taken from one of her windbreaker pockets. Gripping the pistol firmly with her right hand, she pulled the fuse with the other and scrambled clear of the door. Three seconds later, the charge detonated, and Foley burst through the door, searching through the smoky haze for targets.

A man stood up from a small table in the kitchen area. She aligned the pistol's tritium sights with his head and fired the weapon, instantly confirming a hit by the dark splatter staining the white cupboards behind him. She shifted her aim to his chest and fired twice, pushing him backward into the crowded kitchen counter. His lifeless body slid to the green linoleum floor, bringing an electric frying pan down onto him and knocking a glass into the sink, shattering it. The spilled grease sizzled as she scanned for the remaining Iranian.

Unable to immediately find her second target, she processed what she knew from her three seconds in the apartment. Two plates filled with food sat on the table, untouched from what she could tell. Glasses of water looked full. Something had been cooking in the frying pan. All of this led her to believe they were a few minutes away from starting dinner. She recognized the man she'd shot from intelligence photos provided by Karl Berg and Viktor's *bratva* surveillance teams. Vahid Mahdavi, the Iranian intelligence operative assigned to watch over Ehsan Naghadi was no longer a threat. So where was the Iranian scientist?

Viktor's teams confirmed that he was in the apartment, which left few options. The apartments were all configured the same—small common area shared with the kitchen and one bedroom with attached bathroom. Her mind had settled on the only possibility before Mahdavi's body hit the floor. Her pistol was already aimed at the open bedroom door situated in the middle of the wall. She walked silently to the left, squeezing through two tattered armchairs and a flimsy wooden coffee table. A full ashtray and several cans of energy drink littered the water-stained tabletop. Her back brushed against the television set, rocking it gently on the stool used as a makeshift entertainment stand. She kept the tritium sights trained two thirds of the way up the door, gradually moving herself to a point along the wall.

She heard some commotion in the hallway outside of the apartment and realized she was running out of time. She had really hoped to catch them together, watching television or playing cards. Whatever two Iranians would do on a Sunday evening in a foreign country. Now she had one of them in the other room, well aware that something was wrong in the apartment. At least she was dealing with the scientist and not a fully trained Iranian intelligence operative. The voices in the hallway grew louder. Time to try a different approach.

"Federal Security Service! Put your hands above your head and walk forward through the bedroom door or we'll use tear gas and high explosives!"

Erin lowered her body into a crouch after issuing her counterfeit warning. She had carefully crafted her words to accomplish two goals. To confuse the Iranian scientist and to buy her more time with the neighbors. The words "Federal Security Service" should be enough to send onlookers scurrying back into their apartments.

Feet scampered in the hallway, as onlookers scrambled to remove themselves from the possible line of fire outside of the apartment. She listened for any signs of movement in the bedroom. Nothing. This was not looking good for her. If Ehsan Nagdhi was armed, she stood a high chance of taking a bullet charging through the doorway. She took a shallow, quivering breath, fighting every natural instinct to walk away from the apartment. Gripping the pistol tightly, Erin pushed aside her hesitation and decided to go in low on the count of three. The wall above her exploded in a maelstrom of drywall dust and shredded wallpaper before she mentally reached two.

The burst caught her by surprise, freezing her in place. There was no mistaking what had just torn through the thin wall separating her from the bedroom. Fearing that the next burst would be placed lower, she lurched forward into the doorway, searching for a target. She found a man kneeling on the floor with his hands in front of his face, pleading in broken, yet animated Russian, which was muted by the ringing in her ears. She fired three rounds in rapid succession through his extended palms. Ehsan Naghadi's brains covered the wall behind him, no longer a threat to the United States.

She stepped forward to confirm the kill, catching sight of a compact submachine gun lying halfway under the bed amidst several spent shell casings. She kicked the weapon into full view and glanced at the bullet hole pattern on the wall by the door. A smirk started to form under her ski mask. He'd fired a twenty-round magazine from a Skorpion submachine gun and missed her, which was a fucking miracle at this range. The pattern showed how lucky she had been. The first round struck midway up the wall, where she would have been if she hadn't decided to crouch, but that wasn't the extent of the miracle.

Rays of light from the other room poked through the scattered pattern of holes, roughly trailing up and to the right. The highest round had hit the wall near the ceiling. He had no idea how to shoot the weapon. If he'd braced the weapon and concentrated the burst where his first round had struck, two or three of the rounds would have gone lower, striking her in the head.

She was definitely meant to be on that airplane tonight. Any ridiculous notions she had about staying behind to help Farrington had been erased. She had depleted all of her luck on a single, deadly burst of fire from a submachine gun and would probably get hit by a car on Zorge Street leaving this shitty apartment building. No. She was done with Russia. Less than fifteen miles away, a confirmed first-class seat departing for Bangkok, Thailand, awaited her. She'd be in the air before Russian authorities put any of the pieces together here, and out of Russian airspace when Farrington's team hit Vektor.

On the way out of the bedroom, something on the dresser next to the door caught her eye. Something familiar. She slowed down long enough to swipe Naghadi's Vektor security card from the top of the lone dresser in the room and pocketed it. No need to point the police in the right direction too quickly. She took a few steps toward the other room before another thought fired through her head, stopping her. She went back to the dresser and opened the three top drawers.

"Jackpot," she whispered.

The leftmost drawer held the rest of their identification papers. Iranian passports, work visas, folded copies of their lease. She jammed the rest into her cargo pockets and sprinted to the front door, glancing in both directions down the hallway. Nobody wanted to catch a stray bullet. Less than a minute later, Foley stepped out of the dark apartment building into a courtyard leading to the street. A few people had wandered off the street and into the courtyard, attracted by the sound of gunfire, but they paid no attention to her as she walked casually by them. She had reversed her jacket inside and removed the ski mask, once again appearing no different than anyone else.

When she reached the street, she turned right and picked up the pace. Her pickup car was nowhere in sight. She continued down Zorge Street, rapidly approaching an intersection with a convenience store and gas station. They had told her to turn right and look for the car, now she was headed toward a high-traffic area. Just as she was about to turn onto a side street and look for a vehicle to hotwire, a car sped up behind her, screeching to a stop. She wheeled around to see Ivan hanging halfway out of the front passenger window yelling, "Where the fuck are you going? Can't you hear the damn sirens?"

Her ears were still ringing from the close-quarters machine-gun fire inside the apartment. She jogged to the car and got in the back seat. The driver drove toward the intersection at a normal speed, cautiously pulling up to the stop sign. A blue-striped, white police car screamed through the intersection, nearly clipping the front of their car. The driver took his time scanning the street for additional police cars before turning left and accelerating out of the neighborhood. As soon as they were clear of the intersection, Ivan turned all the way around in his seat.

"What the fuck happened in there? We heard a machine gun."

"Thanks for coming to help," she said, digging into her backpack on the seat next to her.

"Viktor's orders were clear…and you can apparently take care of yourself," he said, turning back in the seat.

"One of them was in the bedroom when I crashed the door. The scientist. He fired a full mag from a Skorpion at me."

"He must not have known what he was doing," Ivan said.

"That's the only reason you get to enjoy the next twenty minutes with me on the way to the airport," she said, opening a compact mirror to apply makeup.

"Can I report a successful mission? They're eagerly waiting for confirmation," he said.

"Affirmative. Blackbird's targets have been terminated."

Ivan pulled out his radio and made the report. Less than a minute later, the cell phone in her backpack buzzed. She scrambled to open the zippered compartment containing her phone, digging through her passport and money to retrieve it.

"Blackbird," she answered.

"You all right? Sounds like we almost had a problem," Farrington said.

"I'm fine. Ever have a Skorpion fired at you from less than ten feet away?"

"Old or new model?"

"I wasn't aware of a newer model," Foley said.

"You wouldn't be alive if it had been the new one."

"I shouldn't be alive either way."

"Am I sensing a little reluctance?"

"Nothing a few days on the beach in Phuket can't cure. Is my flight still on time?" Foley asked.

"S7 Airlines, Flight 859 is sitting at the terminal. They start boarding in fifty minutes. Better hurry, or they might push you back into coach. I hear you have to pay for your own drinks back there," he said.

"Ha! I haven't paid for a drink since college."

"I bet. All right, Blackbird, we'll catch up with you in Argentina, if you decide to join us," Farrington said.

"You guys are relentless. Good luck tonight. Bring everyone back," she said and disconnected the call.

"To the airport?" Ivan asked. His normally deadpan face turned to a forced grin before breaking into laughter. "Just kidding. See? I have the American sense of humor too."

"Ivan, you're a piece of work. How does someone with your charm and grace get mixed up with these guys?"

They both started laughing.

"See? We both know you're making a joke. Okay. I have more. A whore walks into a bar with a monkey on her shoulder..."

Foley forced a laugh and settled in for the longest twenty-minute car ride of her life, glad she could barely hear the jokes over the ringing in her ears.

Chapter 43

Thomas Manning turned to Director Copley and the president after a brief discussion with Karl Berg.

"They're good. The Iranians no longer pose a threat to homeland security. No collateral damage and a clean getaway."

"But something didn't go as planned. Am I right?" the president asked.

"One of the targets unexpectedly moved to an adjacent room prior to entry and opened fire on our operative. Nothing our operative couldn't handle," Manning said.

"But now we have an escalated situation with the local police," the president stated.

"The police would have been involved no matter what," Manning said. "We had to blow the door to get inside."

"I thought this was supposed to be a covert operation," Remy added.

Manning hated that pretentious little fuck. He took every opportunity available to dig away at the CIA, Department of Defense…pretty much any organization that represented a potential threat to the administration's public image, regardless of the fact that these same groups sacrificed deeply to keep the real United States safe and Remy's precious job secure for another term. Ironically, placating Remy was one of the distasteful tasks necessary to keep the nation secure. The son-of-a-bitch had the ear of the president and could shut down their operation if Manning wasn't careful.

So instead of telling him to shut the fuck up and let the experts run the show, he went in a different direction.

"We had to kill those guys. They represented a future threat to the United States and our allies. The only other option that satisfied our timing issue was to plant a bomb in the apartment and take down half of the building. Everything is fine. Our operative sanitized the apartment of identity documents. It'll take them a while to figure this one out. By then, Vektor's bioweapons lab will be history."

"I hope it takes them more than two hours," the president said, checking his watch, "or your people might have a surprise waiting for them at Vektor."

"We're watching and listening for a response," Manning said.

"Well, watch and listen closely, because if they boost security at Vektor, operation Black Fist is off. I can't risk the consequences of a failed raid at the compound. The fallout from a successful raid will be bad enough, but I'm willing to deal with that shit-storm, because I agree that the Russian bioweapons program has no place in our world. A failed attempt today will shut us out for good. Months or years from now, after Monchegorsk and the threat of a biological attack has faded from public consciousness in Europe and the United States, I won't be in a position to green light plan B. You get one shot at this, and I prefer that it's taken while the international community is primed to turn a blind eye to this transgression of Russian sovereignty. But no shot right now is better than a bad shot. I'm counting on your agency to make the right call."

"Understood, Mr. President. We have no plans to make a mess of things," the director said.

"I don't mind messy, as long as we're the ones controlling the mess," the president shot back. "Gentlemen, I'll be in my office. Please notify me at least five minutes before the next phase….and good work. I don't take their sacrifice lightly."

Manning watched him walk out of the room, immediately flanked by Secret Service agents in the hallway. Remy stayed behind long enough to call General Gordon out of the room. He didn't like the way the president used the word *sacrifice*, like the team had already been written off. He'd have to keep a close eye on the political side of this operation. The Russians had violated the Kazakh border a few months ago in pursuit of Sanderson's operatives, so it was fair to assume that they might not turn back tonight.

With Remy whispering doomsday predictions in his ear all night, the president might lose his nerve at the last minute and abandon Farrington. Manning couldn't stand by quietly and let this scenario unfold. He'd have to come up with something to turn the tide, even if it meant losing his job as the National Clandestine Service's director. He couldn't think of a better way to retire.

Chapter 44

Anatoly Reznikov leaned back in his Adirondack chair and admired the bright orange sun on the eastern horizon. His chair sat perched on a small rise in the northwest corner of the compound's clearing, well removed from the rest of the buildings, but still visible to the ever-prying eyes of his captors. *Not for long*, he mused. This called for a drink, as did every small task at Mountain Glen. He reached inside his down-lined jacket and removed a flask from the front pocket of his flannel shirt, catching the last vestiges of the day's sun on its polished silver surface. He took a long pull, feeling the warm rush spread outward to augment the sun's early morning efforts. He might actually miss the artificial solitude of his mountain confinement.

The distant sound of an ATV motor spoiled that thought and he turned his head to see what his attendants were up to back at the security station. He saw one of the four-wheel noisemakers headed in his direction, which was unusual. He hadn't ordered breakfast yet.

He drained half of the flask, relishing the clean vodka taste, and prepared for the guard's arrival. The hill was steep at one point, and the best he could hope for was an accident that toppled the ATV. He'd seen a few compound guards roll their toys on less challenging terrain in the past few weeks, as the rains abated and the trails dried. They were just as bored as he had become.

He couldn't imagine a life confined to these grounds. Judging by the advanced age of the other inmates, he guessed that this place didn't appeal to the younger crowd. For someone in their forties, like Reznikov, the thought of spending the next thirty to forty years here would drive you to commit suicide. Maybe that's why the guest population appeared to be well into their fifties or sixties. The younger guests either opted out of the deal or eventually killed themselves. Not everyone had a contingency plan like Reznikov.

The buzzing sound of the ATV grew closer, giving him a brief feeling of disappointment that the driver had chosen the shallow approach from the north. No horrible accident today. The olive-drab machine stopped several feet from his chair, sputtering its noise and air pollution in his direction. If he planned to stay here for any length of time, he might recommend that they switch to electric vehicles. Who knew? They might oblige him if he gathered a consensus from the other guests. They'd dragged this chair up the hill specifically upon his request. If only the American taxpayers knew about this place. He turned his head lazily, feeling the effects of the eighty-proof vodka. The guard dismounted the ATV with a satellite phone.

"Phone call, Mr. Reznikov."

"Here?" Reznikov said.

All of his calls had taken place in the security station, where they could monitor and record his every word. This must be the call he had been waiting for.

"You can either drop it off on your way back, or we can pick it up with breakfast. Will you be dining up here?"

"Sure. My usual, thank you," he said, accepting the phone, along with a small note pad and pen.

He hadn't thought of taking breakfast on his private hill. What a marvelous idea. He had to savor the irony of it all. Unemployment was on the rise, families were losing their homes at a record pace, and he got to enjoy a catered breakfast compliments of the same people. He waited for the ATV to disappear before answering.

"So it has begun?"

"The Iranians are dead. We're setting up for phase two," Berg said.

"Most excellent. What a way for Vektor Labs to start the week," Reznikov said.

"I need this call to be as brief as possible. As you can imagine, we're a little busy over here," Berg said.

"Yes. Of course. I believe you have a series of letters and numbers to pass?"

"Are you ready to write this down?" Berg said.

"Go ahead," Reznikov said, staring at the half-submerged blood-red orb to the west.

Berg read the twenty-digit alphanumeric code, and Reznikov repeated it, not bothering to write it down. His mental capacity was twice that of these mental midgets, with their notepads and electronic devices. He'd long ago committed to memory the cipher needed to interpret this alphanumeric code. He processed the cipher and smiled.

"Are we good?" Berg asked.

"Yes. We are very, very good. Here's what you need to know to ensure the complete destruction of Vektor's bioweapons program. The program was relocated to the basement in 2006 in order to accommodate a special directive issued by Putin. At least it was rumored to have been Putin. They needed a way to quickly sanitize the program, leaving no traces. As you've probably guessed, very few people in the government or Vektor know about the program, which is why they keep the number of scientists and staff working on the program to a minimum. They also don't like to leave loose ends, as your people have already experienced. Someone got very nervous in 2006—"

"Because of your disappearance?" Berg interrupted.

"Maybe. Either way, they built the new lab and installed a failsafe, which even fewer people know about."

"But you know about it," Berg said.

"Of course. I make it my business to know these things, which doesn't come cheap."

"Al Qaeda money?"

"I made significant investments with their payments, and they've paid off nicely, wouldn't you say?"

"So, what do we need to do?"

"It works like this. The lab is a negatively pressurized steel container designed to keep airborne viruses and bacteria from escaping. The lab is separated from the first floor of the building by enough concrete and metal to isolate the effects of a truck bomb detonated inside," Reznikov said.

"How is that possible?"

"The lab is vented by twelve immense heat- and pressure-activated shafts that can channel enough of the explosion's expanding force out of the building to prevent a critical failure of the reinforced concrete and steel sheeting structure. The concept has been tested, and it works. The building would still suffer from the seismic effects, but aside from a severe rumble, all would be well throughout the building."

"That's the failsafe? They have a massive bomb built into one of the lab tables or something?"

"No. That would make a mess of things in the lab, but it might not destroy all of the evidence. Only a massive fire could ensure that. The lab is equipped with eight pressurized propane burners, each fed by a 500-pound tank buried outside of the building. When the system is activated, the burners will shoot fire throughout the sealed lab, raising the temperature to fifteen hundred degrees centigrade within five to seven seconds, instantly incinerating everything in the lab. The vents are designed to open at five hundred degrees centigrade, alleviating the pressure caused by the sudden rise in temperature. The system burns for a total of ten seconds. Activating this system will permanently erase the program from the face of the planet."

"How do we activate the system?"

"It's a little tricky, since they obviously don't want a rogue agent or disgruntled scientist destroying the program," Reznikov said, pausing for a laugh that never came. "No sense of humor, huh?"

"I'm a little pressed for time here," Berg said.

"Very well. You'll need two codes, which I will provide. One is entered into a terminal within the lab, the other at a secure terminal within the main security station. I assume your plan involves taking down that station?"

"It does."

"Excellent. You'll find the secure terminal inside a vault within the station. I recommend taking care of the laboratory first, so your team can put as much distance between that building and themselves as possible. I have no idea where the laboratory vents exit the ground, but I know for a fact that you don't want to be anywhere near one of them when the propane system activates."

"Covering your bases?"

"I'm not familiar with that saying," Reznikov said.

"Covering your ass?"

"Ah, yes. I don't want you to deny my retirement to this beautiful resort because of something I omitted."

"Please continue."

"All right. Your team will find the lab terminal in the southeast corner. It's a standalone computer system built into the wall. The screen will remain blank until the code is typed correctly and you press enter. The screen will then activate and prompt you for the code again. Once the code has been entered for the second time, your team can leave the laboratory. This side of the activation process was designed so anyone working in the lab could be used to trigger the system.

"The second terminal is a bit trickier. It is fingerprint coded and can only be accessed by one of the scientists assigned to the bioweapons program or the P4 Containment Lab's director. There is a key slot, so I assume members of certain special response teams could override the system, but for your purposes, you'll need to grab one these people."

"Luckily for you, we haven't killed them yet," Berg said.

"It wouldn't matter. The biometric sensor on this terminal does not read temperatures. You could chop off one of their hands and use it," Reznikov said.

"As it happens, we'll have one of the scientists with us. You neglected to mention that a fingerprint scanner protected the lab. Heat sensitive," Berg said.

"Biometric security is standard procedure for sensitive areas of an infectious disease laboratory. I just assumed that would be understood," Reznikov said.

"Be careful what you assume," Berg said. "It could mean the difference between lobster Benedict for breakfast and moldy bread."

"Do I need to remind you that there might be armed security patrolling the grounds?" Reznikov spat.

"Which finger do we need for the secure terminal?"

"Right index finger. You'll have to enter the code twice and confirm that you want to activate the system. Once confirmed, it cannot be stopped. Thirty seconds later, mission accomplished. Here are the codes," he said.

Once the codes were transferred and confirmed, Berg abruptly hung up, which suited Reznikov just fine. He despised the man, despite the fact that the unsuspecting CIA agent had helped realize one of his longstanding dreams. He might pay Karl Berg a visit in the future, accompanied by some of his new friends.

Reznikov reviewed the deciphered code in his mind and smiled, staring off into the clear blue skies. He'd have to enjoy his last sunset on the hill with drink service from the lodge. A nice dry martini would cap off the evening perfectly, especially when it was paid for by the U.S. government.

Chapter 45

9:15 PM
Oktyabrsky City District
Novosibirsk, Russian Federation

Tatyana Belyakov gently kissed her two children goodnight and tiptoed out of their shared room, closing the door behind her. The kids were tired from a long Sunday running through Sovetsky Park, near the State University, where her husband taught molecular biology. Days spent at the park reminded her of meeting Arkady in Moscow during her undergraduate university studies. Fifteen years later, memories of those carefree years with her future husband were buried, brought briefly to the surface by the sight of students lounging around her husband's campus.

He didn't take them to the university very often, and he'd never brought them to his office, which he claimed was crammed into an unsafe industrial basement area of the Biology and Chemistry building. They lived outside of university-supplied housing and rarely socialized with other members of the faculty; a necessity he stated was necessary to maintain some semblance of work-life balance.

She couldn't complain too much about their situation. His salary and housing allowance gave them the luxury of a small home, which was twice the size of the university-supplied apartments and included a tidy yard and garden. The neighborhood left a little to be desired, but the area was generally safe, something that couldn't be said about many of Novosibirsk's suburbs. They had been here for eight years, never once experiencing a break-in, which was why Tatyana couldn't immediately process the scene that unfolded in front of her as she entered their family room.

Four men with black ski masks and guns blocked all of the exits to the room. One of them held his index finger to his lips and shook his head slowly, aiming a suppressed pistol at her head.

"Ssshhhhh. We wouldn't want to wake up the children," he whispered.

Her legs nearly buckled at the mention of her kids. She held it together and looked at her husband, who looked confused and frightened.

"Andrei and Milena will be fine as long as you don't wake them. They must be tired from a long day playing in the park," he said, a little louder this time.

She felt her world spinning. They knew the children's names and had been following them all day. This wasn't happening to them. Why was her husband just standing there, doing nothing? Saying nothing?

"You can have anything you want here. Please, leave our children alone. We won't say a word of this to anyone," she said.

"The only thing I came to take is your husband. We need to borrow him for a few hours. I'm going to leave a few of my friends to watch over you. Their orders are to kill your children if you try anything stupid, like try to call the police. In about an hour and twenty minutes, my friends will leave and you are free to do whatever you please. Can you manage to behave for eighty minutes?"

"Yes. I promise. Please don't hurt them. Please don't hurt my husband."

"The safety of your children lies solely with you," he said, pointing at her. Don't fuck with me on this. I specifically didn't give them instructions for what to do with you. I'll leave that to their imagination. Dr. Belyakov, it's time to go. You'll need your security card."

Her husband froze in place. "Where are we going?"

"Where's the card?" the man barked, shifting his pistol back to Tatyana.

"Just give him your badge," she said, putting her hands up in a useless gesture.

The man glanced at her husband and started walking toward the hallway leading to the bedrooms.

"Maybe it's in the children's room," the man said.

She reacted instinctively and moved to block him, but one of the other men stepped in and pinned her against the wall, placing the cold barrel of a sawed-off shotgun under her chin.

"No. It's in my car. Don't hurt her," Arkady whispered.

"Arkady, don't mess around with them! Your university badge is in the kitchen," she said.

"You have no idea, do you?" the man said to her, turning to Arkady.

"Start walking, or I'll just fucking kill them and save my men the hassle. I'm sure they have better things to do right now than guard your wife."

"All right, all right. I'm going. I love you, honey. This will all be fine. Y-you'll see," Arkady stuttered, moving toward the man.

"What did we do to deserve this?" she whimpered, as they put a dark canvas bag over her husband's head.

"Trust me. I'm doing you a favor," he said, walking over and putting his face right in front of hers. "Your husband is a very dangerous man. Very bad for the mother Russia," he hissed and walked away.

His breath had reeked of tobacco and rotten meat, almost making her gag. She barely registered what he said about her husband. Whatever he had done, she just wanted all of this to go away. When the men finished handcuffing her husband, they pushed him through the kitchen and out the side door. Several seconds later, she heard car doors shut, and her husband was driven away to whatever fate awaited him. She wondered if this had something to do with his job at the university or the faint suspicion she always harbored that he didn't really work there.

"Take a seat," one of the remaining men said, gesturing toward the couch with a sawed-off shotgun.

She carefully walked to the couch and sat down, trying desperately to make as little sound as possible.

"How about some television?" the other man asked. "You have satellite?"

"I don't know if that's a good idea. Can we just sit here quietly, please?" she offered meekly.

"Turn the television on. Don't you watch shows after the kids go to bed?" he said, pointing a mean-looking pistol at her.

"We usually read books. We have a whole bookcase of them."

"Fuck that. Turn the television on."

She gripped the remote and pointed it at the flat-screen television with shaky hands. Her kids listened to shows at high volume, and the television defaulted to one of the all-day children's channels. Turning the television on could jar them out of their sleep, killing them all. She hesitated.

"Press the button," he insisted.

She hit the red button, and the television came to life. Her fingers furiously pressed the volume button in an attempt to cut off the sound. The volume started high, but died immediately, emitting a single burst of children's mayhem.

"Not this shit. How about some pay-per-view? Do you have the porno channels?"

"No. Just the basic lineup," she said, grateful that they hadn't upgraded their satellite subscription.

She couldn't imagine pornography leading to a good outcome. These guys looked and sounded like ruffians. Probably mafiya. She'd try to find something on network television or some of the Western channels. Anything to keep their minds off killing her children for the next eighty minutes.

Chapter 46

Major Daniel "Boogie" Borelli steadied the helicopter thirty feet above his assigned refueling position, aligning Black Magic "Zero One" with ground-based infrared markers visible to night vision equipment. His flight helmet had been fitted with a Heads Up Display (HUD) integrated L-3 GPNVG-18 (Ground Panoramic Night Vision Goggle) system, giving him a ninety-seven degree field of vision, compared to the traditional forty-degree field offered by dual-tube sets. The HUD integrated L-3 represented a breakthrough in helicopter night-flying technology, merging four separate image intensifier tubes into a wider image and superimposing vital flight information directly into the pilot's field of vision. The system vastly increased his situational awareness outside of the cockpit, which was critical to the dicey approach he currently faced.

FARP "Blacktop" had been situated on a small plateau, concealing the equipment from prying eyes, but exposing them to the violent sweeping winds common across the Kazakhstan steppes. The FARP had been arranged according to the prevailing winds and weather predictions to accommodate landing into the wind. Unfortunately, the winds had not cooperated since they arrived, gusting from the northwest, buffeting them with a nasty crosswind. The three helicopters had plenty of lateral space between them to avoid a collision during one of the wind gusts, but setting this clunky bird down in any crosswind posed a considerable risk.

The designers had traded some of the original airframe's aerodynamic stability for stealth, which gave these helicopters a certain level of unpredictability during the relatively unorthodox flight maneuvers common to Special Operations missions. They had hovered over the site for five minutes, timing the gusts and gauging their comfort level. There was no room for error here. A disaster at this FARP would leave operators stranded. Even the loss of a single helicopter would seriously jeopardize the team's chances of exfiltration. He had no idea what the team's mission might be, but judging from the fact that Washington was willing to send these helicopters anywhere near Russia emphasized the importance of retrieving Blackjack.

A heavy gust swayed the helicopter, breaking his alignment with the IR markers. He fought his urge to overcompensate, instead making dozens of minor adjustments to the cyclic and anti-torque pedals to keep him from drifting horizontally. Once the gust abated and the heavy dust cleared, he repositioned the helicopter over his landing zone and gave his task force the order to land. They should have at least another forty seconds before the next gust.

He eased up on the collective, and the helicopter slowly descended. A member of the Combat Control Team aided the descent by signaling his proximity to the ground. The night vision goggles gave him decent depth perception, and the aircraft's radar altimeter was spot-on accurate, but adding a third, subjective component reduced the chance of mishap to nearly zero. Boogie felt the landing gear settle and locked his controls into place. He stared through the starboard side window past the copilot to confirm that the other helicopters had landed without obvious incident. Everything looked good, and the Combat Control Team hadn't reported a problem.

"Welcome to the middle of fucking nowhere. Let's shut her down," he said into the helicopter's intercom.

As the copilot started to shut down the aircraft, he opened the encrypted frequency used to communicate with SOCCOM.

"Control, this is Black Magic. The package arrived intact at Blacktop, over."

A few seconds passed before the satellite communications system brought the reply.

"This is Control. Copy, Black Magic intact at Blacktop. Radar and electronic surveillance aircraft reports a clean ride. Refuel and stand by to commence run to Holding Area Alpha. Break. Clarified rules of engagement follow. Do not depart Alpha without clearance from Control. Once cleared to depart Alpha, under no circumstances will Black Magic cross the border or engage hostile forces located across the border. If hostile forces cross the border in pursuit of Blackjack or employ weapons to engage Blackjack from across the border, Black Magic will maintain a two-kilometer standoff distance from hostile forces. How copy, over."

"This is Black Magic actual, copy and understand rules of engagement, over," Major Borelli said.

"Control, out."

"What kind of bullshit is that?" asked Captain Graves, his copilot, over the internal circuit.

Before he could answer, his crew chief, Sergeant First Class Papovich, chimed in over the system. "Cover-your-ass bullshit. That's what."

"D.C. does not want to lose one of these helicopters on Russian soil," the major said.

"I get that," Sergeant First Class Papovich said, "but the two-kilometer standoff crap is pure political horseshit. If the Ruskies are in hot pursuit, they'll never open the distance to two kilometers. I wonder if Blackjack is aware of this."

"I'm sure they are. These birds aren't configured for a fight. Blackjack will slip quietly across the border, and we'll extract them without incident. In and out, undetected. That's what we do. That's why they picked us," the major said.

"You don't really believe this is going to be quiet, do you, sir?" Papovich asked.

"Not really. We'll work within my interpretation of the rules, as usual."

"Then I recommend some mental stretching while we wait, sir, because I get the distinct feeling that this mission is going to test the limits of your ability to interpret the ROE."

"You and me both," the major replied.

He raised his night vision goggles and stared out into the sheer darkness. A thin, dark blue line on the western horizon broke the black veil beyond the cockpit, but that was the extent of what his eyes could perceive. He wouldn't be able to see the flurry of human activity around his helicopter for several minutes, as his eyes slowly adjusted to the dark. He sat there and contemplated Papovich's words, wondering just how far he would have to push the limits of his rules of engagement tonight.

Chapter 47

10:38 PM
State Research Center of Virology and Biotechnology (VEKTOR)
Koltsovo, Russian Federation

Jared Hoffman ("Gosha") pointed a suppressed semiautomatic pistol at Arkady Belyakov, contemplating the man's fate. The scientist had given them absolutely no trouble since his handoff from the Solntsevskaya mafiya. In fact, he'd nearly tripped over himself to be helpful up to this point, offering practical advice about approaching the parking lot this late at night. He clearly had no idea that this was a one-way trip for him. Belyakov was on the short list of personnel Reznikov had identified as critical to the bioweapons program. The rest on the list had already been killed by the Solntsevskaya crew. Belyakov was still alive because of the biometric fingerprint scanner in Building Six.

"You're not Russian," Belyakov said in decent English.

"What makes you say that?" Gosha replied, in a seasoned Moscow accent.

"Something," Belyakov answered.

Misha held up a fist from the driver's seat, which was barely visible by the light cast from a distant street lamp.

"Quiet time," Gosha said.

Misha listened for a few moments, then spoke into his headset in clear English. "Copy. We're moving. Black Magic is at the FARP. We're up," he said to Gosha.

"I knew this wasn't an internal operation," the scientist said. "Even the Russians wouldn't use mafiya scum."

Gosha didn't respond. The SUV lurched out of its hiding place in a shadowy corner of the parking lot adjacent to a darkened three-story apartment complex. The town of Koltsovo, on the outskirts of the Vektor complex, had shown few signs of life when they arrived forty-five minutes earlier, shortly after dusk. Koltsovo served mainly as a feeder community for the sprawling scientific facility and a few nearby industrial businesses, but contained few amenities like grocery stores or restaurants. Beyond nine o'clock in the evening, there was very little reason for anyone to be out on the streets, which suited their plan well.

The facility's lights appeared ahead of them, less than a kilometer down the access road leading from the edge of town. Misha used Belyakov's security card to pass through the unmanned vehicle gate and proceeded to the empty parking lot in front of the Virology compound, choosing a space offset to the right of the main entrance. Once they were in place, Misha turned in his seat.

"Dr. Belyakov. You and I are going inside—"

"At 10:40 in the night? They will be highly suspicious. They're probably watching us right now, calling for reinforcements," Belyakov said.

"No. They can't see us here. This is a blind spot for their cameras. We'll approach together. You in front, me in—"

"This won't work. Each person has to swipe a card to gain access to the building. If you try to step inside with me, they'll trigger the alarm and my family will die," Belyakov pleaded.

"I have another card that will work. I just need to get inside without them setting off any alarms. Keep thinking about your family, Dr. Belyakov. If anything goes wrong, they die along with you."

"I understand," Belyakov said.

"All right," Misha said. "Showtime."

"Lower all of the windows," Gosha said.

He wanted unrestricted fields of fire for the short period of time he would be stuck in the car. Once Misha and the scientist were on their way to the entrance, Gosha wrestled his primary weapon from a large duffle bag in the rear compartment and settled into the back seat of the SUV. He rested the suppressed AK-107U in his lap and actively scanned the lighted parking lot for any signs of activity. His orders were to engage and neutralize any security patrols that approached before Misha neutralized the main security station.

෨෯

Vasily Rusnak watched the two men dressed in civilian clothes approach the main entrance and huffed. He didn't recognize either of the men, but that didn't surprise him. He'd worked the overnight shift from the very beginning of his employment at Vektor nearly seven months ago. Nighttime entry to the Virology complex was rare, unless there was a national epidemic or pandemic emergency. They had been extremely busy in April, when rumors of some kind of epidemic in Monchegorsk had kept scientists and government officials running in and out of the building at all hours of the day. All of that had died down by now, leaving him to read books and sleep most of the night. He really hoped this wasn't an emergency.

His hope dwindled when the first card was swiped in the external lobby. He examined the picture that appeared on his security monitor above the man's basic information. Arkady Belyakov. Senior Research Scientist. P4/A. The "A" stood for "all access," which meant that he was important. Vasily quickly matched the face on the camera to the monitor.

"Straighten up," he said to the guard next to him, "This guy's a senior scientist in Building Six. Might be the beginning of a long night."

"Shit. Not again," the other guard said, finishing up a text and pressing send.

The second card swiped eliminated any doubt that they would be in for a series of long nights. Pyotr Roskov. Research Scientist. P4.

Rusnak sighed. "Another P4. We're screwed."

"Should we give the team outside Building Six a heads-up?" the other guard asked, standing up to straighten out his uniform.

"Not yet. Maybe one of them had some kind of brilliant flash of genius that they needed to work on right away. Who the fuck knows with these guys?" he said, taking a second look at Roskov's digital photo.

"This guy needs to update his security picture..." he started to say, before stopping in midsentence.

It wasn't the same man at all. He looked up from the monitor, catching three 9mm armor-piercing projectiles in the face. His body hadn't begun to sway in its chair before his partner's head absorbed a similar burst.

෨෯

Misha turned to Belyakov, keeping his suppressed PP2000 submachine gun trained on the door leading into the main facility from the security station. The senior scientist stared off into the middle distance, his face frozen in place by the unexpected act of violence. He snapped his fingers in front of Belyakov, breaking the trance.

"Have a seat in the waiting area. One wrong move, and you end up like them. Go," he said.

While the scientist scurried to a small seating area to the right, he passed word to the rest of the team through the specialized communication system under his clothing. They had opted to use a modified throat microphone system, which sat lower on the neck than traditional systems and could be worn with a collared shirt or mock turtleneck. The earpiece was affixed to the inside of the ear with a natural resin that could be detached using the right chemicals, but would stay in place and function under water. Best of all, the entire system operated wirelessly, communicating with a transmitter/receiver that could be placed anywhere.

This convenience eliminated the need to run wires through their clothing, which became problematic if they had to shed outfits. The CIA had express-mailed the gear to Viktor when it became apparent that the Solntsevskaya Bratva wasn't familiar with the technology. Based on what Misha had seen, they didn't seem to be big on technology at all. It was clear that they had outsourced the assembly of the computer network he had used in their warehouse. Nobody could answer a single question about it.

Gosha arrived at the door, which he had jammed open with a small backpack. He carried a similar submachine gun under his brown leather jacket, the suppressor visible along his right thigh.

"Can you bring that bag?" Misha said.

Gosha removed the bag, and the door pneumatically hissed behind them. He tossed the backpack over the security counter to Misha, who had just kicked the dead guard out of the chair. He barely caught it, giving him a momentary scare.

"Take it easy with this shit," Misha said.

"Nothing that can break," Gosha replied.

"I'm not worried about it breaking."

While Gosha guarded Belyakov, Misha set about the task of disabling the security systems relevant to their mission. He had already embedded a Trojan horse virus that would allow him to access the full security suite from any computer hooked into Vektor's intranet. He traded the bloodied chair for the one used by the other guard and started typing. Within thirty seconds, he had accessed one of the subdirectories and activated the back-door entry.

He now had complete, unfettered access to every system except for the self-destruct protocol. He started by deactivating the motion- and pressure-activated lights along the triple-layered perimeter fence near the assault team.

"Yuri, this is Misha. You are clear to breach the perimeter fences."

"Roger. Assault team moving."

Next, he proceed in a logical order to disable every security system that could lead to the assault team's detection as they broke into Building Number Five, which was connected to Building Number Six by a windowless, above-ground, reinforced hallway. He was mainly concerned with the motion-activated lights. Lights tripped by the assault team might attract security to the area, where they were sure to discover a broken window. All of the other systems triggered an alert in the main security station, where nobody would see them.

Chapter 48

10:51 PM
State Research Center of Virology and Biotechnology (VEKTOR)
Koltsovo, Russian Federation

Richard Farrington ("Yuri") held the breach in the chain-link fence open for Sevastyan Bazin ("Seva"), the team's demolitions expert. Once Seva had squeezed through, he released the fence and attached gray zip-ties at several points along the cut, pulling them tight and trimming the loose ends. From a distance, the section would look perfectly intact to one of the highly infrequent roving patrols. Up close was a different story, but they didn't plan to be around long enough for that to be a problem. Finished with his handiwork, he turned and located the team through his Russian made PN-9K night vision goggles. They were huddled at the corner of Building Five, scanning the darkness between the inner fence and buildings. He arrived at the corner after a dead sprint and positioned himself behind Grisha, taking a moment to catch his breath.

"Anything?" he whispered.

Grisha shook his head. Farrington leaned over him and examined Building Six. Windowless for the first two of four stories, the target building showed no signs of life through his night vision goggles. The front of the building was attached to the concrete enclosed tunnel that connected it to Building Five. There were no more buildings beyond Building Six. The Virology complex was configured as a series of six connected buildings.

Each consecutive building represented a higher level of security, providing a simple, progressive security arrangement. An employee cleared to work in Building Five could access areas appropriate to their duties anywhere between the main security station and the entrance to the access tunnel leading to Building Six.

Likewise, in order to ultimately reach Building Five, that employee would have to pass through each consecutive building in numeric order, forward or backward. Each building was separated by one of these enclosed tunnels, protected by security card readers. The system kept track of their security card use and verified that no security point was skipped. Employees authorized to work in Building Six had to endure additional security measures.

A manned security station in the lobby of Building Six monitored the entrance to the tunnel, actively granting or denying access. The door leading into the tunnel from Building Five was constructed of bullet-resistant, shatterproof glass surrounded by a thin, reinforced metal frame, allowing the security station to visually verify that only one person stood in the card reader vestibule, without relying on security cameras. The cameras were mainly utilized to match the identity of the security card user with their Vektor profile.

The final measure only compounded their problem. Building Six's security system included a few cutouts from the main security program. Most important, the alarm system was independent, sounding directly at the Vektor Quick Reaction Station (QRS) and alerting mobile patrols via electronic tablet. This added security feature posed a challenge for his team. Misha could disable the cameras and the door, but there was nothing he could do within the security system to hamper the guards' own vision. The sight of armed men huddled outside of the tunnel would guarantee the quick arrival of at least a dozen ex-special forces security contractors, which is why he had been more than happy to include the breathing version of Arkady Belyakov in the most updated plan.

"Misha, confirm that the alarms for Building Five are disabled," he whispered.

"All security features through Building Five have been deactivated, with the exception of the cameras outside of the access hallway."

"Good work. We're accessing Building Five. Send Gosha and Belyakov."

"Understood. Gosha is en route."

Yuri patted Grisha on the back and went to work on the nearest ground-floor window with Seva.

∼✦

Dressed in one of the custom-fitted Vektor security uniforms provided by the mafiya, Gosha peered through the security station's front window into the parking lot, checking for any signs of a roving security patrol. *Bratva* surveillance confirmed that the roving patrols occasionally checked on the main station, peering through the door. If they arrived and found one guard on duty instead of two, they might access the station and investigate, which would put Misha in a tough situation. They had hastily cleaned the walls of obvious bloodstains visible from the door and changed into the Vektor security uniform provided by the mafiya, but the room wouldn't stand up to the most cursory inspection by anyone approaching the security counter.

They had dragged the bodies into the security vault located behind the counter, but there was no way they could adequately clean the sheer volume of blood that had pumped onto the black-and-white checkered linoleum floor behind them without dragging in janitorial gear. They wouldn't be in place at Vektor long enough to justify a tidy wipe down. Any curious security officers that decided to step inside the lobby would join the pile of bodies in the vault.

"Gosha, you're up. I've deactivated all security through Building Five. Press the green button on the access panels to open doors. Do not enter Building Five until Yuri is in position. The security guards in Building Six will be able to see you as soon as you enter."

"Got it," Gosha said, motioning to the scientist with his hand. "Time to earn your family's release, Dr. Belyakov."

"What are you looking for in Building Six?" Belyakov asked.

"Don't worry about that yet. Just keep your mind focused on what will happen to your family if you fuck this up. Get moving."

Gosha followed the scientist across the lobby, pausing to hand his PP2000 to Misha. The security uniform provided no possible way to conceal the compact submachine gun, and main station guards were not issued weapons. Only the Building Six station guards, roving patrols and Quick Reaction force carried weapons.

A few minutes later, Gosha paused in Building Three. "Hold up," he said.

The scientist stopped and slowly turned around, exposing beads of sweat that had formed on his ghostly pale face. The guy looked like he was on the verge of a nervous breakdown.

"All right. Here's how this will work. Another team is waiting for us in a room next to the access panel leading into the Building Six tunnel. The door to that room will be open. As we approach the transparent security door, you focus on the access panel and only the access panel. Do not look at the men in the open door. Understood?"

"Yes," Belyakov replied.

"One of the men will slide a weapon in front of me on the floor. I will kick this into the vestibule with us. If I kick this into the back of your feet, you do not look down."

"Won't the guards see it?" Belyakov asked.

"No. The cameras cannot pan down to the floor, and the door's frame is thick enough along the floor to block their view. Are we good?"

"Yes. You're going to kill them like the others," he stated.

"That's right," Gosha said.

"You're going to kill me too," Belyakov said.

"I'll kill you if you don't follow my directions. When we approach the access panel, you will use your card," he said, handing Belyakov the security card, which was attached to a lanyard.

"They only allow one person through at a time. No exceptions. This won't work," Belyakov protested. "They won't open the door with you in the vestibule."

"Then you and I will have to convince them to make an exception. Stick to the script."

❧❧

Gennady Lyzlov sat up at his station and examined the rightmost computer monitor closely. One of the camera feeds showed two people walking briskly through Building Five's main hallway. He used a computer mouse to take control of the camera and magnified the image, recognizing the scientist immediately. Dr. Arkady Belyakov. The scientist was no stranger to late-night laboratory work, but he usually arrived with one of his colleagues or lab assistants in tow, not a security guard.

"What do you think of this?" he said to his partner, who had already taken notice.

The second guard, sitting in a chair to the right of Lyzlov, leaned forward to check the computer screen.

"Zoom in on the guard," he said.

The image shifted slightly, panning across the guard's face.

"He's definitely not one of the two guards at the main station," the guard said.

"Let's see what they want. Keep your hand near the alarm," Lyzlov said, pointing to a gray button the size of a teacup saucer located to the far right side of the desk.

❧

Gosha kept three feet between himself and Belyakov as they approached the vestibule. He wanted to give Yuri adequate room to slide the unsuppressed PP2000 along the floor between them. The trick would be to kick the weapon hard enough to get it over the vestibule lip. Too hard and he might flip it, which could momentarily expose the black metal submachine gun to the guard station thirty meters beyond the final door. Too soft and it might not make it over, requiring him to shuffle his feet to push it the rest of the way. Either of these scenarios might draw unwanted attention. Eliminating the guards without raising the alarm would require a near perfect confluence of events, which couldn't be forced.

He watched the scientist pass the open doorway on this right, thankful that he didn't panic. As Belyakov opened the vestibule door, Gosha approached the same point in the hallway, sensing movement in his peripheral vision and resisting the same temptation to look. He heard the metallic clatter of the PP2000 slide across the floor directly in his path. Without looking down, he brought his right foot forward in what appeared to be a normal step and connected with the weapon, sending it forward. The PP2000 slid toward the angled lip, slowing down as it rose slightly. It stopped at the top of the lip, perfectly exposed to the guard station, before it dropped into the vestibule. Gosha's earpiece crackled.

"Take the guard on the left first. His hand is closest to the panic button. Guard on the right is armed with the same weapon at your feet, carried in a sling set across his right back. If you can't convince them to open the door, I'll open it for you, but you'll lose any element of surprise."

He nodded slightly. Element of surprise was a stretch of the word in this case, but he understood what Misha meant. Just the simple act of opening the door would occupy one of the seated guard's hands for a fraction of a second. He would need that time to pull this off. If their assessment of Vektor's security was completely accurate, the guards assigned to this station were rotated from the Quick Reaction team.

Before Belyakov could raise his security card to the reader, a voice echoed through the vestibule.

"Good evening, Dr. Belyakov. Sorry to bother you, but I need the security guard to step out of the vestibule."

"Much to my dismay, this gentleman is required to stay in my presence until further notice. We have a situation worse than Monchegorsk, and the director insists that I be guarded at all times. He escorted me from my home," Belyakov started.

Very nice. Right on script. The guard on the right stood up to face them.

"I'm just following orders. Mr. Ivkin was explicit in his directions," Gosha said, invoking the name of Vektor's security director.

"I spoke with Dr. Rodin and Zaslovsky on the way over, and they have escorts as well. They're a few minutes behind us," Belyakov said. "I'm surprised you haven't been notified. This is a bit annoying."

"I'll have to verify this with QRS," said the guard on the right.

"Hold on, officer," Belyakov said, turning to Gosha. "Can't you leave me here? This is a reinforced concrete tunnel, and unlike you, these guards are armed. I think a handoff at this point wouldn't violate Mr. Ivkin's instructions."

"I don't know," Gosha said, "he was really clear about this. I don't want to lose my job."

"What could possibly happen? You can't follow me around the building. You're not cleared beyond this point. They'll buzz the door, and you can watch me safely enter the tunnel. I'll personally call Mr. Ivkin and notify him that you did your job well and that I arrived safely at the lab."

"I suppose that would be all right," Gosha said, putting on a conflicted face.

Belyakov swiped his card across the reader, turning the door handle LED indicator green. He turned to the guards next and pleaded with them. "Officers, please open the door, and I'll call Mr. Ivkin. He shouldn't put you in a position like this. We have a major disaster on our hands, and we don't have time for this kind of miscommunication. Your station should have been notified immediately. It's not this guy's fault."

"All right, but he stays in the vestibule," said the guard on the right.

"That's fine, as long as you call Mr. Ivkin to explain," Gosha said, tensing for the moment the door buzzed.

His earpiece activated.

"Go," was all Misha said to set everything in motion.

Gosha immediately kneeled to retrieve the submachine gun, beating the buzzer by half of a second. While he raised the submachine gun to his shoulder, Belyakov threw the door open and pinned it to the left side of the concrete hallway with his body, clearing Gosha's field of fire. The operative quickly centered the leftmost guard's head in the PP2000's holographic sight and fired a short burst, not waiting to see the result. He had a margin of milliseconds to engage the second guard, which didn't allow him the luxury of confirming the kill. He shifted to the second guard and fired a longer burst center mass, unaware that the guard had managed to retrieve the weapon slung around his back and put it into action.

The first armor-piercing rounds from the guard's hastily fired burst struck the bullet-resistant glass at a shallow angle and deflected into the doorway, striking Gosha in the chest. The brute penetration force of the remaining rounds shattered the glass, chipping the smooth concrete tunnel surface behind it.

Knocked backward into the vestibule by a sledgehammer-like strike to his chest, Gosha lost his balance and hit the door frame with his head, sending a flash of light across his vision. He wasn't exactly sure what had happened to him, but he slid to the floor confident that the two guards were dead, as evidenced through his blurred vision, by the two massive scarlet stains on the wall behind the security station. He lost consciousness as the rest of his team poured through the vestibule, crunching the glass around him.

Farrington followed his team through the vestibule, assessing the situation. The two guards were obviously hit, but their status was unknown. Gosha lay slumped against the vestibule wall, unresponsive to Seva's attempts to revive him. He hadn't seen any blood or gore in the vestibule, which gave him hope that Gosha had only been knocked unconscious somehow. Grisha reached the security counter and reported.

"The guards are dead. I think they were knocked clean of the desk. I don't see any sign of an activated alarm on any of their screens."

"Misha, can you confirm that they didn't hit the alarm?" Farrington said.

"Hold on. I'm reviewing the feed. A couple more seconds…and, we're clear. Neither guard hit the panic button, unless the back wall is one big panic button. Gosha nailed them both."

"Excellent. We're moving to Building Six."

Farrington turned to Seva, who was still working on the downed operative. "How is he?"

"Vitals are fine. He took one hit to the vest," Seva said, knocking on the boron carbide protective plate insert under Gosha's uniform.

"All right. Pick him up and start moving him back to the main security station," Farrington said.

"Got it," Seva said.

"We have a problem," Sasha said.

Farrington turned to face Alexander Filatov ("Sasha"), who nodded at Dr. Belyakov. The scientist stood frozen against the concrete tunnel wall, holding the shattered door open like a statue. His glassy eyes seemed to be focused on the concrete wall beyond Sasha.

"You can let go of the door now. We need to move," Farrington said, stepping forward to grab the scientist.

"Look at his chest," Sasha said.

Farrington examined him closer, now seeing the tight pattern of red dots stitched across his upper torso. He grabbed Belyakov by the right sleeve and pulled him forward to reveal a gore-splattered wall. Five distinct dents in the bloodied concrete indicated where the armor-piercing rounds had stopped after passing cleanly through his body. The scientist collapsed in a rapidly spreading pool of blood that he hadn't noticed when they first burst into the tunnel.

"Motherfucker. Let's get him to the terminal before his body temperature drops! Misha, open the door to Building Six."

He ripped Belyakov's security card from the lanyard hung around his neck and helped Sasha lift the dead weight onto his back. He hustled ahead to join Grisha at the first hermetic door, which slid open at an excruciatingly slow pace. Blood poured out of Belyakov onto the green floor as they waited for it to close, trapping them between two hermetic barriers. Once the outside door sealed, the inner door would slide open, admitting them to the building. Based on the schematics downloaded from the system, they would have to travel the entire length of the building to the furthest door on the right, which led directly to the bioweapons lab entrance. Farrington wasn't overly optimistic about their chances of getting through the biometric station.

"Seva, I need you back here when you're done. We might need the Semtex."

"Got it. I'm halfway to the main security station," Seva replied.

"How bad is it?" Misha asked.

"Doctor Belyakov lost half of his blood from what I can tell," he replied.

"Should I call this in to base?"

"Negative. We'll get the door open. We just might have to wake the entire neighborhood doing it," Farrington said.

Chapter 49

7:54 PM
Foreign Intelligence Service (SVR) Headquarters
Yasanevo Suburb, Moscow, Russian Federation

Dmitry Ardankin sped through the maze of computer stations in the joint operations to reach his desk. He needed to contact the Foreign Intelligence Service director immediately. One of the analysts had discovered something nearly unfathomable to Ardankin while sifting through a batch of digital pictures sent to the SVR by the Federal Customs Service. The batch formed part of their expanded search protocol, which started with all documented Australian visitors and expanded to citizens of the UK and Scandinavian countries. He dialed Director Pushnoy's direct home line and waited.

"You better have something, Dmitry," the director answered.

"I do. You won't fucking believe this. An Australian woman named Katie Reynolds flew into Vladivostok on Sunday and bought a ticket to Moscow on the Trans-Siberian Railway. She's supposedly a travel journalist. We've been running all Australians through the facial recognition software against known military personnel or agents associated with Richard Farrington. We included the young woman, Erin Foley, who disappeared from the American Embassy in Stockholm. One of our operatives in Stockholm was killed with a knife from behind. Everyone here agreed that this wasn't done by the team that hit Reznikov's apartment and—"

"I assume this is going somewhere?"

"Of course, sir. Katie Reynolds' face is an 88% match with Erin Foley's. Two high-profile operatives from the Stockholm disaster are back in Russia, and they might be headed to Moscow," Ardankin said.

"You have no idea where this woman is?" Pushnoy asked.

"I just received facial recognition confirmation. We're trying to piece this together right now," Ardankin said.

"I doubt very much that they are headed to Moscow. The Trans-Siberian stops in Yekaterinburg, the last known destination for the other agent," Pushnoy said.

"But there's nothing critical there. We've analyzed it and have so far come up empty. No high-ranking visits are scheduled, no sensitive installations worth targeting…hold on a second," he said, covering the receiver.

"I'm on with the director!" he yelled, frantically waving away the analyst knocking at his office door.

The lanky man ignored his protest and opened the door, causing Ardankin to stand up from his chair. He'd kill this man with his bare hands for interrupting a call with the director.

"Katie Reynolds boarded a plane headed for Bangkok, Thailand. The flight left Tolmachevo Airport, Novosibirsk at 9:20 local time. One-way ticket. She's gone, sir. The flight will be over Mongolia at this point," the man said, frowning.

"Thank you. Close the door," he ordered. "The news just got worse. I've just been told that Reynolds, aka Erin Foley, left Novosibirsk ninety minutes ago on a one-way flight to Thailand. Whatever they had planned must be finished," Ardankin said.

"Any sign of Farrington?"

"Nothing yet."

"Keep looking. Something tells me he's still around. Start making an assessment of possible targets in Novosibirsk and report to me when you've compiled a list. I may have to bring this higher up the chain of command," Pushnoy said.

"Yes, sir. I'll keep you posted," Ardankin said to an empty line.

He didn't like the sound of this. The only person higher in Pushnoy's chain of command was Putin himself.

☙❧

Pushnoy had figured out the target before he hung up the phone. It all made perfect sense in the context of Farrington's original mission to abduct Reznikov and the recent biological attack in the United States. Ardankin would likely include the site in his list of targets, but he was unlikely to connect the dots. He didn't possess the same information about the site's capabilities. The situation would definitely require a call up his chain of command, which he didn't relish, but first a more practical step.

He opened a secure internet connection to SVR headquarters and searched for a phone number only his private database could provide so quickly. Several options appeared on his screen, and he selected the number with the highest probability for Sunday evening. He put on the headset hanging next to the computer monitor and dialed the number through an encrypted VoIP system that would sanitize all identifiable aspects of the call.

"Hello?" a female voice answered.

"Good evening, Marina. This is an extremely important call for Alexei Ivkin. I need to speak with him immediately," Pushnoy said.

"Hold on," she said, and he heard harsh whispering over the line.

"Who is this?" an angry male voice said. "How did you get this number?"

"Listen to me very closely, Mr. Ivkin, and do not hang up..." Pushnoy said.

"This is an invasion of privacy. Why is your voice garbled?"

"My voice is garbled for the same reason you claim to be on duty at Vektor every other Sunday. To hide something. Now shut the fuck up and listen. I have solid intelligence leading me to believe that Building Six may be the target of a terrorist attack."

"Building Six? Impossible. Nobody can get inside."

"I suggest you make a call or head over there yourself," Pushnoy said.

"If there's a problem, they'll call me. I think you had better identify yourself," Ivkin said.

"I work for an organization powerful enough to know that you're fucking the twenty-five-year-old housekeeper right under your wife's nose. Make the call or I can guarantee a visit from your wife within the next twenty minutes." Pushnoy hung up.

Chapter 50

Misha opened the door to the security lobby just as the phone rang.

"Set him down on one of the couches," he said, returning to the desk.

While Seva set the unconscious operative down on one of the lobby couches, Misha reviewed some basic information about the duty roster and the evening's assigned duress codes. Satisfied that he hadn't missed anything, he picked up the phone.

"Building Six," he said.

"What the fuck are you two doing over there? How long does it take to answer a phone? Never mind. Have you seen Mr. Popov tonight?"

"Mr. Popov" was the trigger word for a series of verbal exchanges confirming that the main security station hadn't been eliminated or taken hostage.

"Mr. Popov is on vacation in Sevastopol. Mr. Mirokin has taken his place."

The combination of "Sevastopol" and "Mr. Mirokin" told the Quick Reaction Station that the speaker on the phone was one of the guards assigned to the post, but there was still the possibility that the speaker was answering questions under duress.

"How long will Mr. Popov be gone?"

"Six days," Misha said.

Six days meant everything was fine. Any other number would lock down Vektor.

"Very well. I'm sending over four men to reinforce security. Two men will stay in the main station. The others will join you."

"What's going on?" Misha said into the phone, mouthing "go" to Seva, who disappeared into the building.

"The security director received unconfirmed intelligence regarding a possible threat to the facility. I'm increasing the number of roving patrols and stationing guards at both the main and pedestrian gates along the access road."

"All right. Maybe we should conduct a sweep of the building," Misha said.

"I'm sending a group to examine the outside. Mr. Ivkin doesn't want anyone to access the building."

"He doesn't trust us?" Misha said, fishing for more information.

"He has no idea what we might be up against. He said this could all be a bunch of bullshit, but he's not taking any chances. The reinforcement team should arrive in about five minutes."

"Got it. I'll notify the idiots at the front station," Misha said.

"Perfect. That will save me a headache."

The call ended, immediately followed by Yuri's voice through his earpiece.

"What are we looking at?"

"Four men arriving in under five minutes. Someone passed unconfirmed intelligence to the security director about a possible threat. Nothing specific, or they would be going ape-shit right now," Misha said.

"We don't have much time. I'm sending Sasha back to help you take care of the Quick Reaction team. Keep it as quiet as possible. Seva, what is your ETA?" Farrington said.

"I'm halfway through Building One."

"We're entering the room with the biometric scanner. If this doesn't work, we'll blow our way inside. One way or the other, the Russian bioweapons program ends tonight. Misha, call this into base. Berg needs to know that the cat might be out of the bag. They need to watch the local military response closely."

"Got it."

Before calling base on his satellite phone, he decided to move Gosha. The lobby was visible from the internal door, and the sight of a guard lying in a heap on one of the couches was sure to cause a problem. While lifting

Gosha off the couch, a thought flashed through his mind. Their SUV had been the only vehicle in the parking lot. On any other night, the vehicle might not get a second glance, but given a possible terrorist threat, it was sure to attract attention. The vehicle had deeply tinted windows protecting the rear compartment from prying eyes, but he couldn't remember if they had left anything suspicious in the passenger compartment. Fuck. He'd have to check it out or move it out of sight if he had time.

He deposited Gosha's limp body on the floor in front of the couch and walked to the front entrance, swiping the dead security guard's access card. The card reader flashed green, and he heard the door mechanisms turn.

"Yuri," Misha said, "I'm headed out to check on our vehicle. I can't remember if we left anything in the passenger compartment that might be a problem. QR is guaranteed to check it out. Sasha. Where are you?"

"I just passed Seva in Building Three at a dead sprint," Sasha replied.

"Shit," Misha muttered, "all of the windows are down."

⁊⟋⟍⟋

Farrington copied Misha's last transmission, but didn't respond. Misha could handle whatever showed up at his doorstep. Right now, he was focused on scrubbing Belyakov's right index finger clean of the blood that had poured down his arms while slung over Sasha's back. He held the finger under Grisha's flashlight, barely satisfied with the job done by a combination of spit and his jacket sleeve.

"Move him over to the scanner," he barked.

Grisha lifted the blood-slicked corpse by the armpits and dragged it to the biometric reader. Farrington followed, keeping the hand raised above the body to prevent blood from pouring over it. Farrington leaned over the body, still holding the hand high, and swiped Belyakov's card, activating the access panel. The screen greeted the deceased scientist and asked that he press his right index finger in the scanner below. Farrington obliged the machine and waited. His hope for a successful mission faltered when the screen flashed, "Access Denied."

"Shit. Access Denied. Misha, do you have any ideas?"

"I'm a little preoccupied at the moment. We have guests," Misha replied.

Grisha kicked the wall next to the machine. "I'd microwave his fucking hand if I thought it would help."

"His peripheral temperature probably dropped like a rock as soon as he was hit. His body did everything it could to preserve the critical organs, which included redirecting blood from the extremities. Fuck!" Farrington said.

"Stick the finger in one of the bullet wounds," Grisha said.

Farrington could hear Seva's footsteps in the hallway outside of the room.

"That might work, but we'll have to clean it again," Farrington said.

"You could stick it in your mouth," Grisha replied.

"To clean it?"

"No. To warm it up."

Farrington stared at Grisha for a moment, unable to come up with any reason why he shouldn't stick Belyakov's index finger in his mouth. He really wanted to come up with one. Without hesitating another moment, he grimaced and inserted the finger in his mouth, fighting back an incredible urge to vomit.

"I hope this works. I don't want this to be one of my last images of you," Grisha said.

Farrington managed to mumble a few obscenities, just before Seva entered the door a few seconds later, out of breath.

"Good thing he didn't suggest sticking it somewhere else," Seva said.

"That might work too," Grisha added.

Farrington removed the finger, spitting in disgust, and placed it against the scanner glass. Nothing happened for a few moments, and Farrington started to shake his head. Suddenly, the screen turned green and flashed, "Access Granted. Welcome back, Dr. Belyakov." He turned to the two operatives.

"Fuck both of you," Farrington said.

"Seva, remove Belyakov's right hand with the hatchet in your pack and deliver it to Misha. We shouldn't be more than a minute or two behind you."

છ~જ

Misha heard Yuri over the net, but was far from celebrating their success with anything beyond a subtle smirk. The Quick Reaction force had pulled into the parking lot earlier than expected, and caught him getting out of the driver's seat of the SUV. They pulled up ten meters away, perpendicular to the SUV, and switched to high beams. He could barely see them as they climbed out of the car. His only confirmation that all four had exited came from the sound of four separate doors slamming shut. He glanced up at the main entrance to Vektor, but saw nothing that gave him any hope that he would survive this encounter. He carried a suppressed pistol behind his back, tucked into his pants, but had no chance of successfully taking down four trained men that he couldn't see. If they asked him to turn around, he was screwed.

"What the fuck are you doing out here? We have a situation. Didn't they call you?" one of the guards demanded.

He had already planned his response. "They did, but I wanted to get something out of my car before this place turned into a madhouse."

"Are you out of your mind? Wait a minute. How did you get a car onto the campus? None of us are allowed to drive inside," the guard said, stepping forward far enough for Misha to see him.

The sight of full body armor, ballistic helmet included, was not an encouraging sight. Neither was the shortened AKS-74U, fitted with a reflex sight, slung across his chest in a ready position. Misha's pistol might buy him enough time to get behind the SUV, but that would be the full extent of its usefulness. He hoped someone was listening to his one-way conversation and had figured out a plan to neutralize the situation quietly. He decided to continue with his ruse, stalling for a miracle.

"All right. It's not my car. My girlfriend works in building one as a lab assistant. That's how I got this job. She wanted to come by. This is her car," Misha said.

"And she's inside? What did you forget, condoms?"

"Nothing ever happens on this shift," Misha said.

"Well, you picked the wrong night for this shit. I'm going to make sure both of you lose your jobs. Get back inside the building."

The lead guard turned and yelled to one of his men, "Call this in, and check out the SUV."

Misha stepped sideways out of the glaring light, careful not to expose his pistol. Now he could see the entire group. One of the guards on the far side of the white four-wheel drive security jeep walked toward the SUV, while the others started walking to the Virology compound entrance. The lead guard stopped and stared at him incredulously.

"Are you going to stand there all night? Let's go. Open the door."

He had stalled the inevitable as long as possible. Where the hell was Sasha? As if on cue, a voice spoke up in his earpiece. "Take the guard talking to you first, then the one by the SUV…on three, two…"

"I'm talking to you!" the guard yelled.

"One," Misha said, reaching behind his back with blinding speed.

The guard failed to react as Misha fired three hollow-point 9mm projectiles at his indignant face. Two of the rounds struck less than a centimeter above the lip of his ballistic helmet, deflecting into the night sky. The third struck the bridge of his nose, dropping him like a rag doll onto the dark pavement. He swung the semi-automatic pistol in the direction of the guard walking toward the SUV and concentrated his fire on a point high on the distant man's torso. As the rounds started to strike his intended target, he was vaguely aware that the other two guards had fallen like the first.

The jacketed hollow-point ammunition in his Russian-made GSh-18 pistol had no chance of penetrating the guard's body armor, so he went with a different strategy. Saturation and shock. The GSh-18's magazines held eighteen rounds, which he used to pummel the man while advancing close enough to deliver a coup de grâce. The guard stumbled backward, trying desperately to remain standing, but unable to withstand the pain and kinetic energy imparted by a maelstrom of copper-lined, lead-core projectiles striking his chest and arms at 1,750 feet per second. Misha reserved the two remaining rounds and calmly approached the downed guard.

"Please. Don't kill me. This is just a job. I have a family. Three kids. Don't do this," the guard sputtered, unable to raise his shattered arms.

Misha considered his words for a brief moment and fired the last two rounds at point blank range into the pavement next to his head. He had no doubt whatsoever that this man would have gutted him if the tables were turned, but there was no reason to execute him. He was unaware of the bioweapons program hidden in the basement of Building Six, and judging by his wounds, he posed no threat to the team. The man stared up at him, unable to respond. Misha kneeled next to the man and rolled him onto his side. He ripped his P25 radio out of its holder on the backside of his ballistic vest and yanked out the coil cord connected to the man's shoulder microphone. He rolled the guard onto his stomach and turned to face the main entrance. Gosha stood in the open doorway, covering the parking lot with Misha's suppressed PP2000. Sasha was running across the pavement, headed in his direction.

"I need the keys. We're almost out of here," Sasha said.

"Where were you?" Misha said.

"Gosha had it under control by the time I arrived. You were in good hands the whole time," Sasha said, catching the keys thrown at him.

Misha jogged to the doorway, anxious to finish the job at Vektor. The suppressed weapons had created an unmistakable racket across the quiet campus, certain to attract any nearby roving patrol.

"Look who's back from the dead," Misha said, punching Gosha in the shoulder.

"Just in time to save your ass. What were you doing out there?" Gosha said.

"Rolling up the windows you left down."

"I didn't have the keys," Gosha replied.

They were interrupted by Seva, who stood at the security counter holding a severed hand at arm's length away from his body.

"Ladies, I don't mean to interrupt, but I have a special delivery," he said, slapping the hand on the counter.

Misha rushed to the counter and grabbed the hand, which felt like a slab of meat in his grip. He handed the P25 radio to Seva, who accepted it reluctantly.

"Press the transmit button to hot mic the system. It'll give us a few minutes of confusion on their end. Just don't give away any operational details while you're transmitting."

"No shit," Seva said.

"Yuri, where are you?" Misha said, heading to the secure vault behind the counter.

"Thirty seconds from your location. Go ahead and activate the system. Get everyone else into the car. Welcome back, Gosha," Yuri said.

"Glad to be back."

❧

Less than five hundred yards away, behind Building Six, a pair of security guards doused their flashlights and crouched.

"You hear that?" one of them said.

"Barely. Sounded like suppressed semi-automatic fire. Definitely something," the guard to his right replied.

He agreed. The gunfight lasted fewer than three seconds, ending with two distinct snaps. He couldn't get a directional bearing, since the sounds were so faint, but there was no doubt in his mind.

"I'm calling it in. Watch our six," he said.

While his partner backed up against the building and turned to face the way they had just come, Mikhail Blok whispered into his shoulder mic.

"Raven's Nest, this is Raven Three-One. I report shots fired in the vicinity of the Virology compound. I say again. Shots fired in the vicinity of the Virology compound."

He waited for several seconds, scanning the darkness over his rifle.

"No reply," he whispered.

"Check the radio," his partner replied.

Blok knew the radio worked. He had tested it with base and the other teams standing in the QRS ready bay. He checked anyway and quickly discovered the problem.

"Motherfucker. Hot mic," he said.

"This is screwed, man. We're too exposed out here," his partner said.

"Hold on a second. You know what I just realized?" he whispered.

"What?"

"The motion lights should have lit us up when we came around the back of the building," he said.

"Fuck. We need to get out of here. Right now."

Blok reactivated his LED flashlight and swept the beam along the perimeter fence thirty meters away.

"What the fuck are you doing? Turn the fucking light off," the other guard hissed.

"I'm looking for a breach. That's why the lights are out."

Bathed in 900 lumens of light, the contrast in color between the chain link material and the plastic zip ties was noticeable to the trained eye. He quickly found the L-shaped pattern in the fence.

"Right there. See the outline of the cut?"

"Yeah. Now turn off the fucking light."

"I need you to verify the breach while I activate the emergency broadcast on this radio," Blok said.

"To hell with the radio. You cover me until I'm back," he said.

"All right," he said and slapped his partner on the back.

The slap catalyzed the guard, who sprinted across the open area and paused at the fence area in question. Blok felt a slight rumble vibrate from the building, which he first mistook for an explosion somewhere on the Vektor campus. The other guard stopped examining the fence and started to sprint back.

What Blok saw next would stay with him for the rest of his life. Yevgeny Gribov disappeared in a thick plume of blue flame that reached forty feet into the sky, instantly super heating the air around him. He could see three more plumes spread out along the back of Building Six in his peripheral vision, but his vision was fixed to the blue shaft of flame that had entombed Gribov less than twenty meters in front of him. Frozen in terror, Blok watched the outline of his body change shape, shrinking and twisting.

Ten seconds later, the blue plume was replaced by a puffy white explosion that launched the incinerated guard's body twenty feet in an arc through the air. As the ash particles floated down around Blok like delicate snowflakes, Gribov's scorched, sizzling remains crashed to the ground less than three meters away, causing him to recoil in terror. His eyes met the hollow, black sockets of Gribov's skull for a brief second, causing him to flee. He hugged the building wall the entire way, not wanting to suffer the same fate as his friend.

❧

Farrington caught sight of the blue plumes from the parking lot, unwilling to leave until he confirmed that the system described by Reznikov had worked. The propane-fueled shafts of fire illuminated the parking lot, bathing them in an eerie cerulean blue glow.

"Holy mother," he muttered, hopping into the front passenger seat.

Sasha had started backing the vehicle as soon as Farrington's feet cleared the pavement, throwing him forward into the glove box.

"Sorry. We need to get out of here. Hang on," Sasha said, turning the SUV sharply in reverse.

The maneuver would have tossed him out of the open door if he hadn't heeded the warning. Instead, he found himself braced against the doorframe, anticipating Sasha's next move. At this point, they needed to move forward as fast as the vehicle would take them. Farrington centered his body on the car seat just in time to avoid whiplash as the SUV lurched forward toward the main gate.

"Guards at the gate!" Sasha yelled.

Everyone reacted at once, extending the barrels of their weapons through the open windows. Farrington reached between his legs and retrieved his PP2000 submachine gun, getting it out of the window in time to join the rest of his team in the slaughter. At a range of fifty meters, Gosha started firing short bursts from the rear passenger side window with his AK-107U assault rifle, scoring immediate hits on the guards. Farrington fired a sustained volley of armor-piercing 9mm projectiles, adding to the carnage as they closed the distance. By the time they pulled to a stop at the motion-activated gate, the three heavily armed security contractors had stopped moving, their bodies contorted in positions of agony along the checkpoint.

"I don't see anyone in pursuit!" Seva yelled from the rear cargo compartment.

"Roger. Head to the first switch-out point."

Sasha lowered the night vision goggles strapped to his head and drove for several seconds before making a sharp left turn onto an unmarked jeep trail fifty meters along the access road. The trail's entrance had been marked earlier that evening with two infrared glow sticks visible only to night vision. They would travel along the dirt path for two kilometers, emptying onto an improvised road south of Vektor, where they would find their first cache of vehicles and equipment. The detour took them away from Koltsovo in an unexpected direction that would hopefully provide enough of a head start to arrive at their second cache undetected.

There were no high fives or "hooyahs" in the black SUV, just the sound of weapons magazines being changed and the quiet resignation that the hardest part of the mission still lay ahead of them.

PART FOUR

BLACK AND BLUE

Chapter 51

Thomas Manning held his breath, waiting for visual confirmation that the bioweapons laboratory had been destroyed. The National Reconnaissance Office had positioned two satellites in geostationary orbit over the area to provide detailed pictures of Vektor. They stared at two muted gray images of the facility on the bank of massive flat-screen monitors. One remained motionless, providing an overview of the Vektor campus, centered on the Virology compound. The second view shifted and magnified at the request of the CIA operations center. Right now, it remained focused on Blackjack's vehicle in the parking lot. The massacred security team nearby was plainly visible to everyone.

"What are they waiting for?" Jacob Remy asked.

The first screen flashed to white momentarily before the infrared image settled back to what they had been watching seconds ago. The new image showed eight white-hot plumes surrounding the Virology compound.

"That," Manning said and turned in his chair to face everyone. "Mr. President, Russia's bioweapons program is officially offline."

"Fantastic work, everyone," the president said. "I hope this closes the book on a nasty chapter in modern human history. Biological weapons have no place in the world, and neither do the people who work to create them."

"This should close that book for a long time, Mr. President," the CIA director said. "With Vektor gone, the Iranians will experience a significant setback in their plans to enhance Iran's biological weapons capability. This was the right call given the attack we suffered last month."

"What are we looking at in terms of a local or regional response?" Remy asked.

Manning pressed a button on the touchscreen computer monitor imbedded in the table, opening the communication channel with CIA operations. He placed his headset on and adjusted the microphone.

"Karl, great work. That comes right from the top. Pass that along to the team when you get a chance. Has NSA picked up any unusual chatter yet?"

"Nothing yet, but I'm worried about one of the reports passed by the team a few minutes ago. One of our operatives intercepted a call meant for the security guards at Building Six, alerting them to a possible terrorist threat. That's why we had a flurry of security activity during their last few minutes at Vektor. The head of security, Alexei Ivkin, apparently received an unconfirmed intelligence report regarding the threat. This can't be a coincidence. Someone figured out what we're doing," Berg said.

"But they were too late."

"Too late to save Vektor, but this doesn't bode well for Blackjack. Whoever called this in isn't connected to the Russian Federal Security Service. Trust me on that. I'm guessing high-level SVR. If they know, you can rest guaranteed that Putin knows. This could get ugly. We need to get Black Magic to the holding area."

"I'll let General Gordon know," Manning said and removed the headphones.

"Is everything all right, Thomas?" the president asked.

"Everything is fine, Mr. President. NSA has not picked up any unusual communications chatter, but it's early. The team is en route to their first checkpoint, where they'll hide the SUV used at Vektor and switch to two cars for the next leg of their journey. It looks like they've made a clean break from the facility," he said, pointing up at the screen.

Both images had zoomed out far enough to encompass the entire Vektor campus and the immediate area surrounding it. Blackjack had just veered off the main road leading to Koltsovo, heading south through the trees, which partially hid the vehicle from the satellite's cameras. In front of the Virology compound, two vehicles pulled up next to the dead security guards and their abandoned jeep. The road leading to the main gate remained empty.

"Maybe we'll get lucky and they'll make a clean break from Russia," the president said.

"It's always possible that they could make it to the border undetected," Manning replied, "but I'm not counting on it. General Gordon, we need to move Black Magic to Holding Area Alpha. If they continue to move undetected, they could be at the border sooner than we expected."

He watched General Gordon's reaction closely. Earlier this morning, Jacob Remy had pulled Gordon out of the Situation Room for a private conversation with the president. Manning knew this because he had excused himself to use the restroom and watched the combatant commander of U.S. Special Operations Command disappear into the president's private office on the other side of the watch floor. This meant one thing to Manning. The president and his chief of staff wanted to privately clarify the rules of engagement for Gordon's helicopters…or modify them.

"I'll notify SOCOM immediately," the general said.

He sensed a slight hesitation in Gordon's response, which might have gone unnoticed under different circumstances. Manning's request flowed through an additional filter in Gordon's mind, which had caused a nearly imperceptible delay. He anticipated a problem if the Russians mobilized significant assets to locate Farrington's team.

Chapter 52

Richard Farrington scanned the road ahead for any signs of trouble. They would travel along this two-lane road through the Sovetskiy City District, at the far southern edge of Novosibirsk. The road connected with Highway M52, which was the most logical escape route out of Novosibirsk, leading south and feeding into several roads that pointed toward the nearby border with Kazakhstan. It would also be the first road that the Russians would scour to find them. Instead, they would cross the highway and continue west a few kilometers to the edge of the Novosibirsk Reservoir, where they would turn north and cross the Ob River at the dam responsible for the reservoir. Their second checkpoint lay several kilometers from the dam, along the northern shores of the reservoir. If they managed to cross the river undetected, they stood a solid chance of surviving the night.

The six operatives had separated into two nondescript, high-performance sedans at the first checkpoint. They traded their limited-range submachine guns for an assortment of compact, modern assault rifles equipped with the latest optics. Rucksacks filled with essential gear, along with weapons and ammunition, had been staged in each car. Each member of the team fulfilled a specific role and their gear had been distributed accordingly.

Farrington's AK-107U was jammed against the door, resting under his right arm, where he could put it into action quickly if necessary. At this point, they were mainly concerned with a local police response, which he hoped they had successfully evaded by heading away from Koltsovo. Crossing the Sovetskiy City District would pose a risk, but most of the district consisted of businesses and housing complexes that supported the two universities situated within a few kilometers of each other. He didn't expect any trouble they couldn't handle.

A lone street lamp appeared in the distance, ahead of the lead car, as his sedan followed a tight curve and emerged from a stretch of tree-lined road. Grisha reported from the car thirty meters ahead.

"Approaching the first roundabout. Looks clear."

"I see it. Take it slow," Farrington said.

Once they cleared the rotary, they had six more kilometers until they reached another rotary on the outskirts of the city district. They would have to be careful after the second rotary. The roads twisted and turned throughout the city district, dead-ending in large apartment building complexes or university parking lots. Driving would be tedious and confusing, requiring several turns to navigate the poorly designed university area before finding the road that would take them across the highway.

His satellite phone activated, bathing the front seat in an orange glow. He retrieved the phone from the center console.

"Blackjack actual," he answered.

"This is Berg. Sanderson wanted me to pass NSA intercepts directly. They caught a high-level transmission emanating from the Koltsovo area. Encryption conventions and codes phrases correlated to known Vympel protocols."

"How long ago?" Farrington asked.

"One minute after Vektor burned. They must have a response team in the area. Watch your back," Berg said.

It made sense. Vympel Spetsnaz units formed the backbone of the Federal Security Service's counter-sabotage capability, tasked to protect key strategic installations across the Russian Federation. Major transportation centers, crucial industrial hubs and nuclear facilities fell under Vympel's protective umbrella. Experts themselves in the art of sabotage and deep-penetration operations, Vympel operatives were among the most highly trained and lethal instruments in the Russian Federation's current inventory.

"We'll be looking over our backs all the way to the border. Any word on Black Magic?" Farrington said.

"They'll arrive at Alpha within three hours and shut down until you're closer to the border. Remember, Black Magic will RTB thirty minutes prior to sunrise. That gives you a little under five hours."

"We won't be posing for pictures along—"

Farrington stopped in mid-sentence. He'd detected something moving fast in his peripheral vision, headed toward the rotary from the right. A car on this road wasn't cause for worry but something had triggered an internal alarm. He peered through the thick row of trees lining the road that dumped into the rotary from Koltsovo, wondering for a brief moment if he hadn't imagined it. At the same time he detected the red glow of the brake lights in front of him, he saw it again, but this time closer to the intersection. His mind interpreted the danger within in instant. A large SUV, driving without headlights, was headed into the rotary at high speed.

⁂

Senior Warrant Officer Grigory Limonov gripped the ceiling handle above the front passenger window as his driver accelerated the UAZ Hunter into the rotary. His detachment of eight men had been woken by a direct alarm activated within Building Six at the Virology compound. All of their beepers sounded at once, triggering a prearranged response that brought all eight men together at the main intersection of Koltsovo within ten minutes. On the way to the rendezvous, he placed two phone calls.

The first call went to Vektor's security director, Alexei Ivkin, who explained the situation. Deadly biological samples had been stolen from Building Six in a sophisticated operation, leaving several guards murdered and the basement of the building destroyed. Guards at Vektor reported seeing a single SUV speeding out of the gate.

He placed the next call to the Federal Security Service's Center for Special Operations. The alarm set off in Vektor had already set things in motion at headquarters, and he was immediately transferred to a surprisingly senior government official. By the time he arrived at the intersection to join the detachment, Vympel Spetzgruppa "Victor Two Three" (V23) had its orders from Moscow: capture or kill the terrorists responsible for the attack. Retrieval of the stolen biological samples had not

293

been mentioned, but was implied within the constructs of the primary order.

Since it was obvious that the terrorists' vehicle had already passed through Koltsovo, he separated the detachment into two groups, sending one north along the road leading to the town of Baryshevo. If the terrorists planned to seek shelter in Russia's third largest city, they would have to pass through Baryshevo. As soon as his operatives sped north, he alerted local authorities in the town, with the hope that they might be able to stop the terrorists. At the worst, they could buy his team some time. By his calculation, the terrorists had a twelve-minute head start.

He'd put his own car on the road leading south, in case the terrorists decided to connect with Highway M52 and flee in that direction. This was the less likely scenario in his mind, but he had to cover both directions without splitting the team too thin. When he first saw a set of headlights appear on the east-west road, heading to the rotary, he had a strong suspicion they had stumbled onto their suspects. As his SUV cleared the line of trees obscuring a clear view of the approaching vehicle, he had a sudden moment of doubt. Guards at Vektor had reported an SUV. This was a sedan.

He grabbed the wheel to yank them out of the way, but spotted a second, nearly identical car emerge from the same direction. Two cars speeding along a back road after 11:00 PM on a Sunday? He turned the wheel into the crash, adjusting the center point of their impact from the sedan's engine block to the front passenger door. He needed to kill or incapacitate everyone in at least one of the cars to give his men a chance to succeed, even if it cost him his own life.

⌘

Farrington dropped the satellite phone and issued a quick warning to the lead car, which he could already tell would be pointless.

"Grisha. Contact right!"

The brake lights disappeared momentarily, giving him the false hope that they might accelerate past the speeding SUV. The rotary had slowed Grisha's vehicle to one third of its original travel speed by that point, making it an easy target. In the orange glow of the single street lamp jutting from the center of the rotary, he helplessly watched the SUV "T-bone" the sedan with horrific results.

The two vehicles plowed into the grassy center of the traffic circle as one mass of warped steel and shattered glass. Misha braked hard and turned left, exposing the car's right side to the wreck, in a semi-controlled slide that ended at the edge of the rotary. Anticipating Misha's maneuver, Farrington had braced his assault rifle against the bottom of the open passenger window, trying to line up the weapon's sights for a shot.

He didn't bother trying to use the ACOG scope, instead opting for the iron sights mounted at a forty-five degree angle along the weapon's rails. He canted the weapon slightly and fired in full automatic mode at the SUV. Gosha's weapon started firing three-round bursts at nearly the same moment.

The AK-107's Balanced Automatics Recoil System performed as advertised, allowing him to keep the weapon well controlled at its cyclic rate of 900 rounds per minute. Within two seconds, Farrington had pumped thirty rounds of 5.45mm ammunition into the SUV, shredding the metal frame and obliterating any remaining glass. He opened the car door and crouched low, sprinting beneath the barrel of Gosha's rifle, which continued to fire controlled bursts of steel at potential targets within the traffic circle.

Farrington reached the rear of the sedan and reloaded his rifle, inserting a fresh thirty-round magazine as he took up a position on the unexposed side of the vehicle, behind the trunk. Misha had already settled into a crouch behind the engine, firing his AK-107 over the hood in quick bursts to cover Gosha's retreat through the back seat of the car.

Once all three of them were behind the sedan, Farrington made a quick assessment of the situation and issued orders. With only one working vehicle in the intersection, he had to take action to preserve their only method of escape. As the hollow sound of punctured metal started to fill his ears, he realized that they needed to quit using the sedan as cover.

"Gosha, cover us while we approach Grisha's car," Farmington said, sliding down the length of the sedan. "You ready?" he said to Misha.

"Now or never," the operative replied.

"Cover fire!" he said over his shoulder, putting the sniper into action.

Bullets snapped overhead and beside them during the twenty-meter sprint across the open grass. Fortunately, the SUV's survivors were at a disadvantage huddled behind their vehicle. Once Farrington and Misha had covered half of the distance, the mangled sedan effectively blocked the attackers' line of sight, and the volume of gunfire slackened. Farrington lifted his rifle and aimed through the canted sights, searching for movement beyond the sedan.

"Target. Front of your sedan," he heard in his earpiece.

He shifted the weapon left and aimed at a point beyond the driver's side door, across the hood. A bloodied face appeared in his sights, aiming over the roof of the car in the direction of Gosha. Farrington fired two quick bursts that knocked the man off his feet and flipped his submachine gun onto the hood. Edging forward along the car, he reached the driver's window, noticing that Seva's head was leaned up against the doorframe. The rest of his body was obscured by a deflated, blood-sprayed airbag, which rendered a quick damage assessment impossible. The blood splatter, along with the gash on the side of Seva's head, wasn't an encouraging sign for what he might find under the airbag. Three distinct semi-automatic rifle reports caused him to duck instinctively.

"Shooter down. Headshot. That's three confirmed, including the driver and the one you smoked in front of the sedan. I didn't see anyone else get out of the SUV," Gosha said.

"Got it. We're pressing forward to investigate," Farrington said.

The traffic circle grew eerily quiet, despite the constant hum of the wrecked sedan's sputtering engine. He signaled for Misha to go around the other side of the vehicle, so they could approach the SUV from two sides. He risked a glance behind him and saw Gosha scanning the wreckage through the scope on his assault rifle. He edged forward, crouching at eye level with the car's crumpled hood, his rifle aimed at the SUV's half-intact windshield.

He rounded the front of the car, spotting three men splayed on the grass. The closest man lay on his back, his eyes wide open in a blank, glassy stare straight up at the overcast sky. Blood trickled from his mouth down the side of his jawline. Farrington had fired at least ten 5.45mm projectiles into his body, overwhelming the man's body armor and killing him instantly. The other two bodies lay behind the SUV. One of them had clearly suffered a headshot, probably from Gosha's rifle. A massive exit wound marred the side of his head exposed to Farrington. The other lay motionless, face down in the grass a few feet from the partially opened front passenger door.

"Three down behind the SUV. One in the driver's seat. We leave in thirty seconds," he said, realizing this meant making a few tough decisions regarding the men in the wrecked sedan.

Farrington started to turn when he heard a static crackle, followed by a Russian voice. His attention was drawn to a handheld radio, which lay a few feet away from the facedown Russian. The man suddenly lunged along the ground, reaching for the black handset. Several steel-jacketed bullets from Farrington's AK-107 punctured the soft armor portions of the downed operative's ballistic vest, penetrating deep into his torso and preventing any further movement. Farrington sprang forward and smashed the radio under his boot. The Spetsnaz operative spit a mouthful of blood onto the grass and coughed before expiring.

He turned the man onto his back and examined his gear, concluding that he must be part of the Vympel detachment assigned to guard Vektor. Type IIIA ballistic vests, thigh holsters, throat microphones, hand grenades, dozens of spare magazines for his OTs-14 bull-pup-configured submachine gun. All of it professionally rigged in a manner demonstrating years of operational experience. The fact that they had intentionally crashed into their lead vehicle sealed his assessment that they were Vympel. He just wondered if they had managed to get a warning out to the rest of the detachment or the local law enforcement network.

The sound of a muffled scream brought Farrington sprinting back to the passenger side of the sedan. He found Sasha stretched out on the ground, battered and bloodied, his left arm bent at the elbow in an unnatural angle. His right leg bled profusely through his dark brown cargo pants. He met Gosha's eyes and raised an eyebrow.

"Not good. Compound fracture. Lower right leg. Arm is fucked. Misha's getting one of the first aid kits. We'll have to stabilize this shit before we move."

Farrington looked into the driver's seat, coming to terms with the possibility that he'd lost everyone in the car. As far as he was concerned, Sasha was done. They'd bring him as far as they could, but only a perfect exfiltration scenario from this point forward could assure his survival. Based on what they'd just experienced, the night was guaranteed to be anything but perfect. Sasha's twisted limbs would prevent him from any serious attempt to flee over ground, and unless the Russians let them drive across the border, he was a dead man.

He opened the door, expecting to catch Seva with both hands. Instead, Seva's limp body hung in the seat, suspended by the shoulder strap of his seatbelt. From this angle, the underside of the airbag looked clean, giving him hope that Seva had been spared. He reached across the airbag to disconnect Seva's seatbelt, catching a brief, horrible glimpse of what used to be Grisha. The SUV had struck Grisha's door with enough force to instantly drive the metal door three feet into the sedan, pulverizing the operative in a tangle of broken steel and limbs. There would be no need for a second look.

Lowering Seva carefully onto the grass, he noted a complete lack of external injuries beyond the shallow gash on the left side of his head. He felt for a pulse and checked respiration. Seva's vitals were strong.

"Let's get these two into the car. Ten seconds. I want all rucksacks and ammunition. We'll have to change frequencies en route to the next checkpoint. We don't have time to look for Grisha's communications gear. Misha, torch the car when everything is clear," he said.

"What about Grisha?"

"His body isn't going anywhere, and we can't leave him behind to be identified," he said.

Chapter 53

Karl Berg stood up from his station and looked around the operations center.

"What just happened? I lost communications with Blackjack," he said, trying to raise Farrington on the net again.

"Blackjack. Come in, Blackjack."

He waited several seconds and tried again with no response.

"Fuck! Are the comms going through?" he yelled.

"Diagnostics look fine, Mr. Berg. It's a simple satellite connection," said one of the techs from the front of the room.

"There's nothing simple about any of the connections in here," Berg snapped.

He was worried. Farrington had cut out in midsentence, and he thought he had heard gunfire. An ambush wasn't out of the question with the Vympel detachment activated.

"Is there any way we can find them with satellite?" he said, knowing that this wouldn't be easy.

Satellite tracking didn't work like the movies, where savvy ground-station operators could follow a car for hundreds of miles using a joystick to pan the camera. Current technology allowed for imagery and camera control, but on a more limited scale, subject to satellite positioning and object-tracking algorithms that take into account moving object estimation, target behavior modeling and target match processing. Much of the process was automated due to the complex mathematics involved, and restricted the satellite's imaging capacity to a small fixed area around the target. They had decided from the outset not to restrict their satellite capability by tracking the team's vehicles.

"I can coordinate a search along the road leading from their last checkpoint. It'll take a few minutes," said a dark-haired woman a few computer stations away.

"No. I don't want to lose the bigger picture. We already have one satellite moving to a better position over the border-crossing area, and we need to keep an eye on the military base outside of Novosibirsk," he said, sitting back down.

He tried the team again, but received no response, switching over to Sanderson's communication net.

"Base, I lost communications with Blackjack during the middle of a satellite phone conversation. Can you make contact?" Berg said.

"This is base. Stand by."

Ten seconds later, Sanderson came back on the line. "The call won't go through. What happened?"

"I don't know. Blackjack was in the middle of a sentence and that was it. I thought I heard gunfire. NSA confirmed Vympel signalled intelligence less than a minute after Vektor burned," Berg said.

"The self-destruct system must have triggered their activation. I can't imagine they could have caught up with our team," Sanderson said.

"I don't know. Maybe satellite communications are down. If we don't hear from them within the next few minutes, I'll redirect all satellite assets to find them. Until then, there's not much we can do, aside from keeping our fingers crossed. It would be a real fucking shame to lose them at this point," Berg said.

"You should have a little more faith in my people, Sanderson chided. "They haven't let you down yet."

"I just want to get them back. I owe them that much," Berg said.

"We'll get them back."

A few seconds later, Farrington's voice returned to Berg's headset.

"Berg. Are you still there?"

"I'm still here. What happened?"

"Part of the suspected Vympel detachment rammed the lead car, killing Grisha and severely injuring Sasha. Seva is still unconscious, but his vitals are strong. We're back on the road in one vehicle, headed to the reservoir," Farrington said.

"I'm sorry about Grisha. Are you able to continue with the exfiltration plan?"

"Affirmative. We're on our way to the second checkpoint."

"That's good to hear. We're going to get you out of there. Contact base to report your status," Berg said.

"Understood. Blackjack out."

Berg turned to Audra Bauer, who shook her head slowly.

"Grisha's dead, and Sasha is severely injured. Seva is unconscious, but appears to be fine," he said.

"Shit," she muttered. "We'll have to pass this on to Manning."

"Nothing for them to get worried about. The exfiltration plan remains the same."

He knew that the mission couldn't suffer any more unexpected setbacks without jeopardizing the helicopter exfiltration option. The president had been skittish about using helicopters from the very beginning. His most recent restrictions to Black Magic's ROE underscored the delicate situation. It wouldn't take much at this point for the president to send Black Magic back to Kyrgyzstan without Blackjack. He'd need to put his own secret play into action soon. It might be Farrington's only hope.

Chapter 54

Farrington leaned inside the car and released the emergency brake, starting their car on a slow descent down the neglected public boat ramp to the dark waters of the reservoir. Gosha helped him expedite the process by joining him behind the vehicle's open trunk and pushing. By the time the car reached the water, it had gained enough momentum to continue all the way into the gently lapping waves of the manmade lake. The car floated into the lake for several seconds, hissing as the cold water filled the remaining air pockets in the chassis. Once the black water started to pour into the open windows, the car gave up and plunged to the bottom, temporarily erasing any trace that they had come this way.

In his estimation, the concrete boat launch hadn't been used in decades, and their car would probably remain hidden for weeks, depending on the level of the reservoir. Of course, he was probably wrong on that account. Nearly everything in this part of Russia either appeared to be in a state of decades-long disrepair or had been hastily cobbled back together without the benefit of an architect or skilled labor, including the community of lake homes they had passed in Leninskoye on their way to this isolated stretch of lakefront—thirty miraculously uneventful kilometers from Vektor.

So uneventful that Farrington could scarcely believe their good fortune after the disaster outside of Koltsovo. The Vympel team clearly hadn't expected to find them so close to Vektor, instead stumbling upon them out of sheer random coincidence while travelling south. No detailed calls had been made to law enforcement units in the Sovetskiy City District, as evidenced by the complete lack of even the most rudimentary police presence. The streets had been deserted, as expected on a Sunday night in a university town, but to completely avoid running into one patrol car had been nothing short of a miracle, especially driving around in their shot-up sedan.

One close look at their car would have been enough to raise the suspicions of even the most apathetic police officer. One of the side mirrors had been sheared clean by a bullet. The windshield had been peppered by at least four hits. The side windows along the right side of the car were down in forty-degree weather, mainly because the multiple bullet strikes to that side of the car had shattered the windows inside the doors. They had tried to roll one of the windows up, but it had jammed after a few inches, yielding nothing but broken safety glass. Finally, their left front headlight had been destroyed, making them an easy target for a police officer looking to make a few dollars with a warning ticket. Then again, he mused, their car didn't look half bad for the streets of Novosibirsk. Maybe two officers sitting in a well-hidden patrol car had watched them pass, each shrugging at the sight of another beat-up car on the road.

Farrington ran with Misha along an overgrown dirt path to a flat stretch of sandy beach fifty meters down the shoreline. Their mafiya contacts had picked this spot for its isolation along the northern shore, and its correspondingly rare shallow-entry sandy beach. Hard-to-find spots like this along the lake were usually accessed by boat, which gave them some hope that the car wouldn't be found by someone trying to back their boat trailer into the water tomorrow morning. Early June was still a little cold for recreational boaters, but in Siberia, a fifty-degree day in June was treated with more enthusiasm than a seventy-degree day in July. Either way, they should be on a helicopter headed to Kyrgyzstan by the time anyone decided to take their boat out for the day.

Emerging from the tall grass at the edge of the beach, Farrington was greeted by the business end of Gosha's OTs-3 SVU sniper rifle, extended over the bow of their boat. The 23-foot whaler sat slightly canted on the sand with its engines idling. Gosha stood up and took station behind the whaler's center console, while Farrington and Misha waded up to their knees in the frigid water and lifted themselves over the side of the boat.

Before he had a chance to think about taking a seat, the engine roared, pulling them off the sand and into the deeper water of the reservoir. Gosha lowered his night vision goggles and pointed them in the direction of the southwestern end of the reservoir. Moments later, their boat accelerated to thirty knots, or roughly thirty-five miles per hour, skimming the surface of the lake.

The boat travelled significantly slower than a car and would eat into the precious block of time left to reach the border, but it afforded them a few advantages they could not ignore. The reservoir and the wide river beyond it could not be easily blocked like a road. Russian authorities wouldn't expect them to travel by fast boat, and by the time they started to consider the possibility, Farrington's team would be back on dry land. While not the fastest way to reach the border, travelling southwest across the entire length of the reservoir was the most direct route to their next checkpoint.

One hundred kilometers from their starting point on this beach, the reservoir turned south, emptying into a wide river delta, before narrowing again and becoming the Ob River. They would swap the boat for two SUVS hidden on the delta's western shore. From there, they faced a 160 kilometer journey across dirt roads and rolling hills to the border, passing north of Lake Kulunda, a massive salt lake surrounded by industrial facilities.

Viktor's Solntsevskaya scouts had mapped the entire route with GPS, claiming that it could be done in less than two hours. Farrington had his doubts about their estimate, given that they had conducted the dry runs during full daylight, when the SUVS could be pushed to 50 miles per hour on dirt roads. His team would make the same trip employing night vision, more than likely restricted to 35 miles per hour. It could take them nearly three hours to arrive within striking distance of the Russian/Kazakhstan border. At their current speed, they would arrive at the next checkpoint at 1:35 AM, giving them little leeway for the three-hour land portion of the exfiltration plan.

Sunrise was at 5:25 AM, but he had to subtract thirty minutes from that time, since the helicopter pilots had been ordered to turn back at civil twilight. D.C. wanted their precious birds clear of any inhabited areas by sunrise, which left him with a drop-dead arrival time of 4:55 AM. Three hours and twenty minutes to travel 160 kilometers, leaving him less than twenty minutes to deal with the unexpected.

He took the seat next to Gosha, which provided him some shelter from the thirty-knot artificial wind and gave their situation some thought. They'd have to make up some time on the open water. He glanced back at Sasha, who lay across the back of the passenger compartment on the deck, supported and surrounded by cushions taken from the seats and various life jackets found stowed throughout the boat. Seva sat behind him on the rear cockpit bench along the stern of the boat. Seva had regained consciousness after they crossed the Ob River dam, complaining of blurred vision and a throbbing headache. Since a strong possibility existed that he had suffered a concussion, he would rest and tend to Sasha's comfort during the crossing. Only three out of six operatives remained fully combat-ready with nearly five hours left to go. The odds were not stacked in their favor.

He leaned over and yelled into Gosha's right ear. "Open this thing up to just under full throttle. We need to make up some time."

Gosha nodded and pushed the dual throttle forward as far as it would go, notching it back just slightly to avoid a full redline situation. Viktor's men had assured him that the boat was in top condition, but running an engine at its full RPMs for an extended period of time was tempting fate, and he couldn't imagine any of them had much karma left to spare at this point. The boat accelerated across the water, reaching 43 knots. He examined the dimmed chart plotter on the navigation screen and noted their new estimated time of arrival at checkpoint three. 1:10 AM. Twenty additional minutes to deal with the unexpected. Staring out into the impenetrable darkness, he couldn't escape the sinking feeling that they would need more time.

Chapter 55

The president paced in front of his desk in his study, considering what Jacob Remy had just suggested: sending the helicopters back to Kyrgyzstan and letting Sanderson's team fend for themselves inside of Kazakhstan. Remy's logic was cold, but had been built on the realities of the situation. He needed to war-game this more, to make sure Remy wasn't exerting undue influence. Remy had made it clear from the very beginning that he didn't want to use U.S. military assets for any phase of the operation, but Sanderson wouldn't budge without the guarantee of a military-supported extraction. Since everybody wanted to see the Russian bioweapons program destroyed, the limited use of military assets was approved. Now they were all having second thoughts.

"What are we looking at if we send the birds back to Kyrgyzstan?" he said.

"We avoid a potential disaster. This whole helicopter thing was just appeasement from the beginning. We can't allow the birds to cross the border to pick up the team, so Sanderson's people were always working under the assumption that the team would have to figure out a way to get into Kazakhstan. Shit. If they can get into Kazakhstan, we can send some fucking cars to pick them up at the nearest gas station. Anything but risking one of those helicopters."

"Mr. President, Mr. Remy," Lieutenant General Gordon said. "Two things to consider here. First, we gave Sanderson our word that his team would be picked up at the border and flown to safe—"

"Not if half of the Russian Army is on their heels," Remy cut in.

"I don't remember any conditions to their extraction, other than it taking place on Kazakhstan soil," Gordon countered.

"This just got far more complicated than just a simple handshake," said James Quinn, the National Security Advisor. "Light elements of the 21st Guards Motor Rifle Division in Altay have been activated, along with the 122nd Reconnaissance Battalion in Novosibirsk. We're talking a lot of Russian soldiers combing the area with crappy command and control. If Sanderson's team gets caught up in a fight, the Russians might not stop at the border. We can't put those helicopters in that kind of a situation."

"I understand the complexity of these missions better than anyone in this room," Gordon said. "Trust me, I'm not blind to the possible consequences here."

"Then you can see why we can't afford to lose one of those helos. Especially to the Russians," Remy said.

"Maybe you shouldn't have insisted that we use them, if you weren't prepared to lose them," Gordon said, directing his comment at the National Security Advisor.

"The task force has to fly within detection range of Semipalatinsk Airport to reach any of the possible extraction points. We can't do that with conventional helicopters. You said it yourself," Quinn reminded him.

"Well, we can't undo this now without betraying the men and women who stuck their asses out to do us a favor," Gordon said.

"These aren't U.S. troops," Remy said. "We're talking mercenaries at best."

"I wouldn't go that far, Jacob," the president interjected. He was painfully aware of the delicate line they all walked trying to classify Sanderson's people, and he didn't want to have this discussion with General Gordon.

"It doesn't matter who they are. What we need to decide is whether we're going to leave them hanging out to dry or use these helicopters for their intended purpose. We have to test them at some point. This is as good an opportunity as any," Gordon said.

"We stick to the plan for now, but if this gets any hotter than it already is, I'll strongly consider sending them back," the president said.

He could tell that Jacob Remy wanted to continue the debate, but had decided to shelve it for now. When everyone had left the study, Remy closed the door and stared at him with the same look he'd given him for nearly ten years throughout his meteoric rise to the presidency.

"It'll get hotter, and you know it. There's no way they can avoid these units long enough to slip over the border. This is going to end badly for everyone," Remy said.

"So we send the birds back and it only ends badly for Sanderson's people?"

Remy shrugged his shoulders, not wanting to utter the words. The president hated this about his chief of staff. He'd put the knife in your hand and walk you right up to his intended victim, shrugging his shoulders with that "you know what to do" look plastered on his face, but he'd never be the one to do the stabbing.

"We'll see this through to the end. If they have the entire Russian army at their heels, I'll get our helicopters out of there," the president said.

"I hope that won't be too late," Remy remarked dryly.

Chapter 56

1:08 AM
Ob River Delta
Altai Krai, Russian Federation

The sleek white boat slowed to a crawl along the tree-covered shoreline to give Farrington the best chance of spotting their checkpoint without making another pass. The two SUVs had been hidden near the checkpoint early this morning by Viktor's crew. In addition to providing Farrington with a GPS waypoint marking the location along the riverbank, the *bratva* soldiers had hung several infrared chemlights from the trees at the proposed landing site. The chemlights would fade significantly, but should provide more than enough illumination through night vision to enable a quick discovery.

"Got it. Come right slowly," he said, feeling the boat sway. "Dead ahead," he added, when the dangling green lights seen through his goggles reached the bow.

"I see them," Gosha confirmed, steadying the boat on course.

Farrington made his way forward to join Misha on the bow to guard the approach. They scanned the dense, murky vegetation for signs of an ambush, sweeping their assault rifles in long arcs as the boat approached a worn path through the foliage. When he felt the hull scrape along the rocky bottom, he slung his rifle over his back and climbed over the side, landing on spongy ground less than a foot from the water. Misha passed him the bowline, which he hastily tied to a thick tree trunk planted several feet into the brush.

"I'm going to scout ahead and locate the vehicles. I want everything and everyone offloaded in two minutes," he said, hearing the team's immediate acknowledgements over his earpiece.

He shouldered his rifle and peered over the holographic sights. The path leading away from the riverbank was dim, even with the help of night vision goggles. He'd walk several meters and stop, listening for anything that didn't belong along an isolated stretch of the Ob River at one in the morning on a Sunday, besides his own team. After repeating this process three more times, he arrived at the edge of a small clearing in the trees and searched for more faded IR chemlights. Swiftly locating the dying green lights, Farrington moved toward them, keeping his weapon trained toward the jeep trail that emptied into the clearing from the west.

He reached the SUVs, which had been hidden from view by several thick, richly foliated tree branches, and conducted a quick visual inspection of the tires. He opened the driver's seat door of the nearest vehicle and found the keys under the driver's seat. Everything appeared as advertised.

"Team. I found the vehicles, and I'm heading back in your direction. I want to be on the road in less than five minutes. We have a lot of ground to cover."

"Roger. We're already moving up the path," Misha said.

"How much gear is left at the boat?"

"Your pack and the spare with extra ammunition and explosives."

"Got it. I'll call this in and get a SITREP from base," Farrington said and took off for the path.

He removed the satellite phone from one of his tactical vest pouches and called base to get an updated report regarding enemy movements in his immediate area and along his exfiltration route. He temporarily switched off his intrasquad radio so his conversation wouldn't block his own team's communications. Sanderson answered immediately.

"This is base."

"Base this is Blackjack. We've reached checkpoint three. The vehicles are here as advertised. We're a few minutes from stepping off. Any change to the disposition of hostile forces?"

"Unfortunately, the situation has worsened. Elements of the 122nd Reconnaissance Battalion have arrived along highway 380 from Novosibirsk, on your side of the river. They're spreading out along the road, leaving vehicle checkpoints all the way down to Barnual. The 21st

Guards Motor Rifle Division hasn't fielded any units, but we've seen indications that they'll put light armored vehicle platoons at border checkpoints. With access to the main roads, they'll have these in position within an hour or two."

"I'm more concerned with the reconnaissance units. Is this armored reconnaissance?" Farrington said, moving out of the way for his team to pass along the path.

"Negative. No signs of BTRs or anything like that. Mostly Tigers or lighter," Sanderson said.

"The Tigers might as well be armor given what we're carrying for weapons. We'll have to avoid them just the same. Any good news?"

"No helicopter activity so far," Sanderson said.

"That's really good news."

"So far. Intelligence analysts are pretty sure that most helicopter assets have been shifted west and north in response to Monchegorsk. With things simmered down up there, they've conceded that it might be possible for some of these units to have returned. Novosibirsk airport was home to a squadron of Mi-8 Hips, so you might have to contend with airlifted troops near the border," Sanderson said.

"Wonderful. I don't suppose anyone at the Pentagon knows where the Mi-28 Havocs are based? I seem to remember one of those in this neck of the woods a few months ago."

"I can't get a straight answer about that. I don't think they have any idea where it came from," Sanderson said.

"There's nothing we could do about it anyway, so there's no point in worrying about it."

"Exactly. I'm going to send you all known positions of hostile units, based on communications and satellite imagery. The CIA is analyzing the areas relevant to your projected path. Make sure to keep your RPDA (Ruggedized Personal Data Assistant) handy. We'll continuously update this information on the RPDA's digital map. From what I can tell right now, you're going to have a problem about two kilometers down Highway 380. Two Tigers are sitting next to the road you plan to take west. I'd avoid that route," Sanderson said.

Farrington thought about the location of the Tigers with respect to their exfiltration plan. The improvised dirt road represented one of the few westerly passages they could use to travel over thirty miles per hour until they reached some of the small townships halfway to the border. Their other options lay south of the Tiger checkpoint or several kilometers to the north. Driving north would add too much time overall, forcing them to work their way west along less desirable roads. They could always head straight across Highway 380 from their current position and try to find a jeep trail that connected with the original road, but satellite imagery had steered them away from this option early in the planning process, and he'd be hard-pressed to force it on himself now. There was always another option.

"We'll have to take out the checkpoint. I need to be on that road if we're to have any chance of making it across the border before the helicopters turn back," Farrington said.

"You can use the jeep trails along the riverbank area. They connect to other clearings in the trees and sort of leapfrog to a hidden area directly east of their position. You'll have to cross over four hundred meters of open space between the Tigers and the trees, but that shouldn't be a problem. They won't be expecting you to come from the river," Sanderson said.

"Sounds like you had this worked out ahead of time," Farrington said.

"I knew you wouldn't give up on that road," Sanderson said.

"Am I getting predictable?"

"Just the opposite. You're starting to get interesting. How is Sasha doing?"

"As long as we don't have to travel by foot, he'll be fine. We've started to administer morphine to dull the pain. I wanted to hold off so he could work a gun, but there's no way he'd be able to withstand the SUV ride," Farrington said.

"All right. Does it make sense to pack the team into one vehicle?"

"It makes a lot of sense tactically, especially with Sasha, but practically, I need to run two vehicles. It's darker than shit out here, and we'll be moving fast. Anything more serious than a blown tire would put us out of business with one vehicle," Farrington said.

"See what I mean? I predicted you'd go with one vehicle."

"Keep a close eye on those Tigers. We'll be headed out in two minutes."

Farrington lifted his assault rucksack onto one shoulder and Grisha's pack onto the other, finding his balance before heading off for the vehicles. His own pack was heavy enough, filled with water, batteries, ammunition, rope, medical supplies, and a variety of grenades, but Grisha's pack pulled him down even further. They had emptied Grisha's rucksack on the boat and refilled it with ammunition magazines, Semtex and two Claymore mines, all of which combined to weigh far more than his own pack. He heaved the weight along the path and caught up with the team at the SUVs. Sasha was already situated in one of the vehicles, propped against the left passenger door by rucksacks.

"Change of plans, gentlemen," he announced to the dark cluster of operatives.

"Base found something in our way down the road. We'll have to do a little housecleaning before we can proceed west."

Chapter 57

Gosha sighted in on the rightmost GAZ-Tiger vehicle and adjusted the picture for maximum contrast. At 397 meters, the ATN Thor 6X thermal scope on his sniper rifle gave a crisp, high-resolution black-and-white digital image of the Tiger. He shifted his view to the second Tiger on the left and conducted the same drill, scanning the thermal image for personnel in the open. The gunners for each vehicle sat half-exposed in the roof hatch, scanning the highway to the north and south. From his few minutes of observation, he noted that they paid no attention to the dirt road leading to the river, which was fortunate. Farrington and the remaining two operatives had covered the open ground at a fast jog, counting on the slightly raised road to shield them from view by the gunners.

A ghostly white image appeared from the back of the vehicle on the right and walked toward the west, along the road Farrington insisted they would need to get out of Russia. The man stopped for a moment, facing away, and Gosha could tell that he was urinating. He was unarmed, which gave the sniper an idea.

"I have one target taking a piss to the west of the vehicles. No rifle. One target visible on top of each vehicle. This might be as good as it gets. We have a ten-second window of opportunity."

"Let's take it. Same plan as discussed," Farrington said.

"Roger. Stand by," Gosha said.

From his position in one of the trees, Gosha centered the reticle on the white image of the soldier standing behind the Pecheneg light machine. The machine gun represented the biggest threat to the three operatives lying on the other side of the road. If the gunner was quick to react, the Pecheneg's high rate of fire could put them out of business quickly. Seva would focus his suppressed rifle fire on the second vehicle's gunner, who sat behind an AGS-30 grenade launcher.

He relaxed his hand and started to apply pressure to the trigger. The 7.62X54mm steel jacketed projectile left the barrel while the crosshairs drifted over the target's upper chest.

"Shot," he said and shifted to his second target.

He didn't relish the thought of shooting a man while he was taking a piss, but the man was dead either way, so what did it matter?

☞☜

Farrington pushed himself up and sprinted for the Tiger. The bullet would take less than a half second to travel the distance, probably striking before he could fully raise himself off the gravel. He heard Seva's suppressed AK-107 snap two short bursts, followed by the report of Gosha's rifle. Through his night vision, he saw the gunner tumble out of the first vehicle. As he barreled across the two-lane road, he felt a projectile snap over his head.

"Target on ground is down. Sorry about the haircut," Gosha said.

Farrington continued sprinting toward the vehicle several meters away, glancing briefly to his left to verify that the gunner of the second vehicle was no longer a threat. The soldier moments ago leaning against the grenade launcher had disappeared, so he didn't break stride. He reached the Tiger just as a commotion broke out inside the vehicle.

Not wasting a second, he jumped onto the rear tire and grabbed the steel bar at the edge of the jeep's roof, heaving himself onto the roof. He landed on his stomach and quickly rolled to his side to access one of the grenades on his vest. He tore the safety pin out of a fragmentation grenade and released the handle, throwing the grenade through the open hatch. A discordance of screams and panic erupted inside the vehicle.

Farrington stood and fired his AK-107 through the hatch, adding to the mayhem. After firing the extended burst, he jumped off the Tiger and rolled on the ground to face the jeep, emptying the rest of the magazine at anyone attempting to escape through the passenger doors. The grenade detonated inside the Tiger with a muffled thump that exploded the windows and knocked open the rear hatch. Nobody appeared to have escaped. The second Tiger suffered a similar fate less than a second later.

He quickly lifted himself off the ground and checked the other side of the smoking jeep. A mangled corpse hung upside down from an open door, its lifeless hands barely raking the hard-packed dirt below the vehicle. He didn't expect to find any survivors. The effects of a fragmentation grenade in such a small space could be devastating.

"Tiger one is clear," he announced.

"Tiger two clear," Misha said.

"Copy. Let's load up the bodies and get these vehicles out of sight. Gosha, keep an eye out for unexpected company on the road."

"Already scanning. Looks clear."

Farrington yanked the blood-slick body up by its vest and pushed it through the front seats into the back of the Tiger. The inside of the vehicle looked ghastly through his NVGs, still sizzling and smoking from the intense damage done by the grenade. He counted three bodies, including the driver, all blasted beyond recognition, much of them adorning the seats and equipment. He flipped the starter switch and the diesel engine roared to life, which was a small miracle after the grenade blast. He stopped for a moment and examined the back of the Tiger again, pausing to look up through the hatch at the overcast night. Instead of driving off with the other Tiger, he climbed over the dead driver and stood up through the hatch, examining the Pecheneg machine gun. He pulled the charging handle back and aimed down the road, firing off a burst.

"You got something?" Gosha asked.

"Negative. Just thinking," Farrington replied, looking at the second Tiger crossing the highway.

"I'm thinking the same thing," Misha said.

"That we just traded in our unarmored SUVs for heavily armored jeeps?" Farrington said.

"Exactly," Misha said.

"Sounds like a plan. Let's transfer all of the gear and get out of here."

Six minutes later, they were packed into one of the Tigers, headed west along the improvised road at nearly 65 miles per hour. They'd lost nearly fifteen minutes dealing with the checkpoint, but they could make up all of that time in their new transportation. If anything, they might even gain time. Similar to the "Humvee," the Tiger was a high-mobility, multipurpose military vehicle, equipped with a powerful diesel, turbocharged, air-cooled engine. Independent torsion suspension, telescopic shock absorbers and regulated-pressure tires gave it a top speed of 55 miles per hour over rough terrain and up to 90 miles per hour on the road.

The Tiger's unyielding endurance for poor road conditions left Farrington confident that they could condense the team into one vehicle. He'd chosen the jeep with the grenade launcher because the weapon presented a capability they didn't have organic to any of their weapons— long range high-explosive munitions. The Pecheneg machine gun would have been nice, but the ability to fire 30mm grenades at a rate of two per second would come in handy if they ran into any more armored vehicles. He could almost guarantee that these wouldn't be the last Tigers they ran into out here. He just hoped they didn't bump into any light armored vehicles from the 21st Guards Motor Rifle Division. The 30mm grenades would be useless against those, along with everything else they carried.

Chapter 58

Karl Berg removed his headset and turned to Audra Bauer, who was examining satellite footage on her two screens.

"They're clear of the checkpoint, moving west in one of the Tigers," Berg said.

"Smart move taking the Tiger," she commented.

"They're going to need all the help they can get. The Tiger might give them the edge they need to pull this off. They won't have to stick to roads or trails when they get near the border, which is a major improvement to their plan. They should be able to slip through the 21st Motor Rifle Division units along the border," Berg said.

"Speaking of the 21st, satellite imagery and electronic intercepts confirm that a brigade from the 142nd Motor Rifle Regiment has started to deploy from their base in Biysk. Estimated time of arrival along the border zones for the bulk of the brigade is two hours. Early elements will arrive within the hour," Bauer said.

"Shit. We're looking at BTRs, BRDMs, Urals and Tigers. Anything with wheels. They can't move the tracked infantry fighting vehicles into that area fast enough. How many are missing from the base in Biysk so far?"

"They're still counting. At least thirty BTR-80s and seventy Tigers, along with a dozen utility trucks. All headed west."

"Add that to the 122nd Recon Battalion's sixty plus Tigers to the east and we can conclude that somebody's pissed back in Moscow," Berg said.

"Audra, can you direct one of the satellites to babysit the checkpoint Blackjack just eliminated? Eventually, someone is going to wonder why the checkpoint isn't responding and take a look. I want to give Blackjack a heads-up when that happens," he said, standing up.

"Sure. You headed somewhere?" she said.

"I need to make a call," he said.

"Your guy in Russia?" she said.

"Could be a woman. I was a hot ticket back in the day," he said, winking.

She shook her head and started typing instructions to the NRO satellite handlers, leaving Berg to his phone call. He was glad she quickly assumed he was calling Kaparov. It made sense given the fact that Vektor had been attacked. At some point during the night, if it hadn't happened already, Kaparov would be awakened with the news that a facility containing samples of biological material suitable for weaponization had been breached. Of course, there would be no mention of the bioweapons laboratory. Kaparov would be asked to analyze the threat posed by the possible theft of viral samples like smallpox and avian flu. He'd wait for Kaparov to call with the "shocking" news.

No. Berg had a different call to make. One he couldn't make in the CIA operations center. If anyone discovered what he had arranged behind all of their backs, he ran the risk of losing the asset before it could be employed. It was better that they discovered his plan when the consequences of shutting it down outweighed letting it proceed.

He exited the "Fishbowl" section of the operations center and walked toward the exit, eager to retrieve his cell phone.

"I need to make a call outside of the operations center," Berg said, addressing the two security guards manning the entrance station.

Less than a minute later, he stood in the hallway outside of the operations center. He walked through the deserted hallway and speed-dialed the number he needed. He waited for the call to connect, which took several seconds, since the signal had to travel halfway around the world and negotiate encryption protocols at its destination.

"Weatherman standing by for you to authenticate."

Berg pressed the ten-digit combination of numbers assigned for the operation.

"Good evening, Mr. Berg. Black Rain is spooled up and ready for launch."

"Good timing, Weatherman. Launch Black Rain immediately and proceed to holding area over Lake Kulunda."

"Roger. We'll have her airborne in a few minutes. Time to station estimated at 0425 local."

"Copy 0425. I'll open a channel in the operations center for terminal control at approximately 0400 local. Have a safe flight," Berg said.

"We always do. I'll expect to hear from you at 0400 local. Weatherman out."

Berg put the phone back in his jacket pocket and leaned against the wall, breathing heavily. He was extremely nervous about the next three and a half hours. If he got lucky, Farrington's team would slip through the Russians' net and drive right across the border to be picked up by Black Magic. Black Rain would never be used, and it would be high fives all the way to the White House. Berg was no stranger to luck, but his breaks didn't come so neatly wrapped. Three and a half hours and this would be over, one way or the other, and nobody could accuse him of shortchanging Sanderson's people. He could live with the consequences of putting Black Rain into play to give Farrington's team a fighting chance.

Chapter 59

2:35 AM
Kamen-na Obi
Russian Federation

Lieutenant Colonel Maxim Odenko ran his finger along an unfolded road map of the Altai Krai region, squinting to make out the details. Battle lights bathed everything within his command vehicle in a dull red glow that preserved the occupants' night vision, but cast a monochromatic film over his map. He could barely make out the terrain features, not that it really mattered. He didn't have the resources to start scouring small valleys or posting units on hilltops. He barely had enough vehicles to cover the roads adequately.

He had the three hundred kilometer stretch of Highway 380 between Novosibirsk and Barnual locked down to the best of his battalion's ability. Sixty-three vehicles were spread along the highway at ten to twenty-kilometer intervals, covering all of the major western roads or trails they could identify using local maps and satellite imagery. A smaller number of vehicles had been dispatched along Highway M52, but the local law enforcement response from towns along the highway had been swift to respond, blocking the north-south route at Cherepanovo and Tal'menka within thirty minutes of the terrorist action against the state institute in Koltsovo. Unless the police were full of shit, there was no way the terrorists could have travelled Highway M52 quickly enough to make it through those cities before the roadblocks were established.

His bet was on Highway 380, not that he thought it mattered at this point. Unless the perpetrators had taken an hour-long nap on the side of the road, they had already cleared these roads and headed west. He'd requested permission to start moving his units along the roads they were guarding, but the request had been quickly denied pending updated intelligence. Orders from the 41st Army commander had been explicit, and in true bureaucratic fashion, it was too soon to consider a shift in tactics, regardless of the obvious.

His battalion would seal the highway from Novosibirsk to Barnual and let the 21st Motor Rifle Division and Border Guard Service barracks in Karasuk handle the border...despite the fact that the terrorist attack had taken place nearly two and a half hours earlier and the perpetrators had not been seen since the ambush outside of Koltsovo. His patience was starting to wear thin with headquarters, especially at two thirty in the morning. Sitting on this road was a waste of time, and everyone in his command knew it. Now it was apparently taking its toll on his men.

"How long since checkpoint twelve reported?" Odenko said.

A bleary-eyed lieutenant holding a radio handset answered from across the small table. "They missed the one-thirty check-in, so it's been over an hour at this point."

"That's too long, damn it! I'll hang the sergeant in charge of that group and relieve his platoon commander if we find out they fell asleep. Send that useless fuck over to check on his men. I shouldn't have to tell him to do this! Or you!" Odenko said.

"Zulu Three this is Alpha Zulu, over," the lieutenant said over the command net.

"This is Zulu Three, over."

"Send one of your vehicles to investigate Zulu Two Five's position and report their status immediately, over."

"This is Zulu Two actual. We're trying to raise radio contact with Zulu Two Five, but suspect communications gear issues or possible atmospheric interference, over."

Odenko swiped the handset from the young lieutenant and responded. "This is Alpha Zulu actual. You need to quit suspecting every reason under the sun for their failure to follow orders and get someone over there to confirm what happened. I want a report within ten minutes, out."

He heard the communications net key a few times, as the lieutenant on the other end of the line debated whether to respond. He'd closed the loop on any response by ending his transmission with "out," which he hoped ended the conversation.

"If he says one word, I'll call an airstrike down on his position," Odenko said.

"Do we have air assets on station, sir?" the lieutenant asked.

His battalion master sergeant snickered from the front passenger seat as Odenko stared at the lieutenant in disbelief. "Did any air assets check in with you tonight?"

"Negative. There are no air assets. I answered my own question," the officer said, clearly intimidated by his plum assignment to the battalion command vehicle.

"Next time answer it before you ask it!" Odenko said, noting that the master sergeant had not stopped his muffled laugh.

"Don't laugh, Master Sergeant. It only makes me more irritable," Odenko said.

Given the level of dysfunction he had witnessed so far, he'd have to schedule more night training for the battalion. The battalion barely received enough fuel to conduct basic daytime maneuvers, but he didn't care if they just sat in a field and counted the stars. Mobilizing the battalion out of a deep sleep had been a painful experience he did not care to repeat. He could foresee many emergency recall drills in the upcoming months. Twelve minutes later, the radio came to life.

"Alpha Zulu, this is Zulu Two actual. Zulu Two Four reports that Two Five is not at the checkpoint, over."

"What do you mean they are not at the checkpoint?" Odenko said, well past using proper radio protocol.

"They're missing, sir."

"Well, you need to find them!"

"This is Zulu Two. I'll shift vehicles and start a search of the area, over."

"I'm coming myself. We're less than fifteen kilometers away. Out," Odenko said.

This was a regular clusterfuck. He didn't know who had screwed up at this point. Was Zulu Two Four looking in the wrong place? Or was Zulu Two Five sitting in the wrong spot, oblivious to their error…and apparently the radio? He'd soon find out.

"Kamarov, let the other vehicle know that we're headed to Two Five's checkpoint location," Odenko said.

Eight minutes later, Odenko spotted a lone vehicle on the road through his night vision goggles, crushing any hopes of finding Zulu Two Five along the road. According to his handheld GPS, they were less than a kilometer from the assigned checkpoint location, so the lone vehicle had to be Zulu Two Four. Now he started to worry. He couldn't think of any reason why they would be off the highway. He lowered himself into the hatch, out of the 65 mile per hour wind buffeting him.

"Can you confirm that's Two Four up ahead?"

"Wait one, sir!" the lieutenant replied.

Odenko climbed back up and gripped the Pecheneg machine gun for stability against the gale-force wind created by the Tiger's speed along the highway. A few seconds after that, Odenko saw the vehicle's headlights flash twice.

"It's Two Four, sir. They just flashed their lights!" the lieutenant said through the hatch.

"Got it!" he replied.

Not good. Two of his Tigers, carrying eight of his men, had vanished into thin air, either leaving their checkpoint without authorization or never arriving. He started to climb down into the vehicle to talk with the Tiger on the road, when his night vision goggles flashed bright white, effectively blinding him. He immediately raised the goggles attached to his helmet and tried to pierce the darkness with his degraded sight. The deep sound of an explosion reached him seconds later, just as his vision had cleared enough for him to determine that a fireball had erupted behind a line of trees to the east of the highway. He pulled back on the Pecheneg's charging handle and swiveled the mount in the direction of the dissipating flame. He felt someone climbing through the hatch and looked back to see Private Second Class Marakev squeezing through.

"I got this, sir!" the private said.

Odenko grabbed his shoulder. "Scan three hundred and sixty degrees. We have no idea what we're dealing with!" He struggled to yell over the wind.

Private Marakev lowered his night vision and squeezed by to take charge of the machine gun, relieving Odenko of his duty to protect the command vehicle from immediate threat. Odenko dropped into the rear compartment of the Tiger and took the handset from his lieutenant.

"Two Four, this is Alpha Zulu actual. What is your status? Over."

"This is Two Four. I sent two men on foot to investigate Tiger tracks heading toward the river. They had just reported finding one of the Tigers when the explosion occurred. I've lost contact!" the sergeant said frantically.

"Sergeant, take a deep breath, and get a hold of yourself. My unit will investigate the explosion and bring back your men. Stay alert and watch the road. This could be a diversion of some sort. Out."

"Master Sergeant, get us over to the explosion. Lieutenant, I need you topside with your rifle."

He popped back through the hatch just as their Tiger started to slow to make the turn at the checkpoint. Through the pitch-dark night, he could make out the shapes of both soldiers on top of Two Four's Tiger. His driver gingerly dropped them onto the shoulder and pointed the Tiger in the direction of the treeline. Odenko lowered his night vision goggles and immediately saw the bright green glow of a burning vehicle through the trees. The Tiger moved forward slowly.

"Watch your targets. We have two friendlies in the immediate vicinity of the explosion," Odenko said.

"Yes, sir," the private replied, scanning the darkness with the machine gun.

Odenko lowered himself into the vehicle just as the lieutenant arrived at the hatch, tightly gripping an AK-74.

"You cover any direction Marakev isn't watching," he said, adjusting the young officer's night vision goggles and patting him on the shoulder.

He had no idea what they were headed into behind the rapidly approaching tree line, but as a reconnaissance battalion, scouting the unknown was their primary mission, and he was excited to finally do what he had trained a lifetime to do. He just hadn't expected his vehicle to lead the way on the battalion's first combat reconnaissance mission since he'd taken command two years earlier. If he'd known this ahead of time, he would have put a few more experienced soldiers on the guns of his Tiger.

Chapter 60

Farrington stared intensely through the night vision goggles at the featureless green road ahead of them. The chilly night air blasted his face through the missing windshield, pelting his cheeks and neck with stinging pebbles. A small price to pay for a better off road vehicle and armor that could stop most small arms fire. He strained to see as far ahead as possible and make what little sense he could of the deeply rutted dirt road.

Travelling at thirty-five miles per hour along this confusing jumble of jeep trails for the past twenty minutes had put them into the trees twice, costing them precious time. He desperately wanted to avoid any more involuntary off-road trips, but he had no intention of slowing down any further. He needed to close the distance to the border while they were alone on the roads. Once they started to attract company, travel would become perilous and require more caution, which was why they had detoured slightly from his original plan twenty minutes earlier and found themselves on these miserable trails.

They had just completed a shortcut through a small hamlet of dirt roads and corrugated tin huts called Verkh Payva, in an attempt to link up with a road that could support another high-speed run. They hadn't seen a single light in the village as they sped through at seventy miles per hour. Every small settlement they'd encountered west of Highway 380 had been the same—eerily quiet and dark, just the way he liked it.

His original plan had been to travel north of the town and continue on what had turned out to be a reliable jeep trail, but he had become hopelessly addicted to travelling at seventy miles per hour. They'd already made up the time lost at the checkpoint and gained a few minutes on their exfiltration deadline. The road they sought through the thick trees and washed-out trails ran for fifty miles to the town of Znamenka, on the northern tip of Lake Kulunda. If he could hit sixty miles per hour on the road ahead, he could gain more time. Based on Sanderson's last report, elements of the 21st Motor Rifle Division had started to set up roadblock positions in the towns closest to the border. Znamenka was thirty miles from the border, so he didn't anticipate anything more than local law enforcement.

The Tiger's chassis crunched and shook as they hit a sizable washout along the road, seriously testing the vehicle's supposedly undefeatable suspension system. He wasn't sure how many times they could plow over a downed tree or crash through a washout at forty-five miles per hour before they threw an axle or bent a pin, disabling the vehicle permanently.

"You can slow down if you see stuff like that," Farrington said, "no point in walking the rest of the way."

"I was hoping you'd say that. I'm not sure how much more this thing can take," Misha said from behind the wheel.

Farrington's satellite phone rang, and he plugged it into his communications rig.

"What are we looking at?" Farrington answered.

"I noticed you took a little detour," Sanderson said.

"I'm going to make up some time on the road between Verkh Sayva and Znamenka," Farrington said.

"Just be careful. The 121st Recon battalion started moving west a few minutes ago, which means they found the ambushed Tiger. You bought some extra time with the booby traps, but they know you're headed west. High-profile roads might not be the best idea. The 21st Motor Rifle Division will respond accordingly and likely expand east from the border area. We can't track all of these units."

"I understand. Has the 21st shown any movement?"

"Negative, but it won't be long, and you have a Border Guard barracks in the area. They know the area better than you do. If there's a quick way to get to that road you're taking, they'll show the 21st the way. We'll keep a close eye on Znamenka."

"That's all we can do. Two hours and this is over," Farrington said.

"And there's no wiggle room. Berg is worried that the White House might yank the helos early if things get too hot. We still have a few cards to play, but I don't have a trump card this time," Sanderson said.

"Understood. Is Black Rain still online?"

"Affirmative. ETA 0425 over Lake Kulunda. We'll track your progress and adjust accordingly. It looks like you'll be past the lake by 0425, so we might head it straight to your position. That should shave a few minutes off the ETA."

"I think that's the best plan. I'd send it to Slavgorod," Farrington said.

"You're not punching through Slavgorod."

"I'm not planning on that, but I estimate that we'll be somewhere northwest of Slavgorod at that point. At least I hope so. If not, we're fucked."

Slavgorod was fifteen miles from the border, but not directly connected to Kazakhstan by a major road. Hundreds of jeep trails and unmarked dirt roads snaked west into the fields and rolling hills, crisscrossing and emptying directly into Kazakhstan. They anticipated a sizable military presence in Slavgorod, so the plan was to run well north of the city through the myriad trails winding through trees, streams and mild gradients. Once they reached a point less than a mile from the border, they would turn due west and take the Tiger on a true off-road journey, relying on Berg and Sanderson to avoid any final patrols. If they hadn't swung past Slavgorod by 4:25, they were unlikely to reach the border in time for pickup, especially travelling north of the city.

"All right. I'll reroute Black Rain to Slavgorod. How is Sasha holding up?" Sanderson said.

"He's holding up better in the Tiger. We have him lying down, strapped to one of the troop benches. His vitals are stable, but we have him fully drugged up on morphine. The road would have killed him," Farrington said.

"And Seva?"

"Severe concussion from what we can tell. His vision seems fine, and he's one hundred percent mission-capable, but he's started to vomit frequently. I'll be glad to get these two on a bird heading home."

"I want *all* of you on a bird heading home. Be careful on that road," Sanderson said, ending the call.

"I think this is our road," Misha said, slowing the Tiger down to a crawl.

Farrington grabbed the RPDA and activated the screen, scrolling to a tighter view of the digital map. Examining the map for several seconds, he agreed. "I concur. Viktor's people ran this road at sixty miles per hour during the day, so what do you say we try fifty?"

"That's all?" Misha said.

"Feel free to push it if you can keep us on the road," Farrington said, feeling the Tiger accelerate onto the wide dirt road.

"You up for sixty, Seva?" Misha asked.

"I might get some splash back from my own puke at sixty. Ten would be nice," Seva said, eliciting a laugh from the team.

"Might get some splash back? I'm already getting a taste up here. Maybe you could aim lower?" Gosha said from the gun turret.

"I'll send the next batch right up your way. Sixty it is," Seva said.

"Fucking great," Gosha said.

Once the Tiger stabilized on the road, Misha rocketed them forward at a speed that brought a smile to Farrington. He leaned over to examine the speedometer. Sixty-three miles per hour. At this speed, they'd cruise through Znamenka before any of the 21st's vehicles could mobilize.

Chapter 61

4:01 AM
Outskirts of Znamenka
Russian Federation

Farrington didn't have time to further articulate his decision to run the blockade. Their Tiger was rapidly approaching the maximum effective range of the weapons likely to be mounted on the vehicles at Znamenka, and he didn't have much time to coordinate a strategy before 30mm grenades started raining down on them.

"We're running it. I'll call you once were through, out," he said, jamming the satellite radio into the center console.

"Gosha! Anything yet?" he said.

"Nothing. I don't see shit!"

Sanderson reported the sudden appearance of three vehicles on the edge of Znamenka. Two Tigers with multiple weapons mounts and one Ural 4320, heavy off-road trucks capable of transporting an infantry platoon. All of this was supposedly in the open, but nobody in his Tiger had been able to spot the blockade force through their night vision goggles. Still more than two kilometers away, the unmagnified NVGs couldn't provide a crisp enough image to pick them out of the background. He also wondered if the rolling hills didn't play a major role. If the vehicles were situated in a small depression outside of town, they might not see them until the last second. He wanted to believe that the Russians would have the same problem, but he knew better.

"Seva, take over for Gosha on the gun. Gosha, try to pick them up on your thermal scope," Farrington said.

"Got it," Gosha replied.

The maximum effective range for an AGS-30 automatic grenade launcher was 1700 meters, but he didn't expect the Russians to engage his Tiger that far out. The 30mm grenades fired by the system travelled at 183 meters per second and would take an eternity to arc down onto target at that range, rendering impossible the task of adjusting fire on a fast-moving target. The automatic grenade launcher was designed to engage static or slow-moving targets with overwhelming firepower, so he anticipated a strategy better suited to the weapon starting at 1000 meters.

Tactically, the best way to stop an approaching vehicle with an area weapon like the AGS-30 was to create a wall of fragmentation and high-explosive detonations at a fixed point in front of the vehicle and let it sail through. He planned to exploit this tactic to get their lone vehicle past the initial grenade threat unscathed. After that, it would come down to speed and firepower, as it always did in open combat.

"Slow it down to fifty miles per hour, Misha," Farrington said.

The Tiger immediately decelerated, launching him forward against his seat belt.

"Shouldn't we be speeding up?" Misha said.

"Not yet. I just had an idea. Be ready to floor it."

❧

Gosha sat on the back lip of the hatch and peered through the thermal scope at the bouncing purple image. He was thankful they had slowed down because the jolting and bumping at seventy miles per hour would have made this task impossible. He had changed the digital scope's settings from black-and-white to color, in order give him the best chance of picking up warm engine blocks, hot exhaust pipes and personnel in the open. Thermal returns would appear in the orange to yellow range, with yellow signifying the hottest sources. He expected to see the Ural's exhaust pipe first, since it was located high above the cabin, followed by the gunners manning the weapons on the Tigers. His scope showed nothing but a sea of purple.

"Negative on the thermal scope. They must be masked by a hill," Gosha said.

Seva sat on the right side of the open hatch, trying to remain clear of Gosha's view. He swayed on the edge, which made Gosha nervous. Seva had vomited at least five times in the past hour, yielding little more than the water he was trying desperately to force down to stay hydrated. He lowered the scope for a moment to grab Seva's vest and pull him closer.

"I'm good, man. I'm good," Seva insisted.

He was far from good. The operative was fading fast, suffering from a severe concussion and possibly a cerebral blood clot. He needed to be strapped into the bench across from Sasha, receiving intravenous saline, but they had neither the saline nor the luxury of retiring his gun until they reached the extraction point.

"Hang in there, brother. Less than an hour to go," Gosha said, slapping him on the shoulder.

He lifted the rifle back into position and scanned the deep purple image, sweeping left to right along the perceived level of the horizon. The Tiger hit something in the road, slamming the scope into his eye socket and dazing him momentarily. The road smoothed out again, and he got the sensation that they were climbing a gentle hill. He put the scope to his face, afraid of taking another mind-numbing punch to the head and prayed the hill's elevation would give him the view he needed. Nothing appeared for several seconds as he anticipated the Tiger's next jolt. Suddenly, he saw the entire formation. Three unmistakable vehicle heat signatures and a dozen smaller yellow specks surrounding them.

"Contact confirmed. Three vehicles. One Tiger on each side of the road. Utility truck behind the Tiger on the right. Marking targets," he said, moving forward in the hatch to a position next to the grenade launcher.

He activated the AN/PQS-23 Micro-Laser Rangefinder (MLRF) and triggered the narrow beam, centering the thermal scope's crosshairs on the rightmost Tiger. The laser was invisible to his thermal scope, but would appear as a crisp, bright line to his team's night vision goggles, leading directly to the hostile vehicles. Unfortunately, the Russians would see the same laser and know that their blockade had been spotted.

"Got them. Three vehicles," Farrington said.

"Same here. Give me the first target," Seva said, suddenly flush with energy.

"Range to right Tiger?" Farrington said.

"Hold on," he said, fumbling with the MLRF's rubberized buttons.

The green LED readout on the back of the MLRF gave him a distance of 1700 meters, but he wasn't sure the laser had been centered on the Tiger, since he couldn't see the laser in his scope.

"Confirm that my laser is on target. On three, two, mark," he said.

"On target!" Farrington and Seva yelled simultaneously.

"Sixteen hundred meters!" Gosha said.

"Mark the right Tiger for Seva and watch your rangefinder. Our first salvo goes out at 1000 meters. I need to know the instant they start shooting," Farrington said.

"Copy that," Gosha said. "You ready, my friend?" he said, nudging Seva.

"As long as you don't nudge me while I'm firing," he replied, sounding much like the smart-ass Seva he knew.

⤳⤳

Lieutenant Mikhail Greshev lowered his rifle in utter disbelief. Standing on the hood of his Tiger, he had been watching the vehicle's approach through the night vision scope on his rifle for over a minute. The vehicle had disappeared behind a hill for several seconds, and when it reappeared, a bright green laser connected his vehicle with the oncoming Tiger.

"They're marking us, sir!" said the sergeant manning the automatic grenade launcher.

"I can see that," he grunted, jumping down onto the hard ground.

"Do they have air support?" his platoon sergeant said from the window of the Tiger.

"Nothing was reported. They're probably ranging us," Greshev said. "Radio!" he said, fuming that his radioman had suddenly gone missing.

A soldier trotted up to him from the darkness and pushed a radio handset into his shoulder.

"Intrasquad net," Greshev said, swiping the handset.

"Yes, sir."

"Master Sergeant, make sure he's sighted in on the 700 meter mark. Fire on my command only," he said, sending the same command over the radio to the other Tiger. "Battalion command net," he ordered.

"Right away, sir," his radioman said.

He was in the middle of reporting contact with the suspected terrorist cell when one of the soldiers across the street started screaming, "They're shooting at us!" He raised his rifle and stared through the scope, watching in horror as the grenade launcher on the approaching Tiger flashed bright green several times.

"Incoming!" the gunner screamed behind him, scattering everyone standing near the Tiger.

He did the math in his head, like he had been trained to do. The incoming fire would be inaccurate and likely ineffective at first, but the hostile force could rain grenades down on him for another fifteen seconds before his first grenades arched skyward. The terrorists had started firing well outside of the 700 meter marker. Even an ineffective barrage could cause mayhem throughout the platoon, disrupting his carefully laid plan. All of this information collided inside a brain well aware that an unknown number of 30mm high-explosive projectiles were a few seconds away from possibly landing on top of him. Suddenly confronted with conflicting information, under threat of annihilation, he did what any newly minted officer might do in a similar situation. He panicked and tried to make a last-second adjustment to a plan that would have served him well.

"Gunners, add 200 meters and fire! Add 200 meters! Fire!"

He searched for his radioman, but couldn't make anything out in the darkness. He had been using the night vision scope on his rifle so frequently throughout the night that he had practically forgotten about the night vision goggles attached to his helmet. He took off running for the road, screaming his orders to the second Tiger and colliding with one of his own soldiers. Knocked off his feet, he regained his footing just as both of his own Tigers started lobbing grenades down the road.

He crouched in place on the side of the road and waited for the hostile rounds to land in his position, showering the black sky with glistening body parts and glowing metal fragments. Instead, the first salvo of projectiles from the inbound Tiger struck 100 meters short of their position. By the time the deep, rhythmic thumping of multiple high-explosive impacts reached him, he realized what he had done. He had effectively killed his platoon.

❧⚘❧

"Enemy rounds out! 900 meters to target," Gosha screamed, keeping the laser centered on the rightmost Tiger.

"Reloading!" Seva yelled.

The AGS-30 was fed by a detachable drum that held twenty-nine grenades. With a rate of fire exceeding 400 rounds per minute, the weapon was good for four to five sustained bursts before reloading. Unfortunately, they didn't have a spare operative to help with the procedure.

He felt the Tiger lurch forward on the road as Seva disappeared, straining at its top speed of 90 miles per hour along the improvised road. His rifle bounced everywhere as the speeding Tiger jarred him against the hatch, rendering his efforts useless.

"Help Seva reload! I need that gun back up in twenty seconds!" Farrington said.

Gosha slung his rifle and swiveled the launcher ninety degrees to the right to facilitate reloading. Twenty seconds was a tall order for a crew that had just practiced loading and reloading this system for the first time an hour and a half ago on an even road. He detached the empty drum and tossed it over the back of the Tiger, catching multiple flashes in his peripheral vision. He turned his head over his shoulder, watching in awe for a brief second as several dozen bursts of white light, surrounded by brilliant orange sparks, decorated the road behind them.

"Multiple impacts. 100 meters behind us," Gosha said, grabbing the ammunition drum handed to him from inside the Tiger.

Now he understood what Farrington had done. He had lured them into overshooting somehow and very likely emptying their ammunition drums. At 90 miles per hour, their Tiger would reach the convoy in less than thirty seconds, which might not give the Russians enough time to put their grenade launchers back into action. His team's biggest concern from this point forward would be vehicle-mounted machine guns and small arms fire, which was no small threat to their lightly armored vehicle. Fortunately, they would have twenty-nine rounds of 30mm ammunition to even the odds. He attached the drum and secured it tightly, stepping to the right to put his laser back into action. Seva finished the job, pulling back on the charging handle and searching for the rightmost Tiger through the 2.7X sight attached to the AGS-30.

Green tracers raced past them, snapping closely overhead and bouncing off the ground in front of them.

"300 meters!"

He winced as a tracer bounced off the grenade launcher mount, sizzling the air between their heads. Unfazed by the close call, Seva put the AGS-30 back into action, concentrating the 30mm maelstrom on the two heavily armed vehicles. Through the thermal scope, Gosha saw several yellow blossoms envelop the rightmost Tiger, which was immediately followed by a similar digital light show on the left side of the road. His entire scope image suddenly turned bright white, causing him to lower the rifle. A massive fireball rose in front of them, indicating that one of the Russian vehicles had been destroyed by a secondary explosion. The AGS-30 coughed several more rounds and fell silent amidst the chaos of inbound tracers, supersonic cracks and the sound of bullets striking metal.

"Switching to rifle!" Seva yelled, indicating that the launcher's drum was empty.

Gosha ejected the spent magazine in his rifle and reloaded another from one of the pouches on his vest, firing at the bright flashes seen through his fuzzy thermal sight, keeping only his shoulders and head exposed through the hatch. Seva took the same position on the right side of the Tiger, and they both fired furiously at the quickly approaching cluster of soldiers on the ground.

ᔛᔗ

Lieutenant Greshev hugged the ground, flattened by the explosion of the Tiger and simply afraid to stand up. From his position on the side of the road, he could see the darkened hull of a Tiger speeding directly for him. In less than a minute, his platoon had been destroyed because of his error, and now he lay behind the bullet-riddled body of the soldier he had knocked down running blindly through the dark. A series of small explosions ripped through a small knot of brave soldiers trying desperately to put one of the platoon's light machine guns back into action. He could see all of this now through the night vision goggles that he had forgotten about earlier. He could also see that nothing moved in his command vehicle, which had been obliterated seconds earlier by the same weapon that just killed the few surviving members of his platoon. He couldn't imagine any of the soldiers near the light machine gun surviving the simultaneous detonation of several high-explosive grenades in their midst.

As the Tiger raced toward him, he made a split-second decision to atone for his failure and bring honor back to the platoon. He tensed his body and made sure that the safety on his AK-74 was not engaged. When the Tiger reached a point less than thirty meters away, he jumped to his feet and fired his rifle from the hip in the general direction of the speeding vehicle beside him. His lifeless body hit the ground without knowing what he had accomplished.

అఁ

Using his rifle's angled tritium sights, Gosha fired a hasty burst at a soldier superimposed against the flames of the burning vehicle. Before he could assess the effects of the burst, a hammer-like impact dropped him through the hatch into the rear compartment. Seva's body followed him through the hatch, landing directly on top of him and dislocating his right shoulder, which had been pinned underneath him by the fall. The pain in his shoulder flared so intensely that he momentarily lost track of the fact that something had knocked him off his feet. He lay there for a second, unable to process what had happened, until the Tiger jolted, tearing at his dislocated shoulder.

"Motherfucker!" he said, pushing Seva with his left arm.

He could tell that Seva was dead. The operative's body moved with little effort, displaying none of the stiffness or resistance indicative of someone still in control of his or her body. The clanging of metal projectiles against the Tiger's hull suddenly shifted to the rear of the vehicle, settling on the back hatch and dissipating with the few seconds it took Gosha to regain his bearings.

"We're through," Farrington announced.

"Seva's hit. I think I'm hit too," he managed to say, cringing from the pain caused by the Tiger's coarse ride.

"Slow us down to sixty," Farrington said.

Farrington raised his night vision goggles and climbed between the seats. A bright light filled the compartment, focused on Seva, who lay on his back. The light shifted to Gosha's face, causing him to raise his left hand.

"He's gone. Where are you hit?"

"Right leg, maybe. My shoulder's on fire too," Gosha said.

Farrington helped him up onto the bench opposite of Sasha, being as careful with him as possible in the back of a dark, cramped compartment

337

moving at sixty miles per hour down a glorified jeep trail. The experience nearly caused Gosha to momentarily black out, mainly fueled by the pain in his right shoulder. He stared at Sasha's glazed-over eyes as Farrington examined him with the flashlight, wondering if he had survived the firefight.

"I think I dislocated my shoulder," Gosha said.

"Let me see."

Farrington raised his limp arm at the elbow, rotating it across Gosha's stomach and probing along the dislocated shoulder. The pain caused by the movement of this arm caused him to grimace, but paled in comparison to what Farrington had planned for him. Without warning, he firmly swung Gosha's forearm one hundred and eighty degrees in the opposite direction, causing him to scream. The pain subsided within moments, restoring full mobility to his arm.

"All fixed. You have a laceration across your right thigh from a bullet that ripped through your holster. Nothing too nasty," Farrington said, aiming the light at a red slash visible below a rip in his bloodstained khaki cargo pants.

"Patch that up with a compress, and reload the grenade launcher. I need to contact Sanderson and figure out what we're looking at to the west."

"Got it. How long until Black Rain is on station?" Gosha said.

"Fifteen to twenty minutes. We'll hit Slavgorod right as they arrive."

"We're going around Slavgorod, right?"

"Going off-road this far from the border will give the Russians time to redeploy the bulk of the 21st in our path. We can't get into a running gun battle with BTRs on twisting jeep trails with no cover. They'll tear us to shreds from a distance. Black Rain will get us through Slavgorod. Then we go off-road," Farrington said.

"We can't survive another encounter like that."

"I know. Patch yourself up, and get ready. We'll be there in less than fifteen minutes, unless our air is late."

"All right. Let's do this," Gosha said, not sure what to make of Farrington's lightning advance along the most predictable route to Slavgorod.

Chapter 62

Karl Berg watched the satellite feed closely, speaking in hushed tones to Sanderson through his headset. He didn't want Audra to figure everything out until it was effectively too late to stop what he had planned. He glanced over the top of his computer station and caught the watch floor supervisor's attention. Almost time. Audra leaned over and pointed at a cluster of vehicles on one of his screens. Her index finger rested on the thermal image of four BTR-80 armored personnel carriers hidden behind a thick barrier of trees north of Slavgorod. She slid her finger east along the main approach road to the city and stopped on a pair of Tigers less than a half-kilometer away.

"They need to take evasive action immediately. That's a reconnaissance element looking to hand off targets to the BTRs. The rest of Farrington's nine lives will be used up pretty quickly if the BTRs catch him in the open," she said.

She was dead right, as usual. The single 14.5mm gun in each BTRs turret had an effective range of three kilometers and could fire a variety of armor-piercing or high-explosive projectiles, all of which could penetrate the thin armor on Farrington's vehicle with little effort. There was no way Farrington could approach Slavgorod with the BTRs guarding the road.

"I'll notify Sanderson immediately," he said, feeling guilty about the subterfuge circling the air between them.

"Base, this is control," Berg said. "I am passing positive control of Black Rain to your station. Satellite imagery confirms the presence of four BTR-80s and two Tigers on the approach road. I recommend using ordnance sparingly. Additional units have entered the city from the south and may present a challenge."

"Which unit is Black Rain?" Audra said.

"Hold on," Berg said.

He didn't meet her gaze, knowing he couldn't lie directly to her face. He concentrated on the screen and activated the communications link to Weatherman, a CIA drone operator working out of the mobile control station at Manas Air Base. Berg had managed to surreptitiously deliver one of the CIA's MQ-9 Reaper drones to Manas, hidden amidst the logistics equipment necessary to support the temporary presence of three top-secret helicopters. The secrecy surrounding the helicopters kept prying eyes off the delivery manifests, drawing little attention to the arrival of one additional C-17 Globemaster III heavy transport aircraft from Jalalabad Air Base.

"Weatherman, this is Berg. Standing by to transfer tactical control of Black Rain."

"This is Weatherman. Wait one."

"Karl, who are you talking to?" Audra insisted.

"This is Weatherman. I have positively authenticated the request for tactical control of Black Rain. ETA 0418 local."

"Good luck and happy hunting," Berg said, ready to come clean with Audra.

He turned his head toward the watch supervisor and nodded, watching her immediately transmit an order over her headset to one of the technicians in the operations center.

"Karl, I need you to explain what is going on here," Audra said.

"I've arranged an insurance policy for Sanderson's crew," he said.

"Please tell me you didn't put one of our drones over Russia."

"You know I have a bad track record with drones," he said, hoping she might find the humor in his comment.

"I don't find that amusing, Karl. Not in the least. Your track record involves losing drones. We can't lose one of those on Russian soil, for many reasons," Audra said.

"I'm not going to lose this one."

She glanced around and moved her seat closer. "It's already lost," she said, looking at him for agreement.

She tilted her head and managed to look even more incredulous, which Berg didn't think was possible at this point.

"You sent a Reaper?" she demanded.

"The Predators don't have the range to make the round trip," Berg said.

"That didn't stop you last time."

"See? I'm becoming more responsible."

"What was all the head nodding with Ms. Halverson about?" she said, gesturing toward the watch floor supervisor.

"I'm cutting the satellite feed to the Situation Room for a minute or two," he said.

She shook her head and leaned back in the chair. "I don't know what to say, Karl. You've gone too far on this one. I think this might have to be our last operation together," Audra said.

"You mean you're not going to fire me?" Berg said.

"How could I fire you? I can't sit here and pretend that this isn't partially my fault. I've encouraged you for far too long. I've swept enough of your operations under the rug for one career. I need a break from that kind of stress. Our friendship needs a break from it," she said.

"I'm sorry to have kept you in the dark on this, but I wanted to give you and Manning some plausible deniability here. I need him to look the president and the director in the eye at the White House and convincingly tell them that he has no idea what just happened. I need to keep them all confused long enough to get Farrington to the border."

"You better pray that Black Rain doesn't get shot down over Russia," she said.

He was moments from making an ill-timed joke about purposely crashing the drone, but Audra beat him to it.

"And I don't care how bad it gets out there, you will not turn one of our Reapers into a kamikaze like you did before. Are we crystal clear on that?"

"I've already built that restriction into the parameters. Sanderson can only pick and prioritize targets. Once the eight Hellfires are expended, the drone is back under our control," he said, wondering if he needed to further clarify this with Weatherman.

Chapter 63

5:17 PM
White House Situation Room
Washington, D.C.

Thomas Manning stood along the back wall of the small conference room and watched the satellite feed with curious interest. Reports from Karl Berg over the communications feed evaporated when Sanderson's team sped past the first possible detour point, six kilometers from the city. He'd spent the next few minutes urgently trying to reach Berg, as the Tiger continued to barrel down the road, skipping several more opportunities to deviate from a suicidal engagement with Russian armored vehicles, and sending the president and his staff into a general uproar.

When Berg didn't answer his repeated requests, dozens of scenarios swirled through his head, none of which held promise. Did they lose communications with Farrington's team? Did someone sabotage the CIA operations center? Was Farrington ignoring orders, thinking he could take on armored vehicles?

The Tiger continued to close on the city, bringing everyone to the edge of their seats. Farrington's vehicle suddenly stopped three and a half kilometers from the Russian BTR ambush site, eliciting a collective sigh of relief from the room. When the Tiger once again accelerated at reckless speed toward the city, the president stood up from his seat and turned to CIA Director Copley.

"They're never going to make it through! What are they doing?"

"I don't know, Mr. President. I can't get through to my operations center," Manning interrupted.

"The BTRs are on the move, heading east to intercept on the road. They'll be within gun range in less than thirty seconds," Lieutenant General Gordon said.

Manning confirmed the armored vehicles' movement on the screen. All four BTRs had moved in a column onto the east-west road running from Znamenka to Slavgorod. In a few seconds, the vehicles would spread out into a "line abreast" formation, exposing Farrington's Tiger to four 14.5mm guns. If the Tiger didn't alter course within the next few seconds, they would all bear witness to a massacre. He wondered if this was Farrington's plan, if Sanderson and Berg had uncovered information over the past few silent minutes that had sealed the team's fate, and Farrington intended to go down fighting.

"Isn't there any way to communicate with the team? I thought we were talking to them just a few minutes ago?" the president said.

"I've lost communications with the group controlling Blackjack," Manning said.

"Well, somebody better warn them that they're about to be taken out! I think we should send the helicopters back to Manas immediately. Something isn't right here," the president said.

"Mr. President, the helicopters haven't been detected. There's no reason to send them back prematurely," General Gordon said.

"It's not a premature decision, General," the president said. "Those men are as good as dead."

"We can send them back in a few minutes, Mr. President. What's the range of those guns again? 3000 meters?" Jacob Remy asked.

Remy's cold statement wasn't lost on Manning, or anybody in the room. Lieutenant General Gordon penetrated him with a look of disgust and hatred that might have caused Remy to lose voluntary control of his bladder...if the president's chief of staff had bothered to take his eyes off the wall monitor. Instead, his gaze remained glued to the massive screen, eagerly waiting to watch the thermal image of Farrington's Tiger blossom into a bright white circle. Before anyone could answer Remy's question, the two screens displaying the operation's satellite feeds went blank, catapulting the room into chaos.

"Operations, this is Thomas Manning. We just lost our satellite feed in the Situation Room. What's going on over there?" he demanded.

"We're not sure. Some kind of technical difficulties with the satellite link. Should be back up in a minute or two. Everything is under control," a familiar voice replied.

He almost screamed into the headset that nothing appeared under control, but something gave him pause. The voice belonged to Karl Berg, and he'd answered immediately. Manning thought about the events leading up to this moment and the incredible risk they had all undertaken to coordinate the team's extraction. The possibility of encountering light armored vehicles in their path hadn't been a surprise. In fact, Pentagon and CIA analysts had accurately predicted the response and deployment of the Russian assets on nearly every level. The strong likelihood of a sizable roadblock north of Slavgorod had been part of the early briefings. Now it made sense to him. He stopped with that thought and whispered into the headset.

"Berg, you devious son-of-a-bitch."

"Did you get through to your operations center?" the president demanded.

"I did, Mr. President. They experienced a problem with the satellite link. Should be back on-line in a minute. They don't know what happened."

Without hesitating, the National Security Advisor suggested the possibility that the Russians had disabled U.S. satellites with a directed EMP blast. His declaration plunged the already agitated room into further chaos and temporarily yanked him out of the spotlight. Manning looked up at the director, struggling not to grin. The director wore an emotionless face, but he could see it in the director's eyes. Like Manning, the director was engaged in an all-out battle to internalize his suspicions that the timing of the satellite link failure was far from random.

Chapter 64

4:18 AM
3 Kilometers outside of Slavgorod
Russian Federation

The wind punched through the missing windshield, mercilessly ripping through the Tiger's cabin as Misha increased their speed to eighty-five miles per hour. The frost-heave-damaged asphalt road connecting Znamenka to Slavgorod had left his spine rattled and his stomach in knots. Despite the shattering discomfort, successfully navigating the entire road at highway speed had far exceeded his expectations for the Russian equivalent to backwater USA. Based on what he had witnessed during their trek westward to the border, backwater was a generous description of the isolated network of villages and trails defining their southwestern Siberian experience. He couldn't imagine a commerce-related reason for the government to pave the road between these two towns, but was grateful that some nameless Communist Party bureaucrat had at one time persisted in his or her pursuit of the precious bitumen surface his vehicle travelled.

He stared at the monochromatic green image of two Tiger vehicles less than a kilometer ahead, partially obscured by a thin stand of tall trees extending north. The line of trees, planted long ago by Slavgorod city planners to cut the frozen winds sweeping across the Siberian steppes, rapidly grew in his viewfinder. At this speed, it took less than thirty seconds to travel a kilometer. Sanderson was cutting it a little close.

"Stand by to engage targets!" Farrington said.

"We can't keep slugging it out like this," Gosha replied.

"Have some faith, boys," Sanderson said over the communications net.

For the final phase of their exfiltration, Farrington had patched the satellite phone directly into his comms rig, adding Sanderson to the intrasquad feed. With elements of the 21st Motor Rifle Division pouring into the city from the south, the ride through Slavgorod would require quick communications and multi-sensory input from all members of his team.

Of course, if Black Rain didn't immediately produce some bad weather for the approaching Tigers, they might not reach Slavgorod. He scanned the northwest horizon, looking for any sign that they would not have to engage in another close-range gun battle. He couldn't imagine the Russian gunners making the same mistake twice. A single flash erupted on the horizon, followed by multiple flashes.

"Missiles away," Sanderson said over the net.

"Gosha, distance to targets?" Farrington said.

"Less than five hundred meters!"

He did a quick mental calculation involving estimated missile time of flight and flipped up his night vision goggles.

"Get inside the Tiger!" he said.

Less than a second after he heard Gosha drop into the cabin, a brilliant flash illuminated the landscape ahead of them, immediately followed by a shockwave that rattled their 12,000 pound armored vehicle like a toy. Misha kept the Tiger steady on the road as they sped toward the inferno.

A few seconds later, the heat radiated by the burning wreckage on the side of the road became too intense, forcing him to shield his face with his hands. Through his fingers, he caught a brief, ninety mile per hour glimpse of the carnage wreaked by the Hellfire's 100-pound high-explosive warhead.

One of the vehicles lay upside down but mostly intact against the burning trees, smoke and flame pouring from its windows. The other Tiger hadn't moved from its original position, but there was little left to indicate what it had been before the Hellfire missile had plunged through the thin armor. Through the flames dancing in the grass, all he could discern was a twisted, smoking chassis. The drone operator had assigned one missile to the pair of Tigers, correctly assuming that the force of the warhead would effectively destroy both of the tightly parked vehicles.

Two fireballs ascended skyward on the horizon, in the vicinity of Slavgorod's city limits, drawing his attention away from the grisly destruction. Additional flashes closely followed, momentarily exposing several small buildings previously shrouded in darkness.

"Black Rain reports good hits on all targets. Four BTRs and two Tigers destroyed on the road. Three Hellfire missiles remaining. Black Rain will remain on station until all ordnance expended," Sanderson said.

"Copy. Just make sure Black Rain keeps us positively identified throughout the city. We're driving a Tiger and I just saw what a Hellfire missile can do to a Tiger," Farrington said.

"Roger. Recommend that you activate your IR strobe once inside the city. That'll keep Black Rain off your ass. Use the lowest intensity setting. Remember, the Russians can see that strobe with their night vision. Black Rain is repositioning to cover you from the top down."

"We're less than a minute from entering the town. Any chance of a straight shot across?"

"Not likely. I'm looking at eight Tigers and five BTRs less than two kilometers from the northern access road. Even if you did slip by, they'd be all over your ass on the way to the border. You could have avoided all of this drama by staying on the trails," Sanderson said.

"And we'd be forty kilometers from the border instead of fifteen, with little chance of reaching our pickup. We weren't making enough progress," Farrington said.

A few seconds of icy silence hung over the net before Sanderson spoke.

"Let's get you through the city undetected. You'll have to slow down as soon as you reach the first houses on the left. You'll need to take a left on a dirt road just past the seventh house. This road will curve to the right and put you at a dirt intersection with homes on all four sides. Take another left at the intersection. We'll assess enemy vehicle movement from there," Sanderson said.

"Solid copy. We're passing the destroyed BTRs right now," Farrington said, tracking the wrecked convoy through his windows.

The first armored vehicle remained upright on eight surprisingly intact wheels, burning brightly through the blown side and top hatches. A massive hole above the troop compartment poured thick smoke and sparks into the darkened sky. The second and third BTR on the road had fared no better, belching flame through every opening into the Siberian air, evidence of torn metal and burning material scattered on the road between them. The last BTR had been knocked onto its side by the force of the explosion that inflicted a three-foot wide hole in its left side and blew the turret at least fifty into the field. Misha swerved to avoid the smoking chunk of metal as they passed down the left side of the road, giving Farrington a view of the twisted gun barrel sticking up from the grass. Looking back as the Tiger rejoined the road, he could see an area the size of two football fields softly illuminated by dozens of small fires and burning fragments thrown from the obliterated vehicles. The glow receded as their Tiger reached the first house and Misha started counting the houses out loud. Misha found the dirt road and slowed to make the turn.

"Gosha, activate the strobe," Farrington said.

"Strobe activated," Gosha replied.

A few seconds later, Sanderson's voice echoed through his headset.

"Russian vehicles are starting to deploy east through the town in response to the explosions. If they keep going east, you'll run into them trying to break through to the west. We're going to hit the first one to reach the northern road with a Hellfire and try to draw them away. I've just been told that Black Rain has identified your strobe and marked your vehicle as friendly. You're looking good. Keep heading south on that road."

It now seemed that the only people who didn't know where the vehicle was headed, were the people actually in the vehicle. Farrington stared at the green image ahead, trying to make sense of the dirt road that barely stood out from the rest of the landscape. Several scattered houses forming the rough outline of a road guided them, but for all he could tell, they could have been driving through a row of backyards.

"Coming up on a right curve. Make sure you take a left at the first intersection after the curve. Once you take that left, keep going and don't turn west until I tell you to. You'll be off-road at that point, but there's a massive windbreak on the eastern edge of town that will keep you hidden. Keep pushing south," Sanderson said.

"Got it. Misha, can you see a curve?" Farrington said.

"I can't see shit."

"Coming up in thirty meters. On my laser. You might want to slow down," Gosha said.

Both of them saw a bright green line mark the start of the curve, which gave them a better frame of reference, but did little to help either of them identify the turn. Misha slowed at the point and started to gently turn.

"Sharper turn! You're gonna roll us into that ditch," Gosha said.

Farrington felt the vehicle lurch to the right, as Misha turned the wheel suddenly.

"Nobody said a fucking thing about a ditch!" Misha replied.

"This looks good," Farrington said, pretty sure they were straightened out on the road.

A few seconds later, they reached the intersection and turned left, continuing south into the fields behind a large barn and several unlit homes. He saw the thick row of trees Sanderson had mentioned past the houses, and directed Misha to work his way along the field until they found an opening in the tightly sown windbreak.

"Missile away," Sanderson said.

Farrington leaned forward and craned his neck to the right, trying to catch a glimpse of the inbound Hellfire. A bright flash reflected off the treetops and the top of the barn, blinding his night vision goggles, followed by a massive crunching sound.

"Scratch one BTR. Find a path through the trees and stand by to make a high-speed run due west," Sanderson said.

"Follow my mark, Misha," Gosha said.

Misha accelerated toward the tree line, chasing Gosha's laser. He stopped the Tiger less than twenty meters from the opening.

"Russian units are speeding to the site of the destroyed BTR. We're going to fire one more at a building north of the city. As soon as you hear the explosion, take off looking for an east-west road. All of them cut directly across the town. Deactivate your strobe," Sanderson said.

"Strobe deactivated," Gosha said.

"We're at a break in the trees," Farrington said.

"Stand by...missile away," Sanderson said.

Eight seconds later, Farrington saw a bright green flash to the north. He slapped Misha's shoulder, and the Tiger rocketed forward before the sound of the explosion reached them. Misha turned the jeep left on the gravel road just beyond the trees, searching for a westerly route. Farrington spotted what appeared to be a wide turnoff coming up on the right.

"Try that," he said, pointing uselessly at the turnoff.

"Where?" Misha said, slowing.

"Right there. Looks like a car parked at the corner, or some kind of—"

"Got it," he said, swinging the car onto the road and speeding up.

"You're clear to punch through town. The closest units to the south are three kilometers away, just entering Slavgorod," Sanderson said.

A few minutes later, Misha brought the Tiger to a halt in unfamiliar territory on the far western outskirts of town. They needed to connect with one of the major jeep trails headed southwest, which would feed into a network of smaller westerly trails that emptied directly into the border less than twelve kilometers away.

"Anyone following us?" Farrington said.

"Not that I can tell," Gosha said.

"You look clear from where I'm standing," Sanderson said, eliciting a few tired laughs.

"Anything ahead of us?" Farrington said.

"Nothing heavy. We've spotted a few Tigers running up and down the border, but we'll help you get past those. I'm going to notify control, so they can release Black Magic from the holding area," Sanderson said.

"Copy. We're moving out."

Farrington looked at his watch and smiled. *4:27*. They had nearly thirty minutes to travel twelve kilometers over flat terrain, with nobody in immediate pursuit. Maybe this hadn't been the suicide mission he expected after all. Then again, it was too early to start thinking like that. A lot could go wrong in twelve kilometers.

"Head out on the trail to the left at fifty miles per hour. If it stays southwest, increase your speed. Stay frosty, gentlemen. We ain't out of the woods yet."

Chapter 65

3:39 AM
CIA Compound, Manas Airbase
Manas, Kyrgyzstan

Dean Canales stared at the shifting infrared image of the Tiger on his screen and manipulated the joystick at his station to decrease the magnification and display a more panoramic view. Based on the Reaper's sensor input, Blackjack was less than three kilometers from the Kazakhstan border, with a clear path ahead of them. The nearest enemy vehicle, a heavily armed Tiger, sat four kilometers southwest of them at the end of the jeep trail in front of the border. Blackjack had jumped the trail a few kilometers back, heading due west at a conservative off-road speed that would put them on Kazakhstan soil in six minutes if they didn't blow a tire. Even if they blew a tire at this point, they could limp across the border in time to meet their pickup.

"Let's do one more sweep for hostiles. Climb to three thousand feet and start a three sixty centered on Blackjack's current position," Canales said.

"Roger. Climbing," the other CIA employee said.

"All right. Let's see who's out there," he said, adjusting his joystick to sweep the area north of Blackjack.

Commands transmitted from the mobile ground control station took 1.2 seconds to reach Black Rain through a satellite link, which made operating the drone an interesting exercise in forward thinking. Nothing happened immediately, and high-stress situations required an odd form of time-delayed patience. Former pilots had a difficult time adjusting to a video-game-style flight mode that didn't immediately respond to their "stick" movements, and were rarely transitioned to UAV programs. The CIA preferred to steal previously trained drone pilots from the Air Force, or in the case of Dean Canales, train them from scratch.

The Raytheon AN/DAS-1 Multi-Spectral Targeting System (MTS-B) mounted under the Reaper's nose responded to his commands, sweeping north and panning out to an even wider view than previously established. Canales focused on the MTS-B's infrared sensor's input, which gave him the best chance of detecting any threats within the sensor's view. The Siberian landscape had retained little of the previous day's heat, providing a near perfect backdrop for the passive infrared sensor. The heat signature of a human or recently run vehicle starkly contrasted with the cold ground, making his job relatively simple. The system's software did the rest, automatically locking onto these signatures for further investigation by human operators. Canales would make a quick assessment, based on system recommendations and his own experience, whether the Reaper needed to do a closer sweep over a detected signature.

With his eyes fixed to the screen, he reached for an insulated coffee mug on the floor with his unoccupied hand. He found one of the mugs and lifted it, quickly determining that it was too light to be his backup supply of caffeine. He moved his hand around under the thick leather swivel seat in frustration, finally deciding to take his eyes off the screen for a brief second. He turned the seat to the right and leaned his head over the side, immediately finding the tall black mug and lifting it from the floor. Now he was back in business.

He had crashed hard ten minutes ago, coming down off the incredible adrenaline rush initiated by the brief one-sided battle over Slavgorod. He'd fired more than his fair share of Hellfire missiles against Al Qaeda operatives or other "extremists," and was no stranger to questionable drone missions, but what they did over Slavgorod was something different altogether. Whatever Blackjack carried in that Tiger had to be absolutely critical to national security because he had just committed an act of war against the Russian Federation to defend it.

He couldn't imagine the agency debrief for this operation and all of the paperwork he'd have to sign swearing this to secrecy. The only immediate upside he could foresee would be an instantaneous transfer out of this shithole back to the United States. He expected to be on the first flight out of Manas after landing the Reaper, which suited him fine. Manas Airbase was a miserable assignment that he'd reluctantly agreed to take for the hardship pay.

When he returned his gaze to the multi-sensor input console, his eyes caught something exiting the bottom of the screen at high speed. He didn't see enough of the image to determine what had crossed the screen, but based on the sensor's orientation, it was travelling north to south. He nestled the coffee mug between his legs and checked the system for a software tag. Finding it at the top of the queue, he hooked the tag and clicked on the icon to slave the MTS-B turret on the Reaper to the heat signature. One point two seconds later, he experienced an adrenaline spike that felt like more of a heart attack. Two Mi-8 Hip helicopters had passed under his Reaper, headed toward Blackjack.

Chapter 66

4:40 AM
2.5 Kilometers from Kazakhstan Border
Russian Federation

The Tiger dropped into a shallow ditch, jamming Farrington against the four-point harness that had kept his body inside the vehicle over the past several minutes. The vehicle suddenly angled skyward and cleared the ditch in a violent lurching motion.

"You gotta watch that shit! We can't get stuck!" Farrington said, fully aware that he was letting the conditions get the better of him.

"You didn't see the fucking ditch either! I've been driving this motherfucker in the dark for four hours. I could use a little help watching the road!" Misha said.

"Check out the eastern horizon," Gosha said, temporarily diffusing the tension.

Farrington raised his night vision goggles and risked a look out of the passenger window. The horizon indeed displayed a faint blue glow, which signified the beginning of nautical twilight. Soon enough, the landscape surrounding them would start to appear without the aid of night vision, exposing them to simple observation by border patrols or aircraft. He hoped to be flying across Kazakhstan in a helicopter by that point.

The vehicle bucked again, slamming the side of his head into the metal doorframe.

"Son of a bitch," he muttered.

"Serves you right," Misha said.

The left, front side of the vehicle dropped and rebounded, shaking the entire vehicle, but sparing Farrington any further physical damage. Sasha moaned from the rear compartment, feeling the full impact of their off-road voyage, strapped against the thinly cushioned troop bench. His morphine had started to wear thin before reaching Slavgorod, but they didn't feel comfortable giving him more painkillers without a better assessment of his condition, and so far they hadn't been able to spare the time for a more comprehensive examination. He was moaning, which meant he was still alive, and that was about the best they could manage at the moment.

Farrington's satellite phone vibrated, and he immediately answered.

"Blackjack, this is control station. Black Rain has detected helicopters inbound from the north—"

"Is this our pickup? We're not over the border yet," Farrington said.

"Negative. Two Mi-8 Hips at low altitude. Scan north to northeast of your position. We're trying to find them on satellite…shit, check your four o'clock!" Karl Berg said.

"Scan four o'clock for hostile helicopters!" Farrington yelled.

"Scanning!" Gosha yelled.

"Where the fuck are my helos, control?" Farrington said.

"En route to primary extract. ETA three minutes," Berg said.

"You need to redirect them to our position. We can't fight off armed helicopters," Farrington said.

"I'll do what I can. Until then, I have one last parting gift for you," Berg said.

❧

Gosha spotted the helicopters and swiveled the grenade launcher as far to the right as possible, unable to line them up in the launcher's sight. Unlike the American "Humvee," the GAZ Tiger didn't feature a fully rotatable gun ring enabling gunners to engage targets in a three-hundred-and-sixty-degree arc. He was limited by the Tiger's forward direction of travel.

"I have two helicopters coming in low at four o'clock," Gosha said.

"How far?" Farrington said.

"Not far enough."

He couldn't guess their distance in the dark and had no intention of taking his hands off the grenade launcher to try and mark them with his rifle-mounted laser. By the time he determined the range, projectiles of various calibers would start arriving. He assumed the helicopters hadn't been armed with air-to-ground missiles, or they would have fired them already, serving up the same result as the Hellfire missiles fired from the drone overhead.

Without air-to-ground missiles, the transport helicopters would have a limited number of attack options, all strictly dependent upon the types of guns installed. The most typical weapons arrangement for the Mi-8 Hip troop transport involved door guns, which would leave them with two options: high-speed strafing runs alongside the Tiger or standoff gunnery at low speed. The Tiger's grenade launcher could outrange most of the weapons mountable in the Hip's doors, making a slow or stationary standoff attack unlikely. One 30mm grenade could cripple the lightly armored Hip, and the pilots would be unlikely to take that chance. Gosha counted on them to favor less accurate, high-speed tactics which, combined with the one Hellfire missile still owed to them by Black Magic, gave them a fighting chance to reach the border.

Almost on cue with this thought, the lead helicopter exploded in midair, spinning ninety degrees and dropping to the horizon. Upon impact with the ground, a secondary detonation expanded skyward, blinding his night vision goggles. He couldn't tell if the explosion had simply masked the second helicopter from sight or enveloped the second helicopter in the storm of shrapnel and fire that illuminated the countryside. He prayed for the latter. He raised his NVGs and scanned for any sign of a second crash site, unable to see past the firestorm that appeared well within his grenade launcher's range.

"Splash one helo! I don't have a visual on the second," he said.

"Second helo peeled off in a wide arc," Farrington said. "We might have caught a break. Get us to the border, Misha. I don't care how you do it."

Misha accelerated the Tiger forward through the rough terrain, making a final push for the border. They travelled several seconds before Farrington broke the bad news over the intrasquad radio.

"Control reports that the second Hip appears to be back in the fight, approaching from our seven o'clock. They have a bird's-eye satellite view of the situation and can estimate range. We'll turn into them at 2000 meters so you can engage with the grenade launcher," Farrington said.

"How far to the border?" Gosha asked, pushing his NVGs down over his face.

"One point five kilometers. We just have to stay in the game for three minutes! Control is telling me to stand by to maneuver. Three, two—" Farrington said.

"I don't have a visual," Gosha said, scanning the indicated sector for a dark object hovering over the horizon.

"Hard left! Accelerate!" Farrington said.

The vehicle banked left, swinging Gosha into the metal lip of the hatch and breaking his grip on the grenade launcher's handle. When the Tiger straightened on its new southerly course, Gosha swung the launcher left, expecting to see the Hip lined up within a few degrees to either side of the weapon's barrel. Instead, he saw nothing in a one hundred and eighty degree arc.

"I can't see it!"

Before Gosha figured out his error, a continuous line of green tracers hit the ground in front of the Tiger, ricocheting in every direction. Misha managed to turn the vehicle out of the rapid-fire onslaught less than a second before the flow of 7.62mm projectiles hit them. The buzz-saw sound of the Hip's minigun filled the air, competing with the general panic on their internal communications net, as he followed the last line of tracers back to the source. The helicopter had attacked them from a high angle, which he clearly hadn't expected.

Misha's quick maneuver had saved them from certain oblivion. This Mi-8 Hip was fitted with GShG 7.62mm miniguns, capable of accurately firing 6,000 rounds per minute out to 1000 meters. The gunners aboard the Hip only needed to line the Tiger up in their minigun sights for one second to shred the Tiger with over one hundred steel-jacketed projectiles. While his grenade launcher could saturate a stationary target at twice the range of the minigun, hitting a moving target was a different story altogether. The grenades took forever to reach their target and didn't travel in a straight trajectory, making it nearly impossible to calculate the necessary trajectory to successfully lead a fast-moving target. He wasn't the least bit optimistic about hitting a helicopter moving at 150 miles per hour with one of his grenades. Not before they were torn to pieces by the Hip's miniguns.

Instead, they would have to work together to dodge the obtrusively lethal green line of tracers. If they could maneuver wildly enough at the last moment, the gunners would have a hard time lining up a shot. The last gun run had lasted fewer than three seconds, which was all the time the Russian gunners would get if the pilots continued to play it safe and conduct high-speed strafing runs. He watched the Hip bank left and commence a slow turn, while Misha pointed the Tiger toward the border and floored the engine.

Chapter 67

The president turned to General Gordon and demanded an explanation for what they had all just witnessed on the screen.

"Did one of our helicopters just crash in Russia? I did not authorize the extraction force to cross the border!" he said, turning to Manning next. "Find out what the hell is going on there!"

"That was not one of our helicopters. Black Magic is sitting three kilometers west of the border. I'm talking with the SOCOM air controller right now," General Gordon said, putting his right hand over his ear to drown out any noise from the room. "I've just been told that Black Magic saw the explosion. They also report another helicopter in the area firing on Blackjack."

"Mr. President," Manning said, "Blackjack reports that they are under attack by Russian helicopters. Heavily armed Mi-Hip transports. Blackjack is less than a kilometer from the border and requests immediate extract."

"Black Magic Zero One is armed, Mr. President," General Gordon said.

"We don't know how many Russian helicopters are out there. What if there are more? We don't even know where these helicopters originated!" Jacob Remy said.

"Our analysts are pretty sure they came from the airbase at Novosibirsk," Manning replied. "Probably helicopters in transit to Georgia or Murmansk from a squadron based in Irkutsk. They feel confident that this is all we'll see."

"All I heard was 'pretty sure' and 'probably,' Mr. Manning. We can't afford any more surprises here. General Gordon?" the president said.

"Yes, sir?"

"Get Black Magic out of there. Roll the whole package back to Manas."

"Understood, Mr. President."

Manning couldn't believe what he was hearing. Against all odds, Farrington's team had made it close enough to the border to get within visual range of Black Magic, and they were still going to pull the plug on the operation.

"We could have them onboard our helos in less than three minutes, Mr. President. We've come too far to give up at this point," Manning pleaded.

"Correction, Mr. Manning. We've gone too far at this point. I'm responsible for a trail of Russian corpses extending nearly two hundred miles from Novosibirsk to Kazakhstan, and now we've just added a Russian transport helicopter to the list. I'm already facing a hard fucking day on the diplomatic front tomorrow. I won't risk compounding the situation with the loss of an American helicopter on Russian soil, especially not one of those prototypes. I don't know how I let any of you convince me to authorize their use. General Gordon, are those helicopters heading back?"

"They just received the order, Mr. President," the general said.

"You're making a big mistake leaving them behind, Mr. President," Manning said. "If any of them are captured alive, you'll be facing more than a bad day on the diplomatic front."

"Stand down, Mr. Manning," Director Copley said.

"I want him out of here," Remy said, prompting Manning to stand up.

The Secret Service agents standing at the door stirred, responding to Manning's sudden movement. He wondered if they would physically remove him from the room if he refused to leave, and found himself not caring. He activated the communications channel to Karl Berg and passed information that he knew would result in his immediate expulsion from the Situation Room.

"Berg, this is Manning. The president refuses to send the helicopters to assist Blackjack. Black Magic has been ordered to return to Manas Airbase. Make sure they know who's responsible."

"What in the hell are you doing?" the president said.

"Informing Blackjack that they've been abandoned, so they can properly adjust their tactics," Manning said. "I suggest we all cheer on the Russian helicopter gunners at this point," Manning said.

"And why is that?" the National Security Advisor asked.

"Because if I was in that Tiger, I'd sell this pit of vipers out to the highest bidder if I managed to survive," Manning said. He paused to listen to his headset for a moment and responded, "Negative. It appears they never had any intention of extracting the team. They're on their own."

"That's a bald-faced lie!" Remy yelled.

"Good luck convincing anyone of that. I've sat here for the past hour watching you do everything short of breaking out the beer and chips to cheer on the Russians at every roadblock. You looked like you'd just seen a ghost when we restored the satellite feed," Manning said.

"Director Copley, I don't want to see this man again," the president said. "Get him out of here."

Manning handed his headset to Director Copley and raised his hands above his head, easing his forced departure from the conference room. The Secret Service agents grabbed his shoulders, forcibly guiding him from the room. Director Copley wore a grimace that indicated he was powerless to step in. Manning understood why. The CIA couldn't afford a presidential coup within Langley, and the simultaneous removal of the CIA Director and National Clandestine Service Director would create a power vacuum that the White House would be eager to fill. Copley wouldn't make it that easy for Remy. Not after this fiasco.

"Good luck explaining the Russian mafiya connection!" Manning said over his shoulder at the doorway.

"What is he talking about?" the president said, directing his question at Director Copley.

"I have no idea, but it sounds like something you might want to ask him yourself," the director said.

"Hold on. Bring him back!" the president said. "What are you talking about?"

"Who do you think helped Sanderson's team set up the entire operation within Russia?" Manning said.

"I thought it was an activist group. Some kind of eco-terrorist network," the president said.

"Unfortunately that fell through. We had to pay the Solntsevskaya Bratva several million dollars to arrange the logistics, surveillance and assassinations necessary to complete the mission," Manning said.

"You set us up!" Remy said.

"I think it's time to crack out the chips and salsa, Jacob, you've got a lot of cheering to do for that Russian helicopter," Manning said. "I'd hate to imagine what the survivor would do with that information, not to mention Sanderson."

"Don't think you can scare me with this last-minute revelation," the president said. "I don't care if you contracted with Osama Bin Laden to take down Vektor. After the biological attack against U.S. citizens less than a month ago, I could nuke Novosibirsk and not raise an eyebrow at home. A Russian mafiya connection? Grow up, Mr. Manning. Sanderson's operatives understood the risks involved. Sending helicopters into Russia was not part of the deal. Get him out of here."

Manning was struggling against the Secret Service agents' efforts to push him through the door when Director Copley's voice broke through the commotion. Manning planted a foot in the doorframe, temporarily arresting his rapid departure so he could hear what his boss had to say. Copley was a man of few words, but his brief discourses typically held far more sway than his quiet nature might suggest.

"I suggest we keep the helicopters in place so that we have the capability to honor the deal if they cross into Kazakhstan," Director Copley said.

"What if the Russian helicopter doesn't back off at the border?" the president asked.

"Let's cross that bridge when we reach it."

The president considered his comments for a moment and turned to General Gordon. "Rescind my previous order. Black Magic will remain on station until the pickup time has expired."

"What about the enhanced rules of engagement?" the general asked.

"We'll cross that bridge when we reach it," he said, staring at Director Copley.

Manning released all of the tension in his body and allowed the agents to whisk him away down the hallway, satisfied that he had done everything possible to give Farrington's team what little chance they might have to escape Russia.

Chapter 68

4:46 AM
3 Kilometers from the Russian Border
Kazakhstan

Major Borelli eased Black Magic Zero One into a hover forty feet above the ground and glanced through one of his left cockpit windows. Through his panoramic night vision goggles, he saw Zero Two's dark green form pull even with his helicopter, roughly one hundred meters away. Zero Three remained two kilometers behind them, watching the area to the west and standing by to replace either one of them at a moment's notice. They were back in position to extract the special operations team. He had no idea what was going on at SOCOM, but he was glad to be back. It didn't feel right to abandon the team so close to the end.

"Blackjack reacquired," he heard through his helmet's communication suite.

The Forward Looking Infrared (FLIR) pod mounted in the nose of his MH-60K Stealth Hawk had quickly found the friendly Tiger. The 160th Special Operations Aviation Regiment (SOAR), aptly named the "Night Stalkers," had taken possession of the three prototype stealth helicopters ten months ago, putting the highly modified Black Hawk frames through hell and back for U.S. Special Operations Command. Major Borelli had been quietly assigned to lead the assessment, which still remained a secret within a secret at the 160th SOAR, frequently vanishing with his handpicked flight crews to Area 51, where the prototype helicopters were hidden from prying eyes.

The birds looked ungainly sitting on the ground, built wider and longer than the standard Black Hawk to accommodate the angled hull designed to defeat aerial search radar waves. In the air, the Stealth Hawk performed reliably, though the controls behaved sluggishly compared to the MH-60K. Built on the Black Hawk frame, designers still struggled to distribute the additional weight of the extended hull in correct proportion to the original design. Every time they returned to fly the prototypes, the helicopters looked different. Still slightly unstable, the helicopters had come a long way since his initial flight.

"Distance to Blackjack?" Borelli asked.

"Twenty-six hundred meters," the sensor operator replied.

The Stealth Hawk was configured with an electronics warfare console mounted directly behind the copilot and manned by a specially trained member of the 160th Special Operations Aviation Regiment. The console operator controlled the FLIR pod, monitored hostile electronics emissions, and managed their outgoing radar profile, freeing the pilot and copilot for the near impossible task of flying nap-of-earth through enemy territory at night. If necessary, the console operator would join the crew chief and man one of Zero One's M134 miniguns to defend the aircraft or provide suppressing fire during a "hot" extraction.

His helicopter was the only prototype fitted with an organic weapons platform. Zero Two and Zero Three were unarmed, except for the personal weapons carried by the crew. SOCOM planners had wanted to send all three helicopters into Kazakhstan unarmed, but Borelli had pressed the issue, insisting that the task force have some defensive capability other than stealth. SOCOM compromised by arming Zero One with two M134 systems. A stream of tracers appeared above the horizon and bounced off the landscape in a cascade of green sparks several meters to the north of Blackjack.

"Mills, track that hostile contact. I don't want any surprises."

"Tracking," his sensor operator said.

"Are we heading over to help, Major?" Sergeant First Class Papovich asked.

"My orders are to wait for them to cross the border," Borelli said.

"Don't forget the two-thousand-meter restriction, Boogie," his copilot said.

"And that," Borelli mumbled.

"The two thousand meters only applies if they're under fire from a hostile force," Papovich said.

Another line of tracers raced to the ground in the distance, sputtering skyward after impact with the ground.

"They're engaged by a hostile force, Pappy. I can't touch them," Borelli said.

"Then we might have to remove the hostile force, so we can comply with our rules of engagement," the crew chief said.

"I'm not even going to ask how you came up with that."

"Simple, Major," Papovich said. "It gets pretty confusing on these operations and this is a prototype aircraft prone to bugs and glitches. As long as we bring them back, nobody's gonna give a shit how far we were from the border."

"Distance to Blackjack?"

"Twenty-four hundred meters."

With the Hip conducting gun runs, the Tiger wasn't making enough progress to reach the border in time, and there was no way he could keep the Stealth Hawks on station past 4:55. He needed a thirty-minute high-speed run before sunrise in order to clear any inhabited areas near the border and arrive at FARP "Blacktop" undetected. There was no way the Tiger would make it if they didn't intervene. He nudged the helicopter forward at a steady fifty miles per hour.

"Revised distance to Blackjack?"

"Twenty-four fifty. They lost some distance zigzagging," Mills said.

"Pappy, help him with the laser rangefinder, I'm getting some strange readings on my helmet-mounted HUD," Borelli said.

"Roger that, sir," Papovich replied. "I never did trust all of the gizmos in this thing. I'm reading nineteen hundred meters and closing."

"Can you confirm that, Mills?"

"Affirmative. Nineteen hundred meters and closing," Mills said, finally climbing onboard the bullshit bus.

"Gentlemen, my sensors indicate that Blackjack has crossed into Kazakhstan," he said, keying the taskforce communications net.

Chapter 69

350 meters from the Kazakhstan border
Russian Federation

Richard Farrington's shoulder slammed into the front passenger door as Misha yanked the wheel left to avoid the Russian helicopter's next fusillade of projectiles. Halfway through the turn, he heard the AGS-30 automatic grenade launcher start to discharge rounds at its cyclic rate, in a futile attempt to disrupt the attack. The Hip's pilots and gunners had conducted five gun runs at this point, and it was only a matter of time before they figured out how to compensate for Misha's evasive tactics. If his Tiger didn't reach the border within the next seven minutes, the Russians would have all day to figure it out. When a second stream of tracers struck the ground in front of their vehicle immediately after the first, he realized the chase had come to an end.

The entire cabin erupted in a blinding green light as tracers bounced off the hood and streamed past his face. His night vision goggles disappeared in a flash of heat. His ears filled with an incredible racket that sounded like multiple jackhammers pounding away at the sheet metal. Human screams competed unsuccessfully with the intense noise, barely registering. A warm spray blurred his vision…and the storm ended just as quickly as it started, leaving him stunned in his seat.

The Tiger slowed to a stop, with smoke pouring from its partially open, punctured hood. It was still too dark to see inside the cabin without night vision, but he didn't need to visually confirm the fact that they were combat ineffective. Misha's head leaned against the steering wheel, his hands still tightly gripped in the ten and two o'clock position. He muttered unintelligibly, or maybe Farrington was still too dazed to comprehend what he was saying. He glanced over his shoulder and saw Gosha lying on the deck of the rear compartment, trying to raise himself up on an elbow.

The deep thumping sound of the Hip's rotors jarred him back into action, and he opened the door, gripping his AK-107 rifle. He hopped down from the vehicle, expecting to fall into the tall grass on useless legs, but instead landed in a steady crouch. Grateful that he had somehow escaped the maelstrom unscathed, he reached instinctively for his missing night vision goggles. Failing to find them attached to his helmet, he cursed and moved to the back of the Tiger, hoping to spot the lumbering beast against the early dawn sky.

He caught a glimpse of the dark shape moving right to left and considered climbing up the side of the Tiger to use the grenade launcher. He knew it would be pointless. The Russians would engage the vehicle from behind, rendering the AGS-30 useless. His only course of action at this point was to drag his team clear of the vehicle and try to reach the border. The thought was insane, given what he had seen inside the Tiger, but it was the only plan he could conjure while tracking the Hip's movement against the royal blue strip of horizon. The terrifying buzz saw sound of the Russian helicopter's miniguns filled his ears, causing him to involuntarily brace for the inevitable green storm that would unceremoniously tear him to shreds three hundred meters from the Kazakhstan border. They'd almost made it.

The sound of rapid gunfire continued, but he didn't disintegrate along with the Tiger. Instead, a long line of red tracers raced toward the Russian helicopter, bouncing off the Hip's metal hull like a Fourth of July sparkler. The visual effect gave the deceptive impression that the Hip was impervious to the gunfire, but Farrington knew better. For each tracer that bounced off the Hip's thin aluminum hull, at least fifteen 7.62mm steel jacketed rounds pounded the helicopter in a continuous stream of kinetic energy. The three-second burst of tracers put well over three hundred high-velocity projectiles into the Hip, most likely killing it.

A second crimson stream reached out and connected with the Russian helicopter. Before the minigun's deadly echo had faded, a tremendous explosion lit the ground to the east, briefly exposing the black helicopter that had undeniably saved their lives. Farrington turned to the Tiger and opened the rear hatch, using the light from the burning wreckage to survey the damage. The blood-slicked deck didn't buoy his hopes.

"Blackjack elements, report!" he yelled, checking Sasha's pulse, which was strong.

"I'm hit in at least two places," Gosha whispered, "left shoulder and hip."

"Looks like you got hit in the head too," Farrington said, searching his vest for a flashlight.

"Doesn't surprise me," Gosha replied.

"Misha?" he said, getting no response.

He slid along the left side of the Tiger to the driver's door, directing his flashlight through the smoke to assess the damage. The hatch showed several sizable, paint chipped dents, where rounds had bounced harmlessly off the vehicle's armor plating. The window frame showed similar damage, which made him wonder how many of the projectiles had passed through the open window, potentially striking Misha. A bloodied hand appeared and gripped the bottom of the window frame.

"Misha?" Farrington repeated, exposing the operative to the bright LED beam.

"Yeah, I'm fucked up," he grunted.

"Can you move?" Farrington said, trying to open the door, which was stuck.

"I don't think so. I'm hit all over," he whispered.

Farrington pulled on the door several times, finally dislodging it. Misha's assault rifle tumbled to the ground, landing under the Tiger. Glistening scarlet ribbons lined the instrument panel and center column, extending across the dashboard to the passenger side. The operative turned his head toward the light and smiled weakly. In the bright LED beam, Misha looked pale and listless. A deep gash ran across his chin, dripping blood onto the bottom of the steering wheel.

"We made it," Misha said.

"Somehow," Farrington said. "Let's get you out of there."

A gust of wind poured through the cabin from the open passenger side door, pelting his face with dirt. Squinting to see through the door into the murky darkness beyond, he detected the presence of something big lowering to the ground beyond the Tiger. Not wanting to take a friendly bullet between the eyes less than three hundred meters from the Kazakhstan border, he put his hands over his head and stepped back from the vehicle. Moments later, six heavily armed, dark-clad figures sprinted through the swirling cloud of dirt and descended on the vehicle.

"I need two stretchers!" one of them yelled, hopping down from the rear hatch and walking up to Farrington.

"We need to get out of here, sir. The entire 21st is headed right to this grid square. I don't know what you did, but you sure as shit pissed them off!" the commando said.

"You have no idea," Farrington said.

He grabbed the Delta operator's shoulder before the man had a chance to turn.

"I'll take care of the KIA," he said.

Farrington slung his rifle and helped the soldiers lower Misha onto one of the foldable stretchers produced by the helicopter's extraction team. By the time he had finished securing Misha to the stretcher, the rest of his team had been spirited off into the night. He pulled Seva's body out of the Tiger's troop compartment and heaved it over his shoulder in a fireman's carry. *No man left behind.* He raced through the choking swirl of Siberian dirt to catch up with the men loading Misha's stretcher onto the strangest helicopter he'd ever seen.

Eager hands pulled Seva's body into the troop compartment, grabbing him just as quickly. The ground lifted away from his feet before he had fully entered the helicopter.

"Sorry about that, sir, but we really need to get moving," the Delta operator said, gripping Farrington's combat vest.

The helicopter banked left, giving Farrington a sweeping view of the Siberian steppe. The dark blue eastern horizon had started to show a faint, blood-red hue under the thinning clouds. The helicopter's crew chief reached out and pulled the sliding door shut. Dark red lighting bathed the compartment, exposing the urgent effort to stabilize Misha. Toward the rear of the helicopter, one of the Delta soldiers methodically stripped away his body armor and outer garments, while another prepared several IV drip bags. On the bench in front of him, a third operator pressed a medical compress to Gosha's leg. Sasha's stretcher lay at his feet, jammed into the compartment. The helicopter's hasty departure hadn't allowed for an orderly loading process.

"They're in good hands, sir. This is one of our combat trauma teams," said the Delta operator next to him.

He noted that the compartment resembled a stripped-down version of a Black Hawk, configured with eight troop seats and a sophisticated medical station equipped to handle two casualties. An additional station behind the copilot's seat resembled something he'd seen inside a command-and-control Stryker vehicle.

"What is this thing?" Farrington said.

"Highly classified. That's about all I know. They didn't want to send these in after you," the lead Delta operator said.

"I'm glad they changed their minds," Farrington said.

"They didn't. Our task force commander made the call. They're probably choking on the hors d'oeuvres back in Washington."

"I hope so. Saves me from having to choke them," Farrington said.

Chapter 70

The president closed the door and took a seat on the leather couch, ready to jump down Jacob Remy's throat if the man said another word about the helicopters. Yes, they had all watched Black Magic violate the established rules of engagement to the fullest extent possible, by not only crossing into Russian airspace but also destroying one of the Russian helicopters. And yes, this could have ended badly, with the wreckage of a prototype stealth helicopter and the bodies of a dozen or more American servicemen strewn across the Siberian countryside. But none of that mattered because it didn't happen. None of it had *ever* happened, and Jacob Remy needed to get that clear. The operation succeeded, leaving no physical evidence behind, and the Russians were in no position to press the matter.

"Well?" he said, shrugging his shoulders at Remy.

"We've got a bigger problem than two Russian helicopters," Remy said.

"I don't really care at this point," the president said.

"You have to care, sir. The CIA has gone rogue. Manning has lost control of the National Clandestine Service. I want to show you something."

"Go ahead."

Remy activated one of the large flat-screen monitors, which displayed satellite imagery. He sat behind a small computer station in the corner of the study and zoomed in on one of the images.

"This was taken over Slavgorod right after the mysterious blackout. Thermal imaging confirms the wreckage of seven armored vehicles. All six vehicles situated along the approach road to Slavgorod were destroyed. There's no way that Blackjack could have done this. I was willing to believe that they had somehow slipped away, but this is clearly the work of something else. Either a drone or stealth bomber," Remy said.

"General Gordon decided against the use of surveillance drones over Kazakhstan," the president said.

"Right, and I don't think anyone stole a stealth bomber. The Pentagon tends to notice when things like that go missing. Do you know what this means?"

The president shook his head apathetically.

"The CIA put an armed drone over Russia without your permission and attacked Russian army units en masse. Renegade special operations pilots destroyed two Russian helicopters," Remy said. "We're looking at fifty plus Russian casualties, easily. This thing spiraled way out of control. We should have taken action earlier to limit this."

"How? By sending our own drones in to take out Blackjack on the Ob River? Or maybe passing along Blackjack's exfiltration route to the Russians? After they successfully destroyed Vektor, of course," the president said.

"That's not what I meant."

"Really? Because I'm beginning to wonder. Jacob, I learned a valuable lesson tonight. Something I've lost sight of. Politics has no place in an operation like that. We either check our politics in at the door, or we don't walk into the room, because the men and women carrying out these missions don't care about any of that crap. They execute the mission. End of story. If we can't support them one hundred percent, then we have no business asking them to do our dirty work in the first place."

"We didn't come up with the idea to take out Vektor," Remy reminded him.

"Once we put our stamp of approval on it, we owned it. Thomas Manning, the helicopter pilots, and whoever made the decision to put an armed drone over Slavgorod? We owe them a debt of gratitude for correcting our mistake. Don't ever forget that, Jacob."

Jacob Remy remained silent for several seconds. By not offering an immediate contradictory statement, his chief of staff indicated that he understood the president's point and would abide by it.

"We should meet with the secretary of state and White House counsel within the hour. They're going to need most of the night to prepare for tomorrow's fun," Remy said, closing the link to the satellite picture.

"Let's call them in, though I'd be surprised if tomorrow held much drama for us. I predict that the Russians will quietly sweep this under the rug. Bioweapons are an ugly business."

"So is invading another country," Remy said.

"Agreed, which is why we're going to politely hold the rug up for them. The sooner this goes away, the better," the president said.

Chapter 71

Karl Berg shut down his computer and locked his KSV-21 Crypto Card in his desk. He stood up and removed the sport coat draped over the back of his chair, eyeing the small carry-on bag next to his open office door. He needed to be on a non-stop flight to Burlington, Vermont, that left Ronald Reagan Washington National Airport at 10:10 PM. He'd rent a car and check into the closest hotel, hopefully settling in by one in the morning. He'd wake up early and drive to the Mountain Glen Retirement Facility, where he would personally put an end to the last twisted legacy of the Russian bioweapons program.

Thomas Manning appeared in the doorway before he could turn off the brass-finished banker's light on his desk. Shit. He had really hoped to avoid Manning tonight. Based on the NCS director's last transmission to the CIA operations center, Berg got the sense that Manning's career had just suffered a severe setback. The fact that Director Copley handled all communications from that point forward further reinforced the hypothesis. Whatever happened between Manning and the president triggered a series of events that brought the surviving members of Farrington's team home. If Manning was willing to torpedo his own career to do the right thing, Berg had no intention of making excuses for the drone stunt. Shit rolled downhill, and Audra had made it clear that she would no longer protect him from the avalanches of shit he called down on himself. He'd take whatever Manning came here to deliver, standing up like a man.

374

"Karl, do you have a minute?" Manning asked.

"Of course, Thomas. I have a 10:10 flight to Burlington, but I can't envision the drive taking me more than thirty minutes on a Sunday night. Interesting day, huh?"

Manning stepped into the office and gently closed the door. "That's one way of describing it. We did some good today."

"We certainly did. It's been a long few months since I received the first tip that the Russians were looking for Reznikov. I'll be glad to put this whole thing to rest tomorrow," Berg said.

"You did an unbelievable job with this, Karl, which is why I'm willing to overlook the fact that you hijacked a twenty-million-dollar drone from Afghanistan and declared war on Russia's 21st Motor Rifle Division."

"And one helicopter," Berg added.

"I was wondering. Why not both helicopters?"

"We used one of the Hellfires to create a diversionary explosion in Slavgorod. If we'd saved that missile, the end wouldn't have been so dramatic," Berg said.

"Sanderson's men are in stable condition at the FARP," Manning said. "SOCOM will fly the whole package back to Manas after nightfall."

"He seemed pleased with the outcome. I think he expected to lose more of the team."

"I think he expected to lose all of them," Manning said. "This was always a one-way trip in my mind, which is why I didn't hold back when they broke through Slavgorod. I knew what was going on as soon as the satellite feed died, and I wasn't about to let the president and his weasel-faced chief break their promise to those men."

"I told Sanderson what you did. He owes you one."

"No. Once again, we owe him. Keep your eyes and ears open, Karl. Not that you have any friends in the White House. Jacob Remy will throw Sanderson to the wolves if the opportunity arises. The least we can do is run interference."

"You'd be surprised who I know and who Sanderson knows," Berg said.

"Good. Between you, me and Audra, we should be able to make good on that debt."

"I don't think Audra and I are on speaking terms any longer."

"She'll get over it. I'm transferring you to the Special Activities Division's Special Operations Group as the new acting deputy director.

Jeffrey McConnell is slated to take over the entire division by the first of next year, which should give you more than enough time to familiarize yourself with his job."

"His job as director of SOG?"

"I could really use someone with your planning ability and instincts over there," Manning said.

"Isn't this technically a demotion?" he said jokingly.

"Considering the fact that I basically created your current position under Bauer out of thin air? No. This is a promotion. Actually, it was Bauer's idea," Manning said.

"Wow. She really *is* pissed at me," Berg said.

"I don't think that had anything to do with her recommendation. She submitted your name two weeks ago," he said, pausing for a moment. "I'll let you get going. Good luck tomorrow."

"I shouldn't need any luck," Berg said, "hopefully."

"There's nothing easy about killing someone. That's why we usually have other people do it for us. They can take care of Reznikov's 'retirement' you know."

"I know," Berg said, turning off his desk lamp.

Chapter 72

7:45 AM
Mountain Glen "Retirement" Facility
Green Mountains, Vermont

The SUV slowed to a stop, and Berg heard the vehicle's front doors slam shut. They had arrived at the compound. Moments later, the right passenger door opened, exposing him to the same drizzly, overcast day he had experienced on the entire drive from Burlington. Berg gripped his black nylon briefcase and nodded to the serious-looking man holding his door. The security agent escorted him to the colonial-style structure, where Gary Sheffield waited.

"You're turning into a regular up here," Sheffield said, shaking his hand.

"This should be my last trip for quite some time. Running across someone like Reznikov is pretty rare in my experience," Berg said, stepping inside the hallway foyer.

"I'm glad to hear that because he's by far the creepiest inmate we've ever had the displeasure of housing. I don't particularly care for any of the guests, but I'll be extremely glad to see him go. Something about him is really off."

"That's truly an understatement in his case. I can think of a lot of people that share your sentiment, which is why I'm back so soon."

"Can I get you some coffee or breakfast?" Sheffield said.

"Maybe after I'm done."

"I'll put something together. Shall we?" Sheffield said, motioning toward the end of the hardwood hallway.

The compound's quaint façade ended several steps into the house. Through the door leading left out of the front hallway, he saw wall-to-wall flat-screen monitors organized around a half-dozen workstations. Security personnel monitored the sensors and cameras installed in the residences and public buildings from here. The doorway to the right was closed, but he knew from previous visits that Sheffield's people kept an eye on the external sensors and communications from that room. Sheffield walked past these rooms and approached a metal door flanked by a biometric fingerprint scanner. He pressed his thumb down first, then his ring finger, holding it there until the door clicked and opened a few inches.

"What do you do if there's a power failure?" Berg said.

"We have generators to keep that from happening, but the door automatically opens if the house loses power for more than ten seconds," Sheffield said.

He pushed the heavy door open to expose a walk-in-closet-sized room lined with racks of military-grade weaponry.

"Expecting an invasion?" Berg said.

"Some of our guests commanded private armies in their previous lives," Sheffield said.

He reached to the right, just out of sight and withdrew a semi-automatic pistol fitted with a short suppressor. He pulled back on the slide, locking it in the open position before handing it to Berg.

"This should do the trick. Sig Sauer P250 compact. Magazine holds fifteen rounds, not that you'll need that many…I hope."

"I'm not that bad of a shot," Berg said.

"Not saying you are. There's no safety on this pistol, so—"

Berg released the slide, chambering a round. "Double action only?"

"Correct. But it's a light pull. 5.5 pounds."

Berg placed the pistol inside an easily accessible Velcro pouch within his briefcase. The nylon bag held a mock file and a 750 milliliter bottle of expensive vodka, which Reznikov would never taste.

"All right," Berg said.

"Perfect. Reznikov has ordered breakfast for 8 o'clock, which is earlier than usual. I'll send a cleanup crew down instead," Sheffield said.

Berg nodded, feeling suddenly anxious about what he had calmly envisioned doing for the past month. The look on his face must have betrayed his apprehension because Sheffield put a hand on his shoulder.

"You don't have to do this. In the three years I've been here, we've retired eight guests. Nobody from Langley has ever showed up for one of the retirement ceremonies," Sheffield said.

"Do you really call it a retirement ceremony?"

"That's what they've always been called," Sheffield said.

"This guy doesn't deserve the euphemism. I'll take you up on the coffee and breakfast when I get back. I might have a shot of this vodka too," Berg said.

"Fair enough, Mr. Berg. I'll show you out."

A few minutes later, Berg turned down path number five and entered a thick stand of pine trees that concealed Reznikov's soon-to-be-vacated residence. He rang the doorbell, expecting to wait several minutes for the drunken maniac to answer. Reznikov had used his fifth satellite phone call yesterday afternoon to confirm that Vektor bioweapons program had been successfully destroyed. His Solntsevskaya contact confirmed that the operation had succeeded at the laboratory. A brief description of several simultaneous plumes of fire at the site had been enough to convince Reznikov that Berg's team had succeeded. Sheffield said he celebrated well into afternoon before passing out without ordering dinner.

Berg was caught slightly off guard when Reznikov opened the door. He'd expected to find the scientist stumbling around in a cotton robe, nursing a massive headache and rubbing his perpetually bloodshot eyes. Instead, Reznikov looked rested and alert, wearing an outfit suitable for a day hike in the mountains. Something seemed off about this.

"Oh. It's you?" Reznikov said.

"Going for a walk?" Berg said.

"Uh, well. Now that I am a permanent resident, I figured it might be time to embrace my surroundings. So, I suppose congratulations are in order?" he said, glancing nervously over Berg's shoulder.

"They are. I thought we'd celebrate," Berg said.

Berg withdrew the bottle of vodka from his briefcase and offered it to Reznikov, who accepted it reluctantly.

"I really do feel like getting some fresh air this morning. I celebrated a little too hard yesterday afternoon," Reznikov said, taking a step forward.

Berg blocked the doorway, flashing a disingenuous smile. "I insist that we take a moment to celebrate. It should help you take the edge off. You look like you've seen a ghost."

Reznikov took a moment to consider Berg's offer, displaying an anguished look out of character with someone who routinely downed a bottle like this before ten in the morning. The Russian's eyes shifted to the forest again before he finally relented and stepped back into the cottage.

"Where are my manners? Of course. A quick toast, then I really should get out for some fresh air. You're welcome to join me," Reznikov said.

Berg pulled the door shut and followed him inside, sliding his hand into the black nylon briefcase. He felt for the Velcro flap that covered the hidden compartment, suddenly hardened for what he needed to do.

ớ∞ó

Greg Marshall yawned and rubbed his eyes. A few more minutes and his eight-hour shift monitoring the compound's remote sensor network would come to an end. He'd eat a massive breakfast and crash out for several hours upstairs, until his natural biorhythms forced him out of bed. He closed his eyes and imagined the grease-laden farmer's breakfast waiting for him in the sunroom. Security work at the compound might be tedious, but the food was plentiful and he had plenty of time between shifts to work it off. He could imagine worse work within the agency.

When he opened his eyes, he immediately saw that one of the eastern-based sensor arrays had detected movement. Damn it. Now his watch turnover would be delayed by at least fifteen minutes while a team was dispatched to investigate what would undoubtedly turn out to be another bear. The system could eliminate most non-human signatures based on speed, size and thermal characteristics, but it had a hard time differentiating between a young black bear and a human being. The system would track the bear accurately while it ambled along on all fours, but suddenly flash an alert when it rose up on its hind legs to pick berries. Now his breakfast would have to wait. He pulled his chair up to the desk and started the checklist.

The fifty-inch LED screen mounted at eye level in front of his desk displayed a digital map of the area surrounding the compound. Two sectors showed movement, which was a little unusual. He moved his hand to the red phone at the edge of the workstation and considered ringing Sheffield. Not yet. Sheffield hated when they rang him without gathering any information. He dragged the cursor over to the closest red sector and double-clicked, activating the two screens flanking the center monitor.

The top screen displayed multiple camera feeds from the sector, which he could change from traditional full color day view to thermal imaging. The bottom screen presented information from the motion sensors, pressure plates and thermal scanners in numeric and map form. The sector boundary map on this screen indicated that the signals were rapidly approaching the fence line. Multiple signals. The data flowing next to the map told him which cameras to search for a view of the targets, presenting hyperlinks that would change the view on the top screen to reflect what he had selected. He clicked on of the links and momentarily froze in his chair. *What the fuck?* Two heavily armed men sprinted toward the only section of fence exposed directly to the security complex beside the front gate. He didn't bother to check the second sector before charging the entire eastern fence line and picking up the red phone.

❦

The former Russian GRU Spetsnaz soldier raced toward the ten-foot-high section of chain-link fence directly ahead of him and threw himself to the ground several feet in front of it. He quickly extended the bipod attached to his RPK-74S Light Machine Gun and pressed the weapon firmly into the ground. Through the 3.4X ACOG sight attached to the RPK's top rail, he sighted in on the front door of the gray two-story house and disengaged the weapon's safety.

His partner had already stopped several meters back, having found a thick tree stump to support his .50 caliber sniper rifle. They would both start engaging targets as soon as it became apparent that the alarm had been sounded. The RPK would be used against security personnel, while the .50 caliber sniper rifle would initially target the building's communications array. Based on the second team's progress, they would breach the fence and provide close-up support as requested.

Nearly on cue with his arrival, three men spilled out of the front door onto the gravel driveway. One of the men peeled left and crouched against the front bumper of a black SUV, aiming an assault rifle in his general direction, while the other two took off in the opposite direction. He fired a sustained burst through the fence at the man next to the truck, kicking up gravel around the truck and connecting with the SUV's metal frame. The man flailed backward, obviously hit by at least one of the rounds, so he shifted his aim to the two men fleeing toward an outcropping of dark ledge near the house.

A massive detonation sounded in the distance on his right, rippling the fence as his next burst of bullets caught the first man and sent him tumbling to the ground in a tangle of collapsed limbs. His partner stopped and crouched low to return fire, but was struck in the head by a well-aimed, short burst from the machine gun.

The RPK's longer and heavier barrel, designed to allow accurate, sustained automatic fire in an infantry support role, combined extremely well with the combat telescopic sight to yield an effective sharpshooting weapon. He reacquired the front door of the house and demonstrated the light machine gun's true purpose on this mission, pulling the trigger and cycling through the remaining seventy seven rounds of 5.45mm in long sweeping bursts that raked the front of the house from top to bottom, splintering the cedar siding and shattering all of the windows.

❧

Karl Berg's hand froze when he heard the first muffled staccato burst of gunfire. His first thought was that Sheffield had picked a really shitty time to conduct target practice for his security team. He dismissed that thought when the house shook violently, followed immediately by the thunderclap of a nearby explosion. He put it all together before the next burst of gunfire tore through the compound. Reznikov had somehow led the Russian mafiya to Mountain Glen.

He fumbled with the Velcro flap in his briefcase, almost missing Reznikov's sudden attack. The thick bottle of vodka he'd given the scientist appeared overhead, plunging toward his head. Berg abandoned the effort to draw his pistol and raised the briefcase upward to deflect the heavy glass bludgeon. With most of his hand-to-hand combat training years behind him, the CIA officer's instinctual response was far from graceful.

The bottle crashed into his forearm with a sickening thump, driving his arm down below his head. Reznikov raised the bottle to strike him in the head, but Berg kicked him in the sternum, disrupting the attack. The Russian stumbled backward, dropping the bottle onto the hardwood floor, where it shattered. Berg considered trying to retrieve the pistol from the briefcase at his feet, but Reznikov charged the door, and he had no intention of losing the Russian that easily.

The Russian grabbed the doorknob with both hands, unable to defend himself from Berg's front kick, which was aimed at his hands. Berg's sturdy hiking boots crushed Reznikov's fingers against the brass knob, causing the Russian to recoil from the front door, howling in agony. Less than a second later, a klaxon sounded in the house, and Reznikov threw himself at the door, screaming. Now Berg understood why he had been so focused on the door. The house could be put into lockdown mode from the security station, which would complicate whatever plan the lunatic had conjured.

Reznikov yanked at the door to no avail and quickly scrambled left to one of the picture windows. Berg glanced at the window to his immediate right and saw metal shutters descending outside of the windowpanes. He heard glass shatter and turned his attention back to Reznikov. The crazed scientist had cracked the other window with the base of a table lamp. Judging from the shutters' rate of descent, Berg wasn't worried about Reznikov escaping through the window. The security shutters next to him had already blocked most of the light from the outside. In a fit of rage, the Russian repeatedly struck the window frame in an ineffectual display of fury, yelling orders to his hidden rescuers.

Berg decided that this would be a good time to grab his pistol. Trying to ignore the excruciating pain in his left arm, he opened the flap and withdrew the pistol, just as a fusillade of bullets tore through the door and the drywall next to him. The CIA officer dropped flat against the floor and fired three hastily aimed shots through the cloud of obliterated drywall dust at Reznikov's silhouette. Another long burst of gunfire penetrated the front of the house, ripping through the furniture and collapsing the closest end table.

He hadn't fully processed Reznikov's verbal tirade, which had obviously directed indiscriminate automatic weapons fire into the left side of the house. He needed to get clear of the free-fire zone before Reznikov directed the next barrage right onto him. Searching for a target with his pistol, Berg scrambled forward, quickly reaching the archway to find the library room empty. He heard a chair scrape across the kitchen tile and turned his attention to the doorway leading out of the library and deeper into the house.

Before he could process the thought any further, he heard two separate Russian voices outside of the house yell, "Clear!" Berg's options at this point were extremely limited, but one of them wasn't standing in the library, exposed to the front door. He passed through the doorway less than a millisecond before a small explosion shook the house. The explosion cleared his mind and engaged some of the mind processes buried under years of bureaucratic deskwork at Langley. He hoped this temporary reboot would be enough to keep him alive.

He'd been one of the CIA's premier case officers in Europe during the Cold War's final decade, sidelining as a "black ops" field supervisor long before retired Special Forces operators filled those roles. He knew what would come through that door, and that his chances of walking out of here alive were poor, but Berg was a survivor, and he still had plenty of fight left in him. He immediately started forming a strategy.

Reznikov's Solntsevskaya benefactors would have used highly trained professionals for this job, most likely former Russian army Spetsnaz, which didn't bode well. Spetsnaz operators were notoriously savage and barely restrained by rules of engagement within the Russian military. As hired guns for the Russian mafiya, there would be no limit to their brutality. The only factor working in his favor at this point was an intimate familiarity with Special Operations tactics.

Special Forces teams worldwide could attribute their incredible success rate to training. Repetitive training. Especially in close-quarters combat. There was little variation in training and tactics, which is why he wasn't the least bit surprised to hear metal objects hit the hardwood floor somewhere in the front of the house. Flashbangs. He glanced toward the staircase off the kitchen and made a quick calculation. He had at this point all but forgotten about Reznikov, who was nowhere in sight.

৵৵৽

A long burst of distant gunfire preceded the multiple flashbang detonations inside the house, reminding Yergei that the compound's security team was still in play. He didn't need to cue the two men that flanked the door. They had practiced this drill hundreds of times together as a Russian Spetsnaz direct-action team and several dozen more times as private contractors. The only real difference between the two was that he routinely got paid more for one of these privately funded operations than he made in an entire year as a Russian army sergeant.

The four-man team assembled on Reznikov's doorstep had worked exclusively together throughout the world for the past three years, making money hand over fist doing business with some of the nastiest people alive. Assassination, kidnapping, extortion, blackmail…all for sale to the highest bidder, and the Solntsevskaya Bratva was by far their best customer.

When the flashbangs exploded, the assault team's point man peeled away from his position next to the smoldering doorway and slid into the house. The operative on the other side of the door started to follow, when two gunshots knocked the point man's lifeless body back onto the granite porch in a cascade of brains and blood. The second man fired a burst from his shortened AK-74 into the house, which instigated mayhem. Yergei heard screaming, followed by several rapidly spaced pistol shots, all of which competed with the sound of crashing furniture.

"He's upstairs, you fucking idiots. He shot me in the face!" yelled a Russian voice from inside.

"Watch your fire!" he yelled to the team.

His instructions had been clear. If he didn't recover the scientist alive, they had no reason to return to Russia. They would be out of business, simple as that, targets of the next team standing in line to take their place…and there were many. Their *bratva* contact had made this painfully clear, which underscored the importance of the mission and better explained the exorbitant fee they had been able to negotiate. Reznikov was critically important to the Solntsevskaya Bratva.

"Hit the upstairs," he said, pointing at the cottage's shuttered dormer windows.

The two remaining operatives sprinted several meters back from the house and turned, each firing an entire magazine at the second floor. Yergei charged through the door during the mayhem and headed right, hearing the snap of a bullet pass inches from his head. The pistol's report was lost in the hammering of automatic weapon's fire from just outside the house, but he had caught a glimpse of the shooter on the staircase.

He spotted Reznikov sitting against a floor-to-ceiling bookcase, precariously close to a splintered doorframe he presumed to be fully exposed to the shooter who had just fired on him as he entered the house. Reznikov muttered to himself, holding a blood-covered hand to his face while repeatedly hitting the bookshelf with the back of his head. Scarlet fluid oozed through his fingers and dripped into a widening stain on his right thigh.

Yergei aimed his rifle high along the room's interior wall, pointing in the presumed direction of the staircase off the kitchen. He fired several controlled bursts through the thin drywall while advancing toward the scientist. He arrived at the splintered doorframe next to Reznikov with enough ammunition in the rifle's thirty-round magazine for a short, well-aimed burst at the staircase. As he fired the rifle, two more bullets snapped past, missing his head by inches and striking the wall behind him. He yanked his head back, satisfied that he had done enough damage to the shooter to escape safely with Reznikov. A sizable bloodstain had appeared on the wall at the top of the stairs.

"We're getting you out of here," Yergei said, reloading his weapon.

"Team. Inside left! Watch the stairway!" he said.

Within seconds, the two operatives appeared inside the house, fanning to the left and occupying the corners of the room. He pointed at the ceiling above them and gave the hand signal to open fire. The men crouched and aimed at the ceiling, firing wild bursts of automatic fire into the drywall above. Yergei joined them, sending most of the steel-jacketed rounds from his fresh magazine into the remaining ceiling areas that didn't show significant damage. He always retained a few rounds just in case.

"We're done here!" he said to his men, walking back to Reznikov.

They didn't have any more time to play around with the mystery shooter. They had less than five minutes to secure a landing zone behind the security building, which still presented a considerable obstacle to their success. The constant sound of small arms fire, intertwined with the deep boom of a .50 caliber sniper rifle, reminded him of why they had been paid so much for this job. Nobody said it would be easy.

"You have to make sure he is dead!" Reznikov said.

"We don't have time for that! My job is to get you out of here alive! So stand up and move out! I don't see anything wrong with your legs," Yergei said.

"You could at least be polite about it," Reznikov protested.

"I don't get paid for that, so don't push your luck. Get on your fucking feet and move!" he said, spurring Reznikov into action.

He pushed the scientist through the front door and activated his shoulder microphone.

"Support team. Move up on the house. We're on our way."

꙳

Berg pressed his hands against his ears, wincing from the pain that radiated through his left arm. The flashbangs detonated moments later, whitewashing the kitchen in a six-million-Candela flash, but essentially causing no distress to his eyesight. Similarly, the one-hundred-and-seventy-decibel subsonic deflagration emitted by the grenade was reduced to a tolerable level by his hands. The suppressed gunshots fired from his pistol moments earlier had produced significantly more discomfort. He sprang into action and crossed the kitchen, torn by his decision to seek safety instead of hunting down Reznikov. He was in pure survival mode at this point, with little on his mind beyond getting upstairs, where he might be able to put up a better defense.

Reaching the center hallway, he didn't hesitate to lean out and search for targets. His experience told him that the men entering the house would rush through the "fatal funnel," or front doorway in this case, and immediately clear the front corners of the house. Their attention would not be focused forward directly upon entry. A heavily armed operative suddenly appeared in his sights, oblivious to his concealed presence dead ahead. Berg fired two 9mm hollow point rounds at his head, stopping the Russian cold. Based on the crimson explosion behind the man's head, Berg had no doubt that he had scored a lethal hit. Unwilling to press his luck, he sprinted toward the stairs, barely avoiding a burst of rifle fire centered on the hallway.

Before he reached the stairs, Reznikov burst out of the walk-in pantry to his right, holding a kitchen stool and shrieking like a madman. He sprinted past Berg, swinging the stool at his head, but missing by inches. The CIA officer extended his right hand and fired repeatedly at the fleeing scientist. At least one of the rounds connected, knocking Reznikov against the far wall, but before he could line up a kill shot, Reznikov spilled through the doorway leading to the library.

He had missed his last chance to kill Reznikov, a fact he knew would condemn thousands, if not millions of lives in the near future. The thought of this epic failure kept him from fleeing up the stairs, which probably saved his life. The upstairs landing disappeared in a storm of drywall and splintering wood, as the sound of automatic fire echoed throughout the house. Movement near the front door attracted his attention, and he brought his pistol to bear on a single intruder. He managed to squeeze off one shot, missing by inches, before the commando vanished into the library.

Bursts of automatic fire punctured the wall on the other side of the hallway and chased him upstairs. He reached the top of the stairs and turned, noting a discernible pattern on the downstairs wall. Each burst had shifted left across the wall, indicating that the gunman was moving toward the back of the house. Berg crouched low and steadied his hand against the stairway corner, aiming at the kitchen doorway as bullets continued to pour through the wall. Through the smoke and drywall dust, a head appeared, and he fired twice, never seeing if his rounds connected. He was struck in the upper left shoulder and spun into the bathroom behind him. He landed on his hands and knees, physically stunned and unable to breathe…but fully aware that he was a dead man if he didn't move.

❧

Gary Sheffield low-crawled down the blood-slicked hardwood floor toward the front door, urging his body forward against every survival instinct his brain had activated within the past five minutes. Another burst of machine-gun fire swept through the front of the house, spraying him with wooden splinters and bits of drywall. The sound of gunfire seemed closer than before. A second distant explosion had shaken the house less than a minute ago, yielding a temporary lull in machine-gun fire. The team had advanced to a new position inside of the fence line.

He stopped for a moment and leaned to the right, peering through the open front door, still unable to spot the shooters. He had no intention of taking a second look. The headless body lying several feet ahead of him served as a grim reminder that the ceaseless machine-gun fire wasn't the only threat out there. Anyone who exposed a body part for too long or appeared in the same place twice inevitably attracted a .50 caliber projectile. Three members of his team had been gruesomely killed this way.

Satisfied that he wasn't in their line of sight, Sheffield squirmed through the doorway on the left and surveyed the communications room. Greg Marshall's bullet-riddled body sat slumped in a chair at the sensor station. He had been killed in the first full machine-gun sweep, along with Sheffield's assistant. Both of them had been desperately trying to raise CIA headquarters to report the attack, but had not received a response. He suspected that the first few thunderous rifle reports had been directed at their communications dome, knocking out their encrypted satellite connection.

Even if they had managed to contact headquarters, reinforcements wouldn't arrive for several hours. Protocol for this ultra-secret station didn't allow them to contact local law enforcement. In the event of an attack, they were on their own until the CIA could arrange for a team to arrive. Under most conceivable scenarios, his security arrangement would have been sufficient to repel any attempted breach of the facility. This morning's attack had been different, and he couldn't shake the thought that the timing of Berg's arrival had not been a coincidence. Greg Marshall's last report confirmed that the second team had breached the fence line near Reznikov's residence.

The rest of his survey confirmed that nothing salvageable remained in the room. Sporadic rifle fire erupted from the house, attracting another long hail of machine-gun fire and at least two sniper rounds. Several bullets punctured the north-facing wall, indicating a new threat direction and the arrival of the team sent to either kill or retrieve Reznikov. Disregarding the machine-gun fire that poured through the front of the house, he sprinted into the hallway and barreled into the kitchen, stopping at the back door.

"What do you have?" he yelled at the agent crouched in the doorframe.

"Another team moving across the middle. Four men. One of them is Reznikov!"

Son of a bitch. They were trying to break Reznikov out of his compound. The big question was how? He had no idea how they had arrived, but he figured that they had hiked in. It was the only way to approach silently enough to evade early detection. There was no way they could successfully hike back, with or without Reznikov, at this point.

The only other option involved commandeering vehicles based at the compound. He had personally disabled both SUVs with his rifle, which left them with the ATVs parked in the garage. They could use the ATVs to navigate the access road and hijack a car on one of the county roads, but this seemed like a flimsy exfiltration plan given what his intruders had already accomplished, and they were headed in the wrong direction. The garage was located in the opposite direction they were travelling.

"Is Berg with them?" Sheffield said, still not convinced the CIA agent's arrival was a coincidence.

"Negative. Three shooters and Reznikov. Fuck! They have a clear angle on us!" the agent said, raising his rifle to engage the group.

Sheffield leaned through the door and sighted in on one of the partially exposed moving targets through the holographic sight attached to his HK416C ultra-compact. He fired in semi-automatic mode, striking the rocks just behind the shooter. The agent in the doorway fired a long burst at the same man, kicking up dirt and rock chips, but failing to score a hit. The two other agents stationed along the back of the house at the corners retreated toward the back door as return fire from the cluster of shooters started to tear into the west-facing side of the house.

A bullet snapped past Sheffield's head, striking the doorframe above him and forcing his retreat into the kitchen. The rest of his agents piled through the opening as bullets started to slice through the wall, forcing all of them to seek cover deeper inside the house. They had learned the hard way that the structure's exterior walls barely slowed the high-velocity projectiles fired at them. Firing directly through a window while standing near it only made things easier for the compound's intruders. He'd lost at least half of his team to gunfire that passed effortlessly through the exterior walls. The compound's designers clearly hadn't anticipated the possibility of the team getting trapped inside the house.

ॐॐ

Yergei threw himself down against the rocks and hugged the ground, wincing from the pieces of rock that peppered his face. The surviving members of the compound's security team were putting up a spirited resistance. With this kind of incoming fire, there was no way he could risk directing the helicopter to land, and without the helicopter, they faced a long, arduous trek out of here by ATV. The helicopter was less than a minute away.

His machine gunner fired a five-second-long burst of 7.62mm projectiles through the north wall and stopped to reload while the sniper sprinted to catch up with the group escorting Reznikov. The scientist didn't have a clue about tactical considerations in a firefight, and his men had to constantly force him down to avoid incoming fire. For a supposed genius, the guy didn't have the situational awareness of a drunken street bum. When the machine gun started chattering away at the house, he called for their extraction on his handheld radio.

"Eagle, this is Mountain Man, over," Yergei said.

"This is Eagle, over," crackled a voice over the gunfire.

"Commence your run to the primary LZ. LZ is hot. I repeat. LZ is hot. All hostiles are buttoned up tight inside the gray, two-story house in the middle of the clearing. You are cleared to engage the house."

"Roger that. We're inbound. Thirty seconds."

He scurried down the backside of the rocky outcropping, staying as low as possible, until he reached a point where he could see his entire team. His sniper had reached the main group a dozen meters away and grabbed Reznikov. With the scientist out of their custody, the two men turned their attention to the house, directing burst after burst of gunfire into the wood siding below and alongside the windows. He signaled for his machine gunner to catch up, and emptied the rest of his rifle's magazine into the back door.

His gunner dropped to the ground next to him in a state of sheer fatigue from hauling the RPK-74S light machine gun more than three hundred meters over rough terrain.

"Take a break and set up here. I want continuous fire on the back of the house until the helicopter arrives. As soon as the helicopter touches down, you move. Good job so far," Yergei said, slapping him on the shoulder.

"The barrel is dangerously overheated!" the ex-soldier said.

"It can handle another two hundred rounds. Keep firing until the helicopter lands," Yergei said. "Move to the LZ! Thirty seconds!" he said, emphatically motioning for the rest of the team to pick up the pace.

The light machine gun unleashed a furious volley against the battered structure, filling the house with deadly fragments of steel and wood. Yergei reloaded his weapon on the run, headed toward several yellow putting flags crowded onto a closely mowed circular patch of grass due west of the house. A massive post-and-beam lodge loomed behind the landing pad, offset to the right and out of both groups' lines of fire. Three gray-haired, overweight men stood on the deck, bizarrely cheering them on with drinks raised over their heads.

A bullet hissed past him, followed shortly by another as he sprinted for the putting green that would serve as their primary landing zone. He fired controlled bursts at the house while running, letting his machine gunner do most of the work. By the time he reached the short grass, the volume of fire had intensified, kicking up patches of sod around him. He ran onto the soft grass, throwing the flags to the ground as the helicopter appeared over the western tree line.

∂◦⊸

Sheffield fired a few hastily aimed 5.56mm rounds through the shattered dining room window at the group lying prone next to the putting green, quickly shifting his aim to the commando removing the yellow flags. His last shot missed, mainly because he was more focused on getting back down to the floor as quickly as possible. Standing for more than a few seconds nearly guaranteed taking a bullet from the light machine gun pummeling them from a well-protected position less than a hundred meters away.

The agent positioned in the far corner of the dining room rose quickly to his knees and fired an extended burst through the same window. The drywall below the window framing exploded at the same time, showering them both in a chalky white powder residue. He covered his face with his right arm and buried his head into the hardwood floor as the room took another devastating extended burst from the machine gun outside. He heard the agent's body hit the ground hard and scrambled through the chunks of building material to reach him.

Bright arterial spray decorated the walls on both sides of the corner, continuing to jet from the agent's lower thigh. Sheffield instinctively started to remove his belt in an attempt to fashion a tourniquet, but stopped upon further examination of the agent's contorted, twitching body. A bullet had passed cleanly through the middle of his neck, rendering the level of trauma care he could give at the moment utterly pointless. He had to do something to even the odds and take revenge for the brutal murder of his security agents.

"Lopez, Graham. Get ready to go full auto. Full mags. Pour it on the group next to the green and get down!" he said, pulling a fresh thirty-round magazine from his combat vest.

The two men spread across the kitchen, changed magazines, and signaled him with a thumbs-up.

"Pour it on those motherfuckers!" he screamed, rising up in defiance of the steel-jacketed rounds cracking overhead.

All three of them emptied their magazines on full automatic toward the group huddled near the putting green. Within three seconds they had unleashed ninety 5.56mm bullets in a hail of gunfire that struck down the group's leader, who just kneeled next to the group. He saw thick splatters of blood erupt from behind the commando, but that was all he could confirm before dropping out of sight and preparing for the inevitable, overwhelming response. Upstairs, he heard at least one friendly gun continue the shooting spree and something else. Shit. Now he understood.

"Helicopter inbound! Get away from the wall!" he said.

All three of them clambered on their hands and knees for the center hallway in a desperate attempt to move deeper into the house. Sheffield was the last man through the opening before bullets started to tear into the kitchen and dining room at a downward trajectory that would have killed most of them immediately. The deep thumping of the rotors competed with the utter devastation unleashed on the house, rapidly growing along with the intensity of incoming fire.

"Keep going out the front door! Out the front door!" he said, pushing them along until they tumbled down the granite steps and onto the gravel driveway.

Bullets continued to rip through the house, passing completely through the structure and forcing them to huddle behind the thick granite steps and concrete foundation. He just hoped that the helicopter didn't plan to circle the house. They'd have nowhere to go but back inside, where they would eventually die. The machine-gun fire continued, but didn't change trajectory, leaving him with the impression that the helicopter was here for one single purpose. To extract the team.

He turned to the two men, hoping to muster one last attempt to stop Reznikov's escape, but both of the agents had taken multiple hits. None of the bullet wounds looked immediately life-threatening, but he could tell by their eyes that they were thinking the same thought that Sheffield had just pushed out of his head. *There's no point anymore. It's over.*

He crawled along the foundation to the right corner of the house and risked a peek toward the putting green, which was partially obscured by the far end of the house. The helicopter's tail rotor protruded into his view, giving Sheffield hope that he might be able to disable the helicopter. They'd still have to contend with two light machine guns and four commandos, but at least he'd make it a little harder for them to get away. He didn't care how good they were, escaping on ATVs would present a whole host of problems that the CIA might be able to contend with.

He aimed at the tail rotor and fired a burst, seeing sparks fly off the rotor assembly. His burst was answered by concentrated machine-gun fire from rocks northwest of the house. He'd hastily assumed that the machine gunner had already fled for the helicopter. The rounds chewed up the concrete foundation and splintered the painted wood above him, leaving him no choice but to withdraw. He waited a few seconds and leaned to the right, squeezing off three shots at the rocks, which were not met by return fire. He rolled along the gravel until the machine gunner appeared, running full speed for the helicopter. Sheffield found the fleeing figure in his holographic sight and centered it in the red circle. He fired two rounds before the gravel ten meters in front of him erupted, barely giving him enough time to roll out of the way of the helicopter door gunner's fusillade.

He backed up to the porch and prepared to climb inside the house to seek shelter, unsure of the helicopter's intentions. He could tell by the whine of the engines and the deeper pitch of the rotors that the helicopter had taken off at high speed. Seconds later, the sound started to fade, and he stood up, walking back to the corner of the house. He watched a red and white, Bell 427 medium utility helicopter disappear beyond the western tree line.

"Check on the rest of the team in the house, then get the staff in the lodge organized. I want all hands on deck helping out with the casualties. Full prisoner count in five minutes. Get on one of the handheld satellite phones and notify headquarters," Sheffield said.

"Got it. Where are you going?" Graham said, leaning on Lopez's shoulder for support.

"To check on Karl Berg. He was here to permanently retire Reznikov," he said.

He started to jog down the center gravel path, stopping for a moment to survey the putting green. He counted two bodies on the ground, indicating that his final shots had found the machine gunner's back.

Sheffield slowed down once he entered the forest and cautiously approached the residence. Scanning over the barrel of his compact assault rifle, he immediately saw that the front of the cottage had suffered the same fate as the security complex, but that the damage had been contained to the left side. A body lay in a widening pool of blood on the covered porch, which caused him to stiffen, until he realized that the man was dressed in the same camouflage pattern as the rest of the assault team that tore up his compound. There was no need to examine the body. The back of the man's head was missing, giving him some hope that Berg might still be alive inside the house.

He stood quietly for a moment, listening for signs of movement in the cottage. Hearing nothing, he stepped inside, sweeping the rifle left to right to ensure that the attackers hadn't left a wounded man behind. The attack had progressed so quickly from his perspective that he couldn't rely on what they had momentarily seen on the camera feeds. He had counted six men approaching the fence, but his count had been quickly interrupted by automatic fire directed against his Quick Reaction force.

His hopes of finding Berg alive were crushed when he caught sight of the ceiling to his left. Bullet holes riddled the entire surface, leaving very few areas intact. Combined with the damage he'd seen on the exterior of the house, he couldn't imagine any scenario in which Berg had survived. The assault team had made a concerted effort, inside and outside of the house, to take him down.

"Berg! Karl Berg! You in there?" he said, walking toward the kitchen.

No response.

"Karl. It's Gary Sheffield!"

Glancing through the kitchen, he noticed several bullet holes in the far wall, which caused him to point his rifle toward the staircase to his left. He spotted a dark red stain on the wall at the top of the stairs.

"Berg! Answer me, damn it!" Sheffield said.

"I'm up here," a weak voice responded.

"Are you alone?"

"Yes," Berg said.

Sheffield slung his rifle and mounted the stairs, expecting to find him lying in the hallway. The hardwood floor in the hallway was cracked and splintered from wall to wall, covered in a fine dust from the damage to the ceiling above.

"Where are you?" Sheffield said.

"Taking a bath," Berg said.

He peered into the bathroom just off the hallway and found himself staring directly at the business end of the suppressed pistol he had given Berg less than fifteen minutes ago. The top of Berg's head protruded just far enough over the top of the cast-iron, claw-foot tub to effectively aim the pistol. The pistol disappeared into the tub, along with the rest of Berg's head.

"Reznikov?"

"He escaped by helicopter. They had us pinned down from the start," Sheffield said, stepping into the bathroom.

Like the hallway, the bathroom had been effectively obliterated. Most of the white tile floor had been shattered, along with the toilet, sink and mirror. The shower stall's glass door lay in pieces within the bullet-perforated fiberglass enclosure. Karl Berg lay crumpled inside the only safe location on the second floor, bloodied and pale. Sheffield extended a hand to Berg and pulled him out of the tub, helping him to the floor in the hallway.

"Your team?" Berg said.

"I lost most of them in the house."

"Shit, Gary. I don't know what to say. I have no idea how this happened. Mountain Glenn is off the grid. Way off the grid," Berg said.

"Can you move?" Sheffield said.

"Yeah. Just grazed me," Berg said, touching his shoulder.

"Looks more like a through and through. You got lucky," he said, examining the floor and looking toward the bathtub.

The tub's white porcelain coating was chipped in at least five places that displayed minor denting from the shallow angle of impact along the side. Since the tub was located against the outer wall of the bathroom, it probably didn't take more than one or two deeper angle hits against its bottom, which was fortunate. Contrary to popular belief, a cast iron tub wasn't bullet proof. Repeated, high-velocity direct hits could shatter the brittle metal, penetrating the steel curtain and peppering the occupant with metal shards from the inside.

"For the first time ever, I'm glad they didn't spare any expense building this place," Berg said.

"I can think of a few improvements," Sheffield said.

"Surface-to-air missiles would be a good start," Berg said.

"I don't know if that would have helped. Between the machine gun and .50 caliber sniper rifle, we couldn't do shit. What now?"

"The border is less than fifty miles away. If they get him over the border, he's gone," Berg added.

"Then he's gone. You know the protocols for this place," Sheffield said.

"Unfortunately, I know them entirely too well. I updated them three years ago to enhance the agency's deniability. Reznikov is definitely lost...for now," Berg said.

Chapter 73

Under Secretary of State for Political Affairs Philip Regan accepted Minister-Counselor Leonid Novikov's hand in a warmly enthusiastic embrace before gesturing toward the decorative coffee table adorned with a tea service set and a small but opulent selection of bite-sized pastries. Once the two diplomats settled into the two luxurious red leather high-back wing chairs, the dance began, starting with tea and a mid-morning snack.

"Can I offer you some tea?" Regan said.

"Thank you. That would be wonderful," Novikov said in polished, Russian-accented English.

Regan poured him a cup of black tea from a polished bronze samovar presented in the early eighties by the Russian ambassador to George P. Shultz, President Ronald Reagan's secretary of state. Novikov took a sip from the glass teacup and smiled in approval. They both indulged in a few pastries and traded pleasantries about family for the required amount of time before Philip Regan placed his teacup onto a shiny bronze tea service tray and leaned back in the chair.

"I know for a fact that the tea and pastila at your embassy puts this humble offering to shame, so I assume that something important brings you here during the morning tea hour," Regan said.

"I'm afraid so," Novikov said, putting his cup down. "This is a delicate matter," he added.

"You have my undivided attention and discretion," Regan said.

"Last night, we had an incident at the State Research Center for Virology and Biotechnology in Novosibirsk," he said.

Regan pondered the Russian's words for a moment, slowly furrowing his brow in a controlled, deliberate effort to look concerned.

"What kind of an incident?" he said.

"Terrorists attacked the biocontainment facility at Vektor Laboratories," Novikov said.

"Dear heavens. What were they trying to accomplish?" Regan said.

"We don't know very much at this point, but the attack put the entire Novosibirsk region on alert. We lost two helicopters in an unfortunate collision near the Kazakhstan border."

"I'm very sorry to hear that. Please let me know if you need our Centers for Disease Control to help in any way. As Vektor's sister facility, I'm sure they would be eager to lend a hand. Were there casualties at the facility?"

"Several, including a scientific team that was working late over the weekend on a special project," Novikov said, reaching for his cup on the tray.

Regan poured each of them another cup. They were about to broach the matter at hand.

"Their CDC and World Health Organization counterparts will be heartbroken. Such a loss is sure to be profound among such an elite group of dedicated scientists. Do preliminary investigative reports indicate a possible threat to other facilities worldwide?"

"We hope that this is an isolated attack," Novikov said, responding to his hidden suggestion.

"So do we. We stand by to assist your country in any way possible. Given recent events here in the United States, I can assure you that we are committed to keeping facilities like Vektor and our own CDC secure against terrorism. Bioweapons are a frightening prospect on the world scene."

"I couldn't agree more. We'd like nothing more than to put the Vektor attack behind us and renew a joint commitment to stamping out these weapons internationally," Novikov said.

There it was. The Russians wanted a clean slate between them.

"That's very good to hear. I'm sure the American people would strongly support this kind of bilateral effort, and I know that my president is eager to put recent events as far behind us as possible," Regan said.

"Most excellent, my friend. I will relay this to Moscow immediately. Sorry to…how do you say it? Eat and run? But this is a matter of urgency, and your offer of bilateral support will be most happily received."

Both of them stood and shook hands vigorously.

"I'm pleased that we could come together on this one. Don't be a stranger, Leo. Moscow was by far my most enjoyable posting, and I don't often get the opportunity to regale in stories about Russia. Plus, I rarely have occasion to showcase this wonderful gift from your homeland," Regan said, pointing at the samovar.

Novikov admired the samovar and tea set. "Nineteenth century Tsarist Russia, I believe. Very rare, but a shame to keep hidden away for my infrequent visits."

"I'll have to take your advice and keep it out as a reminder of our friendship. Please keep me posted on any developments related to the terrorist attack, and I'll be sure to let you know if we pick up anything on our end."

"Very well, Phillip. We'll be happy to put all of this behind us."

"And so will we," Regan said, showing Novikov to the door.

Once the door closed, Philip Regan settled into the high-backed chair and finished his tea. He had little idea what the exchange had truly meant and suspected the same about Novikov. He had received explicit instructions from the secretary of state regarding the outcome the president desired, which had included just enough information to work out a diplomatic solution in the most vague terms. He knew Vektor Laboratories had been attacked and that the attack might be related to the issue in Monchegorsk, though he had been specifically prohibited from mentioning the Kola Peninsula incident in any way.

Regan had been encouraged to mention the recent bioweapons scare in the United States and suggest that the administration would support any and all bilateral efforts to eradicate the world bioweapons threat. Philip could connect the dots. He had a strong suspicion that the attack against Vektor had been a demonstration of the White House's previous and future unilateral commitment to preventing another attack against the homeland.

Chapter 74

6:42 PM
Federal Security Service (FSB) Headquarters
Lubyanka Square, Moscow

Alexei Kaparov shook his head and smiled for most of the walk back to his office. Maxim Greshnev, chief counterterrorism director for the Federation Security Service, had summoned him unexpectedly for a second time today. The first had occurred at 4:45 in the morning, soon after he had reported to headquarters in response to an urgent roster recall. He had learned that terrorists had attacked Vektor Laboratories, Russia's State Research Institute for Virology and Biotechnology, targeting the biocontainment building. Vektor officials had assured Greshnev that the virology division's infectious disease samples had not been stolen or tampered with in any way.

Kaparov had fought to stifle a grin throughout the early morning meeting, never imagining that he'd have to fight the same battle twelve hours later during a one-on-one meeting with Greshnev. Smiling was not one of Kaparov's strong suits, but today had made him infinitely happy.

He reached one of the doors leading into the Biological/Chemical Threat Assessment Division's cubicle farm and concentrated on presenting the same sour face his agents had grown accustomed to seeing over the years. Normally, his division resembled a ghost town at this point in the evening, but thanks to Karl Berg, the entire counterterrorism department was still a beehive of activity and showed no signs of slowing down.

Thousands upon thousands of hours would be wasted in the Lubyanka Building over the next few weeks, possibly months, and he would have to appear enthusiastic, knowing for a fact that it was an exercise in futility. He was in for a long summer.

Yuri Prerovsky stood up from his cubicle located directly outside of Kaparov's office.

"Anything new to report?" Kaparov said, continuing into his office.

"Center for Special Operations units are mobilizing small teams to assist with the execution of emergency warrants against our high-priority watch-list targets," Prerovsky said, hovering just outside his door.

"Come in. I hate when you linger like that. Do they require any of our personnel in the field?"

Prerovsky stepped inside and closed the door behind him. "Not at the moment, but they're going to run out of agents to chase down everyone on that list, which is what I presume they'll have to do," Prerovsky said, eyeing him.

"Well, given what Greshnev just told me, the entire investigation is about to take an interesting detour. Are you ready for the latest?" Kaparov said, lighting a cigarette.

"Probably not."

"Greshnev asked me to reopen the investigation into Anatoly Reznikov. Information has surfaced suggesting a possible link between the scientist and Monchegorsk," he said and leaned back in his chair.

"You have to be fucking kidding me. May I presume that you did not use the phrase 'I told you so,' at any point in the conversation?" Prerovsky said, taking a seat in the small folding chair next to the door.

"You can't imagine what I was thinking. I could barely keep from laughing in Greshnev's face," Kaparov said.

"This is a genius move on their part..."

"Whose part?" Kaparov said, exhaling smoke toward the nicotine-stained ceiling.

"Whoever decided that this was the perfect opportunity to make lemonade out of lemons. Monchegorsk is an undeniable international public-relations disaster that makes Chernobyl look like a routine ten-car pile-up on the Moscow Ring Road. Linking a disturbed scientist to the terrorist attack on Vektor and ultimately Monchegorsk isn't the prettiest option, but it's sure as hell better than the version of events they're currently peddling to the international community," Prerovsky said.

"I guess I hadn't thought of it that way. I was just wondering how the hell they were going to investigate a dead man."

"That's not a problem for the puppet masters. I'm quite sure that Reznikov will be killed by SVR agents a few months from now, just as he is about to poison another city in Russia. Probably won't be much left of his body after the raid."

Kaparov nodded and took a long drag from his Troika cigarette, exhaling as he spoke. "You're probably right. Until then, we have to go through the motions. Greshnev wants us to prepare a detailed file on Reznikov. Everything we have. We're to activate all protocols previously used to track Reznikov's whereabouts, foreign and domestic."

"None of those protocols had been particularly effective in the past," Prerovsky said.

"I guess it doesn't really matter. We won't be the only ones going through the motions if your theory is correct."

"And Monchegorsk? How should we proceed?" Prerovsky asked.

"I've been told to stand by for further direction," Kaparov said, raising an eyebrow.

"Of course," Prerovsky said.

"Look on the bright side, Yuri. When they find Reznikov, service commendations and medals will shower the division. We should celebrate. Drinks are on me tonight."

"Sounds like a plan, as long as your idea of drinks on the town doesn't involve a park bench," Prerovsky said.

"Of course not. I only drink on park benches during weekend afternoons." Kaparov laughed. "If you'd give me some privacy, I need to make a quick phone call. Business-related. Overseas."

"Yes. I'll be right outside. Can I start sending agents home, or are we in here for the night?"

"Start cutting people loose at seven. I want the entire department back on deck by five in the morning."

"Understood," he said and departed, leaving Kaparov alone in the office.

Kaparov pulled a cell phone from his briefcase and dialed the number Karl Berg had given him, which bounced his call from a legitimate Moscow number to the CIA officer's cell phone. All he had to do was speak a four-word phrase to activate the transfer. Otherwise, the phone would continue to ring at the ghost location somewhere in Moscow. The call rang long enough for Kaparov to wonder if Berg had finally abandoned him. When the CIA officer answered, Kaparov could tell by his voice that something wasn't right.

"I'm glad you called. We lost him," Berg said, sounding tired.

"Lost who?" Kaparov said, hoping he didn't mean Reznikov.

"I can't spell it out on the phone. Science type."

Kaparov tried to process what Berg had just said, but was having a hard time closing the loop in his mind. He couldn't imagine any scenario in which the CIA simply *lost* one of the most dangerous people on the planet.

"What do you mean by lost? I thought he was in one of your most secure locations, which I assumed to be a dark cell, deep under the fucking ground? Better yet, why isn't he dead?"

"It's complicated. He was in a very secure location," Berg said.

"Obviously not secure enough. Dare I ask what happened?" He quickly lit another cigarette, noting that there were not enough Troikas remaining in the pack to calm him down from what he had just been told.

"The compound was hit by a small army right after I arrived. I escaped with a gunshot wound to the shoulder. The rest weren't so lucky. We lost fourteen men trying to stop them," Berg said.

"How the fuck did this happen? I told you to be careful with him. He's not to be underestimated."

"We couldn't have pulled off the raid without his help. We had to make some concessions to keep the information flowing, but we were extremely careful. I can't for the life of me imagine how he pulled this off."

"This information couldn't come at a worse time. I've just been asked to reopen his fucking file! They're going to blame him for the recent events, including the one you just pulled off," Kaparov hissed.

"They can't. How could they possibly pull that off at this point?"

"Shall I march into the Kremlin and demand an explanation?"

"I don't know what to say. This is an utter disaster on both ends," Berg said.

"Disaster is an understatement. It appears that we will have to hunt him down for real. I just need to find some credible leads before they cough up a body to satisfy the world," Kaparov said.

"I'll do everything I can to help you with that. This is my responsibility."

"You can start by pointing me in the right direction. Do you have any idea who was responsible?"

Another long pause ignited Kaparov's suspicion that he wouldn't get the full story.

"We took down three of the shooters. Tattooing suggests army Spetznaz and a possible *bratva* connection," Berg said finally.

"Let's just hope there is no connection to the latter group."

"Unfortunately, it's a distinct possibility. We contracted with some of their assets to make certain logistical arrangements," Berg said in a defeated voice.

"You have no idea what you've unleashed. This is the worst-case scenario. I'll need to see every detail you can provide. You can no longer keep anything from me. Is that understood? At the very least, I have to prove he is still alive before my government produces a corpse and shuts down my investigation," Kaparov said.

"I didn't tell you about the *bratva* because I wanted to keep the information compartmentalized, given what was happening in and around your office."

"If I had known they were involved, I would have told you to cut your ties immediately, even if it meant shutting down the mission. You have unwittingly made the world a much more dangerous place. I'll call you tomorrow to set up an arrangement to receive any information you have on our friend. This changes everything. I have to go…oh, I hope your shoulder is all right. Goodbye," he said and hung up.

"Prerovsky!"

Kaparov's assistant deputy burst into the room with an alarmed look, which immediately turned to confusion. "I thought you might have finally caught fire in the mess," he joked.

"You'd like that, wouldn't you? Shut the door and take a seat."

"This doesn't sound good. Is the celebration cancelled?" he said, following Kaparov's instructions.

"The celebration is cancelled, but I still plan on drinking myself into a coma, and after you hear what I've just learned, you'll want to do the same," Kaparov said.

Epilogue

2:14 PM
Caribbean Sea
Five nautical miles north of Cartagena, Colombia

The smell of diesel fuel and industrial disinfectant permeated the air, sticking to his clothes and saturating his hair. Even his skin reeked of it. Six days hidden away in a cramped cabin aboard a Liberian flagged container ship hadn't exactly been what he had envisioned for his first week of freedom. His dreams of booze and prostitutes, compliments of his new Solntsevskaya friends, had been replaced by strict house arrest under the watchful eyes of three stern-faced commandos, who continued to remind him that they lost three of their comrades because of him.

Fucking babies, he thought. They should be celebrating. Now they had more money to split among themselves. He guessed they were too stupid to do basic math. To add insult to injury, the quack doctor hired to examine him in Halifax had insisted that he avoid excessive alcohol consumption throughout the healing process, which his "captors" had interpreted to mean no alcohol at all. How was he supposed to heal without drinking? None of it made any sense.

He stood up and glanced at his watch. The ship had slowed several minutes ago, on their approach to the port. He had been assured by the ship's captain, who was well aligned with the Solntsevskaya Bratva, that he would be free to move about on his own once they cleared customs and spirited him off the ship to a waiting van. He apologized for the second-class treatment, saying that the instructions for his transit had been clear.

He was to avoid contact with members of the crew, who could only be trusted as far as their paychecks lasted.

The Port of Cartagena had a bad reputation for draining a sailor's wallet, and despite the *bratva*'s influence throughout the dock area frequented by ship crews, the Americans had no problem throwing money around through their proxies. They needed to get Reznikov as far from the port area as possible. He was still highly recognizable at this point, thanks to Karl Berg.

He turned to face a small square mirror fixed to the bulkhead by two metal clamps. The dirty surface revealed a gaunt, slightly jaundiced face covered in stubble. His left cheek was buried under a large, dingy medical dressing that ran from the edge of his mouth to his ear. He gently pulled the gauze tape from his chin and lifted the bandage to expose Berg's handiwork. A long, jagged red scar extended across most of his cheek, the skin still held together by black stitches.

He received little more than basic first aid until they arrived in Halifax, several hours after his escape from Vermont. By then, the deep slash caused by one of Berg's bullets had started to fester, making it nearly impossible for the sham of a doctor the Russians had kidnapped to neatly sew his face back together.

The thought of living with this hideous scar for the rest of his life evoked a murderous rage against the backstabbing son of a bitch who had come to murder him that morning. There was no other explanation for the suppressed pistol Berg produced at a moment's notice. He should have known better than to trust the man who had authorized his torture at the hands of two maniacs in Stockholm and then had the nerve to put him in the same room with one of them in Vermont. His heart had nearly exploded at the sight of the dark-haired, smarmy psychopath, who so casually toasted to stuffing his head in a toilet. He'd eventually find all of them, starting with Karl Berg. Nobody fucked with Anatoly Reznikov. No matter how long it took, he would patiently wait for the right moment to make them all pay.

THE END

Author's Note

If you've made it this far in the series, I can only assume that you've enjoyed reading the *Black Flagged* world as much as I've enjoyed creating it. Thank you! Without dedicated readers, the daily "zero dark thirty" wakeups would wear on me very quickly. Because of you, I look forward to tiptoeing around my house in the morning, careful not to wake the rest of the clan. Of course, I would love to dedicate more of my time to the writing. One of the simplest and most effective ways you can help me achieve this dream of writing full time is to leave reviews on Amazon.

These reviews accomplish two things. First, they give potential readers the confidence to spend their hard earned money on a new author in their favorite genre. Second, a well-reviewed book draws attention from readers and book industry professionals. All of this brings me "that much" closer to achieving my goal of writing full time and releasing three to four books a year, instead of two. See. This benefits you too! Consider leaving a simple review on Amazon for one or more of the *Black Flagged* books. You don't have to write a novel, or anguish over what to say like I do. A basic expression of satisfaction speaks volumes to potential readers. Thank you in advance.

To sign up for Steven's New Release Updates, send an email to:

stevekonkoly@gmail.com

Please visit Steven's blog for more on *Black Flagged* and future projects:

www.stevenkonkoly.com